HOW TO KILL A GUY IN TEN WAYS

Eve Kellman is a fiction editor, lecturer, and writer. She lives in Bristol, UK, with her partner and two adorable dogs. *How To Kill a Guy in Ten Ways* is her debut novel.

HOW TO KILL A GUY IN TEN WAYS

EVE KELLMAN

avon.

Published by AVON
A division of HarperCollins*Publishers*
1 London Bridge Street
London SE1 9GF

www.harpercollins.co.uk

HarperCollins*Publishers*
Macken House
39/40 Mayor Street Upper
Dublin 1
D01 C9W8

A Paperback Original 2024

1

First published in Great Britain by HarperCollins*Publishers* 2024

Copyright © Eve Hall 2024

Eve Hall asserts the moral right to be identified as the author of this work.

A catalogue copy of this book is available from the British Library.

ISBN: 978-0-00-862097-4

Typeset in Sabon by Palimpsest Book Production Limited, Falkirk, Stirlingshire

Printed and bound in the UK using 100% Renewable Electricity
by CPI Group (UK) Ltd

This book contains FSC™ certified paper and other controlled sources
to ensure responsible forest management.

For more information visit: www.harpercollins.co.uk/green

To my sidekicks Rita and Roxy.

I have done a thousand dreadful things
As willingly as one would kill a fly,
And nothing grieves me heartily indeed
But that I cannot do ten thousand more.

Titus Andronicus
Act 5 Scene 1

PROLOGUE

The first man I ever killed was my father.

But we're not there yet. That's not even really part of this story. All you need to know about that, is that a) it was sort of an accident and b) he deserved it. If you must know more about that sorry affair, then I'll have to tell you about it another time. Because really, this isn't about him, it's about me. And a few things I have done recently that may be considered 'wrong' and 'illegal' and the rest.

I've always thought that morality is a grey area and the law is open to interpretation. Still, the things I have done are not the sort of stuff you go shouting from the rooftops about. So why am I telling you? First of all, you are just a tape recording that no one will ever hear. Hopefully. Until I die myself perhaps. The idea of a tell-all confessional tape being released days after my death that shocks everyone to their grey, middle-class core is appealing to me. Gauche, I know, but fame, notoriety, and a certain fuck-you-all glamour is *right* up my street, even if I'm not around to see it. Right now though, this is far from over. Mission incomplete. So, I really shouldn't go around making too many plans for what happens after the end, when I'm still smack bang in the middle.

Another reason I'm telling you this, is to get my own head straight. I don't want to put myself down here, my head *is* on pretty straight already, considering everything that has been happening. But I'm a big enough person to admit that things did get ever-so-slightly out of hand last night, and so taking stock isn't the worst idea.

And lastly, if everything comes to light, some people out there deserve the truth. So, hello future me, my dearest friend, my little sister, or whoever else is listening to this. It's a cold November night, and I'm sitting in my kitchen, drinking a glass of expensive red wine, and counting my sins. Or wins, depending on where you're standing.

I've already said that it didn't start with my father. It probably started with Karl. Or maybe Katie. But when I close my eyes and think, the image I get in my mind is of two girls in the back seat of my car. Short skirts, shaking with nervous laughter. There were often girls in the back of my car (calm down, not like that). But the picture of those two, in particular, is imprinted there. There's also Rose's hair against the white pillow, Katie's arm peeking above the covers, the Liverpool scarf on the curtain rail. But for me, I guess it starts with those girls in my car. And so that's where it's going to start for you, too.

We'll get to the rest.

CHAPTER ONE

I *never* looked that innocent. Even when I was tiny, I'm sure of it. The girls are chatting away in the back seat, but all I can focus on are their too-short, too-cheap skirts and their bare legs with fake-tanned, goose-pimpled skin. The blonde has *glitter* on her eyelids.

It upsets me that they have clearly dressed up for the evening and instead of dancing with wild abandon and then eating cheesy chips on the night bus, they are being driven home at 10pm by a five-foot-nine vigilante in a Nissan Micra. Not upsets me, *angers* me.

'We probably could have taken him, Rach,' the brunette is saying, nudging her friend. 'I could have stilettoed him!' She mimes a brutal attack with an imaginary shoe and keeps going until her friend smiles. Soon they are both shaking with laughter, but then tears start running down their faces. It's relief that does that. The moment of safety, when any tiny joke gives your body permission to release that pent-up adrenaline as hysterical laughter. They are still sitting closer than I assume they normally would, holding on to each other.

Rachel is the one who texted me. She can't weigh more than eight stone, and she looks like a broken bird cowering in the back seat on the way to the vet. A home dye job has left her hair brittle and straw-like, devoid of any moisture, and it frizzes around her petite face like a lion's mane. Her unnamed friend is more robust, both in body and mannerisms, taking on the role of mood-fixer with gusto.

Does she always find herself cheering up others? Making jokes in bad situations? Sorting out her friends' messes with a smile on her face? People pick their group roles long before they're adults, and it's hard to reinvent yourself later in life. If these two drift apart one day, the brunette will find another friend to comfort.

An Audi beeps from behind and I realise my speed has dropped to a crawl as I've been watching the girls. *Fine. Fine, you fucker.* I put my foot down slightly, but stick rigidly to the speed limit on the empty roads as the driver angrily revs up behind me, eager to get to his destination a few precious minutes earlier.

I had a cat once who was hit by an Audi. That sounds almost like the car acted of its own accord, so let me start again. I had a cat once, that a man drove into with his Audi. And then the man continued to drive away despite my lovely tabby Kevin Bacon twitching on the tarmac. I'll never forget the sight of poor Kevin lying there. I saw it from my bedroom window when I was thirteen. Afterwards, I'd walked around the neighbourhood with my pocketknife, scratching a line down the side of any Audi I could find. I bet the guy from the bar the girls were in tonight drove a bloody Audi.

4

My phone – stuck in a plastic holder attached to the dashboard – tells me that when I take the next left, I'll have reached my destination. As I pull up, the girls are full of thanks, the brunette giving me an awkward one-armed hug over the car seat before she gets out. When they are safely behind the door of the house, I take a deep breath and put my forehead on the steering wheel.

What pricks these men are. They are out there, wandering around like you and me, but under the surface they are cruel, power-hungry bastards, preying on women who are really too young to even be out this late. On the vulnerable. On people like those glitter-eyed girls, or my sister, Katie.

I contain my rage, because learning to do that is part of growing up in this society – especially as a woman. It takes me a moment before I feel my phone from the dashboard. Flicking off Google Maps, I see a screen full of notifications.

Shit.

Six missed calls and nine WhatsApp messages, almost all from Nina. It's gone 9pm, and I was supposed to meet her over half an hour ago. Time flies when you are on a rescue mission.

As I'm looking at the screen, it comes to life with her name and photo. I answer because I'm not a coward, but also because Nina is the most understanding person you could ever hope to know.

'Oh! It's the marvellous missing Millie! So good of you to answer!' she rasps down the phone, her rumbling voice heavy with sarcasm. I can hear the wind buffeting the microphone as she walks.

'Nina, I was *about* to leave and then—'

'Don't tell me. You got a Message M text?' She sighs. Nina never stays mad very long. Maybe that's why she is still my friend. She is a Good Person. Someone who forgives and forgets with alarming alacrity. A jumble of contradictions, she is simultaneously a terrifyingly efficient lawyer and a total sweetheart with an unexpected streak of naivety. 'I know it's important. I know you are trying to help. But you've stood me up. Again.'

'I know. I'm sorry. I am in the car and can be there ASAP. I'm not actually sure where I am, but I'm probably not even that far away!'

'Don't worry about it, I'm already on my way home.' I hear the rattling inhale of her vape and can almost smell the sweet watermelon flavour through the phone. 'We'll speak tomorrow. It's fine, honestly.'

The line goes dead, and I stare at my reflection in the windscreen, feeling suddenly exhausted. To keep some level of anonymity, I have my hood pulled up, and half of my face is hidden by sunglasses I don't need at this time of night. Nina isn't mad, she is disappointed. Ouch. But if there is a choice between someone's feelings being hurt and someone's body being hurt, feelings have to be put aside. Trust me, I should know.

My phone flashes again. Duty calls.

Saturday mornings are good for lots of things – long lie-ins, short coffees, slow sex, and quick runs. Being single, I'm fitting in all but the third point before I see my sister. Reclining on the small sofa in my garden, I take a sip of my espresso – strong, black, hot – and close my eyes. The caffeine does its part to wake me from the dull atrophy that I feel every single morning. It was a late one last night. When I received another message – someone thinking they were being followed – I spun around to find the caller and pick them up.

The Message M phone line isn't my real job. Or, more accurately, it isn't the job that I'm paid to do. But the phone line *is* my real job in that it is the one I define myself by.

It started out small a little less than a year ago, born out of anger, and it snowballed. Now, I've got signs in the toilets of all of the bars and pubs around the area, reading:

Are you on a date that doesn't feel right?
Can't shake that creepy guy at the bar?
Worried you're being followed home?
Message M.

And, if someone needs me, what can I do but be there? If some scared young woman texts me for help, am I supposed to say, '*Sorry, I'm having cocktails with Nina, best of luck though!*' No. I can't. I have responsibilities to these people. I can't have them end up like Katie.

But on a Saturday morning, when all the party-goers are sleeping off their hangovers from the night before, there is sweet silence. If only it weren't for that absolute cretin Sean who lives next door. I am opening my favourite book – Stephen King's *Misery* – and raising my coffee to my lips when I hear the dreaded sound of his throat-clearing cough.

'Well, *hello* there, young Millie.'

Oh God. Please. Please no.

'Sean. Hi.'

'Methinks you have a relaxing set-up there on this fine morn!'

I would gladly rid the world of the entire part of the population who say 'methinks'. And I'd be sure to do it brutally.

'Yes. Peace and *quiet* on a Saturday morning.' It's a miracle he doesn't hear the sarcasm, but as I'm never exactly thrilled to speak to him, he must assume that's just the way I sound.

'Ahh, you enjoy that while it lasts! Once you have a few little 'uns running around, you can kiss peace and quiet goodbye!'

I would also gladly rid the world of anyone who says 'little 'uns', *and* those who rudely talk about other people's fertility. Sean is like the centre of my death wish Venn diagram. With his shining head and the top part of his fat little face sticking over the fence, Sean looks exactly like one of the smiling stone goblins you sometimes see for sale in garden centres, bought by God knows who. His nose is bulbous, and his piggy eyes are, I suppose, *friendly*-looking. But that desperate friendliness drives me spare. He's lonely, I get it. But really, that's a him problem.

As I'm deciding if it is possible to shake him off, or if I should just give up and go inside, my phone flashes with a text from Nina. Other than my sister, Nina Lee is the only person on earth that I care for and whose opinion means anything at all. And so earlier I'd sent her a text apologising again for yesterday evening.

Hey pal! That's ok. I was pretty tired anyway
so there's no harm in an early night.
Good old Nina.

The vague noise of Sean's babbling is still wafting over the fence. He's going on about his grandchildren now, who he purports to love but who clearly don't return that emotion or else they'd pop round once in a while.

'Callie was a *much* better swimmer, I'll tell you *that* for free. But that chubby little Indian girl *cheated*, I *saw* her push off before the whistle. I told Callie, I said don't let—'

You are def coming to lunch tomorrow though yeah?

Fuck. I have a semi-regular Sunday lunch date with Nina and our two friends from our final year of school, Angela and Izzy, both of whom I find low-level annoying these days. I'd been hoping to get out of it this week, but I can't say no now that she's forgiven me.

Sure!

Because it's time for you to *finally* meet Hugh!

Extra fuck. I've been putting off meeting Nina's latest boyfriend because he, frankly, sounds like a tool.

'But that *bloody* teacher of hers,' continues Sean, 'wouldn't see sense. I just wasn't having it. So, I went right over there and I said—'

I'll book a table at that pub near yours. The Spotted Cow at 2

'The cheek of her! I mean, I'm paying her wages! So, I told her—'

There is a crash of porcelain as I leap up, my body clearly deciding that it's had enough of Sean's shit. My coffee cup – a nice one that Katie gave me – is cracked in two on the paving. I'm adding it to Sean's list of crimes that I've been mentally compiling since moving into this house eleven years ago.

'Sorry, Sean,' I cut across him. 'Have to dash.' I dart inside before he can ask any questions.

Without slowing, I pull on my trainers, and give my Norwegian Forest cat, Shirley Bassey, a quick stroke. Then I head out into the world, pausing on the doorstep to start a new run on my Strava app.

As I quicken my pace, the air against my skin brushes away my remnant sluggishness and the irritation that Sean has ignited in me. I push myself harder.

But the glitter girls from the night before are still firm in my thoughts. Some guy had been following them bar to bar, not taking no for an answer. In the last one – a sticky-floored All Bar One full of dead-eyed bar staff and drunken punters – he had gotten handsy, and Rachel, the blonde, had seen the promise of aggression flash in his eyes.

'Scary like,' she'd said. 'Like – like he could do whatever he wanted? You know?'

Yeah, I knew. I've seen it first-hand, and I've heard similar descriptions over and over. When I got there, he was still at the bar, his chubby fingers caressing a drink. He was wearing a shiny blue shirt and too-tight jeans, and his bald head was reflecting the red lights of the bar. He looked rather remarkably like a sentient potato, minus the sentience. Knocking a large pink drink into his lap then ushering the girls into my Micra while he flapped around for a tissue was quick and easy, but their fragility has stuck with me.

Rounding the corner of the road, the footpath opens up before me and I leave tarmac behind. The path climbs steadily, and the soft thump of my feet on the earth steadies my heartbeat, each footfall pushing the picture of the girls, with their wide eyes and spindly limbs, further out of my head.

When I reach the top of the hill, the trees open to one side to reveal Clifton Suspension Bridge reaching across the river Avon, magnificent and overly grand. I allow myself to stop, putting my hands on my knees and bending down to catch my breath. A man with a bushy beard and too-tight vest jogging in the opposite direction passes me and I edge to the side of the path. He smiles as he passes, and raises his hand in a two-finger salute that makes my stomach turn. It is the calling card of a tech bro.

Thankfully, he doesn't stop to talk, but he gave me the creeps, so I turn and jog back in the direction I came from, speeding up again to try and silence my mind. I need silence sometimes, need to process everything bubbling away under the noise. The constant, insufferable noise of other people.

But no matter how fast I run today, sweat dripping down my nose and down my back, I can't stop thinking of the girl in my car at 2am, gushing her thanks as we pulled away from a drunk guy in the suit. The gangly sixteen-year-olds laughing with relief at leaving potato man behind. The many, many texts and calls for advice and reassurance I'd had over the course of this week, this month.

And behind it all, always behind it all, is Katie. My dear sister.

CHAPTER TWO

I'm slowly driving to my mother's house; it's already past midday and my speed decreases as I get closer. If I keep going like this, then I'll never actually reach the house. That's basic maths. Or I thought it was, but it's failed because I can see the damn road now, and I appear to be pulling up in front of 112 Ladbroke Drive. Oh well, guess I'll try a different tactic next time.

My mother is not who I'm here to see, but it's hard to avoid her entirely if I want to see Katie. Other than Nina, my little sister is the only person who I truly, truly love and would do anything for. Ten years my junior, it's my mission in life to keep her from harm, though I've not done too well as of late.

Katie has always been the pretty one in the family, the smarter one, too. You'd think I'd resent her for getting the deeper part of the gene pool while I paddle at the edge, but I never have. When Katie got into Durham, I was so proud. My little sister, from my shit hole of a home, getting into one of the best universities in the *world*. Her face when she opened that letter was unforgettable. She turned white, then red with shock. We're smart, the Masters girls. But unlike me, she took that brain of hers and applied herself in the right way. She was going to make it. But *he* took that from her.

The front door of my mother's house is plastic, and I've always hated it. Cheap looking even in its hay day, it is now grey rather than white. The 112 is the same 112 that has been there as long as I can remember, and the 2 is rusting. I let myself in with my key, calling out as I walk over the threshold.

'Hello? It's Millie! Katie?'

My mum comes out of the kitchen to my right. Not who I called, but fine.

'Hi. How is she doing?'

'Oh, she's okay. You know, a bit tired. How are you, my love?'

A bit tired. Mum is the queen of downplaying things, so this assessment doesn't fill me with hope.

'Has she eaten today?'

'Hmm? I'm not sure, love. I've put the kettle on if you'd like some tea?'

'I'm going up to say hi.'

The décor in this house hasn't changed in years. Not since my father died and Mum went on a mad spree with some yellow paint in a futile attempt to 'brighten things up'. The paint was cheap and so the walls ended up looking like the peel of a waxed lemon. It reflects onto your skin and makes you look like you've got jaundice. At least it's clean though. She's always been clean, my mum. She focuses on specks of dust to ignore the sandstorms.

My room is different. No one goes in it these days, including me. While mum doused everything else in yellow, I'd painted my walls bright, gleaming white, hung new ruby-red curtains across the window and bought all new bedding. It didn't work though, I still can't stand the place.

At Katie's door, I pause for a moment to steel myself and then call out sweetly, like I'm enticing a kitten. I stare at my boots on the clean, worn-down carpet while I wait for signs of life.

Nothing. I try again.

'Katie? It's Mill. Can I come in?' After what seems like a lifetime, I hear a murmur from inside that I take as a yes, so twist the handle and gently push open the door. My sweet sister is in bed, peering out over the covers like a hibernating hedgehog who has just been disturbed mid-January. If it wasn't so heart-breaking, it would be funny.

Katie makes an effort, pushing the covers down, blinking hard, and hoisting herself up on her elbows. It's ingrained in women, this need to 'make an effort', no matter what the circumstances. You could be bleeding out on the tarmac, having just been hit with an eighteen-wheeler, and you'd still worry about the underwear you're wearing. *Should have made more of an effort today* must be so many women's dying thought.

My sister's smiles are scarce, so I'm honoured to see a small upturn of her mouth when she sees me.

'Hi Mills. You look fab.' She pushes her body up into a sitting position and leans back against the headboard. 'What time is it? I can't believe I fell asleep again.' She looks at the clock and her pale cheeks colour. 'Shit, it's nearly one. Sorry. I'm a mess.'

I know she's a mess, and she knows that I know that.

And we both know it's not just because she slept in late today. But I roll my eyes and tut loudly, and she shrugs apologetically, and we both pretend like this is a one-off. Because pretending is nicer, and it makes things feel normal. Even though what is more *normal* for us, is this exact situation.

I perch on the end of the bed and we chit-chat about my life, avoiding hers. Seeing as my life is monumentally uneventful – excluding my evening job that she knows nothing about – it's not the most riveting of conversations. Yet, I still cherish these moments with her. Every time she says something about the future – 'I'd like that', 'I'll see' – or cracks a joke, my heart leaps with, not joy exactly, but hope.

'I'll get that framed at Rick's for you, if you like?' I say, nodding at a photograph lying flat on her bedside table that I haven't seen before. Katie's cheeks flush again.

'No. But thank you.'

The picture is upside down, but I can see it's her and her two best friends from school. I wonder if they still try and visit, or if they've given up now too. In it, Katie's hair is shiny and curled, her cheeks full, and she's grinning at the lens with an arm around her friend's waist. I try to stop staring at it, but I can't pull my eyes away.

'How is work anyway?' she asks.

'Eurgh, you know. Rick is obsessed with this new type of glass we have in, which is exactly the same as the old type of glass. Glass is just glass, right? It's see-through. It's nothingness. That's the point of it. But, hey, it's work. It pays the bills.'

The cliché makes me cringe, especially as I remember that I have forgotten to actually pay my gas bill once again. Luckily, I own my house – my uncle Dale helped me buy it with part of Dad's life insurance money – so my meagre wage covers my living expenses with some left over for savings. Even so, I'm chronically forgetful at actually paying the bills because it's just so bloody boring.

'Not all nothingness is the same,' says Katie, and the unexpected heaviness of her words makes us both pause. 'Anyway,' she continues with a smile, 'weren't you thinking of doing a course? Back at . . . back at Christmas? You don't want to be at Picture This forever, right? Answering to Rick?'

By day, I'm a framer. As in, I frame pictures. It's not glamorous, I'm aware of that. I got my A levels and everything, but I never went to university. I wanted to focus on my sister until she was old enough to stand on her own two feet in the world. So I bought a house nearby after I turned eighteen, and I worked at the framing shop around the corner as a stopgap. Then, I just never left.

Part of me loves what I do. For all of the ghastly maternity photoshoots in fields and pathetic prom shots, sometimes, just *sometimes*, my job can be about making beauty even more beautiful.

Very occasionally, I'll be handed a painting that takes my breath away, or a photograph that touches something in my cold heart, and even more occasionally, the customer handing it over won't say 'that'll do' to the cheapest, flimsy pine wood, but will choose something solid and lasting. Mahogany, carved gilt gold, smooth polished oak. Those days make it worth it.

'I'm happy there for now, Kate. Honestly, it's fine.'

'It's not because of . . . You don't have to . . .'

'Katie. I like it. Stop.'

Katie shrinks at my harsh tone, so I force a smile and add, 'And I haven't told you Gina's latest gossip.' After forty minutes of discussing the trials and tribulations of my irritating co-worker, Katie's eyelids start to droop. But this is good, comparatively. She'll feel guilty if she knows I've noticed her getting tired. Guilt is another thing that women feel a lot – even for being *tired*. I once nudged Nina in her sleep and she automatically whispered, '*Sorry*'.

'Right, I need to head. I'm meeting Nina.' It's a white lie. Really, I need to relax for a few hours before the Saturday night buzz of the phone line starts up.

Katie coughs, and her frame shakes like it's about to collapse. When I lean in for a hug, she feels like brittle bones and my chest tightens as I pull away. She looks like she is already falling back to sleep, waiting for me to go before she disappears again. I back to the door with a pasted-on smile and damp eyes.

'Bye! I'll call you later, okay? I love you.'

I shut the door and stand in the hallway, closing my eyes to stop the tears. When I open them, the yellow is there, glowing. Indecently cheerful. And suddenly, my upset is replaced by a cold rage.

Katie has been in that room for nine months now, only leaving when necessity dictates it. She came home from her first term at Durham and never went back. I'm not an idiot, I know she is seriously depressed and dangerously thin, I just don't know what to do about it.

I do know why it started though.

It happened just after one of the best Christmases we'd ever had. Katie had been full of stories – about her course and her grimy student flat and her new friends. She had seemed taller, bubbling with all the new things life was

17

giving her. There had been a moment on Christmas Eve, when I'd thought that it was time for me to do something else with *my* life now that she had started her next chapter. Maybe do that copywriting course Nina was always on at me about.

But she'd gone out on New Year's Eve, while I spent the night in the pub with Nina, Angela, and Izzy, toasting in the new year in genuinely high spirits, and that's when it all went wrong. What was I drinking when it happened? Had we moved on to the tequila by that point? Did it happen while I was holding Angela's hair back in the bathroom? Setting the world to rights with Nina in the smoking area? Had I just ordered the bottle of expensive champagne which I then spilt all over the floor?

You know where this is going. While all of this had been happening, Katie was attacked. Well, to give it its proper term, she was raped. People shy away from that word, scared of its violence. Attacked, assaulted, hurt – they are all much easier to say than the reality. Katie, my baby sister, was raped on New Year's Eve, and now she's a prisoner inside her own bedroom.

Overnight, she shrunk, in every sense. From being an effervescent, smart, joyful young woman to a grey-faced mouse who jumps at a sudden movement. A size ten to skin and bone.

It wasn't my fault. It certainly wasn't hers. At times, I do blame her friends for not looking after each other that night, but I know it wasn't their fault either. It was *his* fault. However, that doesn't stop the guilt I feel day in, day out, for not being there, for failing to protect my sister – the only thing I've ever really tried to do.

Since then, I've also tried to protect other women.

Maybe it's a form of penance, but I'm not a psychologist and have no real interest in discovering why I'm doing what I'm doing. All I know is that I failed at protecting Katie, but while she languishes in her room, I've succeeded in protecting countless other women.

I had hoped she would start coming back to life week by week. But instead, she seems to draw further and further into herself. One day, I worry she will disappear entirely.

I manage to avoid my mother when I slip out the house, though I see her disappointed face appear at the window as the engine of my car roars.

What Katie needs is justice. But justice has been impossible to come by.

CHAPTER THREE

Nina has dreadful taste in men. The last time I met one of her boyfriends, he banged on about his new BMW for most of the evening, and never offered to buy a round of drinks. I found it difficult to restrain myself from pulling his tie so tight his air supply would be cut off.

I saw the BMW parked, badly, outside the pub once I had made my excuses to leave. I ran my house key along its shiny blue door – old habits are hard to break.

But I owed Nina, so I'd agreed to being at The Spotted Cow at 2pm for Sunday lunch. Last night, Message M had been strangely quiet for a Saturday, but I still didn't get into bed until nearly three. This morning I forced myself to go for a run, but I kept checking my phone in hope of a change of plan. What I wouldn't give to be having lunch alone with my best friend, and not having to spend my precious free time fake smiling at Hugh Chapman.

I'm in a foul mood when I walk into Picture This –

your friendly local framing shop – to collect my latest paycheck before I head to the pub. Leaning on the counter, I wait for Rick to come back with the goods, and spot a heap of frames covered in dust that he must have brought out from the back room. Unable to help myself, I grab a cloth and start to wipe them down.

Rick comes out from the back room holding mugs of coffee for us both. He's a decent guy, if incurably dull. He once wrote a novel, bought by no one, and has never recovered. He mentions it at least once a day.

'Ahh well done, Millie. They were looking a right state.' He hands me a mug, and I realise that Rick is the person I spend the vast majority of my life with, which is depressing as hell. 'How is your weekend going?'

I often try and hate Rick, but I can't. Not fully. Yes, he pays me shit all, but it's not like I didn't know that going in. He isn't a pervert, nor a misogynist, nor a run-of-the-mill bastard. He even makes me coffee now and again.

I regret accepting the offer of coffee though as I realise that it comes with small talk, so I continue dusting the frames to blunt the intensity of the interaction.

'Oh, it's been fine, nothing special. These frames new?' I pull out the gaudiest of frames to wipe off the dust. It's large and thick, silver with hundreds of Swarovski crystals embedded all the way around. What artwork would you put in such a thing? I can only imagine that the kind of person who would buy this would put their own boudoir photoshoot pictures in it. It costs £225.

The shop is small, which doesn't stop it stocking the largest variety of frames in the South-West. They are piled in heaps on the floor, leaving a thin path from door to

21

desk. Every week, more arrive from somewhere. They take up every inch of wall space, which is particularly alarming because most of them contain a smiling man or fawning woman. While I work, I'm watched by a thousand judging eyes in fading faces.

As Rick natters on about the new stock, I burn my throat by gulping down my coffee, then make my goodbyes and start towards the pub.

I don't want to be early, so I meander and end up buying a fabulous scarf from the Oxfam charity shop – sheer black with beaded edges – which then makes me late.

I check out my new scarf in the reflection of a shop window, draping it over my shoulder. I'm tall and skinny, but in a way that makes me appear as a collection of sharp angles rather than a graceful gazelle. My skin is pale as paper, and my strawberry-blond hair that curls gently around my shoulders makes me – at first glance – conventionally attractive, but, once you linger, you notice that my face is hawk-like – cruel with harsh lines. Which isn't fair, because I wouldn't say I'm cruel at all. Not if I like you, that is. My nose is sharp with a ridge where it was once broken, my jawbone is square, and my eyes are too small to soften the overall look.

I'm not hugely put out by any of this, it's more an observation. People aren't really my thing, so do I really care if they like my nose? Men don't usually look long enough to see more than a skinny, blondish-haired woman with an okay pair of breasts anyway, so it's never harmed my chances of dating.

Nina is the opposite of me in almost all ways. Short with soft curves, luscious dark hair, and cute chubby cheeks with square, thick-framed glasses usually perched above them, she gets more beautiful the longer you look at her. Her parents are both Chinese and she was born in London before moving to Bristol in her teens, so she has a beautiful accent that is impossible to describe. I stick to monochrome and clean lines, whereas she opts for bright colours and low necklines to show off her fabulous cleavage. She can, quite literally, brighten up a room.

As I walk into The Spotted Cow, I see her sat at a table in the corner, giggling in a somewhat performative way at something her new man, Hugh, has said. Oh Nina. She's so desperate to fall into her own love story that she ends up *jumping* in without looking. Angela is at the bar getting a bottle of red wine and five glasses.

'Millie!' Nina waves, grinning, then tries to rein in the enthusiasm in an attempt to look cool in front of Hugh. 'Meet Hugh.' Nina used to smoke like a chimney and has a voice that's as low and gravelly as an expensive car. She switched to vaping earlier this year, but if anything, she's just taking in even more nicotine.

The man sitting next to her gives me an up-and-down look, which makes me shudder, but then springs to his feet with a sort of half wave that I mirror with awkwardness. Love is Nina's Achilles heel, the potential of it being the only thing that can befuddle her whip-smart brain. So, it's my job to pluck out the weeds that get too close, leaving room for something better to come along.

I hug Nina and pull out a chair as Angela appears in a cloud of chaos and pours the entire bottle of wine into four fashionably large glasses.

'Millie, my babe, I haven't seen you in *weeks*! Not since

Sunday before last, and I was tipsy so can barely remember it! Ha ha!' She glugs at her wine while still standing. 'Cheers! Clink clink! Okay, I'll be back in a sec. Need to pee. Then I have *so* much to update you on.'

Angela is someone that Nina and I went to school with who, I swear, didn't used to be quite this annoying. She speaks constantly, only stopping to gulp drinks as if they are life-saving antidotes to recently ingested poisons. Everything she says is hilarious, but only to her. But Nina, Angela, Izzy and I have all known each other a long time, and despite her quite obvious flaws, she is my friend.

Sometimes I worry that Angela has a lot going on in her own head. She is of average intelligence, with hair that is a mousey-coloured ball of frizz, and milky eyes the size of duck eggs that are too large for her small, chinless face. It may be the case that the abundance of both speech and alcohol she brings with her to every social occasion is an attempt to find a place in a world which would otherwise overlook her. But that doesn't make her any less annoying.

Angela's departure for the bathroom leaves a brief vacuum of silence in which Hugh and I exchange pleasantries, Nina trying to facilitate. She's nervous, and it makes me feel guilty, so I laugh loudly at some remark Hugh makes, then raise my eyebrows in her direction to show I'm impressed. She tries to hide her grin by picking up the menu and suggesting we choose our food. Even though it's a bright day, the pub is dark and there's a candle in the middle of the table providing an illusion of evening romance despite the lads at the bar doing Jägerbombs. The walls have moody, blackened paint, giving the impression that the place has recently recovered from a fire, though it probably cost them a fortune to achieve such a look.

'So, Millie, what do you do?' Hugh asks as he sips at the brimming glass, grimacing slightly at the taste. Clearly more of a beer man. I'm actually rather surprised that he has asked me a question at all to be honest, even if it's a wildly unimaginative one. In the past, I've found Nina's boyfriends to be uniformly self-absorbed.

'I frame. Pictures. I work in a framing shop.'

'Oh. Right.'

Yeah, I guess there isn't much to add.

'And you? Plumber, right?'

'All of it really! No job too small and all that.' Hugh is trying, so he gets a point for that. And he has thick muscles under his t-shirt and blond hair that sticks up at odd angles in a devil-may-care fashion that I know Nina will find endearing. Trying not to stare as I catalogue this new man in my best friend's life, I notice that his heavy-set face is perfectly symmetrical. He gives me a self-deprecating smile.

'He's being modest! He is so talented! He *made* his own coffee table, pal. Honestly!' Nina flicks her poker-straight, glossy hair back in a theatrical way. Thanks to a combination of expensive products and some bizarre genetic quirk, her hair always smells incredible, and she isn't above using it to ensnare. I arrange my face in a way I hope conveys that I'm impressed, even though nailing five pieces of wood together hardly sounds like rocket science. I mean, I know frames are only four, but I'm sure the extra plank wouldn't give me much of a headache.

Angela arrives back at the table, knocking over her glass of wine as she sits down, though luckily, she'd nearly finished it anyway.

'Anyone hear from Izzy? Did you tell her the actual

meeting time, Nina? We were going to start telling her a time half an hour earlier, weren't we?'

'Oh she'll be here when she's here,' Nina says breathily, waving her hand in a nonchalant manner, the kind of casual person who doesn't care about timekeeping. I know if Hugh were not here, she would be rolling her eyes at Izzy's predictable lateness. She slips a vape out of her sleeve and inhales on it subtly.

Gravy-filled plates arrive, along with Izzy in an expensive-smelling fug of perfume full of predictable apologies, and we eat our roasts while Angela bangs on. Nina tries to encourage a fun, relaxed atmosphere by being anything but relaxed, and despite this, Hugh keeps up a steady flow of easy chatter. He asks questions, he laughs at our jokes, and when Nina knocks her fork onto the floor while telling a story, he jumps up to get her another one.

Though I hate to admit it, he does have a certain charm about him. Izzy's perfume and Angela's loud voice are giving me a headache – which I try to drink through. Izzy starts to complain about her babysitter, a common refrain, and Nina and I glance at each other then look away to keep straight faces.

'You coming to Jackie's thirtieth next week, Mills?' Izzy demands to know as the underpaid and seemingly underage waitress removes our tower of dripping plates.

'Um, no? Why would I go to *Jackie's* thirtieth?'

'Because she's our friend?'

'She's *your* friend. I haven't spoken to Jackie in, like, a year.'

Nina sighs and rolls her eyes dramatically, and Hugh leans forward in a mock 'give-me-the-goss-girl' pose, chin resting on the back of an outstretched hand.

'Ooh what happened then? What did this "Jackie" do?'

'Jackie is a wanker,' I inform him. 'Sorry, Izzy. But it's true. She was a wanker in school, she's a wanker now.'

Nina jumps in and turns to Hugh apologetically. 'They had a stupid, drunken argument. Jackie called Millie a stuck-up bitch because she said she doesn't eat from kebab vans. Millie won't let it go.'

'Why should I?'

'Because you cannot hold a grudge forever! I'm always saying, you need to find a proper way to deal with anger. Sometimes, you have to let go of the past and move on!'

'I disagree. Anyway. Hugh. Tell me more about that coffee table. Legs? Four of them?'

Finally, Izzy announces that she has to get back to the kids, giving Hugh an extravagant air kiss and telling him far too sincerely that she *loved* meeting him, before waving down the bored-looking waitress. Angela is looking worse for wear, so Izzy pays both their parts of the bill then forces her out of the pub to be driven home.

The waitress half-heartedly recommends the pecan pie, and Hugh politely explains he is deathly allergic to all nuts, but can always leave Nina and me to it if we want to order one. He really is making an effort. Or maybe he is just a nice guy. Nina declines, which I'm pleased about, and I excuse myself for the bathroom. I've run out of small talk and the Jackie chat riled me up.

In the toilets, I shut myself in a cubicle and take a slow breath as a treat. I sit on the closed lid and read the door poetry.

Sam was here 2019   Caz 4 Jack

Rachel L is a slut

Trans Rights R Human Rights

BELIEVE WOMEN

Shoot for the moon and you may
land among the stars :D

I f**king hate men

Mandy loves cock

In a moment of inspiration, I find a pen in my bag and add, *Jackie is a wanker.* I feel better.

Back at the table, it seems mercifully quiet. I've never been a social butterfly, but as I get older, I'm becoming more introverted, crawling into my shell with my cat and my regrets and my anger. Part of me loves my old school friends, but Nina aside, I have less and less patience for their general bullshit.

'Hugh's bought us lunch,' Nina says with pride bursting from her.

Look, maybe I'm not the one to judge. I've never met a man worthy of this woman. Never met someone that Nina – smart, funny, kind Nina – should want to spend large amounts of her time with, and that includes myself. But she does seem happy, and Hugh hasn't done anything *wrong*, so far. I still don't feel ready to be in the man's debt though.

'Thanks, Hugh, but I would rather pay. Honestly.' I smile so it doesn't feel like a rebuke and scribble my phone number on the receipt with the eyeliner still in my hand.

'Text me your details and I'll send you my share.' He acquiesces after minimal pushback, which tells me that he doesn't really have the money to be freely buying everyone's big boozy lunches, but he wants to impress. It thaws me a further degree. He's a charmer.

However, as I walk home to feed Shirley Bassey, I decide that I'll need to keep an eye on Hugh Chapman. Charm is a dangerous weapon, and I can't relax until I know if the man wielding it has good intentions.

CHAPTER FOUR

I have no desire to spawn children. Occasionally, when life really is that boring or I really am that hungover, I will flick through the Facebook profiles of women I went to school with. Some of them have *multiple* children! We aren't even thirty yet! They will share photographs of a chubby-faced child staring gormlessly at the camera with captions like, 'Can't believe it's been four years of joy with my perfect little family!', followed by thirty-six posts on a local mums' group about the time changes for Mummy and Me Sing Song club.

No thanks. I'll take beer over baby grows, massages over mastitis.

It's not even that I'm too selfish to stand the tedium of running my life around someone else's whims – though I freely admit that I am. It's that I would have no idea how to be a mother.

My own . . . fell short. To put it lightly. I grew up with a father best not spoken of, a mother who was worse than useless, and my uncle Dale who, other than Katie, is the only family member I don't feel actual hatred for. I know exactly how much damage a shit parent can do, and I don't want to cause damage to someone who doesn't deserve it and hasn't asked for it.

It's 2am on Friday night – the hour which sees the boundary between evening fun and night-time terrors – and I'm sitting in my Micra, shivering in my coat, while rain spatters the windscreen. Tonight, I'm wearing a dark wig under my hood. I've pissed off a lot of men doing this job, so I try to keep myself unrecognisable when working Message M.

It's been a fairly shit week. Nothing much has happened – I worked, I played with Shirley Bassey, cooked, avoided replying to text messages from friends. There was a vague plan to see Nina for drinks tonight, but she's cancelled on me to see Hugh. I try not to blame her – I know the first fug of new romance sends people wild. But it meant that I was already in a bad mood when my mother called.

If I had my way, Katie would stay with me. But she says she is happy where she is, and that she doesn't want to leave her childhood room. So, it's up to our mother to try and get her to eat some food, leave her room, and wash her hair once in a while. My mother wasn't a good parent to me, but in her defence, she's always loved Katie more, so she does at least try.

Don't get me wrong, my mother isn't someone who tries to be cruel. She isn't abusive – or I'd have dragged Katie out of that house years ago. But she is passive. She was never the parent. Never took control, made the tough decisions, or even told us off. She just existed, and passivity is a trait that drives me wild with fury. In front of Katie, I keep my opinions on our mother to myself though. They have a better relationship, and right now, it's where Katie wants to live. One day I will persuade her to move in with me.

Leaning back against the headrest, I squeeze my eyes shut and try and still my racing mind. It's easier to be angry at my mum than accept that I'm to blame as well. My job is to protect my sister, and I'm failing.

I went round to see her again on Wednesday. Uncle Dale's motorbike was sitting in the driveway, and I found him in his trademark Newcastle United football shirt drinking beer with my mum in the kitchen. Katie was upstairs in a black hole of depression, looking thinner than ever. So was I surprised when Mum called me this afternoon to say that she had collapsed and been taken into hospital? No. She was sent home again pretty quickly, with firm instructions to put some weight on. My instinct was to ditch Message M for the night and rush over there, but Mum told me Katie was already asleep and I didn't want to wake her when she needs rest.

So, here I am, in the middle of an October night, shivering in my car, willing my work phone to give me lives to save. It's all I can think to do. If I can't help my own sister, I can help someone else.

Hugging my body and pulling up the hood of my coat, I wonder if I should turn the engine on to get some heat, but the petrol dial is low and it feels wasteful. Anyway, the cold feels almost pleasingly punishing. Mum told me Katie only fainted due to low blood sugar. But this is a woman who would put a plaster on a bullet wound. The sharpness of Katie's shoulder blades feels imprinted on my arms, and when I close my eyes, I see her cheekbones propping up dark circles. I suppose that I am kidding myself that she is getting better when really she is wasting away in front of my eyes.

Leaning my head back against the headrest again, I take a deep breath to calm myself. In the darkness behind my lids, I can't stop memories flooding in. I concentrate on my breathing using a technique I learnt during yoga. I was never very good at it. I used to lie on the floor of that studio, trying to 'breeeeathe' and 'empty the miiiiind' but really all I could focus on was trying to make my thighs strong enough to kill a man.

In.

Katie and I laughing hysterically on a night out.

Out.

Me curled up in her bed as children.

In.

Katie getting into Durham University, white with shock and pride.

Out.

Me hugging her the day I brought all of her things home in a van after she dropped out.

In.

Tiny Katie rolling down the grassy hill by our house.

Out.

Tiny me telling her not to worry about Dad.

DING.

Oh, thank God. It's been raining and it's cold, so the night's been fairly quiet, but mercifully someone wants my help. Someone needs me. I skim the text and then slow down to read it again. It's hard to make sense of, like the author is plastered.

Hs lokked hte door.

What?

He srrmd nick buut nw. I feel bad.

I thn smthng ihh my wine.

Something in her drink? Oh God, she's not drunk, she's been drugged. I start to type frantically, needing to know where she is before it's too late. My phone dings again – she's had the good sense to share her location. It's followed by another text.

32

My car is in gear before I have a plan, my head a confused mixture of drugs and girls, blood and wine, Katie and me.

I pull up to a Victorian terraced house ten minutes later. When I'm showing at the same location the girl shared on WhatsApp, I look frantically around and spot a blue door with the number 32 emblazoned on it. Message M usually takes me around the same old bars and clubs, or occasionally I'm contacted by women walking home alone. But now and again, I get called to private houses like this one. These are the ones that send a shiver down my spine, where danger really lurks.

But a simple knock on the door and a request to collect my friend usually works fine – the surprise stalls the man's brain long enough to get her out in seconds. Once I had to call the police. Either way, I usually take a moment to assess the situation so I'm not going to make it worse, or run into a place where I'm getting hurt.

Tonight though, my mind is spinning with thoughts of my sister and her attacker, my mother and my own failure. So, I'm not taking the time to formulate a plan. Maybe part of me *wants* a confrontation. Anger needs to go somewhere, or it just eats you up.

I'm frantic when I get out of the car, jogging up to the front door. This nameless texter has become my sister, upstairs in number 32 Northumberland Road, at the hands of someone who seemed nice but then spiked her drink.

Three loud knocks to the door. Immediately three more, and a kick to the wood. I hear footsteps and eventually, the door creaks open an inch.

Luckily, I catch myself. I need to calm down. This isn't the way this whole thing works. I take a breath and try to smile, though I'm sure it comes off as more of a grimace. The crack widens and I see a man, late thirties. He is shockingly handsome, tall with dark hair lightly curling around an angular face. He has pale brown skin, a smattering of black stubble and large dark eyes. Eyes that could entice many girls into his house, his bed.

The weather is grim and I've pulled my hood up around my face, so he has to peer down to make out whether I'm a man or woman. A threat or a treat.

'Hi! I'm Jessica!' I say it with perky upspeak. All I'm missing is pom poms and a short skirt. 'I'm looking for my friend? She said she was here?' I'm smiling broadly to keep him sweet, but still trying to shade most of my face with the hood of my coat.

'Wrong address.' He smiles down at me to soften the blow.

'Hmm I don't think so! It was definitely here!' I broaden my grin, it's now bordering on manic. I need to get in there. His angular face reminds me of Katie, the sickly pallor of her skin and slight yellowing of her teeth. *Focus*. 'Mind if I come in?'

His soft smile drops and he furrows his eyebrows. He's losing patience already. 'Why do you want to come in?

Your mate isn't here, sorry.' He goes to close the door, but I stick my foot out. The bastard isn't getting away that easily, but I'll stay soft for a moment.

'It's just that her dad is waiting.' I gesture towards some cars. 'She's supposed to be at our friend Jade's house, but if he comes up here and sees she's been with a guy he will be *pissed*. So honestly, it's better if I just get her now.' I give a strangled titter that's aiming at conspiratorial but comes out more like a lawn mower failing to start.

'I said, she is not here,' he says slowly, like I'm stupid, pushing my foot away with his and shutting the door firmly. Damn.

The square of glass in the closed door reflects my sticking-up hair and smudged eyeliner surrounded by a huge puffy hood. Looking demented probably didn't help. This job requires a cool head, and being able to keep a lid on my emotions is something I've prided myself on in the past. Grinding the soles of my shoes into the floor, I push my rage down through my body, through my feet, deep into the earth.

Number 32 is only three houses away from the end of the terrace. I know that I should call the police, but they'll take too long to get here. What would I even say to them? I think of Katie, shaking in my arms on New Year's Day, and know that I have to act fast.

Running to the end of the terrace, I find an easily scalable wall and, before I can chicken out, scrabble over it. It's dark, and hopefully the residents of this house are happily ensconced in their living room watching *Strictly Come Dancing* or *Celebrities Go Fishing* or whatever other crap people watch these days. I'm pleased I'm wearing black combat boots and trousers, but it feels like my white turtleneck is glowing in the dark.

I crash down into the flower bed of garden number two. Silence, no movement. A black and white cat watches from the windowsill of an upstairs room. We lock eyes and it meows, and it occurs to me that, with her white breast and black body, we look similar. I wonder if she's laughing at me.

Lying there in the mud, contemplating all my life choices, the unthinkable happens. My phone rings. I scrabble around to get it out of my pocket and switch it to silent, Nina's name flashing angrily. God love her, she probably wants to tell me about something else 'no-job-too-small' Hugh has done now, but it is not the time. The return of silence feels loud, and I stay stock still, holding my phone, sitting in mud and a partially squashed lavender plant. Nothing happens. Thank fuck. Dusting myself off, I continue and soon I'm in the garden of number 32.

It has those bi-folding doors that everyone, including myself, seems to have now, even though his garden is frankly nothing special to look at. Why bother with a wall of glass to look at a concrete square? All that matters is they are unlocked. I cross the threshold and catch my breath, leaving the door ajar to avoid the potential click of it shutting. The house is quiet except for the soft pulse of music upstairs. My heart is thudding along with the beat. My phone buzzes with a text. Not now, Nina.

Finding myself inside an unfamiliar kitchen – clean, apart from one pizza by the sink – brings me back to earth, and I realise that I still don't have a plan, and what I'm doing is stupid and dangerous. But that girl needs help, and so I'll wing it. I take my phone out and type in three nines, ready to call for help.

Out of the kitchen, I begin to edge up the stairs. It's a stylish house, pale blue walls and wooden floors. It's unexpected. This whole evening is unexpected. When I reach the door that closes in the music, I pause. I'm out of breath, despite having moved so slowly. I'm scared, I realise. And full of pumping adrenaline.

Suddenly footsteps sound from the other side of the door. Fuck fuck fuuuuck. There is nowhere to go and on instinct I stupidly slam my body back against the wall next to the door. By some mystical good fortune, the door opens outwards rather than inwards, almost hitting me in the face but stopping a millimetre short. A burst of laughter comes from the room.

I stop breathing. Potentially my brain worked faster than I realised to hide me, or else this is blind luck, but I'm blocked by the now open bedroom door. I can see the tall figure of the handsome man I met earlier in the crack. He is so close that I can smell his aftershave – Tom Ford.

'Nah, Jay! You ask nicely or you get nothing!' Laughter. Light-hearted insults. 'Okay, Okay, Guinness?' The sliver of the handsome man vanishes and I hear his feet pound down the stairs. My body is frozen solid, my phone damp in my hot, wet hand. For a moment I think of the absurdity of the scene. Imagine the door being pulled back, the man finding me there like a comic suit of armour. What the *hell* am I doing?

Sense slowly returning, I remember why I'm here, and the realisation hits me that I heard *two* male voices. Two. What are they doing to her? I hear crashing around downstairs – this is the time, now, while one of them isn't in the room. I brace myself, check my phone is ready to call if I need help, and peek through the gap in the door.

She's not there. Another man lies on the bed, his face not visible. Three cans of Guinness lie discarded on the floor, and his foot bobs along to the beat of the music. A game of chess lies abandoned, pushed aside by a pizza box. My mind is just trying to make sense of everything when the unmistakable sounds of bounding footsteps begin up the stairs.

'You left the door wide open down there! Cost of living crisis, mate!' The figure darkens the doorway through the crack, me still secreted behind the wood and holding my breath. 'The final Guinness! Aaaaaand the pizza we swore was for breakfast! But we're out of beer so I'm going to run to the shop, because I'm a good brother.'

'Imran! You angel!' shouts the other voice.

The handsome man comes back into the hallway, slamming the door behind him. I'm completely exposed to a thankfully retreating back as he jogs along the hallway and down the stairs. I stand there, frozen, eyes wide. My phone buzzes in my hand again and, not knowing what else to do, I glance at it.

It's Nina calling again, but I also notice another notification on the screen. It's a text from the girl. Sent ten minutes ago.

I mn 34

For fuck's sake. I leave no trace as I slip out of the bi-folding doors.

CHAPTER FIVE

Letting myself into number 34 from the garden, I glance around at a dirty and depressing kitchen-diner. The layout is the same as next door, but the brown vinyl cupboards and chipped Formica worktop screams lack of both imagination and funds, and the pile of plates, saucepans, novelty mugs, and milk-crusted cereal bowls make my stomach lurch. Or maybe it's because I've broken into my second house of the evening. We'll never know.

The house is silent. It smells musty, like you might expect in a house populated by sad boys, which I'm quite sure this is. If not the bare walls, the fruit bowl on the table holding nothing but one shrivelled lime gives it away. Three timetables and a flyer for a night at the union stuck to the fridge tell me I'm in a shared student house.

Maybe I should have gone back around the front and knocked on the door, but this seemed quicker after all the time wasted pissing about at number 32. Or perhaps I'm just not thinking straight. The atmosphere makes my skin prickle as though it can sense danger. This time, I pick a grubby knife from the pile of dishes by the sink and wipe it on a tea towel. I've never seriously hurt someone in one of my rescue missions and I don't intend to start now, but my experience next door reminded me how powerless I am, and I'm smart enough to know that I'm in a dangerous situation. Luckily most people are momentously stupid and therefore, easily confused. If needed, the flash of a blade should buy me enough time to get us out of here.

The hallway is dark, a grubby cream colour, covered in that textured wallpaper you get in old rental flats. Like the skin of a freshly plucked turkey. I slowly place one foot in front of the other on the grey lino, patterned to look (unconvincingly) like floorboards. There are doors to my left and right, but I can't hear a thing.

Moving towards the stairs, I place a foot silently on the grey, wiry carpet, but something makes me pause. I can hear noise, and it's not from upstairs. Unmoving, I strain my ears. There it is, the soft thud of a bass coming from somewhere. Below?

Moving towards the door to my left I press my ear against it and . . . yes this is it. Cracking it open, I see a sliver of light and, as well as the music, I hear a faint shuffling coming from down some concrete stairs. A basement. How fitting for this bottom feeder to be residing underground. I slip through the door and edge my way down a few steps. I can hear someone, but I can't *see* anything. Is *she* going to be there? And if so, what is happening to her?

This isn't a situation I've been in before. Letting my rage override my senses means that I've put myself at the centre of the danger, but it's too late now to back out. As I creep down another few steps, a man's back comes

41

into view. I'm poised as if I'm ready to spring, and I'm barely breathing. A few more steps, and I see her.

She is lying on a bed. Her eyes are closed and her dress is pulled down to reveal her small breasts. Her hair, light pink and dry from over-dyeing, is artfully splayed out around her like a halo, and her bare, pale legs are open. It is a bizarre scene. Beautiful in its own way, if you remove all context. The context being that she is unconscious, and has been posed by a man who is standing above her holding a camera.

A foot either side of her on the bed, he focuses the lens, puts his finger on the button. *Click*. He moves closer. *Click*.

My breathing has completely stopped now, limbs frozen. The guy is around my age, skinny, pale, and is staring into the camera screen with a frown. He reaches for a cigarette poised on the edge of a half-full ashtray, taking a drag before replacing it and running his hand through his floppy, ash-blond hair. He looks like a dirty hipster: someone you might show off to your friends, but wouldn't want to take home to your parents. He leans forward and further fans out some of her blush pink hair, then lets his hand trail down her neck to her breasts. I name her Rose. I see a smirk on his ratty face and bile rushes up my throat. I see Katie in her. So small and vulnerable.

He spins round, and I realise, too late, that a strangled noise has come from my throat. There goes the element of surprise. Blood runs back into my head and limbs, like I've come back from the dead. We lock eyes.

'What the fuck? Who the . . . Who the fuck are you?'

Eloquent as expected, though I'm momentarily taken aback to hear a twang of a Scandinavian accent.

An audiobook Izzy forced me to listen to called something like *Be the Girl Boss You Should Be* once told me that, whatever the situation, you should *lead with confidence*. Capitalising on his shock, I regain my composure and stalk down the stairs. *Lead with confidence* I tell myself.

'I think it should be me asking that.' I point the dirty kitchen knife at him in what I hope is a dramatic and intimidating manner, but I can see the blade quiver. I need to get this over with quickly before he realises that he could easily punch me in the face and be done with it. I don't fancy ending up as March in the creep's annual calendar.

He is still standing on the bed over Rose, camera hanging by his side and mouth open. His eyes are flicking around as his reality adjusts, looking wild and frantic. Then angry. Not scared. Not scared one bit. Ah fuck.

'What the fuck are you doing in my room?!' His voice is loud. If I was indulging my fondness for the dramatic, I would say it was a *bellow*. The girl on the bed stirs.

'I'm here to get my friend.' My voice is shaking, but I'm hoping he won't notice. *Get a grip*. Raising the knife higher, I flick my head towards the bed nonchalantly, like this is, rather dully, how I always collect my friends.

Jumping down from the bed, he flicks off the music and starts walking at me as I back away around the room. It's the classic student-looking basement bedroom. It smells of spunk and damp corners, and pretentious books sit in an unread line on a shelf. The drugged girl posed angelically on the bed is maybe less common in the average student room.

The man starts to shout at me, and I shout back to fill the time and the air. This isn't working out anywhere near like I thought it would. But I suppose, I hadn't really thought about how it would turn out at all. That's the issue.

We both turn our heads as the girl sits up, her eyes unfocused and dress still around her waist. She stares at us both, mouth open. Large, blue eyes look out of a rounded, angelic face and I realise how pretty she is. Not pretty like a model, but a girl-you'd-be-jealous-of-in-the-office-pretty. Her dry, rose-pink hair is sticking up at all angles, the natural brown roots playing peek-a-boo. A poorly covered patch of acne on her chin makes her look younger than I'd originally realised.

'What the . . .?' she says.

Camera creep and I lock eyes again, both of us clearly sensing the same rush of panic. I don't know why I feel like *I've* been caught in the act. I'm the hero of the piece.

I need to embrace the sudden upper hand. She's awake. She might be quite floppy and useless, but it's still two of us against one of him. 'Get up. Get your things. Now.'

Her confusion is fading and fear is setting in. I see her eyes fix on the knife I'm holding.

'Now!'

'Don't you fucking move!'

'Karl?' whimpers Rose. *Karl?*

'NOW!'

She swings her legs off the bed and stands with a wobble, finally pulling up the straps of her dress. The creep lunges, grabbing her wrist, jerking her towards him. Still unsteady, Rose flies backwards, losing her footing.

Smack. The sound that whips through the air is reminiscent of the camera shutter, but this time it's her beautiful pink head against the metal bedframe. There is a whimper, and then silence.

44

'Everyone calm down now.' Karl tries a smile, holding out his hands like I'm some hysterical woman. It's a surprisingly nice smile that transforms his bony face from sinister to attractively boyish like magic. For a second, I imagine sitting across a candlelit table from him in a bar. I might have gone home with him too.

'You've got the wrong idea,' he continues. 'Everyone *calm down*. Ssshh.' Is he actually sshhing me like a baby? A strand of his dirty-blond hair is over his right eye and he pushes it back as he exhales, giving himself a movie star-like air. 'Okay. Good. Okay.'

Karl is thinking through his options. Trying to figure out if he can smooth this over. I glance over at Rose, who is slumped at the foot of the bed to my right. Her eyes are open and she is staring across the room at Karl. At least she seems awake now, wide awake. She must hope she isn't. The three of us are spread out in a triangle across the room, stock still. Rose and I need to get moving before Karl has any brainwaves.

Leaping to my right so I'm in front of her, I thrust my knife in Karl's direction.

'Go now.' Rose knows I'm talking to her, and she crawls at speed to the stairs. On her hands and knees, she looks like a twisted child's toy. Karl lurches forward and I make a wild slashing movement in his direction, forcing him to leap back. With my free hand, I grab a huge copy of *Infinite Jest* and throw it at his head. He jerks to the side and it grazes his ear.

'You fucking maniac!'

From the corner of my eye I see that Rose has started up the stairs. She's still crouched, feeling her way with her hands. At the sound of Karl's shouts, she rises to standing as she disappears up the steps. Her body is still sluggish, but she's fighting it. His eyes are wide in panic, flicking between me and the stairs. My blood is pounding through my body. I've been in exhilarating situations before, but never one like this. Never had a man at knife point while trapped alone in his basement, you may be surprised to hear. It's a power balance so delicate that a gust of air could tip it either way. I hear a clatter of feet and a gargled burst of tears from the floor above – reality is setting in for her. *Get away before you break down, girl.* The front door slams. She is out. She is safe. I, on the other hand, might not be so lucky.

Karl makes a break for the stairs and I throw caution to the winds, jumping towards him waving my knife and yelling. The space feels small, and I get in front of the stairs again, slashing the air with my knife as he backs away. I catch the sleeve of his jumper with the tip of the blade. The hole in the wool blooms and he stumbles backwards, the back of his knees hitting the bed. He falls onto the sad blue striped sheets that his mother probably bought him when he left home, and I take my chance.

Running up the stairs, I hear him leaping up and after me. I make it through the door and the sight of the speckled wallpaper brings me up short, at once calming and infuriating me. This man. This *Karl*. Bringing beautiful, pink-haired, young women back to this disgusting and at-first unthreatening monotony. Taking pictures and keeping them for his private collection, probably sharing them with his friends. Maybe they're weird basement dwellers too, or maybe they're not. Maybe they're estate agents and bankers and shop workers. Normal men, unsuspicious men with nice smiles. Men like Karl, doing what they want. Even when I stop them, they just do the same the next fucking night. I am so tired. I am so mad. I am so sad. I am so powerful.

Instead of slamming the basement door in his face I spin around and grab onto the frame. I lift my right foot high and, as he runs up to meet me, I kick him hard in the chest. Hard enough that the power of his forward momentum rebounds in his body and sends him flying backwards off his feet. That part of what happens is slow, like it's all going on underwater. Slow enough that I see the moment that his mind registers what has happened and what will happen next, and his pale blue eyes widen in fear, his mouth open in comedic shock, his floppy hair lifting. But in reality, the fall must have been as fast as a blink, because the next second I hear a sharp, clear, dreadful, *crack*.

CHAPTER SIX

It's 6:30am on Monday morning. I'm supposed to be getting up for work in a few hours but I haven't slept a wink. The toad from the poster of *The Wind in the Willows* is staring at me from my bedroom wall, proving that I'm safe in my own home, but every time I close my eyes, I'm back in that basement. I see the pink spread of hair, the small breasts, the glint of the grubby knife. And then I hear it, that *crack*.

Once Karl had fallen – or was pushed or whatever – I don't know how long I stood there. At least long enough to know that he wasn't getting up anytime soon. When I finally went back down the stairs, the air was thick with that tell-tale metallic twang. At least it covered up the stuffy smell of male sweat. Swings and roundabouts.

Karl was lying on the floor, perfectly still, his eyes closed, with a pool of blood slowly growing around him, a drop of it at the corner of his mouth. Careful not to step in it, I inched closer. I bent as close to his face as I could, until there was barely a centimetre of air between mine and his. In a film, this would be the point where his eye sprung open, but they didn't. Nothing stirred. No air tickled my skin. Nothing.

I felt a giddying sense of power, standing over him like that, just the way he stood over Rose. I brushed his cooling cheek with a finger. A line from a play I once read at school came back to me.

'A crimson river of warm blood,' I whispered in the stillness of the basement. 'Doth rise and fall between thy rosed lips.'

I shuddered at my own words. That play always made me think of my father. I straightened up and got to work.

I sat on the springy double bed and texted Rose, wanting to make sure she was okay. She replied saying she was nearly home, she'd run the whole way. She sent a string of thank-yous for saving her and sorrys for leaving me behind. All I cared about was that she didn't tell anyone we'd been there. She agreed, because she'd do anything for me in that moment, but then she asked why, and I turned off my phone.

I needed to think.

Compartmentalising my thoughts has always been a talent of mine. You need to break down? Save it for later. Sort your shit out and cry when you get home. Right then, there was most definitely shit I needed to sort out. I ran through a mental checklist:

<u>Pros</u>

I hadn't stabbed anyone.

There were no witnesses (to the final part of what happened anyway).

Really all that had happened was that a man had fallen down his stairs.

<u>Cons</u>

I had most definitely killed a man.

Rose might tell someone about what happened to her, tracing this mess back to me.

There may be evidence I was here.

Things weren't so bad then. I just needed to eliminate all traces of myself, and all that would be left would be a man who had fallen down his own stairs after a few too many cans. Utterly tragic. Going back upstairs, I grabbed a musty-smelling tea towel, wiped the handle of the knife I was still holding, and put it back with the rest of the dishes. Thank God I hadn't used it because things would have been a hell of a lot worse if I'd stuck that bad boy through his jugular.

Rejoicing that the house was empty, I dashed around scrubbing at any surfaces I might have touched. Going back down to see Karl, I couldn't help tiptoeing, as if I was going to disturb him. It goes against the grain, to make noise around the dead.

Sidestepping the blood, I picked up the copy of *Infinite Jest* lying on the floor, wiped it, and placed it back with the rest of his probably unread but oft-carried-around-collection. That would be me erased from this pit. Now for Rose. I plucked a few pink hairs from the pillow, pushing down an urge to vomit. A wine glass with lipstick on the rim was placed on the stairs to take with me when I left. The blood was still oozing across the floor and I was getting jittery, so took a few deep breaths to calm myself, gathered my belongings and left.

When I finally got home that night, I vomited into my sink, clutching the edges as I heaved. The sink was full of thick red blood, dripping from my mouth as mascara blurred my eyes. I blinked, and the blood was gone. *A crimson river of warm blood*. Fuck. Fuck, fuck, fuck. I killed a man. I fucking killed a man. Oh yeah, great, I'd put back *Infinite Jest*, that'd stump Sherlock. No getting past that one. Jesus Christ. I remembered another line from the same play, *'How easily murder is discovered'*.

Wiping my mouth, I wandered into the kitchen. The wine glass sat innocently on my windowsill, rose-coloured lipstick smearing the edges, perfectly matching the strands of pink hair curled up inside. When I plucked a mug from the cupboard to fill with water, the cold porcelain reminded me of his cooling skin.

Before I'd left his basement, I'd found his phone. Manoeuvring his dead, spindly finger to the scanner to unlock it was one of the most surreal moments of my life, which has had multiple surreal moments. Once I was inside, I quickly scrolled through his messages on various apps to check for any communication between him and Rose. Nothing. He must have found her in a bar. Perfect. Wiping that down and pushing it into the pocket of his too-tight jeans, I finally left through the back door.

Next to the wine glass sat the only other thing I'd taken from Karl's house. A camera. Sleek, black and innocuous, with Canon branded across the top and a long lens that can telescope out. I couldn't have left that there, not with Rose inside it. Although, I could have deleted the photos of her there and then. I don't really know why I didn't.

Then I could only wait. To be caught, or not to be caught. That was the question. Either way, waiting is hell in itself. I cancelled Sunday lunch with the girls and spent the rest of the weekend in my house with the curtains closed, my phone on silent. Every car that went down my road made me break out in a sweat.

I have barely slept. The Message M phone has been switched off, texters receiving an automated response with taxi numbers and top tips in place of my direct help.

But it's Monday morning now. The sun is creeping in and the street waking up. The more cars I hear start up and voices carrying on the air, the calmer I feel. Another morning has come. And I have not been caught.

It's not *just* self-preservation that is plaguing me, I wouldn't want you to think I'm some sort of monster. It is also thoughts of Karl. On the one hand, he was a waste of air. An abuser, a beast. On the other, what did I really know about this man? Did he have a sick mother he visited daily? A plan to turn his life around? Probably not, and I saw first-hand the kind of person he was. But even so, did I really have the authority to extinguish him entirely? After all, I could have called the police and let them sort it out.

But what would they have done? I may be a self-confessed cynic, but even the most optimistic idiot must know the rate of conviction for sexual crimes is pathetically low.

*

It's midday when I wake from nightmares of blood and candyfloss. Sitting up in a sweat, I whirl around like I may see a SWAT team leaping out from the cupboard. It's the first real sleep I've had in days, and though I'm still exhausted, I feel better. My phone shows four messages. Three from Nina checking in on how I'm feeling, and one from my boss Rick about missing work today – I told them both I had food poisoning to explain my silence and isolation. Rick's kind well wishes may have produced a pang of guilt about missing work if it weren't for the *slightly* more pressing remembrance of Friday night's murder. I slam my head back down onto the pillow.

Flicking on the TV, I scroll until I find the local news coming to an end on a story about a burst water main. They would probably show a murder *before* the plumbing issues though, so that doesn't tell me much. On my phone, I scroll through BBC News, the *Bristol Post* site, and Bristol 24/7 and any other local news site I can find. Still nothing, just like the last few days. I've been checking these sites obsessively. Perhaps Karl is yet to be found?

In my mind, I wander that house again, run my hands along that speckled wallpaper. There were three student timetables on the fridge and the house was big – he didn't live there alone. The others could be away visiting parents or on holiday. Students are always on some sort of holiday. Maybe even his housemates don't venture into his lair.

I can't go to prison. Imagine the clothing they'd make me wear. Don't get me wrong, I like a jumpsuit as much as the next fashion-conscious millennial, but only in *black* and of decent quality. Preferably one that plunges like that famous *Fleabag* one. I let myself imagine walking into a prison in that outfit, with heels, and deep red lipstick. But that's not the way it is. It's game over, individuality taken, future snatched. It's cold eggs for breakfast and gang bangs for tea. It's no more drinks with Nina. No more silent garden glasses of wine. No more chats with my sister. No more perfectly roasted lamb. I bet I'd even miss neighbour Sean's borderline racist babble. Or maybe that's too far. My fingernails are digging into my skin and, when I force them away, I notice they've left red semicircles along my arm. Would Katie be okay without me?

As well as my fear, there is the other emotion I'm pushing down. Guilt. No matter how vile Karl was, I murdered a man and the blood and shame and sound of the *crack* of his head are reverberating in my mind. In an attempt to silence it, I go for a run to quiet the adrenaline still pulsing through my veins and clear my head. Near the top of the track on my usual route, I see the same bearded man I crossed paths with last week, who gives me the same salute with a grin that reminds me of Karl's. It makes me shudder.

At home, I call Katie just to hear her voice, but my mother answers and tells me she's in the shower. She invites me over, but I don't think I'm ready to speak to anyone face to face. Though I don't get to chat to my sister, the simple act of her being up and in the shower gives me a sliver of hope. It's as though the universe is validating my choices, rewarding me for my actions with Katie leaving her room.

Eight o'clock comes and it's fallen dark outside, which calms me. Another day has passed, and nothing has happened. The sky hasn't fallen in, the door hasn't been knocked down by men with truncheons and tasers. For a delicious moment, I let myself believe that I might be okay. I might get away with this. Padding to the kitchen, I take the camera from the windowsill and bring it back to bed. I've thought about it all weekend, but this is the first time I've felt strong enough to look.

Powering it on, I'm pleased to see that it still has sixty-eight per cent battery. In gallery mode, a picture bursts onto the screen that takes my breath away. Rose, in all her glory. Half-naked, hair spread, eyes closed, lips slightly parted. Like a fallen angel. The next is a close-up of her face. She could be innocently sleeping. Or dead. I slowly click through more than thirty photos of her, ranging from artistic to pornographic. One of Karl's hand, the hand I'd touched when lifeless, up her skirt makes me almost vomit into my mug.

But suddenly, Rose's hair isn't pink anymore. It's blond. And it takes me a moment, too long really, to realise that this isn't Rose at all. It's someone else. It's some other girl, unconscious, on that same bedspread, in that same room. She's in a different pose. Less interesting hair, I guess. This time I do vomit.

The next morning, I go to work. It was stupid not to go in yesterday. If I've learnt anything from crime shows, it's that you must *act normal*. Because when someone looks back and realises that the days following the murder you called in sick, it doesn't look great. There is nothing I can do about that now, other than soldier on and act better. Smarter.

Rick is unlocking the front door when I arrive, bang on time.

'Millie! You star. Come in, let's get you some tea.' My heart swells for Rick. He is a good man.

I've chosen my outfit with extra care today. I want to look good, put together. Partly in case I'm photographed being shoved into the back of a police car, partly because I want to give off the confident air of someone who hasn't just accidentally-on-purpose murdered a man then spent three whole days vomiting with guilt and fear. I've gone for a black shift dress with gold hoop earrings and white ankle boots – classic, yet surprising. As I looked in the mirror, I thought for a moment of one of the girls on Karl's camera in a little black dress with untied spaghetti straps. Girl number six of thirteen.

Rick makes me a herbal tea and insists I sit down, no matter how much I protest that I'm perfectly fine now.

'It was probably the crappy pub food I ate on Sunday. Or a twenty-four-hour bug, or something. Either way, don't worry about it. I am very capable of working.'

'Drink your tea and sit down, there you go.'

Perching on a dusty stool at the counter, I sip at the steaming, tasteless drink while he fusses around opening the shop.

'Maybe you were sleeping all day yesterday, but did you see the news?'

My blood runs cold and I take a deep breath, gripping my Picture This branded mug. 'Have I missed something interesting?' I sip again to hide my face.

'There's only a burst water pipe down on Lydstep Terrace!' I let out a breath I didn't know I had held and tell myself to get a grip. Act normal. I shrug. Normal me would not care about some water flooding a road I know nothing about.

'It's the third this month. That council. Ah well,' Rick rattles on. 'Not the end of the world, I suppose. Did you know, when I was writing my novel, a pipe burst, and the entire street didn't have water for three days? I was on such a roll, so I just stayed there typing away all that time. Writers have to learn to suffer!' I look suitably impressed, and I suppose I *am* impressed that he can bring even the most mundane observations back to his moment of writerly glory.

'Anyway, Mills, if you are feeling well enough today, we've got a few things to be getting on with. I'm finishing off that rather ghastly triptych the Italian fellow brought in, then I thought you could get on with Mrs Baker's new one?' Mrs Baker has roughly eight hundred grandchildren and there is constantly one graduating or getting married or having one of the next generation of Bakers, and each of these gets a new picture and a new frame. Mrs Baker pays our bills.

'Sure, Rick. I'm on it. I'll hold the fort out here while you work in the back this morning, then we'll switch?' He smiles in agreement and retreats to where he is happiest, the back room. And I breathe. I can do this. Thinking about the pictures on that camera – not just Rose but the thirteen nameless girls laid out like playthings – I feel uncertain guilt sloshing in my stomach. If there was only one seat left in hell, would it be given to Karl or me, a murderer?

That night, however, I sleep like the dead.

CHAPTER SEVEN

Days pass and every morning the tension in my chest loosens a bit more. Springing out of bed on Friday, I hum 'Clair de Lune' while I grind coffee beans and pour them into the cafetière. I've laid off Message M this week, have gone running almost every day and slept like never before, so I look and feel grand. While I'm waiting for my coffee to brew, my phone rings on the countertop. Nina. I've been avoiding her and feel guilty about it. I've been able to keep up the charade of everything being normal at the shop – it's easy to lose myself in work – but I'm scared of seeing Nina. She knows me so well, and part of me is fearful she'll see something in my face and just *know* I've done something bad.

But this can't go on forever, so I plunge down the cafetière and pour out a cup while I answer.

'I'm so sorry, pal. I've been so shit with my phone.' Always go straight in with an apology, it disarms people.

'Mills! Finally! I've been trying to speak to you for

bloody *days*,' she rasps, like she has a throat full of lovely, sultry wasps.

'I know. I'm sorry. I've been feeling rough all week. Much better now though.'

Nina is an optimist. She is a happy person. A forgiving person. After ensuring I'm feeling myself again, she slides into delightful babble about Hugh, only ever breaking her stride to suck on a vape which, at 8am, won't be her first of the day. The tension in me eases even further, like a barrier has been passed.

'Nina, my love, I need to go to work. But let's have a drink later?'

'Won't you be *on call*?' Do I imagine that emphasis, like an arched eyebrow? It's the most I'll ever get from Nina to show she has any resentment for how much time the phone line has taken up this year.

'I'll take a night off. Honestly this time. I'll . . . I'll even leave the phone at home.' The phone has been off all week, buried in a drawer with nothing but the voicemail message of top tips and other phone numbers to call to help people. It felt sensible to distance myself from Message M for a few days while I waited to see if the news broke about Karl, and if it was connected to me. Now though, the thought of returning to Message M scares me, and I can admit that it's been good to have a break, even if the guilt of ignoring calls for help is eating me up.

'Oh! Really? Oh cool!' The obvious joy in her voice breaks my heart. I've been a bad friend lately. I've been a bad sister too, I haven't visited Katie since The Incident.

'I need to drop in and see my sister after work, then I'll meet you at The Golden Guinea?'

We say our goodbyes and I sit back on my sofa to

drink my coffee, eat my croissant, and think. It's been seven days since the murder. Life is beginning to right itself. Whoever said actions always have consequences?

Rick is working in the back room and I'm lounging on the front desk, mentally flicking through the photos I found on Karl's camera. I've named each of the girls. All thirteen of them. Each of them has a story. I hope they are okay and they don't remember a thing about what happened with Karl. I wonder what he was like with them in the mornings? I wonder if he made them coffee and gave a little chuckle when they apologised for passing out?

'Don't worry. It happens to the best of us,' he might say with that nice smile of his, sitting on his stairs that broke his skull.

The bell above the door chimes as it's pushed open, and I nearly fall off my chair. Straightening up, I'm taken aback for the second time. Dark eyes and an angular face, a tall frame. I start to shake, feeling sweat breaking out all over my body. But then the man gives me a concerned look, and the dread drains away as quickly as it came, just as it has with each passing police siren over the past seven days. For a second there I thought it was Karl's neighbour, but I've never seen this man before. Paranoia – I believe it's a common side effect of murder.

Smiling to disguise the horror that must have been clear on my face, I steady myself on the desk, feeling my heart rate return to normal. Now my moment of panic has disappeared, my sight sharpens and I realise that he is astonishingly attractive, even more so than his doppelgänger. And I'm standing here with my mouth open like a single-celled organism. *Pull your shit together.*

'Hello.'

Wow, nailed that then. I try to look mysterious, but how mysterious can you be behind a dusty shop counter wearing a name tag?

'Hi! I'm looking for a frame?'

Everyone says this when they come into what is, very clearly, a framing shop. It's that pathetic Britishness in us all – we mustn't appear to be too cocky or sure of *anything* at all.

'Well, you're in luck.' I gesture to the hundreds of frames surrounding us in the cramped front room of the shop, piles of them at my elbows and by his feet.

He is tall and narrow, but solid. A swimmer's body. His features are too big for the slim, chiselled face, and his large mouth grins with the embarrassment of being alive.

'Yeah, sorry. Obviously. I might need one made though. And it's a bit of a rush job, I'm afraid . . . I should have sorted this out days ago.' He shrugs and exhales softly, blowing a strand of his dark, floppy hair into his eyes.

'Tell me what you need.'

There is a pause where his eyes flick down my body and back to my face.

'Something . . . beautiful.'

Are we *flirting*? Is it okay to flirt days after killing someone?

It soon transpires that it's his parents' fortieth wedding anniversary, and he wants some plane tickets framed. As he speaks, I flutter around with notebooks and samples to avoid looking him directly in the face. When I do have to look at him, I focus on his long fingers, tapping rhythmically on the desk.

'It's their plane tickets from when they moved to the UK

– from Bangladesh. Thirty-five years ago now. They met on the flight.' He does that shrug again. Adorable, as is the gift.

I don't want you thinking that I hate all male-kind. I don't. Just most of them. I try to suppress the thought that this guy may actually be nice. He probably has a cupboard full of stolen bras he wanks into on the daily.

'But I need it for next Thursday. That's when their party is. Any chance of that?'

'I can make that happen.' Rick won't be happy. I'll just push back Mrs Baker's job, and that football shirt one. No one has any business owning a framed football shirt anyway.

'Amazing. My brother would kill me if I messed this up. My only job was to sort the present.' He grins again, and then falters. 'I'm James by the way.'

'Millie.'

'I'm aware.' He nods at my badge and I flush, reminded of the inequality of our situation. Server and served. 'James Khan.' He looks at the desk, and I realise that he gave me his name for the form in front of me, not because he cared about knowing mine.

We hurry through the specifics, choosing wood colours and thickness, quality of glass and size of mounting. I push past silver, crystal-encrusted monstrosities to show him an example of classy black wood with a cream mount. He runs his spindly finger across a gilt corner as I speak. As he turns to leave, he falters again, coming back up to the desk.

'I know it usually takes longer than this. I owe you one. Can I . . . Can I buy you a drink? To say thank you?' He smiles and shrugs. I'm beginning to understand the shrug is his embarrassment-tell.

Every time I consider dating, I think of the women I've helped, and of my small, sad sister, and the anger usually pushes away any lust or romance. But for some reason, when James smiles at me, the anger doesn't come. Instead, I feel, could it be, excitement? But it's been months since I've been on a date. Seven days since I've murdered a man probably isn't the time to start.

I mirror his shrug and shake my head. 'Sorry. Company policy.'

I'm at The Golden Guinea at 8pm on the dot. Nina is already here. I don't think there has ever been an occasion where Nina has not arrived first. I'm certain she gets to places an hour early just to make sure. She's already bought me a glass of red and secured the best table. There is a cosy bench against the latticed window looking out onto the street, a table in front of it. The fire is lit to give the cold and drizzly October evening a heart, and a grey-haired man sits in front of it in an armchair, his dog asleep on the floor.

The Guinea is small and dark, and I love it because it's the very essence of Pub. Nina waves, despite only being about four feet away and the pub being minuscule.

'I've got you a rioja.' We hug and I breathe in her wonderful scent of nicotine and Penhaligon's Empressa. My smoky princess. I've missed her while I've been hiding away from the world, and it's been embarrassingly long since I've given her an entire Friday evening without having my phone on the table. I force away thoughts of young women pushing off wandering hands and scared teenagers hiding in toilets, and focus on the pea green of the trouser suit she'd worn to work.

I went to see Katie before The Guinea, and I try my best to compartmentalise that so Nina gets my full attention. But it was another unsatisfactory visit. I'd let myself in and gone straight upstairs, avoiding my mum who was hoovering the living room and dusting the ornaments she's been collecting since Dad died. Nasty little models of dancing women in pretty (hideous) dresses, mothers holding their children close (ironic), and stupid-faced, smooth little dogs (she hates animals). They give me the creeps. God, I hate that house.

Katie was awake, but even less energetic than the last time I saw her. After half an hour of small talk, I asked if she'd eaten that day and she flinched like I'd hit her. It's a hard balance to strike – I want to be the safety she can curl up to, but I also want to push her to get better. Sometimes the latter feels distinctly opposite from the former.

Now, as Nina talks, I'm nodding and laughing in the right places, trying to stay present for my best friend. But when she goes to the bar, errant thoughts flood my mind. Katie's ghostly appearance and monosyllabic answers, the bones poking through her skin. The girls on Karl's camera. The crack of his head against the floor. Although my fear of being arrested has faded, the question of whether what I did was right or wrong has been plaguing me twenty-four hours a day.

Nina returns and bangs a third glass of rioja in front of me. I snap back to reality.

'This might be it, Mills. *He* might be it.' She has a vape hidden in her sleeve which she takes a long drag from, exhaling the perfumed mist into her lap. 'I know you think I'm ridiculous, but *someone* has to be it. And why not Hugh? He is handsome, talented, ambitious. He's planning this business, making fine furniture for rich people? Just needs some capital to kick start it.' I've only been half listening but suddenly I'm on red alert.

'Do not give him money, Nina Lee.'

'Give! Who said anything about g —'

'Do not *lend* him money, Nina Lee.'

'I thought you liked him!'

'Have you already done it? How much?'

'Everyone needs a leg up if they want to be successful. You know that is just the way the world works. I'd do the same for you if you found something you wanted to do.'

That's it then, is it? Mr Coffee Table is after Nina's big lawyer paycheck. My heart is sinking fast. *Oh Nina, Nina, Nina.*

'How. Much. Have. You. Given. Him?'

'Just enough to get started! Get a website up and running.' I stay silent. I know how to get her talking. 'And some material costs, because right now he uses some of his boss's tools, you know? Which he obviously can't do when he sets up on his own.' I sip my drink. 'And in the long run, when we get married—'

Okay, enough is enough.

'More or less than two thousand pounds?'

She looks down into her gin and tonic. 'More.'

I eventually get out of Nina that she has 'lent' Hugh the incredible sum of *ten thousand pounds*. That fucking leech bastard. That grasping weasel prick. That utter piss stain on a turd. My sweet, sweet friend is not only about to get her heart broken, she's going to be paying out the nose for the privilege. I try not to be angry at her, but *who* is so smart and self-sufficient in all areas of life but one? Grinding my hands into fists, I breathe through my nose.

In the bathroom I lean against the sink and breathe deeply. A hawk looks back at me in the mirror. I fix my eyes on the crook in my nose and try to calm myself down. These men. These awful, awful men. I wonder how many other love-starved successful women Hugh has enticed into his muscly arms and taken advantage of. I think of the photos of the girls on Karl's camera. One after another after another.

But Karl isn't going to do that again. Because Karl was stopped. Karl was punished. I meet my own eyes and for the first time since I pushed that bastard down his own stairs, I smile, and mean it. Because, quite suddenly, I'm *proud* of what I've done. It's one of the only things I've done in my life to be proud of. That man did not deserve to live. He did not deserve to breathe my air and share my sunsets, to enjoy a book or get a degree.

I've not just saved one woman; I've saved countless women in the years to come. Because really, what's the point of just interrupting one creep's night out? Someone needs to cut these men off from doing what they are doing.

I think again of Katie, I haven't done enough to help her. I think of the bones poking up through the skin and her pale face above the duvet. It's time Millie Masters stepped up. I'll punish the man who did that to my sister, I just need to find him first. Katie will get closure and start to heal, and he won't be able to do what he has done to her to anyone else.

And Hugh? I'll punish the man who is taking advantage of my friend too.

CHAPTER EIGHT

It is a universally acknowledged truth that runners are cunts. How could anyone possibly enjoy something where nothing happens but your body becoming slick with sweat, your lungs feeling like they've been hacked at with a bread knife? It's boring too, hardly the time to find scintillating conversation or witness hilarious happenings. But these days, I'm afraid to say that I'm one of them.

There is a football game on in a few hours and the roads are busy, cars crawling along full of men in red scarves. The path peels away from them, turning into a dirt track surrounded by trees and brambles and old Carling cans. My feet pound the mud and I pull in my breath faster, harder.

The image of Karl falling down those stairs repeats in my mind like a manic Gif, or one of the nauseating 'boomerang' things that the world's most basic send to each other of them cheers-ing cocktails. Over and over, he tumbles. *Crack*. *Crack*. *Crack*. Running calms that, so I've run every day for the past week. But now, the man in my mind turns into Hugh, money spilling from his pockets as he falls, and someone faceless who hurt my sister.

The path winds around to the left, deeper into forest, and the sound of the road fades away. Nothing but me and the noise in my head that I tramp down with each footfall. I love this part of the route, and I know that soon the fields will open up to my left and they will be full of sheep. Sheep are stupid, famously, but they are also delightful. Although I can't stand idiotic people, I adore stupid animals. What a wonderful life.

If I'm going to get anything achieved, I need to be controlled. I need to think things through carefully. For the first time in a very long time, perhaps ever, I feel like I know my goals and plan. It's simple really.

Find and kill the man who hurt my sister.

That is my focus. But while I am figuring the details of that plan out, I'm also going to have to do something about Hugh.

I don't want you to get the wrong impression. Just because I killed Karl, and I have other murderous ambitions, doesn't mean I'm a complete psychopath. Hugh is not right for my friend, and I *do* need to dream up something suitable to happen to him, but I'm not going to *kill* him. No, I need to break him and Nina up, then I need to make sure he gets his comeuppance.

The trees to my left start to thin and a field full of stupid, white balls of fluff flicker between the branches. One of them lets out a low, plodding Baaaaaa.

I'm reaching eight kilometres when my phone starts buzzing against my arm. Yes, I'm one of those pricks who own specialist running gear now, and my iPhone is in a transparent packet strapped to my bicep. I slow to a jog and then to a stop, resting my hands on my knees. As I'm catching my breath, the bearded man jogs past me, giving me his usual salute.

'Nice speed!' he shouts over his shoulder, disappearing around the corner. I didn't notice that I was going so fast. Murder must spur me on.

By the time my breath has returned enough to hold a conversation the phone has rung off, but I can see it was Nina. I also have a WhatsApp message from Izzy from half an hour ago.

Can we do 2pm for pub lunch tomorrow instead of 1? Babysitter issues. Let's do The Albion xx

If Izzy plans the regular Sunday lunch, she makes sure it's at a fancy pub near her and I often try and get out of it. I'm thinking up an excuse, when another message pops up, from Nina this time.

I've already told them you are def coming. You skipped last week.

Damn her. Maybe this is what she is like at work. Lawyer Nina can hardly go around apologising and being kind all the time. As she brings in the most money in her entire firm – information that I have dragged out of her self-deprecating mouth, syllable by syllable, coated in caveats and excuses – then I suspect she must have a side of her that is as hard as granite under that colourful outer layer.

I suppose it will be good to make sure she hasn't done anything else thick like donate Hugh one of her vital organs anyway. I type out a reply.

I have nothing scheduled this evening. I'm already thinking of buying a bottle of expensive red wine, but in all of the drama of the past week, during which I have mostly worried about myself and at times, Katie and Nina, I haven't spent enough time worrying about the others out there. A pang of guilt interweaves with the stitch forming in my side as I think of the Message M phone in my drawer. One bad experience with Rose shouldn't mean that others should suffer. And was it even a *bad* experience? Wasn't it, in a way, a successful one?

After a week of silence, it's high time that I reopened Message M.

On Sunday, I walk into The Albion at 2:01pm and spot Nina at a corner booth, Angela by her side, clearly already banging on about something dull. They look over and Nina waves while Angela raises her glass at me and opens her mouth wide in faux-glee. Izzy will be on her way, and mark my words, will burst into the conversation in fifteen minutes' time to bore on about the *nightmare* she has had with the babysitter and the *trauma* of getting the baby to sleep and the *horror* or finding a cab.

Angela holds up a bottle of red to show I've already been catered for. I vow to be nice.

'Hi, mate.' Angela half stands up and hugs me across the table. 'You look spectacular, as always. You are *glowing*.' Angela says this sort of thing no matter how one looks, though I must admit that I *do* look good today. I'm wearing a new top – a black silky shirt with too many buttons undone – with black jeans and my favourite black heeled boots with a white leather star sewn on the front. But it's more than the clothes. I probably *am* glowing. Not only did I run 11k at a frankly insane speed this morning, but I am excited for the first time in years. I feel *alive*.

Last night, I had a fairly uneventful night on the phone line. Well, uneventful compared to the *last* shift I did, but I can admit that that one *was* particularly dramatic. I helped a woman on a bad date in a wine bar who didn't feel she could leave, rescued a teenage girl being followed by a man in his forties, and removed a drunken lech from a group of students. No one died.

When I got home, I sat down at my kitchen table with a brand-new notebook. Every woman knows that all good plans start with a brand-new notebook. The one in question was a gorgeous thing with marbled edges that Katie, fittingly, had given me for my birthday this year. As I cracked the spine of the book, a satisfying chill ran down my own. *Crack*.

Nina is pouring me wine when Angela brings up Hugh, pulling me back from the memory and making my hands clench in anger.

'How was last night, Nina? Wasn't he taking you out for dinner?' Angela asks.

'Oh, that . . . didn't happen in the end.'

'Sorry? What do you mean?' I ask. Surely he didn't take her money and bail on her a few days later?

'It's fine. He just couldn't make it.' Nina flashes me a look which tells me to drop it, and uses the ultimate deflection weapon, asking Angela about her boyfriend. Angela can talk about how he won't marry her for days on end.

'It's been, like, six years? Is that normal? Like, I don't get it! How long do I wait?'

I take a large gulp of wine and join in. 'Why don't *you* ask *him*?' With my plan at the back of my mind, I'm finding Angela less annoying. Maybe it's because the rage that usually spills out of me and hits everyone in its path is being channelled into something productive.

'Um, obviously not!' Angela laughs manically without a drop of humour. She downs the rest of her gin and tonic, tips the lime and ice into a half-empty pint glass on the next table, and fills her tumbler almost to the brim with Malbec. 'Like, how awkward would that be?' she says, her huge pale eyes widening in horror to almost take up her entire face. 'I mean, he would probably say yes, but would he *want* to say yes? Like, maybe he would feel he *had* to say yes but wouldn't really *want* to say yes and then later on he might *regret* saying yes and then change his mind and it would be *awful*.'

Angela doesn't have the lungs of a normal person. She can seemingly speak for twice the typical amount of time without taking a breath. I kick Nina under the table so that she knows that I blame her for making me come out. She coughs into her sleeve, into which she was in the process of blowing vape smoke.

'Okay, don't ask him. Maybe you don't need to get married?' Going through the motions is easy because I know this conversation. We have had it many, many times. We all know the options – ask him (no!), give up on the idea (oh-my-God no!), tell him you want to be asked (done that!) or, finally, leave him (come off it!). Today I'm partly thankful for it, especially when Nina takes up the reins on the next phase (give up on the idea). It allows me to mentally fall back into the memory of my kitchen last night, trailing my finger down the page of my notebook and slowly writing out my list. The page is pretty much empty, but that is not the point. It's a start. My plan has started.

'Fuck, sorry, Nina!' Angela has sloshed wine onto the table because she is, predictably, already drunk, and it's splashed onto Nina's jacket. I leap up, protecting my new top.

'We're out, I'll get us another bottle. Everyone good with red, yeah?'

'I'll get it!' Nina shouts, dabbing at her jacket.

'No, it's all good. I've got it.' I wave my phone to show I'm ready to pay and smile at her as I back away. Angela ineffectually pushing liquid around the tabletop. Nina looks at me properly for the first time that night and raises her eyebrow at the new top. She opens her mouth as if she is about to mention it, but is interrupted by the door bursting open and a booming voice filling the space.

'Girls!'

I glance at my phone – 2:24pm.

'Sorry I'm late! Sorry! Eurgh, *everything* went wrong! Hi, Mills.' Izzy kisses me on the cheek and gives me a one-armed hug, then throws her bag down dramatically and turns to the others, seated at the table. Izzy is impressively tall and lean. Even in her casual uniform of straight-legged jeans and a striped t-shirt, she looks successful. It must be the hair.

'I'm just getting the drinks in,' I mutter and slink away, embarrassed, as always, at the excruciating volume of my friend's voice. I can clearly hear her monologuing as I order another bottle of Malbec.

'Honestly there are *no cabs in existence* anymore, I *swear*! I waited for an *age* and it just never came? And do *not* get me started on the babysitter. Oh, Millie!' The volume increases to football commentator without a microphone level, for my benefit. I turn and smile. 'Double G&T?'

'Too late mate! Just paid!' I give the barman a conspiratorial smile as I tap my phone on the card reader discreetly. She may be one of my oldest friends, but fuck Izzy and her three-times-the-cost of everyone else's drink.

At the table I pour everyone a glass – Angela looks sideways at it to show she thinks I'm a stingy pourer – and squash myself into the corner. Izzy's loud arrival has interrupted Angela's flow and, though I can't say I was enjoying it, instead we will now have to listen to the multiple reasons why Izzy cannot possibly, ever, be on time. A large one will be her husband Josh.

Izzy is the only one of us that has tied the knot, and she isn't the best advert for the institution of marriage. As far as I can tell, Josh seems to be more of a hindrance than a help in any part of Izzy's life, which she purports to hate. However sometimes she rolls her eyes in a way that suggests his incompetence and thoughtlessness is, somehow, adorable. Perhaps it's a survival mechanism – if you truly give in to the knowledge that you've married and had a kid with a total twat, what next?

'Mills, I'm just telling the others that my babysitter totally flaked, *again*!' *Yes, Izzy, I would have heard that even if I was in Paris.* 'And then *Josh* had to babysit, but he was *not* happy about it because he was about to text Aaron to go to the pub, but I said I already had *actual plans*, and like, basically legged it.'

Mentally, I added to my Venn diagram of hatred, 'Men who think of looking after their own spawn as "babysitting".' Neighbour Sean seems like someone who 'babysat' his children.

But even if Izzy is unbearably loud and Angela is a boring drunk, I smile to myself. At the next table there is a couple playing scrabble and they have a dog lying at their feet. It's some sort of massive mutant pug, and it is wearing a multicolour striped jumper. Its tongue is hanging out and it looks absolutely, adorably moronic. It's not all bad.

Once we are onto the third bottle, Angela is slurring and Izzy is complaining about people with poor work ethic. She's an event planner, and is often boasting about freebies and canapés and D-list celebs that she has come into contact with. She has been running a fashion event this week, and has been working *so* hard.

'Because I have a *good work ethic*, you know?' She puffs a strand of artfully dyed blond hair out of her eyes and raps her polished fingernails on the sticky tabletop.

'Yeah!' Angela interjects, like a backup in a street fight. Poor thing looks glassy-eyed and messy, but happy at least.

'And the others just were *forever* on breaks. Honestly. Cig breaks, toilet breaks, lunch breaks, emergency phone call breaks. They are just so lazy. What do I pay them for?'

'Yeah!'

'I would feel bad if I made someone pick up the slack, but *they* clearly don't.'

'That's because you are so hardworking, Iz,' drawls Nina in a puff of vape smoke. The sleeve has been forgotten, but the barman is yet to notice. Izzy inclines her head to graciously take the compliment she so clearly set up for herself.

'You're the opposite of lazy!' I haven't spoken in a while so throw my hat in the ring with this mindless comment. Big mistake.

'And how is your job going, Mills? You still at the picture place?' I bristle. She knows I am. There is condescension in her voice that new, post-murder me cannot abide. Not today.

'Yes. But,' I hear myself continue with interest, like I'm watching a film rather than controlling my own tongue, 'not for much longer!'

'Oh!' Nina's ever-expressive eye brows shoot up. 'You never said! What's happened?'

I wink and laugh into my wine glass. God, I regret this.

'Can't say yet. It's not . . . confirmed.' Everyone starts protesting at once and I stand up dramatically. 'Drinks!'

They cheer. I know how to control a crowd. Hopefully they'll forget that in the morning.

It's not even seven o'clock when I get home, but the wine was flowing with lunch and I am feeling lightheaded and happy. I sit at my kitchen island, tapping my toe against the rung of the bar stool. My head is heavy and spinning, but I pour myself a glass of Barolo anyway and sit for a while, soaking up the silence. The notebook is in front of me; it's beautiful, marbled cover glinting, swirling along with my sloshed mind. I open it to page one to find the list I'd made the night before.

Pom Pom's
Bald
Tall
Middle-aged
Red curtains
Magpie Tattoo

Everything I'd managed to get out of Katie about the night of her attack. It is hardly a name and address, but it is a start. In those early days that followed the incident that completely derailed her life, she spent most of her time crying. She didn't speak. We have only spoken about what really happened once. It was four days after, four days and nights that I'd spent in her bed, stroking her hair, passing her tissues. She had refused to go to the police. I'd wanted her to, but understood when she said no. We both knew the chances of them doing anything other than making the situation worse was next to nothing. I *did* want her to talk about what happened though, to a professional, to me, or to anyone really. But every time I asked her for details, she shut down.

On the fourth day, I woke up in the night. It was late – dark and utterly silent. I could tell that she was awake – you just know these sorts of things about your sister – so I found her hand under the pillow and squeezed it.

'A tattoo. A bird.'

'What do you mean?' I remember holding my breath. Desperate to know, but simultaneously terrified of really understanding what had happened. You never know what is worse, facts or imagination, until it's too late.

'I don't remember much, but there was this tattoo. It moved, while . . . while it happened. This fucking magpie tattoo, right here,' she put her hand over her heart, 'on his chest.' Her voice cracked, and I hugged her hard. 'And the red curtains at the window. I just stared at those red curtains like I could fly out of them.' I held her tight, whispering into her hair.

'What else, Katie, what else do you remember?'

What did I want, back then? She wasn't going to the police. Why did I need details? To encourage her to open up and heal? Talking doesn't take away pain, it spreads it. Maybe I knew even then that it would come to this. I know that I felt the murderous hatred, back then as well. I wanted to watch this man burn. I just never believed in myself enough to do it. Until Karl.

The man had been tall, bald and middle-aged, she said, but then she started to cry and her breath came in gasps and sobs and shudders. The whole bed shook. It creaked and whined with our sorrow. 'The red curtains. And that fucking . . . magpie. I have nightmares about that magpie.' I stopped being able to make out words through her sobs and rocked her gently until she fell asleep. I stayed awake, thinking of magpies dashing through red curtains, hounds and men on horseback chasing after them.

The next morning I tried to engage her on it again but she just stared at the floor. When I kept pressing her for just one more detail, she eventually muttered that she'd been in a club called Pom Pom's. The kind of place where sleazy men congregate to prey on beautiful young women with low self-esteem and high expectations of life. After that, she made me swear not to ask again, and her face looked so set that I said yes, and kept the promise.

I underlined each word on the page.

Pom Pom's
Bald
Tall
Middle-aged
Red curtains
Magpie Tattoo

This is the start.

CHAPTER NINE

No one needs to be on time on a Monday, do they? Your head and body are still in the weekend, even if your calendar has moved on. It's *indecent* to expect someone to be on time. And then Tuesday is a non-day, really. You should probably make an effort on Wednesday, that's my bad. But it's now Thursday . . . well that's the weekend again, isn't it?

That is what I tell myself as I do a slow jog to the shop. Usually a pretty punctual person, I've been late every day this week. Since Karl, and my vow to find Katie's attacker, my head has surprisingly *not* been in the framing game as much as it could be. I've been making a plan of action, which includes going into Pom Pom's tomorrow night to start snooping around. I feel resentful that I have to waste my precious time sitting in Rick's shop. I've never thought of life as too short before. On the contrary, it's overly, boringly long. But now, every minute seems precious.

Slowing down, I decide that it's hardly going to make

a difference if I'm forty or fifty minutes late. I've already taken some extra time this morning to call Katie for a chat, and to sort out the bills I've been ignoring for no other reason than lethargy. The electricity company accepted my back payment, though the woman on the phone couldn't resist giving me a speech so patronising it could shatter glass. Every time she called me 'sweetheart' I swear that I could hear shards tinkling to the floor.

'Now you sound young, sweetheart, so I hope you've learnt something from this, yes?'

'Um, don't be poor?'

She gave one of those nauseating laughs that some would describe as 'twinkling'.

'Oh you are funny. Financial planning is important and there are plenty of resources out there, sweetie. Now I don't want to see your name come up again, okay? I know it isn't pleasant getting th—'

I hung up and screwed their letter into a ball in my fist, squeezing it so tightly that my knuckles ached.

'Now, sweetheart,' I told Shirley Bassey, who was sitting on the chaise longue, watching me quizzically. 'Try to control yourself, do you hear, sweetie darling baby? Try not to be too *greedy* with your need for sustenance why don't you? There are lessons to be learnt here!'

When the bell on the shop door tinkles to announce my tardy arrival, Rick looks up.

'You're late again, Millie. Everything okay?'

'Sorry, Rick! Sorry. I overslept. Badly. Won't happen again.' He stares at me and cocks one eyebrow – a talent I don't have and one that Rick uses enviably often. I edge around a stack of frames that I'm sure weren't there yesterday and get to the counter without causing an avalanche.

'Tea? I'll make some. Or coffee?' I breeze past him through to the back room and the galley kitchen. In the cramped, musty-smelling room the paint-splattered kettle is found next to dirty mugs and heavy antique teaspoons which simultaneously look to be worth thousands of pounds and disgustingly, unusably filthy.

Pushing a pile of papers and a random piece of wood to the side, I place Rick's tea – made in the only unchipped mug as an apology – on the counter and smile at him sweetly. 'Sorry again, Rick. If it's alright with you, I'll go finish off what I was working on yesterday. I'm almost done.'

'Okay, Millie,' he says with a sigh, a pushover as always. 'Call next time, if you can? And do let me know if I need to worry about you, or if you need to take time off.'

I retreat into the back room and shut the door, feeling guilty, though that doesn't last too long. Handsome James will be in in a few hours to collect the tickets for his parents' party, and I still need to finish mounting them and polishing up the frame. I admit that this is partly why I'm so late – on the off chance that he *is* the world's last good man, I want to look good.

Gina, who turned up at 12:30pm which is apparently *fine* for her because she works 'flexi-time', is talking my ear off about potentially asking her husband for a divorce. Sometimes, I feel like she comes to work just to bore me senseless. I don't know anyone else who has been divorced, but surely it can't always be this dull. She is a picture restorer, and thinks she is *God's gift*, if not to the world, then at least to the shit bit of Bristol we reside in.

Don't get me wrong, I am usually all ears for women complaining about men, *and* hanging them out to dry in court. But Gina has never being self-aware enough to realise that it takes two to have a conversation. And that gets old.

'I just can't believe this is really happening,' she sighs for, I kid you not, the fourth time *this afternoon*. 'Honestly, Mills, I can't tell you just how awful it feels. You think you have everything sorted, and then one day,' she flings up her hands and mouths *poof*, 'it's just all gone. You are so lucky not to have committed to anyone yet. Don't do it, *that* is my advice! Or least, don't choose a cheating *bastard* like Daniel. Not that it's *confirmed*. But when you know, you know. That message on his phone couldn't have meant anything else! I just . . . can't believe this is really happening.'

Instead of telling her to shut up, my mind wanders, and I imagine smashing her sorry face through a mirror. Getting a hold of my rage – which seems to be consuming my mind since Karl – I push my palms into the desk and try to focus all the frustration I have down into the wood. In short, Gina suspects that her husband, who, I shit you not, is called Daniel Craig, is fucking someone else. As well as Mr Craig acting mightily suspicious by coming home late, going on unspecified 'business trips', and acting 'off', she's now spotted a suspicious message on his phone.

There, didn't take too long, did it? So why am I *still* hearing about it?

'You know *what*? He's never even been that *interested* in sex, so I never thought to suspect this! But then I saw that message on his phone, from someone called Sarah.

Sarah! I mean, please! Well, I'm going to call her. Today. And get to the bottom of all this.'

'Hmmm.' What's wrong with the name *Sarah*?

Rick wafts through from the back room. 'Gina! I thought I heard you. You're working on that Calloway painting today, aren't you?'

'For my sins!' She laughs as if this is an actual joke she has made, which it obviously isn't, throwing her head back in a theatrical way she must have learnt at her posh boarding school. Rick likes Gina, which really brings my opinion of him down, but there you go. They both consider themselves artists and like to make little comments that make them feel as if they are the new Bloomsbury set.

'Well, you look the part.'

Gina holds up her arm to display her paint-streaked jumpsuit in a way that makes me want to drown her in said paint tins. I push down on the desk even more and feel a burn in my biceps.

'You know, you remind me of one of the characters in my *new* novel,' Rick says, as if the character is more real than Gina towering over him. 'You have the same . . .' He waves his hand, looking for words he has clearly already prepared. 'Tragic grace.' Gina blushes as if being called 'tragic' is the new 'thin'. 'I'm going to do some paperwork out here then – you needed the back room, didn't you, Millie? You're getting Mrs Baker's big order finished, I take it?'

'Yes,' I lie. I'll figure that out later. First, I need to get those tickets framed.

'Oh good, we can chat while we work!' Gina trills.

'Greeeaaaat! Great. Great! Let's go, shall we?'

Only four hours and . . . thirty-two minutes until I can leave, I think as I step over piles of old frames, some with faded Post-it notes attached and many parted from their information long ago. Pushing through the door to the back room, followed by Gina, I set myself up at the workshop table and find my notes for the commission. It's dark and dusty in here, no matter how many times I tell Rick that actually being able to see would be helpful when operating power tools. Gina prattles on as I set up, and I let the words wash over me.

'And, when he *did* the washing, he would *never actually put it away,* Millie! Do you *know* how annoying that is? *Do you?*'

An hour before the end of the day, and I can't quite believe that Gina is still talking, despite me barely uttering a word in response. I've been treated to a long discussion on the importance of family and her perfect childhood, how her own father was the king of men and knew how to provide for a family, and somehow, we're back onto the topic of everything that Daniel Craig has done wrong over the last eleven years. I thought we'd covered most of this already.

Gina is someone who speaks in italics. She stresses half of every sentence like it is *the most dramatic thing that has ever been said,* usually accompanied by staring deeply into your eyes, or clawing at the air, palms facing upwards, like she is trying to pry sympathy from heaven. She is also a fan of using one's name. *You don't need to say 'Millie' after every sentence. I'm the only one in the bloody room.*

'Yes Gina. I can imagine how annoying it is, Gina.' In

response, I try to stick to a contrastingly bored monotone, hoping she'll get the hint. I bend deeply over my work to double-check that the corners are perfect and try to block out her rambling drama. I have not seen Gina pick up a paint-brush all day.

'And *do not get me started* about the way he acted on *holidays,* Millie!'

'Okay.'

The door swings open and Rick's bespectacled little face pokes through the gap. 'Millie? A man is here – says his name is James – to pick up a commission? I'm not sure what piece this is though?' Rick quirks his lip to illustrate his distrust even of the man's name. Things happening without his knowledge throws Rick into disarray and he would more readily believe that it was a conspiracy plot.

'Oh yeah, thanks. Can you tell him I'll be right out?'

He frowns, his round head drawing back from the gap as if it was on a stick. I quickly polish the frame and glass, then hold it up for inspection. Grabbing a Picture This paper bag, I slot it in, push my hair up to create the illusion of volume, and stride through to the shop. It's not until the door swings shut that I realise Gina hasn't actually stopped talking as I've made my exit.

James seems even taller than when I last saw him. He smiles at me awkwardly, both of us remembering the polite way he asked me out on a date, then the rather brutal rebuttal from me. I have the decency to blush but I will not look away. A woman shouldn't feel guilty about turning a man down for a date. And yet . . .

'Oh hey, Millie. Hi. I'm, um, I'm here to get those tickets?'

'All done!' I grin at him in a deranged way and hold the bag up in the air. I never grin, why am I grinning? I stop grinning. Gina has now followed me out from the back room and is watching us with interest. Rick's tall frame is hunched over a stack of papers he's pretending to read, but his eyes are fixed on me too. It's putting me on edge.

'Oh wow, amazing. Thanks.' James speaks in charming broken sentences, and I wonder if that only happens when he is feeling awkward. I catch myself thinking about what he is like in the morning. Does he stutter his thanks when you bring him a coffee in bed, his hair flopping down in front of those gorgeous, dark eyes?

'Do you want to have a look? Then I'll bubblewrap it for you.'

He bends closer and inspects the frame. When he smiles, properly, not out of awkwardness, all his teeth show. They are wonderfully white. He runs a finger over one of the corners of the frame, perfectly done, and I feel a rare jolt of pride in my work.

'They are going to love this. Seriously, they will be so happy. And my brother won't kill me for screwing up the gift. So that's also great.' His eyes flick up to meet mine, and I become conscious of how close we are.

'Good! That's good then.' I pull back, taking the frame with me and scrabbling around under the desk for some bubblewrap and tape. I wish Rick and Gina would fuck off.

'We're out for this meal tonight. Been to that new Italian? It's supposed to be good.' He gives that little shrug of his shoulders, and when I don't answer he fumbles in his back pocket for his wallet. 'Anyway, I still owe you money!'

'Let me paper wrap that for you, darling!' says Gina, appearing at my elbow and taking the package. She never usually interrupts me with a customer, but obviously has a sixth sense for intrigue.

I watch James's long fingers with unusually clean nails punch in his pin and imagine them resting on a tabletop as he laughs at something I've said. My God, what is going on with me?

'Well, thanks then.' He shrugs again, and I smile as Gina leans over the desk with the double-wrapped frame. 'See you around . . . or . . . well, thanks.'

'No problem.' I see Rick out of the corner of my eye and then once again give James my distorted grin. 'And thanks for using Picture This!'

He stoops to go through the doorway, presumably out of habit, and the bell tinkles as he leaves.

'What was *that* about?' asks Rick. I duck down to clean up the scraps of tape and bubblewrap and also to avoid Rick's eyes. 'He was gorgeous. Though I don't know how you've had time to do that for him. He said he only dropped it off on Friday.' The rest of sentence hangs in the air, unsaid. *Especially when you've been missing work and coming in late.*

I don't know what has come over me recently. I killed a man, and now I'm flirting with another at work. What next, taking Gina out for dinner? No. That's too far.

Resting my head back on my garden sofa, I exhale into the silence. It's gone eleven, and I'm wrapped in a tartan blanket over my coat, my blond head sticking out the top.

But the October air feels good in my lungs as I breathe in the giddy joy of solitude. The small light on the back of my house lights up the dank patch of ground that I've never bothered to cultivate. There is a beautiful grapevine, left by the previous owner, reaching up from a stone planter, still heavy with inedible bunches of red fruit, but with leaves long since darkened. Other than that, the tiny garden contains just my small corner sofa, coffee table and an array of bushy plants in shiny ceramic pots.

And then there's me, drinking a glass of red wine and thinking about the past.

I'm not usually a melancholy person, or someone who is particularly given to indulgences of nostalgia. If you had a childhood like mine, you probably wouldn't spend much time dwelling on it either.

It's Gina and all that talk of family that's got me feeling sad. Her childhood sounds like something from an ITV period drama – horses and ballet and family holidays to the coast, mother and father and brother all with their own charmed lives. I try to let it wash over me, but after a while it does get difficult. Today, she spent forty-five minutes telling me about a skiing holiday they went on when she was twelve. Sitting out here in the cold, I can't help remembering one evening when I was the same age.

My father was fond of the pub. More than fond, if you catch my drift. I'd dread him going there, but I'd dread him coming back even more. Sometimes his brother, my uncle Dale, would arrive on his motorbike, wearing his Newcastle United shirt and bringing sweets. Dale looked similar to my dad, but he was more successful, less drunk, and less cruel. I used to spend whole nights wishing my mum had married that brother. Dale could contain my dad, or at least keep his mood on track. When Dale joined my dad at the pub, they'd come back laughing.

But when Dad went out alone, his good humour would turn to drunken anger that my mum and I would await in our pokey, sad house. One night, I snuck out of my bed, tiptoed down the stairs, pulled the deadlock across, then slipped back under the covers. Lying there, I kept thinking I should go down and unlock it. Locking someone out doesn't make them go away, just like throwing bills away doesn't stop the bailiff.

When he got back, I'd heard him drunkenly trying to open the door for around twenty minutes before he began to roar and kick at the wood, shouting obscenities. There was nothing I could do at that point. Walk down the stairs and let in the monster I'd angered? I was so scared, I thought I might die. Eventually, my mum's bedroom door opened with a bang of doorhandle against plasterboard. The scurry of her feet accompanied the picture in my mind of her running down the stairs in her ratty dressing gown.

There followed the sound of her sliding back the bolt and letting him in, her stuttered apologies as she took the brunt of his anger. But I still didn't move from under the duvet. I have a lot of resentment stored up in me against my mother. For not protecting us, not loving us more than she loved him. But when I think about that night, there is a cold, hard kernel of guilt.

Swirling my glass of wine, I remember what Nina has said so many times about letting go of the past. With all due respect, she doesn't really have a clue.

My glass is nearly empty, but I'm too lazy to get up

and refill it in the kitchen, so I take bird-like sips and let the flavour of a few drops flood my mouth.

Sighing, I pull the blanket tighter up to my face. Shirley Bassey looks at me from the open back door. A dog would be out here right now, curled up on my lap, but this faithless cat would rather stay warm than support her caregiver. Fair enough, I suppose.

'You look out for number one, Shirley Bassey. Don't you worry about me.' She turns and goes inside.

I'm thinking about following. My head is spinning too much to sleep, but I could watch an episode of *Succession* until my eyes close, and be warm. Tipping the last drops of wine into my mouth, I make to heave my weary bones off the sofa, but pause when I hear a back door open from over the fence. What's Sean doing up at this hour? I assumed he was a bed-by-nine kind of guy.

'Okay, I'm outside. Say that again, from the beginning,' he says in a hushed, hurried voice. There is a long pause. 'I . . . I can't do that. You can't ask that.' Silence again. I can't hear anyone else, so he must be on the phone. Who is calling Sean this late, asking him to do something he can't do? And why has he felt the need to have the conversation outside in the cold? Intriguing.

'Look, my daughter is visiting, I can't be having this conversation right now, I . . . no! You *cannot*, you absolutely cannot. I'm sorry, but no. I just—'

His feet squelch slightly on his small square of lawn as he paces around it, hissing into his phone. The usual cheery bluster has vanished.

'Okay. Look, it's late. She's gone tomorrow. Let's . . . Let's talk this through then, yes? We can reach a compromise. I'm sure we can. Okay then. Goodbye.' The sound of his steps has stopped and is replaced by a long, deep exhale of breath. My outside light, triggered by movement, clicks off. There is no noise at all for what feels like hours. Total silence in the pitch black and freezing cold. Then, I hear him speaking to himself, 'Right! Okay, okay,' followed by the heavy squelching of feet again and the back door being slid open and closed.

Well, well, well. What *can* Sean be up to?

CHAPTER TEN

With my feet pounding the pavement and my AirPods in my ears, I feel totally separate from the rest of the world. Work was annoying today – Gina came in again to 'pick something up' and then dropped heavy hints about James, clearly the only reason she'd turned up.

'So you aren't seeing anyone right now? Anyone you are *interested* in? Anything *bubbling away*?'

I knew exactly why she was asking, but I didn't want to give her the satisfaction. Last night I got a text from James. At first, I assumed he had tracked down my number in the sort of creepy manner men are often so good at. But when I demanded to know how he had it, he'd seemed confused.

Oh, I thought you wrote it down for me?
Sorry If I misunderstood . . .

Um, where and when did I do that?

It was on the paper wrapping of the frame?

It said 'Text me' and had a smiley face?

Damn you, Gina. Once I'd realised James wasn't some boundary-stepping creep though, we had a decent chat. He is funny, and seemed to find my own cynical brand of humour amusing in return. He invited me out for drinks tomorrow, and, with the new me who grabs life by the balls in mind, I agreed. No idea how it is going to go or if his awkwardness and huge smile actually hide a sinister bastard, but let's see.

Even so, I was so annoyed by Gina today that I left at lunchtime, telling Rick I felt sick (though he didn't look wholly convinced). At least it's Friday. Izzy once told me that the good thing about running is that you can set off with your negative emotions as a companion, and then run away from them. Or that's her theory anyway. Anger tends to have far more stamina than I do though, happily jogging along next to me for five, six, eight, ten kilometres until I'm about to drop dead.

Despite the unarguably beautiful orange of the sun setting and the skyline turning a hazy pink, step after step I picture pushing Gina through one of her paintings, and then she turns into the hazy image of my sister's attacker. The man who I am going to try and find at Pom Pom's this evening. The man I am planning to kill. The anger gets louder rather than quieter, but it powers me on. I'm having more trouble, since Karl, in controlling it.

As I round the bend in the path, I see a figure coming towards me. It's the bearded man again. You can tell his entire personality from his silhouette. His hair sticks up at odd angles and is too long. He could quite easily do something about that, but I'm willing to bet money that he thinks it makes him quirky and adorable. It doesn't, it makes him look like an idiot.

Catching sight of me, he waves enthusiastically, slowing his speed. Oh good, he wants to chat. What woman *doesn't* want to stop and chat to a man they don't know on a deserted path?

As I approach him, I twist my mouth into a smile that I'm aware is more of a grimace and raise my eyebrows as a way of hello. He steps right into my path, still with his hand raised in that stupid wave as if I hadn't seen him. Christ alive, there is no getting out of this, is there? I slow my pace because otherwise I would smack right into him, and take out one AirPod in resignation.

'Hi there!' he shouts gleefully in my face. 'Keep seeing you running around here!'

'Yeah, hi. Have a good one.' I raise my headphone to my ear as a signal that this conversation is over and pick up the pace again, dodging around him. But as I'm leaving him behind, just before I seal myself back in my own world of sound, I hear him shout after me. 'See ya another time, Millie!'

How the fuck does this guy know my name?

There are no support groups for murderers. There are groups for addicts and new mums and overweight people, but surely there is enough information out there for them already? There is nothing for those fairly new to the job of killing or for those who may want a few top tips. *The ten best ways to make a murder look like suicide! Take this quiz to find out if you are more of a Stabby Susan or a Poisoning Polly!* Something like that would be great. As it is, you just have to figure it out by yourself. No one ever said life was fair though.

It's 8:30pm and I'm dressing for success. Tonight is the night I'm heading to Pom Pom's – the nightclub where Katie met her attacker – and I'm not leaving until I have some information, or in an ideal situation, blood on my hands. However, one cannot simply walk into a nightclub and stab someone in the back, and, although it was successful in the recent past, one also cannot rely on booting someone down a flight of stairs being fruitful and undetectable. If I'm going to get my revenge and not get caught, it's going to take some thought.

Killing someone in a club, surrounded by people, is going to be difficult, so I think my best option is luring him away from that place to somewhere more private. And for that, I need to look good. Staring at myself in the mirror, I decide that my sleek, black jumpsuit makes me look incredible, but too classy. I need an air of vulnerability.

I'm not delusional, I know the chances of actually finding magpie tattoo man this evening is low. But I'm working on the assumption that people don't *travel* to go to a place like Pom Pom's, meaning that the man lives in the area, had been there before and will go there again. That's all I've got, so that has to be enough.

Heaped on the floor of my closet are clothes that I have mostly forgotten about, unworn for years. I hunt through them until I find something perfect. A simple black dress that is far too short. Stepping out of the jumpsuit, I pull this down over my head, briefly getting stuck in that incredibly unflattering, humiliating way where your arse is out and head and arms are restricted in a tube. But when it's on, I look okay. It fits, just about, and though I feel a little stupid and slutty, I can appreciate that it makes my body look pretty good. And I know what type of man it will help me attract.

In the queue, I shiver and scroll through my phone. Still nothing in the news about Karl. For the thousandth time I think about googling his name, and then stop myself. Not a good look if it ever comes to anyone looking for evidence. I just need to trust that if his death is considered suspicious, it will be reported, and day by day that looks less likely. I wonder who found him? Whoever else lived in that house, I assume. Did they like him? Did they know he was a pervert and a creep? Was there a part of them that was pleased when they saw his hair, matted with blood, his eyes glazed over and lifeless? I bet there was.

At the front of the queue, I give the bouncer what I intend to be a dazzling smile and a silly giggle. Just a fun time girl ready to dance! He gives me an appraising, up-and-down look, lingering on my boobs which are bursting out of the too-small dress.

'Got ID at all?'

I fish around in my handbag for my driver's licence, feeling mildly flattered. When I hand it over with another of my dazzling smiles, my blood turns cold. Bald. Tall. Frequently here. Could it be him? Irish lilt to his voice though, isn't that something Katie would have mentioned?

'Is it your big sister's now? You don't look a day over twenty-one.' He winks at me, and I force myself not to scowl, instead opting for a strained giggle. My hair is different than in the picture, made poker straight in an effort to blend in here. The bald bouncer chuckles to himself, performatively scrutinising my ID. I hate him, because it is utterly pathetic to wield this small, pointless piece of power around like you actually mean something. But I guess everyone needs to get their kicks somehow. I'll get mine by picturing his throat being opened with a kitchen knife.

The bouncer's body is hidden under a large black coat, his identity card on display in a transparent pocket. David Cartwright. I commit the name to memory and plan to look him up when I can. He is broad, and even in the coat I can tell that he has thick, bulging muscles. When he dips his head to look closer at my card, I catch sight of a tattoo climbing up his neck. Would Katie have mentioned a neck tattoo? Could it be the tip of a magpie's wing? At the very least, it hints that there are others lurking under his clothes.

'Ahh, go on with you then. Don't get in any trouble now.' He winks *again* and I mutter my thanks as I take my driving licence back from him. I don't want to be remembered, and staying pliable and silent seems like the best way to do that. As soon as I'm through the door, I fish my notepad out of my bag and scribble down the bouncer's name, just in case.

David Cartwright. Bouncer at Pom Pom's. Large, neck tattoo? Right age and no hair.

The thrum of the bass vibrates in my legs as I approach the bored-looking, overweight woman in her forties behind the desk. Ladies get in free tonight, so without the need for discussion she stamps an ugly, swirling dragon onto my hand in purple ink with unnecessary force. I smile at her with pitying kindness, and she scowls.

Inside, the music is deafening. I suppose that they've made the calculation that no one in here has anything interesting to say anyway. The hairspray in the air is tangibly killing my brain cells, and the number of ugly men staring at beautiful women is making me deeply depressed. Lechery aside, bad clothing always saddens me, and there is that in spades.

Why on earth was Katie even *in* this place? It's so not her. But we all do stupid things when we're young, follow friends into places that we have no interest in because it's hard to say no. Katie has a few dreadful friends, and they are always falling out with each other over stupid things.

There are no windows in here, just purple and blue lights flashing off the bodies already filling the sticky dance floor. The colours make the people indistinct, just writhing flesh, disjointed and separate. To my right, women are shrieking with laughter and raising their thick plastic cups of vodka lemonade into the air, one of them climbing onto a square pouffe and reaching upwards with both hands, as if she could touch the stars in a place like this.

It's a quarter to ten and I'm collecting a glass of barely drinkable Sauvignon from the bar, served in a chunky plastic wine glass. God help me, if you can't be trusted with glass, you cannot be trusted with alcohol. It is somehow too sweet and too acidic at the same time.

Skirting the edge of the dance floor, I start to explore. I quickly find the bathrooms – the men's you could find by smell alone, and the women's, by the shrieking line snaking out of it. I've already spent half an hour waiting by the main bar, and am doing my best to avoid the dance floor, but I find a door leading into a quieter room with a second bar. Fake-leather sofas (plastic glasses, wipe clean furniture, honest to God *this place*) and square pouffes surround impractically small tables full of pints of Heineken and sambuca sodas, while their owners flirt and cackle. At least in here the music is at a volume where I can hear my own thoughts.

A hen party is in the far corner. Quite literally. They are dressed as chickens. But sexy chickens, if you can imagine that. I don't have enough mastery of words to fully describe the sight, but it's hopefully enough to say that there are a lot of plucked legs, feathered arses, and a large cock of the flock being waved around by the woman I assume is the bride. Props to their word play, I suppose.

A group of lads are sitting on one sofa, all wearing clothes too small for them. Their skinny jeans are so tight that it's a wonder they can sit down at all, and their polo-neck t-shirts are designed to show off their steroid-filled biceps. Most have the same short, spiky hairstyle. None of them are bald . . . probably because they haven't hit twenty yet.

After a few more laps of the club, I am getting bored. Most men in here are in their twenties or early teens, with a few tragic thirty-year-olds sprinkled in the mix. I'd thought my problem would be the vagueness of Katie's description, but now I'm here, it's the opposite. There is no one who fits the bill. My thoughts flick back to that bouncer.

I lean on the bar in the quieter room. It's filling up in here and the volume is rising – of both the music and of people shouting at each other over the beat. I've decided that I like the hen party group, who are the best of a bad bunch. Maybe that means it is time for me to get out of here. Disappointment makes me feel sick. I feel my phone buzz in my bag, but when I pull it out there are no messages on the screen. Weird. My bag buzzes again.

Even though I usually keep Message M open on a Friday night, I didn't mean to take my work phone out with me today. It must be a force of habit. But now it's in my hand, and a red number two is showing at the top right of the WhatsApp icon. I may be on a mission this evening, but it's shaping up to be a monumental failure anyway. It was a stupid plan from the start, did I really think I was just going to walk into a club and find the man who attacked my sister across the dance floor? I click to open the new messages.

Hi? Is this the helpline?
I don't know how this works. I'm out, and I've lost my
mates, and some guy is giving me the creeps. He's
been following me all night and keeps putting his hand
on my leg and stuff? I said I'm not interested but he is
freaking me out. I think he put something in my drink
so I poured it away. I'm in the toilets of the club atm
but pretty sure he is waiting for me out there . . .

I take one last look around me. There is nothing for me here, and this girl needs help. I bite my lip in frustration. It hurts to leave with nothing, but clever people know when to cut their losses. I text the unknown number back.

What club are you in?

Three dots appear as she types back.

Pom Pom's

CHAPTER ELEVEN

Endorphins flood my body. Bitter disappointment, rage and anticipation all crash around in my confused mind. Gulping the last of the wine, which no longer tastes quite so foul, I fire back a text telling the girl to wait there and I ask her for a description of the man – not that I really need one. There is one set of women's toilets, and one man clearly lurking outside them. Her reply is confirmation of what I've already guessed.

> He's like 30-ish? Blond hair, curls, and a bit chubby?
> He's wearing a grey shirt.

I look the man by the toilets up and down. Blossoming sweat patches are visible under his jacket, and he is scanning the bodies of the women in the line for the bathroom. With a jolt, I realise I recognise him. A few months ago, I picked up a Message M customer from this very club. Once in the back of my car, she ducked out of sight, gesturing to her pursuer on the pavement. I'd never forget such a smug smirk lurking beneath those golden curls.

I have no plan, just adrenaline. I may have failed in finding the man who hurt my sister, but now I'm setting my sights on someone else. He was probably going to hurt that woman I picked up last time, and he is probably planning on hurting this woman hiding in the bathroom tonight. He has certainly ruined her evening and made her feel unsafe. How fucking dare he reduce a girl on a night out to hiding in the toilet from his creeping hands and aggressive eyes? How *dare* he?

Walking over to him, I keep my eyes averted but I soon feel my body connect with his shoulder. I add in an exaggerated sway of the hips, pulling in my stomach. Leaning against the wall, I sigh loudly. Sensing he is watching me, I blink, as if I'm trying to stop tears forming, then turn to meet his eye. He's got stubble that makes him look dirty rather than ruggedly attractive, yellow curls, and round blue eyes – though the way they bulge slightly makes him look more monstrous than angelic. Maybe it's the combination of the eyes with the lips that are too wide and wet-looking, or maybe it's just what I already know. He smiles at me with sympathy.

'All okay there?'

'Yeah. It's . . . It's just . . . Oh never mind. I should probably just head home.'

'Nah, tell me what's up? It can't be so bad?'

'It's just this guy I am . . . *was* seeing. He's stood me up. I kind of knew he would.' I edge closer to him so he can hear me. He smells of bergamot, of expensive aftershave layered on. The grey t-shirt sports a Ralph Lauren logo. I twist a piece of pin-straight hair around my finger and raise my eyes to meet his, trying to force an electric current.

'He's not worth it,' he says, leaning closer. 'Only a total prick would stand a girl like you up.'

I give a weak smile and look to the side, allowing him a moment to rake over my body. When I turn back to him, his eyes flick back up fast as a cockroach's scuttle. Edging closer again, I lean in to speak directly into his ear over the thumping bass, pushing my chest up to meet his eyes.

'Are you waiting for anyone?' I pull back and I can see his mind whizzing, readjusting to where the night seems to be taking him. 'I can't go home alone,' I add. 'I'd be too sad. And . . .' I bite my lip. 'I'm wearing my best underwear.'

While he is flagging down a cab, I shiver in the night air and take his jacket when it's offered, despite the stale smell of body odour. I text the girl to let her know she's safe.

Already??? That only took like ten minutes?! You're sure?!

What can I say, I provide a good service. Enjoy your night and stay safe!

In the back of the car, he puts his hand on my thigh and I let him, though his touch makes my skin crawl. When I give him a shy smile he starts to inch his hand up under my dress. My heart is thumping, but it's certainly not from sexual desire – it's fury. I pull his jacket closer around my body – despite the stale smell of sweat the fabric is expensive. When the car slows on reaching our destination, I breathe a sigh of relief.

There was no real plan tonight, even before it went wildly off-kilter, and as he shuts the door of his flat, I understand that I'm once again putting myself in a dangerous position. Alone with a strange guy, who I know to be a predator, in his house. No one knows I'm here. There is even a moment when I wonder if I should make my excuses and leave, but lemon-yellow sofa cushions, the same colour as my mother's walls, remind me of Katie, and so I walk forward into the kitchen-living room. In the cab he told me his name was Steven, and I told him mine was Millie. I saw no point in lying.

Stepping into this place makes it obscenely obvious what this man values in life. Framed posters of football players look down on me from all walls and a Liverpool FC scarf hangs from the curtain pole. It's a bright red assault on the eyes that makes the place feel so hideous and teenage it renders me momentarily speechless. *For the love of God, grow up man.*

Underneath the abundant football paraphernalia, I can tell that the place is expensive. It's in a good part of town, with large clean windows. The skirting boards are dust free, telling me this man has a regular cleaner come in to sort the place out, and the kitchen is high-spec. At a guess, I'd say Steven is a banker.

As soon as the door closes, Steven moves towards me, his bulging eyes dilating with hunger, but I step away around the island that separates the living area from the kitchen. The oven looks spotless while the microwave looks filthy, and I start to seriously consider if this person is actually just a gigantic child.

But then his full, wet lips stretch wide in a smile that is more like a leer, and I remember that there is nothing childlike about his interest in women. I realise for the first time that he looks exactly like a toad, and I wonder how far those eyes would bulge if I wrapped that red scarf around his chubby neck. I give him what I hope to be a coy smile.

'You're not going to offer me a drink?' I pout and he laughs.

'Was just gonna do that, hold your horses.' Winking, he turns to open a cupboard behind him.

'I'm just going to freshen up.'

'First door on the right. But I think you look pretty fresh already.'

I leave before I vomit on the floor. The bathroom is weirdly bare, with one black towel hanging on a hook. (Who chooses a *black* towel? Gross.) The porcelain is flecked with bits of hair where he's been trimming his stubble, and the soap dispenser is empty. I lean against the sink and take a deep breath. I don't know why I've come here, it's not like I have a plan, I have just been carried away by my desire for punishment. Racking my brains, I perch on the edge of the bathtub and put my hands in the pockets of Steven's expensive blazer. Then it comes to me.

Steven is putting two glasses of red on the kitchen island when I return. The bottle on the counter looks expensive, but I wouldn't drink something this guy gave me even if he had a gun to my head. I notice that the glasses are slightly different, and I wonder if it's so he doesn't mistakenly drink from mine.

'Hey,' I say from the doorway. 'I just remembered that I have something that's even more fun.' I hold up a small baggy and give him a comical wink. 'If you're game?'

I've surprised him and, once again, he is recalculating the direction of the evening. He can't decide if he is pleased or pissed off that I haven't immediately stripped and climbed into his bed. As his licks his too-wide lips as if I'm a particularly juicy-looking bluebottle, I see him consider before he decides to embrace it.

'Oh yeah? You want to really have some fun, do you?' He laughs and shakes his head in wonder. He's turned the kitchen light on, and the bright fluorescents light up the dark shadows under his eyes and the greying stubble. The sweat patches under his arm have spread. In this light, he looks older, and dirtier. A tired old toad, pulling himself from the swampy marshes. No wonder he isn't saying no to a little cocaine. 'Here.' He thrusts a glass at me. 'You take your drink before we get started and I'll rack up.'

He goes to grab my little bag of magic from me, and I panic momentarily, pulling it out of his reach. I'd rather him not get too close too fast. I employ my special, disgusting little giggle and wag a finger at him to cover the potentially awkward moment.

'Let me do it. You relax.'

'Sure.' He moves behind me and puts his hands on my waist. I try to hold in a shudder. His breath tickles the back of my neck and he presses against me. 'Then it will be your turn to *relax*. Maybe with a massage?'

I can't remember the last time I was so grossed out, but I remind myself that there is rarely any gain without pain. I force the idea of his slimy toady hands out of my mind and turn my head to meet his eyes.

'I can hardly wait. But first, take a seat.'

He sits on the sofa, and I kneel on the engineered wood floor, tipping the little baggy out onto the black glass of the coffee table and separating it into lines with my driver's licence.

'Hey, don't forget your drink!' Steven says, pushing the glass towards my hand. He is very keen I drink that – I wonder why (eye roll). I angle my arm so he can't see exactly what I'm doing, then I lean down with a rolled-up tenner and pretend to quickly snort two lines.

'Whoa, you're keen!' he says with a laugh.

'Yeah, they were big ones too. I'll make you three normal ones, so you're on the same level. You have so much muscle that you probably won't feel a thing otherwise.'

I say it with confidence, filled with the knowledge that a man like this will not want to seem outdone by anyone – especially a woman – and will go with it.

'Yeah, that sounds about right,' he says, puffing himself up, nodding earnestly like it all makes total sense. I smile up at him for a moment and flutter my eyelashes.

I rack up three huge lines and his eyes bulge again momentarily, but when I hand him the rolled-up note his face falls into a smirk. 'Watch and learn, baby,' he says with unbearable swagger, and widens his legs to lean down over the table and snort each line up. One. Two. Three. While he does it, I raise my glass to eye level and spot fine white powder swirling near the bottom. I silently pour half of my drink into the yucca plant I'm sitting next to.

It doesn't take long for the drugs to start kicking in. He encourages me to finish my drink and I pretend to take another slug. He is getting antsy, looking from the drink to me, so I take a wild guess and let my eyelids start to close.

'Wow, I feel sleepy. What time is it?' I say with a slight

slur. When I open my eyes, he is smiling. But a few minutes later, his own eyes start to close.

There is a moment I see the realisation hit him. His mouth slackens and pupils dilate as he meets my eyes. He is conscious, aware, but too weighed down to do much about it. The sweet spot. Getting up, I pull the scarf down from his curtain rail and walk over to where he sits, slumped on the sofa. Hitching up my dress I straddle him. The moment he's been waiting for. Reality doesn't always meet expectations.

'Feeling tired, Steven?' I toy with the idea of tying the football scarf around his throat, but the marks will be obvious and the strength required to crush his thick neck would be huge. 'Yes? Nothing to say?'

His pupils flit around in fear, but his body is unresponsive. He lets out a guttural moan.

'Oh, there we go. You are still in there. Looks like I mixed up my powders! Sorry about that. Turns out it was a drug I believe you are familiar with? It was in your jacket pocket, so I assume you are. Presumably, you had some more stashed somewhere for making our drinks? I've been told they call it "being roofied", which sounds rather jolly, doesn't it?'

I carefully fold up the scarf while I speak so it is nice and thick and padded.

'I want you to understand why I'm doing this Steven. You were harassing a young woman tonight, weren't you? Remember? Not leaving her alone? What was your plan? To slip a little something into her drink and then get her in a taxi back here? Was that it? Is that something you do a lot, Steven? I can't imagine you get a lot of attention at a place like Pom Pom's. But you go there a lot! I wonder why? Is it the young girls, Steven?'

His toad eyes are darting back and forth, and his wide mouth has slackened, falling open and allowing a stream of drool to start its journey towards his chin from the crease of his lips. Staring at him like this, totally powerless, you might think I would feel pity. But instead, I feel anger rising through my body. He disgusts me. Repulses me. I *hate* men like him. Men who think they can do what they want to women with no consequences.

'I have a sister,' I whisper, as if we're the only people in the world. 'She met a man like you once. A vile piece of shit just like you. He raped her. He ruined her life. He took her spirit. Do you feel sorry about that? Are you sorry? And I think you were going to do the same thing to that girl tonight, Steven. You were, weren't you?'

There is no getting any decent conversation from this guy – in any state I imagine. I catch sight of the clock on the TV blinking that it's getting on for 2am. So, I decide to get it over with. Bringing his beloved football scarf up to his face, I put it against his mouth and nose and press down. It's not long before his body starts to buck, and he almost dislodges me, but I grip his waist with my thighs, strengthened from running. A juddering foot catches the edge of the coffee table and sends his empty wine glass flying, landing on the wooden floor. *Crack.*

His toad-like eyes look like they are going to bulge right out of his head, and one of his golden curls has stuck to his forehead with sweat. I stay that way, straddling him with my hands pressed over his face, for ten straight minutes. Until all movement has stopped, and I'm confident it has stopped forever.

CHAPTER TWELVE

Nothing bad happens in the bath. It is a place of warm, luxurious solitude.

I lie my head back on the enamel and close my eyes. It was a long day yesterday, so today I've been taking it easy, though Rick slightly spoiled it. I completely forgot I'd agreed to work today – I rarely do on Saturdays so it didn't cross my mind. By the time I woke up and saw all the messages, he had gone in himself and said that we 'needed to talk'. Telling people off doesn't suit Rick and he knows it, so when I called to apologise he did it in a stuttering voice, reminding me of my contracted hours (which I obviously know) and how the shop needs me (which I know it does not).

Rick likes to think that we're all at Picture This out of some weird love of framing and not because we have bills to pay. As I made to hang up, he asked me in a small, sad voice if I still care about my job, saying *he* cares about it, and hopes I do to.

I felt guilty then, I really did. Rick is a good man. But I didn't have time for his whining. There is a lot going on at the moment. It was a late one last night, and it's not my fault I couldn't get up at 7:30am this morning.

By the time I was completely satisfied that Steven wasn't going to spring up, gasping for air like a breaching killer whale, it had been almost 3am. Then I'd had to sort out the ode to Liverpool FC apartment. First, I washed my glass and stashed it back in the cupboard, then wiped anywhere I suspected my fingerprints may be. I put his cracked, but not smashed, wine glass back on the coffee table, and voila!

Before I left, I took a moment to soak in the scene. Steven was slumped on the sofa, head tipped back, mouth ajar. If it wasn't for the lack of snoring, and wide-open eyes, he could have simply fallen asleep after staying up too late to watch a film. It was a convincing tableau though. White powder marked the naff black glass of the table in front of him, an unfurled ten pound note next to it. One wine glass perched on the edge. A lonely, accidental overdose.

It's an easy mistake to make. Rohypnol turns water a light blue, so I'd been able to check my suspicions in the bathroom before drugging him. But in a line on the table? Hopefully the police won't find it difficult to believe that a man like this would have such a substance on hand and mistakenly grab it rather than his cocaine.

Karl was unplanned, spontaneous. I can't say I set out last night with the intention of murdering a random football-obsessed banker boy, but I also can't pretend it was *entirely* unexpected. It was active. It was a decision.

After Karl, I'd felt sick and paranoid. I'd thought each

siren was coming for me, and frantically checked the news every half an hour for an announcement of murder. But nothing had happened. And this time, I'm *confident* that it won't. Steven was a waste of skin, no one in their right mind would miss him. At some point, a colleague will grow concerned he hasn't submitted any new work. Or his cleaner will let themselves in. His parents will potentially cry, if they are still alive, but really, they should have done a better job of raising him if they wanted a different outcome.

Getting a taxi right from Steven's door would have been idiotic, so I had to walk home, not crawling into bed until four in the morning. So frankly, Rick can chill out; I had a long and stressful night. I'll be better once this is all over.

After a lie-in, a run, and a bath, I'm feeling less groggy than I was when I woke up. Throughout the afternoon I mainline coffee and, despite my confidence, I can't help checking the local news sites more often than usual.

But it's not fear that's driving me, it's excitement. How long will Steven be sitting there, all dignity lost? How little does the world care about him? There is a small voice in the back of my head that asks if I feel guilty. Well, should I? Would you? He was happy to drug me, almost certainly to rape me. Why shouldn't I have done it? It was a preventative measure. At least he died surrounded by what he loved – a woman on his lap, a drink in his hand, and Liverpool FC all over his face. Too good for him really.

No, I don't feel guilty. What I do feel is a slight concern that I am going off-piste. The plan was never to kill every bastard out there, it would be a long old life if that was

112

the aim. It was to get revenge for my sister. But the similarities were striking, and part of me felt – when the last bit of air left Steven's lungs as I pushed my weight down on the scarf – that I *was* getting revenge. I'm sure I was getting *someone's* revenge anyway. But I need to stay on track. No more deviation, and it's become clear that I need more information from Katie if I'm ever going to find this guy. Tonight, I'll blow off some steam on my date with James before getting back to it.

Sinking back into the bathwater I let myself become submerged. A good way to die, I'd say. The water is cool, and when I come up for air, I notice that, as the foam dissipates, the ghostly white of my skin and bony body is starting to show through and distract me. Vivid red circles on my right thigh glow like hot coals against snow. Curiously, I run a finger over them. It has been a long time since I looked at them. I press my finger hard into the skin until it is as white as the body surrounding it.

By 8:20pm, I am feeling humiliated and ready to leave. James and I had agreed to meet at eight in The Portcullis, a cosy pub on the edge of Clifton Village. Despite being in the posh area of the city, this place has managed to avoid turning into an overpriced wine bar that serves small plates (not that there isn't a time and a place for that). It is tiny and almost alarmingly red in decoration, has two cheap meals scrawled on a blackboard for a menu, and from the first of September onwards, has a fire roaring in the grate. It is the sort of place that makes you feel good.

Checking my phone again – nothing – I decide enough is enough. Just as I drain the last of my wine and make to stand up, the door bursts open with a gust of cold air, and a panicked-looking James is scrambling in the doorway. I give him a tight smile, annoyed that he has arrived before I had a chance to leave. I don't like to seem like the kind of girl who will wait for twenty minutes on a first date without a text. The pub is too small, and James too big within it, to make a scene. He collapses into the chair opposite me and leans forward looking earnestly apologetic.

'I am so, so sorry I'm late. I mean – hang on, what's even the time?' He checks his watch. 'Christ, I'm over twenty minutes late. I'm so sorry. Thank you for hanging around. Can I please get you a drink?'

'I did text?'

'My phone died. Work – well work was a whole thing. Are you mad?'

It is an annoying question to ask, because unless you know someone very well you cannot answer it with a 'yes'. He *does* seem sorry, and suitably flustered. His face is creased in concern, his thick, dark eyebrows pulling together, so I suck up my pride.

'I'll have a Merlot. Medium. Please.' His face morphs into that large, gorgeous grin and he jumps up.

'Sure, sure. Sorry again. One sec.'

While he waits to be served, I fiddle with the beer mat on the table that advertises 'the best beer in the world', rolling layers off it and making a mess on the table. At the bar a serious-looking man has asked what flavours of Mini Cheddars they sell and is listening to the answer like it's a political manifesto. There is a pause while he weighs up his options before going for red Leicester.

'So, hi.' James hands me my glass, and his own pint of IPA slops on the table as he sits down. I'm starting to think that this guy is a little chaotic.

'Thanks for this,' I take a sip, and take him in for the first time since he's arrived. He's pulling off his coat, knocking the table and spilling more of his pint, and underneath he is wearing a dark-grey suit and a white shirt with the top button undone. It's a sexy look, maybe even worth the wait. 'So go on then.'

'Huh?'

'*Dreadfully* late, phone dead, wearing a suit. Spy? Or lawyer to organised crime gang?'

'Ha! Not too far off, but less glamorous I'm afraid. Listen, sorry again, yeah? I hate being late. Nice pub though, good choice. I've not been here before.' He slurps at his pint and smiles, doing his little nervous shrug. His long fingers inch towards one of the beer mats, probably to destroy it as I've been doing.

'No worries. And yeah, it's a good pub. Nothing's changed in here as long as I can remember. And I find that barwoman kind of inspirational.' We both glance over at the woman behind the bar. She's tiny, with short grey hair and glasses, and she's gone back to reading *The Idiot* by Elif Batuman. 'She seems so no-nonsense, like no one would dare give her shit, but also she's not a dick.'

'A difficult mix to achieve.'

'Tell me about it.'

'Something tells me you wouldn't take any shit yourself. But you also don't seem to be a dick. So perhaps you are one of the fabled few?'

'I'm afraid I am both a dick *and* have just sat here like an idiot while my date was twenty minutes late.'

He grimaces. 'Ahh don't make me feel worse! I'm sorry!'

'No, no I'm joking!'

'And it's a necessity, that combination.'

'What for?'

'Being a good landlady. You want to run a good pub with a nice atmosphere? You need to take no shit and also be pleasant. Even more so for women. Get the balance off and—' He draws a finger across his throat.

'And what? You are brutally murdered?'

'Well, no. Not necessarily anyway. But you gotta keep people happy and keep them in line. Or it all goes wrong.' I'm enjoying the easy back and forth and the rest of my annoyance at his lateness fades away.

'So, back to my earlier question. From this information, I'm leaning on you being in a mafia protection racket?'

'Ha!' he barks. 'Again, you're not too far off! Just on the other side of the law. Detective. The police kind, not the private kind. More desk work than honey traps.' He barks out a laugh again which feels too loud in the space.

My ears are ringing, and heart has dropped into my stomach. I'm aware I haven't replied, but my mouth is so dry. A *detective*? What are the fucking chances?

'Oh wow. Cool. That . . . must be interesting,' I manage, taking another slug of my wine and promptly choking on it. 'Sorry,' I cough. 'Went down the wrong way.'

'Guilty conscience, aye? It's what I've always wanted to be really. And yeah, most of the time it's a slog but it can be pretty cool and a bit unpredictable. Always on the days you want to get away on time, right! Probably like yours when you get some idiot walking in with an urgent anniversary gift needing framing with, like, no time!' He prattles on and I drum my fingers lightly on the sticky dark wood of the table, mind racing. Okay. It's alright. It's just a coincidence. And most detectives probably work on things like cybercrime, fraud, identity theft. It's only on TV that they are all involved with murder.

'And what sort of "detecting" do you do then? Perverts? Drugs? Bankers?'

He raises his eyebrows in a dramatic fashion, leaning forward. 'Well, my dear Watson, it's actually good old-fashioned *killers*.'

Right. Not ideal. But it's not like he's tracked me down and asked me on a date so he can dramatically arrest me in my underwear. I hope. He doesn't know anything. *Nobody* knows anything. No one even knows there has *been* a murder, or two.

And then it comes to me. Not only am I on a date with an incredibly good-looking man who appears to like me, but I also possibly have an ear on the ground. This could be a good thing, if I play it right. Think positive. *Lead with confidence.*

'Sexy. And is that what you've been doing today? Weren't able to leave work until you'd emptied the city of every one of those big bad murderers? Handcuffed, chucked in the back of the van, and off to the pub?'

He barks his seal-like laugh again and out of the corner of my eye I see the Mini Cheddar eater jump. Maybe we should go somewhere more intimate next time.

'Well, I shouldn't really talk about it.'

'What you mean is you need another pint,' I say, gesturing at his now empty glass with a grin. He thinks I'm joking.

It takes a few drinks before we come back to the subject of work, and though I'm enjoying the way our conversation flows easily, and his loud laugh and easy smile makes me feel warm, relaxed, and witty, I come fully alive when he mentions having been busy.

'Go on then. Tell me what you've been working on today. There hasn't been an actual murder around here, has there? And you've come out to get drunk with me? Shouldn't you be chained to the desk?'

'Ah it's a tricky one.' He gulps at his drink; he's stuck with the IPA and it's making his words looser, but he's still sober enough to lean in conspiratorially. 'Listen, you can't tell anyone this shit, okay?' I raise my eyebrows in answer. 'It's probably nothing anyway. And if not, it's always good to know when to stay vigilant.' He sighs and leans back in his chair, putting his hands behind his head. We sit in silence as he considers where to begin.

'Okay. You know when I came into your shop, yeah? To get those tickets framed for my parents?'

'Yes?' I have no idea where this is going and didn't expect it to start with Picture This.

'I was supposed to bring them in at the start of the week, not Friday afternoon. That's why it was a rush job. And the reason I was late was because, well, my *neighbour* died. I didn't know him very well or anything, just enough to say hi to, you know? Take in each other's Amazon parcels. But one day, I come home and see police cars outside my house. So, I go say hi and ask what's going on. This guy, my neighbour, had been found dead by his flatmate. He'd fallen down the stairs and whacked his head.'

Fuck. I've been confidently walking around thinking there

was no police involvement at all. Nothing was on the news. But all this time, they've been looking into Karl's death?

'Sounds like an accident, right? Maybe he was drunk or something?'

Glancing around, he leans back across the table. I hold my glass to my lips to help hide my expression. When he speaks, I can feel his breath tickling my face.

'Well, yeah. That's the official line. But . . . I don't know. Don't wanna speak ill of the dead, but I always got a bad vibe from that guy. Saw him with pretty young girls a couple of times. Not, like, call-the-police-young. But he was just creepy. We had some girl knock on the door that night too, the night they say he died. Probably a coincidence.'

There is a rushing in my ears, but my voice is somehow cool and calm.

'Did you see this girl? The one who knocked?'

'Nah, my brother answered it. Anyway, that was probably nothing. She knocked on the wrong house. Like I said, a coincidence. She's not really important.' *Not important! How dare he!* 'But it just felt strange.'

Even though my glass is partly hiding my face, my hand is trembling, so I put down the wine and clench my fists under the table. *His brother*. It's so obvious now. It had been dark and I hadn't got a good look at him, but his face and the tone of his voice rang bells that first time I saw James. Of course, it was his brother I met. Fuck, I've been in his house.

'That was a while ago though, if it was before you came into the frame shop. That wouldn't hold you up today, would it? Unless the police are suddenly treating it as suspicious?'

'No, no. They aren't. That's why I can tell you about it. Everyone is busy, and it looks pretty clear that the guy fell. He'd been drinking too. But something else happened today – and, er, this one I probably shouldn't tell you actually . . .'

'My lips are sealed. And like you say, if there *is* a murderer around it pays to be vigilant.'

He still looks conflicted, so I nudge him flirtatiously. '*And* I'll forgive you for being so late if you tell me.' The tension breaks and he returns my smile. Success.

'Well, we get a call, around 10am. A woman has gone into some guy's flat to do the cleaning. Says she always does, says she has a key, right? And he's there, dead! Anyway, that's fine. It looks like a pretty cut-and-dry accidental overdose. Young-ish banker, so it's pretty cliché. But we had to secure the scene and stuff, because it's an unnatural death. Have to look into it a bit. It all overran.'

'Right. Wow. You are busy then.' I start to feel my limbs coming back to life – I didn't notice that they'd gone numb while he was speaking until now. I press down onto the wood of the table and try and slow my heartbeat again. 'But neither of them sound like actual *murders*?'

'Oh, they're probably not. Almost certainly not.' He exhales, puffing a strand of his floppy hair up into the air. His eyes are both bright and dark, the mahogany brown shining intently with his excitement. 'It's just . . . that's two guys dead. Not too far from each other, not too different in age. Both just *dead*, alone in their own homes. It's probably because I'm quite junior that I'm overthinking it – that's what my boss says. I'm on this team, but I haven't really been involved in many actual murders yet, so this is all pretty out of the ordinary . . . Probably sounds stupid to you.'

'Not many people *have* been involved in many murders.'

'So death still freaks me out a bit. The only other thing—' He breaks off, staring at the fire like he is becoming lost in his own world. I try to not sound too invested when I snap him back to the here and now.

'What? What is the only other thing?'

'Ah I really shouldn't.' He drains his glass – is it his third or fourth?

'You have to now.'

'Well, that first guy, my neighbour, you know I said I had a bad vibe from him, yeah? Well . . . okay listen, you swear not to tell anyone? We found some pictures. On his laptop. Of girls. Professional sort of stuff, no iPhone shit. I . . . I won't go into it much. They were unexpected and pretty horrible. It made me feel guilty that I had seen girls going in there that were a fair bit younger than him and had done nothing. Not that there was much I *could* do.'

'Does that change anything?'

'Not really. Not right now. But something I did think was weird? I searched the place. Not just me, but a whole team. And we couldn't find his camera. It was gone.'

CHAPTER THIRTEEN

I'm hungover when I sit down on my sister's bed on Sunday morning. After all the murder talk last night, I drank fast to drown my panic, James matching me glass for glass. We stayed in the pub until it closed and although he didn't tell me any more about Karl and Steven, I picked up some things about how the police investigate murder in general, which is bound to come in useful.

At times, I wasn't sure if I was trying to keep James onside or whether I was just a normal person enjoying themself on a date. But once the wine truly took over and he leant in to kiss me, I went with it. Walking home, I felt giddy – with fear and excitement and lust and wine.

Katie is getting thinner, something I didn't think was possible. I've brought a bag of raisins with me, and when she turns down the offer of one, I put them on the bed between us and take a handful to chew on.

For once, I have something I can tell her about. I fill her in on my date with James, leaving out the tiny detail about his involvement in a murder investigation in which I am the killer.

'Mills!' Katie squeals, and I can't stop the grin bursting onto my face at both the memory and my sister's obvious joy. 'It's been *ages* since you went on a date! I can't believe you didn't tell me about this guy before! Has Nina met him? Is he a friend of her new boyfriend?'

'No, Nina hasn't met him. And there was nothing to tell, honestly! This was the first time we went out, and we'd barely spoken before that. Only when he came into the shop.'

'And Gina slipped him your number, the sly old dog.'

'Oh Gina, the professional meddler.'

'Any update on her Daniel Craig situation?'

'Well, I don't know if you heard, but he has apparently *always been bad at emptying the dishwasher!*'

Katie gasps in a dramatic fashion, covering her eyes and pretending to faint as though she is a Victorian woman bound for the sea air. We laugh, and I see a flicker of life; it feels so good to see her smile. I proffer the bag of raisins and she stops laughing, pushing them away.

'So when are you seeing him again? This James?'

'Ohh I don't know, Kates. When he asks me.'

'I thought you were a modern woman! You ask him!'

'Maybe I will.' We smile at each other, and I forcibly restrain myself from holding out the bag again. When I go, I leave them behind.

I arrive back home with a confused mix of emotions, but they are mostly, for once, positive. Seeing Katie laugh was wonderful, though her appearance makes me desperate to get back to work finding her attacker. Her skin looked so thin today, her wrists so delicate. Her hair, once her pride and joy, looked thin and greasy. Her mention of Nina also reminded me that I'd made no progress on ousting Hugh Chapman from our lives. It was true what I told her about James though. I had really felt something last night.

Usually, on the rare occasion that I get persuaded to give dating a try, I focus in on the minutiae of everything that is wrong with the guy. Maybe they have ugly hands, or sniff too much, or have one crooked tooth. Maybe he mentions a book I find pretentious or takes too long to choose what beer he wants. Bad facial hair, a high-pitched laugh, rests his hand on my leg, likes rugby too much, likes *me* too much, boastful, shy, boring, annoying, too earnest, too cocky, wearing a quirky jumper, V-neck t-shirt, bad glasses, or novelty socks. Tells a Jimmy Carr joke, has nails that are too perfect, works in marketing at a finance company and thinks they count as a 'creative'. Has no opinion or too forceful an opinion. Texts to say they are running late but spells it, 'L8'. Any of the above can be enough to send me running for the hills.

But I didn't have that with James. Even the things he did objectively wrong, like being late or spilling his drink, I didn't really mind.

Perhaps it's because I'm finally finding a healthy way to work out my anger, just like Nina has always wanted me to.

James suggested going back to his, but I obviously couldn't risk his brother recognising me. Even if the vast majority of men are so unobservant that you could cut off your head and replace it with Jimmy Savile's without them noticing. There was also something that felt odd about returning to the scene of the crime. Like I was pushing my luck. I almost invited him to my place, before remembering the camera on the shelf in the kitchen, and the Liverpool scarf under my pillow. Guess I should sort that out.

It's midday now, and I'm cracking eggs into a bowl to whip up an omelette for myself – Nina and Izzy couldn't make the traditional Sunday lunch, and I didn't fancy hanging out with just Angela. I haven't seen Nina for a week, which is some sort of record. But we've both been distracted with men – hers alive and mine dead. I text her while the pan heats to tell her I miss her, then continue mulling over everything I was told the night before.

The revelations about the police involvement had shaken me, but in retrospect, it's positive. Okay, I shouldn't have taken the camera. That was stupid, and I knew it. I should have gone through and deleted pictures of Rose there and then, and left it behind.

But other than that, after the initial panic of hearing that the bodies had been discovered, I felt a thrill run through me.

So both men had been found, catalogued, processed, and suspected as accidental deaths. Even though the discovery of Karl's collection of photographs created some complications, I'm delighted that his true character as a massive fucking creep has been exposed. I hope his friends and family feels sick at the thought of ever speaking to him, and that his funeral is just empty space around an open grave. Though, thinking about it, I don't imagine basement dwellers to have a wealth of friends anyway.

And the cleaner found Steven, as I expected. No loving partner or caring friend popping around *there* for tea. Probably a good thing she'd been booked in for the following day – the poor woman already had to clean his shit up and I wouldn't have wanted a three-day-old rotting corpse to make her day even worse.

My moment of reflection is interrupted by my phone ringing as I slide my completed cheese and tomato omelette onto a plate, abruptly cutting off my audio book.

'Heya pal,' rasps Nina on loudspeaker. 'Sorry I couldn't make lunch today. I'm at work.' The rustle of the wind and rattle of her inhaling on a vape fills the kitchen, and I picture her standing outside her office, huddled against the cold for a nicotine fix. I was sort of excited to tell Nina about my date. She'll have hundreds of questions and will demand pictures and meetings immediately – maybe *she's* the psychopath in this friendship. Although I know I'll quickly tire of it, it's fun to excite her now and again. I'm aware I can be a bit of a drag.

'On a Sunday?' I sit on a stool at the kitchen island and take a bite of my omelette. It's thick with smooth cheddar.

'Yeah. Big case on. Claire is being a right bitch as well.' Claire is Nina's boss. If anyone is really a psychopath around here, it is her. 'She told me I was fat.'

'*What?*'

A rattle and puff through the phone line. Sharp, fast stress smoking. It must be bad. 'I was eating a biscuit. A fucking *biscuit*. And she just appeared like this oversized stick insect and looked at me and said, "Nina darling, you should really lay off the snacks."'

'WHAT?'

'Just because she hasn't eaten a full meal since 1984 doesn't mean the rest of us shouldn't.'

Nina's boss is a terrifying woman. Stick-thin and

glamorous, cruel but oddly kind when people around her don't expect it. She's famed for making inappropriate comments about female members of staff and once told Nina she didn't 'have the figure to pull off' the high-waisted trousers she'd been wearing. It's actually a testament to how brilliant Nina is at her job that she hasn't been bullied out of there. Claire believes that anyone over a size ten is too lazy to be a lawyer.

'Look, Mills, what you doing tonight? I need a drink. Loads of drinks, actually.'

'Sure, sure. Loads of drinks. Just let me know where and when.' I feel a bit guilty that I've been too preoccupied to have done anything about the Hugh situation over this last week, and it will be good to get an update from Nina.

'Let's not tell the others. I just need to rant.'

'Ace. See you later? Eight-thirty at The Guinea?'

After my omelette, I sit down to do some research on my laptop. I absolutely need a plan to remove Hugh – unless Nina wants to meet to tell me she's finished with him – but Katie's attacker is still my number one priority. Finding a bald man with a magpie tattoo was never going to be easy work. Getting revenge for my sister is going to require smart-thinking, organisation and persistence.

Pulling up my internet browser, I search the name *David Cartwright*. The bouncer from Pom Pom's was bald, tattooed, the right age, and would frequently be at the nightclub, and although that is not enough evidence, he is the only name I have so far. Luckily, he is dim enough (who would have thought it!) to have his social media as an absolute free for all. His Instagram and Facebook (who still uses Facebook if they're under fifty?) have basically zero privacy settings, so I can glean a lot from his life within a few minutes of stalking. I'll be honest with you, I don't think 'Big Dave', as his friends appear to call him, has huge depths to plumb.

As well as Pom Pom's, Big Dave works the door at a number of other naff bars and clubs, and has crafted out a personality for himself purely based on his biceps. When he goes out with his girlfriend – a vacuous-looking orange-skinned woman called Kelly – he dresses in a shirt that's too small for his body to give the impression that he is bursting out of it, like the hulk.

There is a Twitter profile, but it's only used to comment on pictures of famous women in bikinis, or to agree with comments that have racist undertones, though incongruously he also likes an extraordinary number of pictures of adorable puppies. Does Big Dave know that this is public?

I'm getting tired of his life after fifteen minutes – imagine *living* it – when I find something useful. A picture of Kelly with a hideously sloppy eggs benedict in front of her captioned 'Brekkie with the babes down our fave local café! #bignightbigbreakfast #sundaymood'. The menu is on the table, just showing in the corner of the picture, and there is the logo. Fork It Up. Did someone really put that on the application for a business loan?

Either way, it gives me something to go on. If he lives near and often frequents Fork It Up for their prison-food-style breakfasts, there is a good chance I'll catch him there and be able to follow him home to find out more. If he has red curtains in his window, then he will have ticked off multiple boxes on my checklist and there is a decent chance I've found my man. God I'm good.

To avoid putting all of my eggs in one basket, I continue my research. The tattoo is a key identifying factor; there can't be *too* many people in the local vicinity with a magpie inked onto their chest. If the man is from this city, there is a good chance that he had the tattoo done here. Google Maps shows around twenty tattoo parlours in the city. It's a bit of a leap. He could easily have had it done on holiday, or perhaps he went to university in another city and got it done then, or at any other time when his sense of taste was otherwise engaged. But hey, I've not got much to go on, and it's a start.

Noting down all the tattoo parlour names in my notebook, I decide to visit a few this afternoon before going on a jog and meeting Nina. David Cartwright's café is probably best left until next weekend, another #bigbreakfast after a #bignight.

On the off chance that this guy is actually friends with anyone I speak to today, I don't want to be recognisable. When he turns up dead, I don't want anyone speaking about the woman with strawberry-blond hair who seemed particularly interested in him a few days earlier. So I root through my bag of old Halloween things and Message M disguises.

Deciding on a black bobbed wig from the time I dressed as Uma Thurman in *Pulp Fiction*, I shove the rest back in the cupboard. I'm already wearing a non-descript black shift dress and boots, so I just pull on the wig and touch up my makeup. I wing my eyeliner so high it almost touches my brows, and add lipstick that I'm aware is too dark for my skin tone and washes me out. But I don't look like me, and that's all I need.

*

The first shop I'm going to is called No Regrets, and I wonder if it's a nod to the classic tattoo misspelling of 'No Regerts' but realise that they are almost certainly not that self-aware. The door is stiff and I have to shove it with my shoulder to open it, meaning that I fall into the shop in a less elegant and more noisy fashion than I would have chosen.

The man behind the counter could be attractive if he hadn't decided to mutilate himself in such an embarrassing and permanent fashion. His left ear is stretched to three times its natural size, a magnifying circle of glass inserted into the hole. Black ink crawls up his neck and down his hands, but it's when he glances up at me that my heart really drops. A spider on his left temple. Seriously?

I'm not against tattoos in theory. You want your grubby little toddler, who doesn't even have a personality yet, to be immortalised in ink by having his name across your left tit? Fine, go ahead. Angela actually has quite a beautiful one of a hot-air balloon on her thigh, and even Izzy has an uninspiring but visually pleasing rose on her ankle. But if you are getting an insect plastered across your forehead don't expect people to not think you're a freak.

I walk up to the counter. Spiderman is still staring at his phone, so I put my hands on the desk and lean down to get his attention.

'Yeah?' Oh, he can speak.

'Yeah, hi. I'm Heather. I'm thinking of getting a tattoo and was hoping to get some advice?'

He sighs so deeply that I'm surprised his entire body doesn't deflate. He does know that he works here, right?

130

I'm sensing that this is going to be harder than I originally considered.

'It would be awesome if I could like, look through a few past examples? Maybe chat about what people have had done before?' He stares at me blankly, so I switch to the perennial backup plan. Flirting.

Giggling, I lean forward on the desk in a way that pushes up my breasts and lightly touch his arm. 'I mean you have *so* many amazing tattoos, so I'm sure you're the guy to help me.'

He sits up in his seat, coming to life, or at least switching on three of his eight braincells.

'Er, yeah. Sure. Like, what sort of thing? You can have, like, anything.'

Fair point, Spiderman. His voice cracks on 'sure', like he hasn't spoken in a long time.

'Well, I *love* birds. And I'm a fan of shiny things.' I giggle like a simpleton. 'So maybe a magpie? I feel like they've got dark souls, like me.' I try to sound offhanded yet suggestive lest he falls back into his stupor.

'Er, yeah. We could do a magpie.'

'Have you got any pictures? Has anyone else had one done here before maybe? It would be great to see what it might turn out like?'

'Er, yeah. I dunno.' I wonder if any brains this man did once have fell out of the holes he has pierced in his face. He sits blankly for a moment while I stare at him expectantly, before he leans backwards in his chair and tilts his head towards the open door to another room.

'Oi, Mo!'

'What?'

'You done a magpie before?'

'Yeah. Why?'

I smile like this is mildly pleasing news, but blood is rushing to my head and I'm starting to feel dizzy. Could it be this easy?

'Chick out here wants to see.'

A sigh to rival Spiderman's comes from the back room.

'It was on Suze. Don't know if we photographed it though. She'll have it on Insta.'

My heart plummets. I'm not at all interested in Suze's Instagram, but Spiderman has his phone out and is slowly, painfully slowly, navigating his apps.

It's another ten minutes before I get out of there after being forced to look at all of Suze's tattoos, most of which are definitely not to my taste. I promise to have a think about it and be in touch.

The next two shops are pretty much the same story, and I can't face continuing today, so I head home to wash off my lipstick and go for a run. Trying to look impressed by all of these people attempting to be different in the exact same way is exhausting. If they want to seem so dark and dangerous, they should try going on a vengeful murder mission once in a while.

CHAPTER FOURTEEN

After my fruitless research into the world of the heavily inked, I decide to take my frustration out with a ten-kilometre run up to the suspension bridge and back. The final tattoo parlour tipped me over the edge. The guy behind the counter leered at my chest, and asked what a 'pretty little thing like me was doing in a bad place like this'. Apart from the obvious cringe of this statement implying the man thinks he is a cowboy in a blockbuster movie rather than an illustrated receptionist, I don't take kindly to being called a 'thing'.

By that stage in the day I was reaching my fake-smile-limit. A woman came out of the back room and she was, arguably, even worse. Wearing baggy wide-legged trousers that I'm sure went out of style ten years earlier along with Avril Lavigne, she almost *audibly* sneered when she saw me. Silver rings climbed up both ears and in one she sported one of the dreaded stretch holes. Don't people know how precious unblemished skin is? How incredible a body is on its own? I long for clear, unmarked skin, and I subconsciously press my hand against the marks on my thigh. If they had been through what I have, they might think twice before doing any more damage.

I didn't kill her though. That would be insane. One cannot go around killing people just because they are rude and sneery and have done hideous things to their ears.

I was frustrated and angry by the time I got home, changing into my leggings, trainers, and running top as soon as I walked through the door.

Pausing before I leave the house, I look in the mirror to tie up my hair and remembered the wig and extravagant makeup. I am me, but not me. Like an alter ego. 'Heather' is my very own Sasha Fierce, or Catwoman. Raising my heavily pencilled eyebrows over my widely flicked eyes gives me a jolt through my body. A surge of electricity, turning the frustration into a dizzying power. The wig feels secure, and I'm keen to get going on my run. Looks like I'll be running as Heather the goth girl today.

Opening the Strava app, I start at a medium pace while I log in. I have a suspicion I am going to break my record today, or *Heather* is anyway. Tattoo shop prowling took longer than I'd realised, and light is already fading by the time I've left the houses and cars behind me, which is when I start to feel my mind focus and sharpen, filing away everything I've learnt so far. David Cartwright's hobbies, girlfriend, the supposed location of his house, or at least his breakfast spot. The so far unsuccessful plan to track down my target via his distinctive tattoo. The red curtains. I'm no closer to sorting out Hugh, but hopefully something will come to me when I speak to Nina later.

I turn the corner and see the suspension bridge in the distance, up a steep climb. It's beautiful, stretching royally across a deep gorge with the Avon River running beneath it. The image is repeated on absolutely anything sold in various tat shops across the city – mugs, birthday cards, calendars, coasters, tote bags. But somehow, this sight, when I come around this corner, always takes my breath away. Picking up the pace, I force myself forward, breathing hard now as I climb the hill.

A flash of colour through the trees catches my eye and I slow my pace. I'm not wearing my headphones today, I left in too much of a hurry, so I hear the thudding footsteps of another runner coming. My heart sinks and something in me just knows it is *him*. The annoying jogger who somehow knows my name. Without really thinking about what I'm doing, I dart to my left and disappear behind a bush.

The slow footsteps get louder and closer until I can tell they are passing right by my hiding place. I hold my breath and stare through the leaves. It's definitely him. He slows to a stop and seems to be looking around. He can't be *searching* for me, can he? How on earth would he know I'm here?

I haven't given much thought to how this man knew my name. I've had more important things to worry about, and just assumed we'd met before somewhere. But now I don't know. What will happen if I'm discovered crouching behind this bush? Will he be angry at me for hiding? This isn't a drunken lout I can easily fool. I'm alone, on a quiet, wooded path, with a large man who seems to have an unhealthy interest in me. But then he moves again and appears to be going back the way he came. *What the fuck?*

I wait for ten minutes until I'm sure he isn't coming back, and then come out from behind the bushes, glancing around and holding my breath. I consider turning back, but why should I let some random man interrupt my plans? If I go home now, I know I'll be so angry with him and myself that I won't be able to enjoy the evening with Nina, and part of me is looking forward to telling her about James. Leaves rustle to my right and I whip my head around, but it's just a breeze picking up. I jump as a strand of jet-black hair whips across my face. Heather.

Afternoon has passed into evening now, and through the trees, I can see the lights of the bridge flicker to life. Stepping out onto the path, I resume the climb towards the bridge at a steady pace. The chance of breaking my previous record is fucked, but like hell am I giving up halfway through the run.

Controlling my breathing, I'm reaching the last part when I turn another bend and nearly have a fucking heart attack.

'Oh, hey!' he says chirpily, leaping up from a bench with a grin on his stupid face.

'Christ, what—' I pull up short and put a hand to my chest to keep in my heart.

'Whoa, new look?' He peers at me with confusion, checking that my face is the one he seemed to be expecting. 'It's pretty cool. Goth, right? I'm Chris, by the way. Up to the bridge?'

'I – yeah. Was planning to.' My mind is still catching up with what is happening, and before I know it, it looks like I am going to jog with this man, this *Chris*, who turns up around here suspiciously often. Still feeling dazed, I set off at a slow pace while he babbles on about the autumn light or some such shit. Had he been waiting for me? He seemed to have come looking for me earlier, and then sat there *waiting*. But surely not?

'. . . I'm more of a weightlifter usually, but I've recently discovered this. The JOY of running!' He shouts 'joy' like a maniac and birds flutter out of nearby trees into the night air. 'It's great to get out into nature, right?'

'You knew my name.'

'Huh?'

'You knew my name. I bumped into you once, on this path, and you said, "See ya another time, *Millie*." How did you know my name?'

His smile falters and his breathing is growing more laboured as we near the top of the hill. I'm certain that there is more to this man than a grinning idiot who just happens to be out on this trail whenever I am.

'Oh, well. Yeah!' He laughs and looks over at me with an embarrassed grin. 'I saw you a few times and thought you were pretty fit. You get less people like *you* in the weightlifting gym!'

Fewer not less, you moron.

'Anyway, thought you were fit, so looked you up on Strava.' My heart sinks. Maybe *I* was the moron. How could I have been so idiotic? I've never thought anyone would, or even could, really glean anything from my Strava. 'And yeah, I got your name through that. It suits you. Or, ah, suited the old you. This new version looks kinda fierce, haha!' He booms out a laugh like a cartoon character.

'Can you see where I am on there?'

'On Strava? Yeah, course! Well, only when you log in, right? When you are on a run, like.'

We're silent while we push on and crest the top of the hill, the bridge coming into spectacular, slightly breath-taking view again.

'So,' I say slowly and deliberately, wanting to make sure I'm completely clear on this, 'when I log that I'm running, you can see that? And where I am?'

'Yeah, you didn't know?'

'Have you been coming out at the same time on purpose?' I ask bluntly.

He has the decency to at least look awkward before admitting to full-on stalking me.

'Well, sometimes. I wanted to talk to you, didn't I? And now I have!'

I feel sick, and not just because I can see the outline of his sweaty balls in his too-tight lycras. For one, why would an app I thought I was using for the wholesome purposes of logging my running speeds be designed to be so easily used to follow someone? I cycle through everything I know about that app, which isn't much. When I signed up, it asked me my name, and it usually shows a map with my route outlined in red. It knows where I haunt with regularity, and the usual times I go. You're telling me that a man can just run by me, like the look of me, and then know my name and where I run, *alone*? While I've been thinking, he's been babbling on through laboured breaths.

'. . . and I followed you . . . on there . . . so I can see . . . when you're heading out. I live . . . not far from . . . the bridge, see? My times . . . aren't as good . . . as yours though, ha! You're speedy . . . Kinda romantic, no?'

We both slow to a gentle jog as the path approaches the start of the bridge, coming to a stop at the same time.

The electric surge I felt earlier is back, pulsing through my body. It's anger, mixed with a knowledge of my own power that has been fizzing in my blood since the night I met Karl.

'Yeah. Romantic,' I answer.

He grins at that, still slightly out of breath. The part of his face not obscured by his beard is red and slick with sweat. He's worked hard to keep up with me. Worked hard for his 'romantic' moment. Probably didn't picture it being so sweaty. Up close, now we've stopped moving, he's older than I first thought. Early forties. There are lines beginning around his eyes, and it's clear that he has tried to hide a weak chin with a full beard.

He exhales and raises his arms in mock triumph. 'Oh yeah! That was good, right?! OH YEAH!'

As well as being loudly obnoxious, he has the audacity to be badly dressed. The worst part of this Neanderthal's outfit isn't even the skin-tight yellow shorts, or the clingy running top that is designed to show off every bulge of his muscles but also shows off every bulge of his stomach and open at the top showcasing a spring of pube-like hair. It is the *bumbag* clipped around his waist – black with go-faster stripes.

I gesture at the view. 'This is pretty romantic too.'

It is perfectly obvious that this man needs to die. Stalking, and ruining a potentially record-breaking run time, cannot be left unpunished. However, I vowed to be more careful than I have been recently, to stop letting my emotions run wild. Getting away with murder takes careful planning, erasure of evidence, feasible alibis, and more. That's what James said.

And yet, it's worked out so far, hasn't it?

139

Strolling over to where the bridge begins, I lean on a wall that looks out over the gorge.

'Wow, *that* is a long way down.' I turn to smile at him, leaning back in a way I hope is provocative. 'It's been fun running with you, Chris. Clever of you to find me like that.'

He smirks. Pleased, I imagine, that I've been taken in so easily by his act of heroism.

'Well, you are worth chasing.'

I push myself up onto the wall and swing my legs up, looking across the bridge. It has a road down the middle, automatic barriers at either end, flanked by a pedestrian walkway. At this time of night, the spotlights embedded in the floor are on, along with the lights strung along the wires of the bridge. It gives the whole setting a vaguely magical air. Clifton shines brightly to one side, the dark of the trees waiting across the other. On the tower of the bridge not far away, I can see a black and white sign.

TALK TO US.
Call Samaritans for free
116 123

Too late for that I'm afraid. I stare out at the trees until I hear the steady thud of Chris's footfall approaching me.

'What a view.' I don't turn, because I just know that he'll be pointedly looking at me rather than the scenery and it will be so unbearable that I'll have to throttle him right here.

'It is. Come sit with me?'

The breeze from earlier has picked up, and I shiver. A spot of rain lands on my nose. The world around us is quiet, and if it wasn't for present company, I'd feel calm. Being up here at this time on a weekend, when it's silent of commuters and the weather scares off any wandering couples, makes me feel like I'm queen of the world. The wind rustles the fake black hair across my face.

'You sure? Why don't we cosy up in a pub somewhere? It's on me?'

Don't tell me stalker boy is scared of heights.

'Just for a second?' I pout at him, and his face cracks into his ugly grin again, curls of wiry hair jutting in all directions from his cheeks.

'Okay, then it's the pub, yeah, Mills?' *Mills?* How dare he.

'Oh absolutely. Then I'm certainly going to the pub.'

He leaps up onto the wall, nauseatingly close to me. His sticky arm touches mine. I edge back and straddle the wall so I can look at him.

'I've got an idea. Give me your phone?' A moment of uncertainly flickers across his face, but he won't say no to a pretty girl with her hand out. 'I need to take a picture. And add my number.' I grin at him wickedly and he laughs again. That irritating 'Ha Ha', like he learnt to laugh from reading. Unclipping his bumbag, he puts it next to him on the wall to unzip, pulling out a phone. Unlocking it with his face, he hands it over and I snap a selfie of our heads close together, before sliding off the wall.

'Stay there! I want one of you!' I take another and move a bit closer. He strikes a muscleman pose. I laugh with encouragement and step closer again. When he makes to get down, I tell him to stop, just one more. He is right on the edge of the wall, above a two hundred and fifty feet drop. I leap forward.

In films, a director can slow down time so the audience can register every emotion cross someone's face. That doesn't happen here, but *I* see them, or fancy I do anyway. His face twists with fear, confusion, and then realisation that this tiny woman is trying to harm him, and his mouth opens into a perfect round O above his bushy beard. His body, lax and unprepared, gives and he tips backwards, his huge arms windmilling, hands clutching at thin air. For a split second, we lock eyes, and I know that this image will be imprinted on my mind for the rest of my life.

But before he actually falls, one clutching hand grasps at the strap of my sports bra, stopping him at the last moment from going over and yanking me forward into the wall.

My thighs smack painfully against the stone and I push back out of instinct, feeling the fabric of my bra slice into my skin as it takes his weight. I start to tip forward with the flailing Chris, the sharp stone cutting my thighs. His other hand smacks at my face and grabs onto my hair. For a moment, I think we are both going over that wall, and Chris certainly seems determined to take me down with him. And then . . .

Crack.

My top snaps. I fall backwards onto the cold, hard ground, and when I glance up, the wall is empty. Staring down over it, I squint into the darkness, only slightly illuminated by the twinkling lights from the bridge. Far down, very, very far down, I can just about make out a flash of neon yellow. Turning back around, I sink to the ground against the wall to catch my breath. My lip stings where he hit me and my shoulder burns from where the strap has cut into my flesh.

I peer over the wall again. No movement. There is no way he'd survive that sort of fall. He's dead down there. I pick up his phone from the floor, mercifully still unlocked, but with an inconveniently cracked screen. I can't hang around for much longer, so I work quickly. Swiping through the photos, I delete the last six that I took, empty the 'recently deleted' folder, and double check that they haven't automatically uploaded anywhere else. Opening WhatsApp, I scroll through to try and choose someone he seems close to. It doesn't take long, because one of them is called 'Wifie ♥'. Their chat is made up of the dull chit-chat of shared living – requests to pick up milk, enquiries of the water bill payment. I wonder if she knows that when her filthy husband wasn't dutifully collecting groceries, he was stalking people down dark wooded paths.

Trying not to think of this woman sitting waiting for him to get back from his run about to read this bombshell, I type out Chris's final message.

I can't do this anymore. I'm so sorry.

Best to keep it vague. As I slip it back into the still-open bumbag, I notice something else, aside from the bank card, keys (an Audi driver! I knew it!), and Vaseline – a shiny red Swiss army knife. Swiping it as memento, I replace the phone and zip it up. Peeking back over the wall, I throw the bag, hoping it will land next to him, turn, and disappear down the path I came from. As I run, I experience a shiver down my spine as I run my thumb over the smooth plastic casing of the penknife.

I'm halfway home when I realise that, when he went over that wall, he took my bloody wig with him.

CHAPTER FIFTEEN

It's 8:20pm and I'm in The Guinea, exhausted and shaken, but here before Nina for once which feels like a good omen.

I'm an idiot. I know I'm an idiot. There are so many things which could go wrong with what I just did. Okay, the text message is pretty convincing. On the surface, some guy texted his wife then jumped to his death. But I know nothing about this man, and if people start to probe deeper, who knows what they will find? People could have seen us together. Yes, it's a Sunday night and it was deserted when I pushed him, but a few cars had driven past before that. And who knows where the wig landed? Hopefully it caught in a tree on the way down and won't be connected with him, but I can't count on that. If it's still in his hand, it's going to look pretty suspicious. What if samples of my DNA are clinging to it? Tipping the last drops of my red wine into my mouth, I go to the bar for another. Time to get a grip.

After the push, I legged it home, quickly showered,

changed and got a cab to the pub. I've barely had time to think, but the hot shower helped calm me, as has my second glass. I exhale slowly and try to pull myself together by cataloguing what I know. Rummaging in my bag, I pull out my notebook.

Pros
No connection to this man
Was wearing a disguise for most of the time spent
   together
Text to wife
Perhaps no reason to look into death any deeper than
   suicide

Cons
Someone may have seen us together
The fucking Heather wig

Well, that's not too bad, is it. More pros than cons is a good thing. Basic maths. The more I think about it, the calmer I feel. The police are busy, they are stretched. Didn't James say as much? They aren't going to spend too long on what seems like a straight-up suicide. The only reason they would even know Chris was seen with someone, someone with *short black hair,* is if they launch some sort of media appeal. And why would they do that?

The other thing that concerns me is how quickly I jumped to the idea of murder. Is this becoming an *issue*? Do I have a problem?

'What ya doing?' I slam the notebook shut with a start and narrowly avoid tipping the rest of my wine over the table.

'Nina! Hey mate!'

'Sorry I scared you. Can't believe you're here before me. I'll just get a drink.'

I stash my notebook and fix my hair, hoping my face looks normal. What does a face usually do when it hasn't just seen someone fall over the edge of a bridge?

Behind the bar, I see the barman pulling a bottle of red wine from the top shelf for Nina and finding two large, clean glasses. The back light comes through the bottles of spirits and hits Nina's shining hair and the gold hoops in her ears. She stands an inch away from the counter, presumably so as not to stain her bright pink jumper with the ale spilt from hundreds of pints pulled that day.

The fire has been lit, but the warmth inexplicably makes me shiver and pull my coat further around me. Rain spatters on the window and I think of Chris's body lying out in the undergrowth, the lycra soaked with water and blood.

Glasses and bottle land on the scratched wood of the table, bringing me back to the here and now, as Nina squeezes into the other side of the booth.

'Fresh glass,' she says, pushing it towards me. 'For the good stuff. It's pay day.' When Nina is about to talk about herself a lot, she buys the most expensive wine on the menu. It's her way of apologising for what is about to happen. This suits me down to the ground because although my heart rate is returning to normal, I'm not in a chatty mood. When Nina smiles at me I look down to my wine. I feel as if I have the word MURDERER written on my face in large, black letters.

'Grim out there,' she says, nodding at the window.

'Grim indeed. Not a night to be caught outside.'

'Not on Message M tonight?'

146

'I need a night off.' We are circling what she needs to say.

'So. Anyway. I need to rant. I'm sorry. I just need to speak about Hugh,'

Luckily, even if I was drenched head to toe in blood, I don't think Nina would notice today. Swallowing a large mouthful of my delicious, expensive wine, I wave my hand in a go-on signal as I settle back against the cracked leather of the booth.

'He's great. He's really great. But I'm feeling a bit . . . I don't know. Not *used* but—'

'So, used.'

'No! *Not* used! But like, you know I . . . *lent* him that money to start his business? Well, like, the other day I asked him how the website is going. And he was all, like, cagey about it? And, oh I don't know. It doesn't help that Claire is being a bitch at work.' Rummaging in her handbag, she pulls out a scarf, a can of pepper spray, a bottle of water, and a hand full of lipsticks before locating her vape. She slips it into her sleeve and inhales it out of sight of the barman.

'Spit it out, pal. You're being evasive.'

'He still hasn't had the website done, and eventually he admitted it was because he didn't have quite enough money for that yet.' She sweeps the debris back into her bag.

'Don't tell me he's asked for more money?' Expensive wine slips down so easily that I didn't notice we'd almost finished our glasses. While she continues her rambling explanation, I top us both up. Fresh guilt floods me. I've been so distracted that I have made zero progress on my plan to remove Hugh from our lives, and now look what's happened.

'It's the way it is though, isn't it, pal? It's alright for me, I'm lucky. I earn enough.'

'That's not luck. You worked hard, you're smart.'

She waves that off, as she always does. Nina speaks as if she's some nepo-baby who has had everything handed to her, rather than a second-generation immigrant whose mum runs a post office. She got incredible grades in school and a full scholarship to university because she is that rare and intimidating mix of fiercely intelligent, impressively hardworking, and wonderfully kind. Everything Nina has, she deserves, and more.

'Anyway, just listen. He said it was all going to cost more than he had thought, and so he was kind of stuck. He said he didn't want to waste it.'

'Basically, he has just kept it. He has taken your money for a specific purpose, then decided instead to just keep it.'

'So, I said that there was no point in that, just, like, sitting on the money until he had enough, right? So I said I'd lend him a bit more. Which is fine, I can do that.' She breaks off to give me a stern look: a warning to not start.

'Okay. So has he started now?'

'Well that's the thing, he hasn't. Yet. But he says he is researching. Anyway, that's not the problem, per se.'

'If the problem isn't the thousands of pounds that he has taken to start a business and not done it, what exactly is the problem?'

'I'm happy to share, Millie. I am. I want that, I want to share a life with someone. But Hugh, he's being quite . . . distant? And we were hanging out the other night and he was on his phone a lot. Like, loads. And doing that thing, you know?' She puts down her wine and picks up her phone, miming reading a message while

148

angling the screen away from me. 'And I started thinking, what don't you want me to see? Right?'

My heart is sinking faster than the post-Brexit British pound. Finally, we are getting there

'Did you snoop?'

Nina has a strong moral compass, and anytime she does something 'wrong' she feels a deep sense of shame which means she beats around the bush for days before spitting out the truth. Depending on the circumstances, it is either endearing or deeply irritating. Today, it's the latter. Time to get to the point.

'Well, I don't know if it counts as snooping. But, well, yeah, I did look. A bit.' She puffs on her vape and I wait in silence. The bag is open now, here comes the cat. Eventually she continues. 'He went to the loo, and I knew I only had a second before the phone locked, so it was like I didn't have time to think and I just acted, you know when that happens?'

'Oh, I know when that happens, Nina. Count yourself lucky you didn't push anyone off a bridge.' My mind is becoming hazy with the wine, and it takes a moment before I realise that I've said that out loud. Luckily, she has barely broken her train of thought. Setting down my glass, I reach for my water instead.

'I opened his phone and the top conversation was with someone called Charlotte. And I didn't open the thread, because he was only gone a second, but I could see it said "babe"'. She pulls so hard on the vape that I'm surprised the whole thing isn't inhaled into her lungs.

'Right.'

'And I guess we haven't said we are exclusive. Should I have checked that? I guess I should have checked that?

And I've been so busy with work recently, so we don't actually *see* each other often. Also, I guess she *could* be a friend? Friends sometimes call each other "babe", don't they?'

Leaning forward, I pin her with my most intensive stare, grabbing her pink fluffy shoulder with my bony talons. 'Nina. Charlotte the babe is not a friend. And no, you shouldn't have to check that your boyfriend you've given, sorry *lent*, ten thousand pounds to is not shagging other women. This is not your fault.'

Nina stares at the table. She looks deeply sad, and it breaks my heart.

'This is not your fault,' I repeat.

'It can't be that. I . . . I can't be that . . . stupid.' She says it in such a small voice that I barely catch it above the pub chatter.

'Wait there.' While I'm at the bar, she doesn't move a muscle but sits staring glumly at the sticky wood, etched with initials and insults of years gone by. Eventually, I see her sadly pull out her vape, blowing it into her sleeve, leaving her thick-rimmed glasses fogged up.

The thud of glass on wood and the smell of tequila makes her look up. 'Sunday's the new Friday, Nina.'

'God, I've not done shots on a school night in a while,' she says, but she reaches for the glass. As the liquid slips down my throat, it burns and feels right. I am ignited with rage. The money was one thing, but this is another. Hugh needs to pay. It's time that took priority.

Rick isn't happy with me when I arrive at work the next morning. Drinking with Nina had taken on a weekend-in-your-late-teens type of intensity, and I woke up late, feeling like death. It really is a marvel that she manages to exist as a lawyer, but then again maybe she can lock herself in her office with coffee and snap at people that she mustn't be disturbed. I have no such opportunity. In my opinion, my appearance, which could politely be described as 'dishevelled', only adds to my story of being ill on Saturday, but Rick isn't so easily fooled.

'You stink, Millie. You stink of *tequila*.'

'I do not!'

'What is going on with you at the moment?' He looks sad rather than angry. Which we all know is far, far worse. He bends slightly to my level to peer into my eyes. 'You know, you remind me of someone in my latest work of fiction – she burns bright, Millie, but it doesn't end well.' Shaking his dipped head in sadness, he looks faintly absurd, like a bullrush waving gently in the breeze. 'Are you sure you're okay? This can't continue, Millie.'

The back door bursts open. 'Naughty naughty!'

Oh good, just what I need the morning after a murder and a thousand shots. 'Hi Gina.'

'I need to borrow you in the back room, darling – sorry, Rick.'

Pulling me by the hand, Gina literally manhandles me into the back room. As the door swings shut, she spins me into the room, my stomach lurching with the motion. The smell in here – of paints, oils, varnishes and wood shavings is comforting though. This back room is a big part of why I'm still doing this job.

'You're *welcome*. Rick was ramping up for a *real* telling off there.'

Reeling for a moment, I realise that Gina has done me a favour and stutter my thanks.

'Girls need to stick *together*.'

I have a sixth sense when it comes to other people's intentions, and my spidey sensor is telling me that there is a reason Gina saved me from Rick.

'Anyway, I need to *talk* to you. I imagine you were out with that *handsome* young man last night? *Late night*?'

There we go.

'No, I was with my friend Nina.' Gina visibly deflates – she thrives on gossip. 'She thinks her boyfriend is cheating.'

She lights back up and opens her mouth to start asking questions, so I quickly move the conversation on. 'How's Daniel Craig and the potential secret girlfriend, by the way? Any updates?'

Gina scowls and turns away to bustle around with her latest project. 'Oh *what* would *I* know. He barely *speaks* to me now. I mean, it's not like I'm his *wife* or anything, is it! But he is getting what is coming to him. You mark my words. I'm *working on it*.' She rattles on without taking breath for what feels like hours while I move things around to look busy. Every movement sends a jolt of pain to my brain that reminds me I'm too old for weeknight piss-ups. To pass the time, I start collecting scraps of wood from the main table into a pile.

After an hour of listening to Gina complain about her soon to be ex-husband, the door swings open to reveal a stressed-looking Rick. He still has a bit of a bite in his voice, but I bet he is on the way to forgiving me.

'Millie, Mrs Baker is here for that graduation picture piece. Is it back here?'

Oh shit. In all the furore about the now *triple* homicide and meeting James, I totally forgot about Mrs Baker. There is a beat of silence, even from Gina, as everyone in the room wordlessly communicates the fact that I have royally fucked up. Rick steps into the room and lets the door swing shut.

'Millie. Please tell me you have done Mrs Baker's frames.'

We both know I haven't, but we're existing in this tortuous purgatory before the words are said, where I may still whip the frame out from under the table with a flourish and a grin.

I rally.

'It's not quite finished, Rick. I've been ill and . . .' Hunching his shoulders, Rick puts his head in his hands as if he is planning to curl into a complete ball from the top down like a deflating party blower, and my speech trails off.

'You've been late pretty much every day for *weeks*. You've called in sick – sorry, *texted* in sick – and then not answered your phone, *multiple* times. You've come in smelling like you've been brewed.' His head is still bowed, his voice muffled through his fingers. 'You've now let down our main customer who is going to go ballistic at me.' Gina is almost vibrating with excitement next to me, soaking in the drama like it's giving her life. 'I don't know what is going on with you, Millie, but this is not good enough. It's like you don't care anymore. This is my *business*. My livelihood.'

A heavy feeling of nausea that has nothing to do with tequila fills my body. Guilt is a terrible thing. Any tingling of unease I felt at the deaths of Karl, Steven, or Chris pales in comparison to this.

But the truth is, my life has changed focus. This place,

Rick, work, even money, has taken a back seat. All I think about now is what I've done to those men, and what I still need to do. My head is full of them, crammed in like maraschino cherries in a jar – lurid red and jostling for room.

I'm aware that Rick has stopped talking and I haven't said anything in response. What is there to say? I *don't* care, he is right. Why would I care about this stupid little framing shop, serving women like Mrs Baker? But I *do* feel sorry for letting down someone who has always been there for me.

'I'm going to sort this out,' says Rick eventually. 'And then we need to talk.'

He sacked me. Of course he did. Gina desperately pretended to work with an intensity I've never seen her actually work with, in case she was asked to leave the room and miss out on the fun. But it was a short and sweet conversation. Rick apologised so many times it was like he'd killed my cat, and I told him not to worry about it. When I left, Gina hugged me tightly, holding me for too long, the smell of oil paint choking me. She was acting like I'd just had a terminal cancer diagnosis.

Personally, I couldn't care less. It's time I got out of that place anyway. I can't stay slogging away at Picture This for the rest of my days. Rick was right – I was just letting him down. Now I can use the extra time for my research and for Message M, which I've stayed away from since the night I killed Steven three days earlier. So I didn't put up a fight and, instead, gathered my belongings lying among the sawdust – abandoned jumpers, a phone charger, a portable coffee cup – and scarpered as quickly as decently possible, the entitled fury of Mrs Baker shouting at Rick, which had wafted through the door moments earlier, still ringing around my head.

Bad news for my bank account, but I have enough in savings to get me by for a short while, and at least I can spend the afternoon doing something productive. Back in my kitchen, I open my laptop to check in on the man who is still my only suspect – David Cartwright – as well as quickly scanning the news to see if there are any updates on my dead men.

I stop, frozen to the kitchen stool. Shirley Bassey meows from the chaise longue, competing for my attention. But I have none left to give, because every ounce of me is focused on the screen, and the headline shouting out from the news site.

LOCAL MAN DIES IN FALL FROM BRIDGE.
POLICE INVESTIGATING.

CHAPTER SIXTEEN

Though my twenty-nine years of life have seen many moments of drama, terror, excitement and sadness, this moment feels well and truly unique. Any traces of sluggish exhaustion vanish in a puff of smoke as I lean forward, as though I can press the information into my brain through the screen. Neither Karl nor Steven were announced in the press like this. Suddenly I realise that I'm up and pacing.

Empathically missing from the article is the word 'murder', but the very fact that it is worth an article at all is obviously a deviation from normal. Look at me, throwing around the word 'normal' like pushing people down stairs to their deaths or suffocating them with scarves is anything of the sort.

There is no indication that the police really think that this death is suspicious though, and perhaps it could just be the public nature of the 'suicide' that makes it notable. The notoriety, even though it's anonymous, has shaken me. However, I've changed since I killed Karl, and the feeling is driving me to act rather than to hide. What's the point in retreating under the covers and waiting for a knock at the door? After a quick shower, I head back out. Much to do, who knows how little time. I feel weirdly alive for the first time in years.

Securing paid employment of some kind must be added to my list of rather urgent things to do, but first I'm going to use the free time to continue my plans. Today, I'll hit up some more tattoo parlours. But before that, I'm going to see Katie. How am I supposed to find one man in a city of nearly 500,000 people, going on the fact that he has a certain tattoo, red curtains, and no hair? The more I try, the more foolish the task feels. A hot shower and adrenaline have dispatched the worst of my hangover, and I'm in my Micra, heading for 112 Ladbroke Drive. This time I'm not leaving without some answers.

Hammering on the door in a way that I know will annoy my mother – she hates a scene – I fish around in my bag for my old key and then let myself in regardless. The banging was pointless as the kitchen is quiet, so I assume Mum is out for once in her life. Probably buying new Jay Cloths or something equally thrilling. Powering on up the stairs I pull myself up short at Katie's door. Tactics. I take a deep breath and gently knock.

'Yes?' The voice is tiny, like it's drifting through mountains from many miles away. But at least she is awake. I creak open the door gently.

'Heya, Kates, it's me,' I say, stepping into the room.

She smiles at me from bed and pushes herself up into a sitting position. I can see a book abandoned on the floor and my heart sings. She seems alert, and she's been reading. A good day.

'Mills! Come in! Why aren't you at work?'

'Wanted to see you.' I decide that I don't have time to beat around the bush. We've been beating around it for far too long already, months. It's resulted in this potent mixture of silence, resentment, and anger – one woman reduced to a shadow of her former self, and the other to a murderer. 'And I wanted to talk to you. Needed to talk to you.'

The way her face falls and her body shrinks back makes me feel sick with guilt, but I force myself on. Perching on the end of her bed, I try to channel the persona of a kind but firm nurse who is telling someone that they need to cut back on the fags for their own good.

'Katie. I need you to give me some answers. I'm sorry, I need you to tell me about . . . *him*.'

'What – what do you . . .'

'Katie.' I wish I came in here with more of a plan, but I quickly think through what information is most vital to me. 'I need you to tell me one more thing, okay? A name, just a first name maybe? Or a location, just a rough one. You need to tell me.'

'Why?' Her eyes are darting around the room, and I know that this intrusion will spark a backwards slide, but it's needed. Bouncing under the duvet, her leg gives away her rising anxiety even if her eyes hadn't already, and it's making her blond curls, which have lost some of their lustre since she stopped taking care of them, jiggle on her head in a way that would be comical, if not for the context.

'You've told me about his tattoo, his hair, and his curtains. Just give me one more, just *one more* thing, then I will leave you, okay? I'll light a candle, make you some toast and tea, and leave you in peace. But until you tell me something, I'm not going anywhere.'

'What the fuck, Mills? *Why?*'

'Because I'm your sister. You are keeping this from me, and you need to tell me more. I . . . I can't tell you more than that. But I will. Later.' I realise that I'm on my feet and try to calm my blood. Katie, usually so small and sad, is watching me with an alertness I haven't seen in many months, and with something else too. Concern?

'Katie, TELL ME!'

She flinches like she's been slapped. 'Millie.' She whispers it, soothingly, and it angers me even more to realise that she is trying to calm *me* down, like I'm a child having a tantrum and not her big sister trying to protect her. Kicking the skirting board sends a sharp line of pain across the top of my foot. Everything feels too much. That this scum of a mystery man has reduced her to this, that I just want to help and know nothing, that I'm failing, that Rick kicked me to the kerb for a few mistakes, that my mother is pathetic, and I am so damaged, that Hugh is so manipulative, Nina is so naive. That all of us are who we are.

'Millie!' She shouts it this time and I stop myself moving. I'm holding something sharp and my hand is wet with blood and something else. There is liquid on the floor and desk, shards of a mug that I've picked up and slammed down so hard it's shattered. My sister's eyes are wide with fear and I feel that familiar stab of guilt. But being nice hasn't ever got me anywhere in life.

'Tell me where he lived.'

'I don't know!'

'Maybe not the address. But you left that house and got home, somehow. You must have an idea, however vague. What part of town? Did you see any shops, restaurants, cafés? Anything at all?'

'I – I saw a restaurant.' Strands of my strawberry-blond hair touch her face as I lean over her, and some base part of me is aware that I may look unhinged, what with the blood running down my forearm.

'Millie, you are scaring me.'

'Katie. I need more.' I take a breath.

'It was called Giovanni's. An Italian. I walked past it, when I was . . . after. I walked past it after.'

I exhale and draw back, whispering the new information to myself. This is everything. This gives me a location. Katie looks like a rabbit in a trap, wide-eyed and pale skinned, but what I've learnt is one of the only things that could be worth that.

'Close by? To the house?'

'Yeah. I think so, yeah,' she whispers, the duvet pulled up over her mouth. 'I think.'

Catching sight of myself in the mirror, it's confirmed that I do indeed look unhinged, with blood flowing down my arm and my eye makeup smudged. Strawberry-blond tufts of hair are sticking up and I realise that I haven't brushed it this morning. *Jesus, Millie, pull yourself together.* Turning back to Katie, I smile.

'Thank you. I'm sorry. I'm really sorry. It's okay. You're okay?' I wipe my hands on my jeans and sit on the bed, giving her a tight hug of apology.

She nods, but when I stand back up her gaze is locked on me like I'm a cornered fox, ready to snap. It hurts to see her judging stare, especially when it's anyone but her I am hunting.

On my way home I pull into The Golden Guinea and sit at the table I occupied last night. I cleaned myself up the best I could before I left Mum's house, but I still get an odd look from the barman. Ordering a tequila shot and a glass of red wine, because I'm unemployed and can do whatever the fuck I want, I pull open my laptop, fire up Google Maps and type in Giovanni's. The result pops up straight away. One in the city, pretty central. Zooming in to look, I imagine walking those streets, searching for a bald head popping out around the red curtains.

Something clicks. I've looked at these streets before. Sliding my phone out of my pocket, I scroll through the Instagram profile of the Pom Pom's bouncer David Cartwright until I find the #bignightbigbreakfast post and zoom in to remind myself of the café name. On the computer, I ask Google to direct me from Giovanni's to Fork It Up. A four-minute walk.

Tattooed, bald-headed, Pom-Pom's-frequenting meathead Big Dave Cartwright lives in the area my sister was attacked.

Jack-fucking-pot.

Back at home, I take a long shower, feeling clean for the first time that day. It's good to take a breath now and again when I'm not caught up in investigating rapists and murdering perverts. Self-care is important.

Slowly I massage my favourite shampoo into my hair and imagine I'm in an advert, hot coconut smelling steam filling my senses. I've not looked at Message M since saving that girl from Steven, so tonight I'll get back to the phone line, even though Monday is usually quiet. I'll have to wait until the weekend to try and find Big Dave at the café, but I'm not one to sit around wasting my life. Seeing as I'm on a roll, I think that I'll tackle the other issue that's been creeping up on my life. Or Nina's life.

Persuading her to leave Hugh was a no-go, I tried last

night. Yeah, she *might* do it, but it would take her a long time. She falls in love hard and fast, and she hates letting go. She's easily placated with a kind word and a vow of eternal love as meaningless as my father's were to my mother. Even if I could persuade her to block and move on, there's the small fact that this would skate over the very important need for revenge.

Changing the blade on my razor, I drag it up my leg to leave it silky smooth, then rinse the conditioner out of my hair. Even though a lot has happened today, it's really rather relaxing, being unemployed. Once you stop worrying about the whole money thing.

When I'm wrapped in a snowy white towel and sitting on my bed, with Shirley Bassey a fluffy curl of a croissant on my pillow, I can begin. It takes me a while to get the phrasing right, because I know there is a risk to this. If he doesn't bite, I'm going to have some awkward explaining to do. I've got until the weekend to start staking out Dave's café, so I can afford to take some baby steps.

Luckily, I still have Hugh's number from when he paid for our lunch, so I open WhatsApp and take a few minutes to compose a simple opener.

> Hi . . . it's Millie, Nina's friend? I was hoping you could help me with something ☺ It's a surprise for Nina though, so it'll have to be a secret . . .

The swoop sounds in the otherwise quiet room to show the message has been sent off into the ether. The ticks turn grey and then immediately blue. Clearly he has nothing better to do than look at his phone tonight.

> My lips are sealed ;)

CHAPTER SEVENTEEN

It's remarkable how quickly one gets used to the unemployed life. Four days have passed since I left Picture This with the few possessions and little pride I could manage, and they have been blissful. I've run every day – with no Chris to accost me – cased out more tattoo shops, visited Katie twice (both with gifts of sweet treats she ignored), and worked Message M every night. Last night was a tough one – one man got nasty with me, and a teenage girl was sobbing so badly I could barely make out her words as she told me how scared she was of the men following her home.

There is also another little project I've been working on in the daytimes. Making a coffee table. Cute, right?

On Tuesday, I went to the hardware store and came back with a collection of screws, tools and pieces of wood. I badly nailed some together, and then waited for my knight in shining armour.

As far as Hugh knows, this started as a surprise for

Nina's birthday next month. He looked at my attempt with pity, and when I pouted and exclaimed that *I just couldn't do it without help* he puffed out his chest and indulged himself in a long explanation of carpentry. It was, he said in all earnestness, harder for women because our brains aren't really hardwired for the exact equations needed.

How could I have ever thought this guy was okay?

Tuesday saw him undo my purposely bad work and give me a lecture while I fluttered my eyelashes and offered him beer. On Wednesday, I took the wood to his house and we cut the angles on his mitre saw. I stood in front of him and let his hands guide mine while I giggled and pushed back against him. I promised to finish the table myself on Thursday – I'd stopped referring to it being Nina's table by this point – and asked if I could come to his to show him the finished result on Friday.

It doesn't actually look too bad, I think, as I lower myself onto the stained Ikea sofa in front of Hugh's own hand-made coffee table. Though I could have done it twice as quickly without his help. I stare at the wonkily hung Ikea print of some crashing waves on the wall in front of me, and am flooded with a heavy sadness. Imagining Nina, glorious, charming, unique Nina sitting in this spot and trying to charm the person who lives *here* is a concrete sign that things are not A-okay with the world.

The man of the hour is fixing us our drinks, and to give myself something to do I start wandering around the living room, investigating the life of such a specimen. It is evening now, my first night off Message M since Sunday, and the light coming in through the windows is orange from the lampposts that had just sprung to life. Inside is lit by that bright, icy light of the chronically poor at decorating.

It is different to Steven's place. Steven the Pom-Pom's-lingerer, for all of his many, *many* flaws was wealthy, and though it was hideous, his place at least felt like his home – his football team glowed from every corner, and he had clearly chosen the furniture carefully, if not well. Hugh's place, on the other hand, looks like the ultimate rental accommodation. The fake beech veneer on the sparse furniture, the grubby carpet that looks like it has witnessed things far worse than murder, the chipped cream paint layered over woodchip wallpaper.

It's like the man has no soul at all.

'Hey up!'

Turning, I see Hugh in the doorway of the room, and I put down the framed photograph I'm studying of what looks like five identical men crowded around a fishbowl cocktail. One of them is wearing a t-shirt that says 'I like my women how I like my coffee. Hot and cheap.'

Smiling, I walk over to take my drink – I kid you not, it's a can of Fosters – from Hugh. I try to look thankful, but it's difficult enough to play nice to this guy without having to drink this piss.

'Don't suppose you have any wine, do you? Or a gin and tonic maybe?'

'Um, dunno. I might have some wine that Nin— that someone has left here. Let me check.' He swaggers back to the kitchen and I put my can down on the shiny black TV stand. I take a deep breath and stroke the smooth surface of Chris's penknife in my pocket. While he's gone, I locate a lamp and turn off the overhead light in an attempt to create some sense of atmosphere.

'Oh ho! This is *nice*.' He smirks at what he clearly assumes to be mood-lighting as he returns with half a bottle of wonderfully expensive red wine that could only have come from Nina. Holding up a stubby tumbler spotted with greasy fingerprints, he sloshes wine in it almost to the rim and hands it over. As we clink drinks, I hold his eyes with mine.

Collapsing back onto the sofa, Hugh huffs out a breath, then smiles up at me as I lean against the windowsill. Nodding at my table, he gives a patronising smile.

'Not bad, for a rookie.'

'I had a good teacher.'

Flirting with Hugh makes me feel guilty and unwell, even though I'm only doing it for her. If I hadn't made the possibility of sex clear, there was every chance that I would never have gotten into his house for the evening. Even so, it's not been pleasant, and I long for the day that I don't have to fear his touch. Luckily, I don't anticipate that being far away.

He tucks the hand not holding his own can of Foster's behind his head as a way to highlight his bicep. A tattoo of a thorn is winding around his arm and it annoys me. Probably the memory of the fruitless hours spent traipsing around the tattoo parlours, which isn't strictly his fault, I suppose. It also annoys me because he is clearly showing off his large, firm muscles, and it's working. I'd be a liar if I said they didn't look good.

'It's been fun . . . teaching you. I'm hoping it doesn't end here.' He begins the sentence by holding my eyes, but can't help his gaze straying down to my breasts, and to my legs. Pretending not to notice, I let him scan me like I'm in airport security.

He taps the sofa with his can.

'Come sit, why don't you?' With a weak smile, I daintily perch on the edge of the sofa – which squeaks as I make contact – far enough from him that he can't start touching me straight away. This close, I see that his hair is damp from a shower he must have quickly taken when I was on my way over here, and his eyes are glassy enough to show that this isn't his first Fosters.

'Anything else you want to learn from a pro?' He says it with a low purr, and leans over to tuck my hair behind my ear. 'Something tells me this wasn't *just* about the table.' The tip of his tongue darts out and moistens his lower lip.

I haven't planned this conversation, so I put my hand on his arm, which he quickly tenses, and squeeze it lightly. 'I can admit that you . . . intrigue me. There are *so* many things I'd like you to teach me. I, well, I can't stop thinking about you. Sorry, I shouldn't have said that.' I turn away in apparent embarrassment, and he takes my chin in his hand, turning my face back towards him.

'No, no. Don't apologise. Do *not* apologise,' he says with a visible swagger. Everyone wants to be the person that someone *cannot stop thinking about*.

'How is your business going?' He looks blindsided. Maybe I went in too serious too soon. 'It's just so fascinating. What you do? You must be so good with your hands.' There we go, back to base.

'Oh I am good with my hands. Very good.' He winks. 'I'm a craftsman. An artist.' *Jesus Christ, alright, Picasso.*

'Tell me more,' I say, eyes wide and impressed. I lean forward, like I've never experienced anyone quite as fascinating as a second-rate handyman in the world's most depressing flat. My phone dings in my pocket, breaking the spell, but the leading lady always sees an opportunity. Glancing at it, I see a message from James that I'm desperate to read, but instead, I frown and look up at Hugh sheepishly.

'Nina,' I whisper apologetically.

'Ah.' He has the decency to look embarrassed, removing his hand from my face.

'Look, I've got an idea. Phone.' I hold my hand out. 'Come on, I want to really get to know you.' I smile suggestively on those last words, and am met with a sudden grin. 'Without any more *unwelcome* interruptions.'

'You're mental, you are,' he says, handing over his iPhone. I sashay to the door that I assume is the bathroom, put both of our phones in a cabinet (having a rifle through at the same time), and come back waving my empty hands, edging back onto the sofa with an ear-splitting squeak.

'There we go! I think you were telling me about your *craftsmanship*?'

He ruffles up his wet blond hair with arrogance masquerading as charm – I thought the pile-of-straw look was accidental but it seems he is purposely trying to create a rough-and-ready appearance.

I try to continue gazing at him in admiration but my attention is caught by a particularly suspicious-looking sofa stain right next to my leg and I try to shift myself an inch away.

Hugh grins at me, noticing my movement and misinterpreting it as me edging closer. 'Want me to show you just how good my hands are?' He leans in, and in a horror that I don't manage to control, I leap up. He sits back in confusion, so I wink at him and start to walk around the living room again, going back to the photos I'd been examining earlier.

'Who are these charming young men?'

'Huh? Oh that's Jackson, Little Tim, Large Tim, Feet, and Lardo.'

'Feet?'

''Cause he always fucking stinks! Ha!'

'Ha! I see!' *I see you are stupider than I ever originally believed.* Though he must have some brains in his head to charm women into giving him their cash, so it's clearly compartmentalised.

'And this?' I gesture to the next picture. It's Hugh, a few years younger by the look of it, with an elderly woman.

'Ah that's my old nan. Wonderful she is.' In my surprise, I have no immediate reply, so he continues. 'She's ninety-four now. Still got it though! I visit once a week, we play dominos.'

I didn't imagine Hugh as a devoted grandson, someone who gives up his time to visit what is, presumably, a vile, bleach and urine-smelling old people's home to play mindless games with (unfortunately) mindless people. A frisson of dishonour runs through me, and I feel a pang of shame. But I push it to the back of my mind and focus on Nina. Who this man is, is someone clearly willing to cheat on his girlfriend with her best friend.

A sound like a mouse being trodden on tells me that Hugh has wrenched himself off the sticky pleather sofa and is making his way over to me. What I don't expect is to feel his hands suddenly on my waist, and I try not to flinch. He leans forward and breathes a Dorito-smelling invitation into my ear.

'So you were saying you wanted me to teach you a

thing or two?' Holding the left side of my hip in one large, meaty paw, he trails the fat index finger of his right hand down the curve of my body. Stiff with fear, I let it happen. The wet strands of his blond spikes tickle my ear as he bends closer, planting a gentle, wet kiss on my neck with a nauseating noise that sounds loud in my ear. Like the gentle cocking of a gun in a silent room.

Coming to my senses, I spin around and edge my way out of his grip. 'First, I have something for you.'

'Ah, you've been teasing me for ages, you have.'

I pout and flick my strawberry-blond hair over my shoulder in what I hope is a coquettish manner.

'I've made you something, I thought you'd like it. Then maybe you can show me the bedroom?'

His grin shows me we are back in business, so I go to pick up my bag from by the door, pulling out a delicate cardboard box. The box is shaking slightly, and I realise it's me. I'm rattled; the place on my waist where he held me and the spot where he kissed me, both burn with the memory. There's nothing like the reminder of your own powerlessness, the realisation that one of those huge, strong hands could knock you out or hold you down without a second thought. I focus on the feeling of the knife in my pocket, heavy against my thigh. My insurance.

'Here. For you.' I open the lid with a smile and a flourish.

Inside the box are six, perfect, pink macarons. His face falls in such a comical way that I almost burst out laughing, the sagging mouth suddenly giving him jowls.

'Ah, what's this?'

Returning to the sofa, it's me who pats the cushion condescendingly this time.

'Come sit, just for a moment.' I wink, and that works despite nothing I've said having any sort of discernible double meaning. 'Now open up!'

He does so, looking bemused, but then suddenly jerks back.

'Hey, you know I'm allergic to nuts?'

'Of course! Nin . . . um, I mean, you, mentioned it at the pub that time. I made these especially for you. Totally nut free.'

My clear dodging of Nina's name must have brought the illicit thrill back into the atmosphere, because he leans forward again, mouth open. I push an entire one inside.

Hugh chews and swallows, a little grimace on his face, then holds out his hand and makes to rise.

'Wait! Just one more. I like to feed my men.' I bit into one myself to bide the time, and Hugh impatiently leans forward with his mouth open like an angry baby bird, clearly deciding that humouring me is the fastest way to get what he wants. I shove another one in and he almost swallows it whole as he leaps to his feet.

'You go through to the bedroom,' I say. 'I just need to freshen up.'

I've read that it can take between a few minutes and a couple of hours for a nut allergy to start taking effect, and I am dearly hoping it to be the former. How I'd manage to hold off the beast touching me again for two *hours*, I have no idea.

Luckily, I am rewarded for my past good deeds. Just moments after the oaf bumbles off into the dark cave of his bedroom, I hear a gasp.

'Millie?'

Hugh stumbles back into the living room, clutching at

his throat. Perching on the arm of the sofa, I'm chewing placidly on a frankly delicious macaron. A red blotch is beginning to stain his cheeks and neck, and his face is already swelling.

'Millie. Epi pen. Coat pocket.' He frantically waves at the coats on the back of the door. When he goes to step towards it himself, I leap up.

'Oh gosh! Oh no! I must have mixed up the batches!'

'EpiPen, now. And call 999. Fuck, I can't breathe. Hurry up.'

His eyes are bulging in their sockets, but his panic is controlled. An attack of this nature is something that he's experienced before – though scary and certainly unpleasant, he knows how to handle it and has the complete faith in the country's medical services of someone who has always been okay in the end. Others have always stepped in to help Hugh. Friends, administering epinephrine via his EpiPen. Girlfriends, transferring him money to get him through the month. Doctors, giving him oxygen and corticosteroids. His mother, who I assume spent her life cooking him special meals, as well as picking up his socks and wiping his spoilt tears. Left alone, Hugh would live in squalor and eat whatever is handed to him. Hugh isn't used to others not doing as instructed, the possibility of it hasn't even crossed his mind yet.

Running to the coats on the back of the door, I fumble through the pockets.

'Come on!' I turn back to see him leaning heavily on the back of the sofa.

'Got it!' I wave it in the air and start to walk back over to him. Here is the moment when this can all go wrong. Mistakes were made on that bridge with Chris, and I'm determined not to let that happen here. Hugh looks weak, like life is being sapped from him moment by moment. But desperation to live can do strange things to a person. Trust me, I know. It can give them bursts of adrenaline, and strength they never knew. And even at half battery, those biceps are large from a lifetime of manual labour.

So even though my natural instinct is to stop and taunt him, I keep a concerned look on my face until the last second, when I dash past him and through the open bathroom door, which I slam shut and lock.

'What – what the fuck?' I hear him wheeze from outside. There is fear creeping in now, enveloping the panic and lack of oxygen. Terror will be starting to overpower him soon. 'Millie? This . . . This . . . isn't a joke.'

'Oh, I know, Hugh! It's not a joke. It's pretty serious!'

'I need . . . that pen.' He's wheezing now.

'Just like ten thousand pounds isn't a joke.'

With my ear against the door, I listen to the rasping rattle of his breath growing slower and louder. My safety comes first so the door stays shut for now, and I try to content myself with just picturing his face in my imagination. In my hands, I hold his two lifelines – his EpiPen and his mobile phone.

A thump tells me that he has hit the floor. Opening his mobile with the code I saw him input a few days earlier, I scroll through to our messages and delete the entire thread. Then I rifle through the cabinet, finding the spare EpiPen that I'd hoped would be kept here and had located earlier.

His voice rasps in the air, making me dash back to the door. I have to focus to catch each word, spat out from a gravel-filled gullet. 'What . . . do . . . you . . . want?'

I'm surprised that he's already accepted this is no misunderstanding. I'd expected denial for longer, but he's not as dumb as he looks. He couldn't be, to outsmart Nina and keep up two relationships. Perhaps he understands that he doesn't have long enough to negotiate, that every second wasted begging is another closer to death. A buzzing of excitement fills my blood and for one strange moment, I'm looking down at myself from the ceiling, crouched low, pressed against the door next to the uncleaned tub and urine-spattered toilet, my strawberry-blond hair curled down my back.

'The ten thousand pounds in cash that you *scammed* out of Nina,' I shout through the wood.

'She . . . gave . . . lent . . .'

Power is absent from his voice now, and I figure that his strength is adequately reduced. This murder has been well-planned, and although I'm aware it's a little melodramatic, I'm not about to miss my chance at being in the room.

Unlocking the door, I peer over at the mass on the floor. His face is bright red and his neck swollen, like a huge joint of pink ham ready for carving. 'She *lent* it to you to start a proper business. And she did that because you convinced her that you loved her. All the while, you were happy to be texting other girls and even,' I gestured to myself, 'trying to sleep with her best friend. That, in my book, is a scam.'

'Psycho . . . path.'

'That may well be the case.'

We stare at each other for a moment, his eyes red-veined and wet. Once again, I view the scene from afar. It's the sort of scene that an ancient Greek may have painted on

174

a vase or carved out of marble. A pathetic lump of a man quivering on the floor, a majestic woman looking down in disgust and triumph. A modern-day Medusa.

'Shoe . . . box. Under . . . bed.'

Tucking the two EpiPens into my bra, I stride into his bedroom and kneel on the floor. I'll certainly have to wash this jumpsuit on a high temperature later. As any man hurriedly preparing to get lucky, he has shoved all of his debris under here – filthy pants and stinking socks, a plate covered in crumbs, wads of tissue which I'd rather not think about. I gingerly poke at the mass of clothes, finally revealing a cardboard box with Adidas written on the side. Pulling it out, I slip open the lid. Bingo.

As I enter the living room carrying my treasure, Hugh's bulging, bloodshot eyes stare up at me from his place on the floor. His face is soaking wet and there are scratch marks on his puffy neck. His left hand is still scratching at his throat, as if hoping to open it for air with his ragged nails, while his right has given up and hangs limply at his side. Now he's given me the money, his red eyes are wide and pleading, full of desperate hope.

Oh Hugh. Maybe you are *as stupid as you look. I can hardly let you live now, can I?* I'd get in *big* trouble for this. Giving his body a wide berth, I make my way to a sticky dining table for two and sit gingerly on a pleather-covered chair where I'll get a good view.

'. . . Pen?' he gasps.

'Oh no, Hugh.' I shake my head in regret. 'I'm sorry.' Opening the box again, I start to flick through the wads of money, counting quickly with red-painted fingernails. He hasn't spent a penny of it, and I wonder what the eventual plan was. Is there a girlfriend somewhere, a real one, one he is saving for a house deposit with? Is he in trouble with a debt collector or drug dealer? Perhaps, most likely, he is just plain greedy, giving himself a lovely cushion to fall back on without lifting a finger. Was Nina the first woman he has tried this with, or are there multiple stashes around his flat, stolen along with women's hearts?

'Now?' His voice makes me jump. For a moment, I forgot he was still in the room. He thinks I've been checking that the money is all there before I help him, which is quite sad, and if I was a weaker woman, it might make me feel guilty. The rattle of his breath has turned to an angry hiss of the underworld, one eye rolling back into his head.

'No Hugh,' I say kindly. 'No.'

Closing the box to give him my full attention, I sit back and watch him fade away.

CHAPTER EIGHTEEN

The walk home passed in a bit of a blur. Strange things stand out vividly in my memory – the bright blue of the plastic barriers around some abandoned roadworks, shining under a streetlight. The large brown rat that flashed across the road from a bush and into the darkness of the park. Razor-sharp screams of a baby from a flat, the window a singular yellow square in an otherwise sleeping building. Deep inhales of breath as I bypassed the corner shop, its windows dark. The greasy, salty smell of chips from a bin that I leant over to vomit.

There were multiple times when, again, I left my body to see myself wandering through the streets towards home, trying to keep upright and sensible-looking. I didn't even register the rain soaking through the brown wig I'd packed for the journey, running down my face, until I was safely in my house.

You must understand, that it isn't shame or guilt. Far from it. When I woke this morning, my mouth tasted stale with the sugary remnants of macarons and vomit, but my head was clear. No, I do not feel anything towards Hugh as a person, nor do I have any second thoughts about my actions. It's not that at all.

But my physical reaction was different to the time following the farewell to Chris, Steven, or even Karl. Partly, it's that this was so close to home. My best friend's boyfriend. It feels ludicrously dangerous, even foolish. The chances that I'll be caught somehow have tripled. Is it that, then?

Mostly, I think, it's the memories. Watching a man die like that. It did bring a lot back.

It's Saturday morning – not that the weekend makes a huge difference to me now that I'm happily unemployed. I'm exhausted and achy, but alas, there is no rest for the wicked. The day has finally come to be at Fork It Up in case Big Dave Cartwright decides to treat Kelly to a plate of cheap sausages and knock-off baked beans. As I pull on my knee-length boots and the black Jaeger coat that arrived yesterday – an eBay bargain – my muscles ache and head spins. Coffee first, I don't want to rely on a place called Fork It Up to have any sort of reasonable bean-grinding process.

I've walked around the area multiple times over the past week, but I have yet to actually enter the café. The chances of Dave being there on a weekday seemed slim, and I didn't want to draw attention to myself by suddenly arriving every day.

The sky displays the perfect autumn blend – a clear, vibrant blue, and sun that emanates an almost otherworldly brilliance, along with that icy air that nips at your cheeks and fingers. It's the sort of day that makes you feel hopeful.

And I *do* feel hopeful. I'm on my way to scope out a decent lead, I've saved Nina from a potential year or more of being sucked dry by a total loser, and got her money back to boot.

Despite the bags under my eyes and aching muscles, I'm feeling gorgeous in my new coat as I march through the deserted Saturday morning streets. The Adidas shoebox containing Nina's money is stashed under my own bed now, and I haven't quite worked out what to do with it. Getting it back to her is the plan, of course. But how to do that without raising suspicion?

Hindsight tells me that I should have repeated the tactic I used with Chris at the bridge. I had the password to Hugh's mobile and should have taken the opportunity to send a text to Nina implying suicide, giving her the location of her money. But we live and we learn.

I won't pretend that there aren't any jitters as well. My body is buzzing. Partly, it's due to the exhaustion and the coffee now rushing through my veins, but it's also because these last few weeks have been . . . interesting. I didn't originally plan to kill Hugh, but when Nina told me about the cheating it felt more than justified. The feeling of taking action against men who harm, or taking the control for myself, is exhilarating. Adrenaline has been pounding through my body ever since I gave Karl that push.

Hugh's murder felt like progression. It was planned and clever, rather than reactionary and lucky. It solidified my determination.

Halfway to the café, a white van passes me, two sharp honks of the horn making me jump. A fat, middle-aged white man leans out of the window.

'Give us a smile, love!'

Small spikes of anger flare, but they dissipate quickly. One cannot kill every man who shouts at them, there's not enough time in the day.

Zero notifications on my phone, which I suppose isn't a huge surprise as I checked it about three minutes ago. This is the difference between what has happened with Hugh and the others. Whereas previously I was keen to check the news sites and see how their deaths had been perceived, now I am on tenterhooks waiting for the inevitable call from Nina.

As I walk, I rehearse how I'll take the news under my breath.

'*What? Slow down, Nina. Hugh is . . . no! You can't be serious! How! Are you okay?*'

She'll do most of the talking. She'll cry, but I just need to remember that this is all for the best. If Hugh had remained alive, she would have ended up crying anyway, as would plenty of other women he'd have met through the years.

Fork It Up is around forty-five minutes from my house and I'm walking rather than driving because I want to pop in a charity shop for a new wig along the way.

The Barnado's on Hengrove Road is depressing in almost every single possible way. The air is thick and stale with dust and sadness. The ancient lady behind the till looks like she is clinging onto the last strands of life, and has decided to spend them here of all places, which doesn't say much for her options. The treasures she presides over are mostly hideous floral skirts from M&S or tatty old Primark crop tops, along with that particular brand of ugly found only in charity shop homeware sections – smiling ceramic dogs.

Flicking through the hangers, I feign interest every now and again by pulling out an item of clothing and frowning at it. I plan to spend eight minutes in here before I can purchase what I'm really looking for. It doesn't pay to look too keen.

Eventually, I approach the woman at the till with a bundle of things I've picked up. She gives me a watery smile and begins fumbling for their cardboard price tags with shaky hands. I bite my lip to contain my impatience. Not to be a total bitch, but when someone is this old, they really should do everyone a favour and stay at home.

'Dressing up, love?' she croaks in a voice that smacks of a lifetime of heavy smoking. How does one get to this age while also smoking forty a day? Maybe she's only forty-five and what they say nicotine does to your skin is all too true.

I hold up the black tutu on the counter. 'Being super prepared for Halloween this year. Going as Natalie Portman in *Black Swan*.'

'Oh, that's nice.' She's folding so slowly it feels like an eternity. If she dies before the transaction is finished it will take even longer. She smiles at me, and I chide myself for being such a cow. This woman is not the enemy. David Cartwright is the enemy. Anyway, luckily, the nice old lady just about pulls through and I breathe in the fresh, clean air with relief as I step outside and continue on to my stake-out location.

Fork It Up is as expected. Owned by someone who, I'm quite sure, describes themselves on Tinder as 'the joker of the group', it screams 'quirky on a budget'. But I've been in worse places with worse people, I tell myself as I slump onto the cold metal chair outside. I'm the first person here and the blue-haired girl behind the counter looks shocked that she has to do something other than tap away on her phone.

A laminated menu is dropped onto the table as I pull out my book from my bulging backpack. I'm wearing the new wig I picked up in the charity shop – most of my Message M ones are too obviously fake to be worn in the daylight – so I'm currently a brunette with elegant shoulder-length hair. The rest of the crap I purchased is shoved to the bottom of the bag – at the time it seemed less suspicious than just walking in and buying a wig.

Ordering a coffee, I tell the bored-looking waitress that I'll keep the menu to 'think about food'. There is no telling how long I'll have to sit here, so I need to draw out the process. My phone is face up on the table, and though I try to focus on the pages of Stephen King's *Misery*, my eyes keep flicking to the screen. When will Nina realise Hugh is missing? How many days before someone kicks down his door? The dark brown mould around the bathtub told me that he obviously didn't have a cleaner. It could be weeks.

The hours tick by and tables fill up with hungover faces in their twenties and thirties. Next to me, two girls laugh over Bloody Marys, dissecting their evening in forensic detail. Who slept with who ('Janet really gets around these days!'), who lost weight ('Can't believe Fat Lizzie is now skinny!'), who humiliated themselves ('Did you see Stuart vomming in the corner of the dance floor?'), and who is never drinking again ('I swear that's it for me').

I continue to eavesdrop while I poke at the pale sloppy eggs on my plate and it gives me a pang of nostalgia for something that I never actually had. A life of light-hearted hedonism with nothing to worry about aside from hangovers and fuddled memories of the night before. Katie had that, briefly. But it's clearly not a life meant for the Masters family.

By the time the waitress is staring at me with pity, I know it's time to give up. Big Dave hasn't shown, and I'm just wasting my time.

I spend the afternoon reading my book in the garden, wrapped in blankets and occasionally dozing. After its morning glory, the sun is now just weakly pushing through the October chill, but it's still pleasant to be in the cool air if you can bear it. The day's been a failure, but one can expect too much, and I do deserve a rest after everything that's happened over the last week. Besides, I'm starting to feel quietly confident about Big Dave being my man, so it's just a matter of time. Sure, there are a few other pressing issues – not having a job, the police finding my DNA in the wig by Chris's body, Nina's money under my bed – but tonight I have a date.

James texted me yesterday, and we arranged to meet tonight, though after taking Friday night off the phone line to sort out Hugh, I swear to myself that I'll log back onto Message M after we've had a drink.

Pulling out my notebook, I start a new page to brainstorm ideas for getting the money back to Nina, most of which are dreadful. Posting it anonymously. Hiding it in her flat. Simply depositing it into her bank account. Trying to pay off a chunk of her mortgage in secret? Just as I'm reliving Hugh's murder and thinking how I could have fixed this with more forethought, the soft scraping sound of Sean's back door opening makes me freeze.

Heavy thuds tell me he is heaving his squat body out of his kitchen into his garden. I'm wrapped in blankets in the corner of the sofa, up against our shared wall, so he shouldn't see me if he doesn't look. It's chilly out here, and most people would be inside, so I'm hoping he doesn't stay – social energy must be conserved for my date, not wasted on people like Sean.

With all of the drama in my own world, I almost forgot about Sean's mystery, which so consumed me that night a week or so back.

A sigh wafts over the wall so deep that I swear I can almost see the trees sway with the gust. I'm barely breathing as I desperately try not to make a noise, and I can hear him shuffling up and down in a rhythmic pacing.

'Okay. Okay,' he mutters to himself with the air of a man preparing to break into a bank. 'Okay.' The beeps of unsilenced phone keys are jarring in the cool air, the noise that tells you a person over a certain age is making a call. Something tells me that he isn't ordering a pizza.

'Hello. Yes, I – no, I – well, I – okay! Look, listen. I have got some of it. Yes, only some! It was impossible! Wait, no you can't, wait! Okay, give me a bit more time, okay? Please. A bit more. Thank you. *Thank* you. If you could just forgive—' Silence tells me that Sean is getting a talking to from whoever is on the other end of that phone, and this is confirmed when it's interrupted by a strangled yelp like a puppy that's been stepped on. 'Okay! Please. I'm sorry. I'll sort it.'

There is a thump, as if Sean has sat down on the ground, and a sniffing that suggests . . . *tears?* I picture him there, sitting in the dirt, his plaid shirt done up to the top, his gnome-like features glistening with tears. It sounds an awful lot like our Sean is being blackmailed. Well, well, well, what has my dear old neighbour been up to?

James looks tired. His hair is sticking up at strange angles and the marks under his eyes are a dark grey-brown. *Get it together, James, at least you haven't been sacked, been on surveillance, partly uncovered your neighbour's blackmail plot, and committed double homicide all in one week.* Thank God for concealer.

We're in a pub again, because we clearly both lack imagination. But a different pub to the last time, because we both like to pretend that we aren't. The Mall is technically nicer, in a way that makes it a less pleasant environment. I'm rather evangelical about pubs. They shouldn't sell good food (unless it's a pie, that is acceptable). They should be small, low-ceilinged, funny-shaped, and populated with the same handful of people on a regular basis. This place fails to meet most of my criteria.

Despite looking exhausted, he is still gorgeous, and he arrived early to make up for last time. His face breaks into that incredible smile when I walk in, and it makes me want to tell him all of my deep, dark secrets.

When we both have drinks in front of us – a red wine for me and a pint of Delirium for him – we start to quiz each other on our weeks. As it would be inappropriate to tell a detective about my recent murder spree, I decide to confess that I'm no longer working, with a few tweaks to how it happened.

'Why? I thought you liked it there?'

'It's not what I want to do. I have some money saved and I've decided to take some time to change my path.' I cringe – I sound like a fridge magnet. 'It was an accident, getting a job in that place, and there was a danger I'd be stuck there for the rest of my life if I didn't do something about it.'

'That's brave. Or stupid. I guess you'll find out.' He grins to soften what is a fair enough blow.

'It's hard to think and breathe when you're working full-time. Which you know, obviously. And I wasn't going to be able to get my next steps straight in my head and start making them unless I took a break.' I shrug awkwardly and take a gulp of wine.

As I say it, I realise that it is true. I've only been trying to fill my half of the conversation obligation, but who knows what will happen next in my life? James is supportive and kind. He even seems vaguely impressed.

'Anyway, what's going on with you? Any news on those deaths? Were they suicides after all?'

'Ha!' He waves his hand with a smile. 'I shouldn't have told you all that last time. You got me drunk!'

'Ah come on, you barely told me anything!'

The charcoal suit is absent, and today he's in dark blue jeans and a plain black jumper – a sensible, sexy, non-attention-seeking man. I cross my right leg over my left to distract him with a freshly shaven and moisturised thigh.

It takes some heavy flirting and three more drinks to get James to circle back to the suicide cases. He is charming, and at least an hour passes when I forget everything that's happened and focus purely on the person across from me – a funny, handsome man who appears to like me. I don't trust people quickly, but there is something about him that makes this feel . . . different. For the past week, I've been telling myself it was good to keep James close because of his job. Though now, sitting with him, I admit to myself that I really do like him.

'Well, listen to this then,' James says at last. He leans forward and I copy him. It's clear to me that he is smart and good at his job, but everyone has a fatal flaw. Hugh's was his need to be desired. James's is his need to be listened to. Mine? Well, I'm quite obviously flawless. He should probably consider a profession where he isn't expected to be so discreet though.

'Did you see in the paper about the guy who fell into the gorge? Near the suspension bridge?'

Furrowing my brow, I cock my head while I think about whether I've heard of such an incident.

'Yessss . . . I'm sure I saw that online. Surely you don't think they're connected?' I laugh and top up our glasses to avoid his eyes. 'Like a suicide epidemic? I swear I've heard of that happening somewhere.'

'Well, I'm not sure. There isn't really a connection between the men that I can find. Ages, jobs, friendships, wealth, family status. They vary, nothing ties them together.'

'Sounds like a coincidence then.'

'It does.'

The pause speaks volumes. I'd bet my own cat that James's superiors are telling him to stop looking for trouble where there isn't any. Let a dead man lie. Not being listened to at work is making him more desperate to be listened to by me and is loosening his lips. But James is clever, unnervingly so. He's also young and ambitious, an idealist with something to prove. I consider moving the conversation on, but decide that it pays to know everything. This is my chance.

'But you don't think so.' It's a statement, not a question.

187

It's the best way to get people talking – removing the sense of interrogation from the words and instead stating knowledge that they can confirm or deny.

'I . . . I don't think so. No.'

'Men kill themselves, James. It's the second highest killer of men under fifty, right? Christmas isn't far away, it's cold, it's bleak, they have no one to speak to. It's not hard to imagine three different men taking that way out. And besides, Karl may have been an accident, right? He could have just fallen down those stairs? And the bridge guy? Stopped for a rest and leant back too far? I think you've watched too much *Inspector Morse*.' As soon as I say Karl's name, I know I've fucked up. I rack my brains for our last conversation. What did he tell me?

'Yeah I know. I know.' His eyes meet mine. 'I didn't even realise his name was out in the press. Karl's.'

Though my palms are sweating, I shrug, taking a sip of wine.

'Something just tells me that . . . there is a connection between these men.'

'Maybe they all did something to deserve it.'

His bowed head whips up and he gives me a curious look. What made me say it? Self-sabotage? Anger at the effort he is putting into figuring out what happened to them, when everyday women and girls are assaulted by men and the police don't bat an eyelid?

'Sorry, I didn't mean that. Bad joke.'

He smiles and shakes his head, breaking the tension. 'No, no. Don't be sorry. I'm getting too deep. And hey, maybe you're right. People die who deserve it all the time.' He raises his glass and clinks mine, and it's almost as if we are toasting to me.

'Anyway. Let's move on. You will never guess what I did this morning. Get your round in first.'

But I don't find out what he did that morning. Because when I pull out my phone at the bar to pay for our drinks, my blood turns to ice in my veins and my head echoes with white noise.

Seven missed calls and a text. All from Nina.

Hugh's body has been found.

CHAPTER NINETEEN

With bags under my eyes that rival those on James last night and unable to stop yawning, I look as deathly hungover as everyone else in this café. The Fork It Up waitress is different to yesterday, which is lucky, but I'm back in my dark brown wig and sleek black coat.

Last night was a wild ride.

Hugh's body was found much quicker that I expected, and that's because his girlfriend, his *real* girlfriend, had a key. Just after eight o'clock on Saturday night, she let herself into the apartment, only to find him very much deceased in the middle of the living room.

Nina only found out about it because one of the first things that said girlfriend did was update Hugh's social media to reflect his new status: dead. Leaving aside the fact that this woman is clearly an Instagram-obsessed freak, this meant that Nina – staying in for the night to work on a case – found out about her new boyfriend's demise by way of a tearful video on his page from someone called Charlotte. Promptly leaping into a cab, Nina had gone to his house to discover what sort of sick prank this was, to be met by a police officer guarding the door and two paramedics loading a covered gurney into an ambulance.

I learnt all of this while sitting opposite James in The Mall, Nina shouting incomprehensibly down the phone. Whether the tears were from anger or sorrow, it wasn't exactly clear. There was also some sort of showdown between her and Charlotte in the street, but the details on that were pretty hazy as I could only understand every other word between sobs.

Downing our drinks, we left the pub after I hurriedly caught James up on what had happened – me heading over to Nina's, and he, trying valiantly to hide his excitement, going into work. By the time Nina arrived home at ten-thirty, I was perched on her front wall with a bottle of wine and a hug.

As predicted, I didn't need to say much. Nina spoke, and when she wasn't speaking, she cried. It was excellent news for us both that Charlotte had been revealed at this crucial juncture. Nina was so furious with Hugh, and with herself, that there was less room for grief, and her anger – more of a volcanic eruption than bubbling – meant that it didn't matter if my face wasn't perfectly mirroring shock.

I slept on her sofa, and left at eight in the morning after barely four hours of broken sleep, blaming the feeding of Shirley Bassey in a text message to the finally sleeping Nina. I promised I'd be back later to check on her.

If I missed my chance at Big Dave today, I'd have to wait an entire week until I could try again to catch him having a weekend brunch. So, despite the heady mix of exhaustion and adrenaline pulsing through my body, I grabbed a shower at home, donned the brown wig, and got here for the café opening at 9:30am, claiming a table outside in case he walks past.

After ordering a coffee, I pull out my phone and reply to a message James sent me the night before.

Sorry. It was quite full on and I didn't get a chance to reply. How was the rest of your evening? Nina is pretty cut up about it. Sounds like he accidentally ate something containing nuts. He was allergic.

I forced myself to type the next line.

Poor guy.

My coffee hasn't even arrived before three dots indicate that James is typing out a reply.

Yeah I heard. Anaphylactic shock. I went to the scene.

Is it usual for a homicide detective to go to the scene of someone who died from a nut allergy? James is still typing.

Something isn't right about all of this, I swear. But the boss won't listen to me. Meet me later?

Interesting.

Hope your mate is alright x

It's eleven when Big Dave walks in, the woman I recognise as Kelly following a few steps behind with a face like a slapped arse. Online in her carefully curated photographs, she looks as polished as a Bratz doll, but in reality, her straggly hair extensions let her down. A second later, the couple come out again and sit at a table just a few over from mine.

'It's freezing out here,' Kelly whines, scuffing her trainers on the floor like a toddler.

'Well it's full inside, babe, what d'ya want me to do?' David Cartwright snaps back. All is not well in paradise. I stifle a yawn and hide my face in the pages of my book. The couple sit in stony silence until the door swings open again, a burst of happy chatter filling the air in the seconds until it thuds closed.

'You guys ready to order?'

'Aye I think so, right, babe?'

'Absolutely!' Kelly and Dave smile like this is the best day of their lives, as if whether the waitress knew they were arguing or not was of the utmost importance. Kelly is wearing Juicy Couture joggers which went out of fashion around fifteen years ago and were vomit-inducing even then. She has long pale pink nails, a fluffy bomber jacket, and she's missed a patch on her neck when fake tanning. Even so, I wonder how she can be with David Cartwright. As I stare at his bulging arms, and his huge hands waving around this laminated menu, I imagine them around my sister's throat.

I realise that my hand is in my pocket, gripping Chris's penknife tightly. With my thumb, I flick out the blade and almost without thinking, I push back the table as I get to my feet.

'You finished there, love? Come inside to pay, yeah?' The waitress makes me jump, and I recover myself quickly.

'Oh, yes. Sure. Thanks. Just using the loo.'

I turn away so my face isn't visible to Kelly and Dave, then scurry to the toilet, hitting my hip painfully on the sharp corner of a table and spilling someone's coffee. In the mirror, I look haunted and drawn. I've been drinking too much and sleeping too little. My hair, though, is sleek and perfect, having come from the wardrobe and been fitted carefully over the tangled, strawberry-blond underneath. Up close, it looks cheap, but not noticeably so unless you are really looking at it.

Brown hair can suit me, but on a day like today when I've had little sleep, it just makes my already milky pale skin look greyer and older. I add some lipstick in an attempt to look less like one of my victims, and order another coffee on the way back to my table, paying for everything so that I'm ready to leave whenever Kelly and Dave set off.

Dave and Kelly are fast eaters, or maybe that is just the case when they are annoying each other. They bicker for a solid thirty-five minutes as Dave ploughs his way through The MegaBrek and Kelly picks at an Avocado Dream Boat. It appears that Dave was out late last night and failed to adequately keep Kelly abreast of his movements. Honestly, sometimes other people make me wish I would lose my sense of sight and sound. After they finish eating, Dave stares at his old yellow iPhone in a moody silence while Kelly rolls her eyes.

But minutes later, my heart is beating again. Partly because I've been mainlining coffee for the past two hours, and partly because we're on the move. Dave and Kelly are about fifteen feet ahead of me and still loudly arguing about Kelly's ludicrous expectations of her boyfriend. This suits me down to the ground; their energy is completely taken up with insulting each other rather than noticing me stalking them.

After about four minutes, they turn down a side road called Malago Close, but when they grind to a halt, I have to swerve and walk right past them. Luckily the road bends and I manage to push my way behind a bush in someone's front garden where I can still hear their voices.

'I don't *believe you,* Dave. I just don't believe you,' Kelly shouts. It's hotting up now, volume rising.

'Ah Jesus. I don't know how to help you there, Kells, I really don't. I was working, then had some drinks with the lads, then I went home. Alone. What more do you want me to say? You want video evidence? You want a bloody time-stamped tracking system updating ya? I. Went. Home. A. Lone.'

'Liar! There were *hours* in between where I didn't hear back from you!'

'Because I was PISSED and HAVING A GOOD TIME!'

This is getting a bit out of hand. It's Sunday morning, for God's sake. I cannot stand people who fight in public, it's so uncouth.

'Fuck you, David. Fuck. You.' Kelly delivers her parting shot in a high-pitched, tearful whine, and I painfully push myself further into the bush as she storms past me. After a few moments, I slowly retract myself from the hedge, straightening my wig and dress, and pulling twigs out of my collar.

There is no way of seeing around the corner to where I left the couple standing, so I'm going to have to take a chance. If I go out now and Dave is still standing there, he'll see me and very possibly realise I was hiding around the corner. If I wait too long, I risk losing him altogether. That can't happen.

I edge out and see him right down the end of the road, marching towards, presumably, his home at an angry speed. I have to do a humiliating jog-walk to catch up. He rounds a corner and I lose sight of him, so I throw caution to the wind and break into an all-out run. I round the bend just in time to see a door slam.

Slowing my pace, I stroll past as casually as I can manage, glancing at the offending property. Number 57 Malago Drive. My eyes flick upwards and my feet stop of their own accord, legs filling with concrete and vision blurring. The house is a classic Victorian terrace not dissimilar to my own, with big bay windows upstairs and down and, above the front door, a smaller, single window. Everything about it looks neat, clean, and unremarkable. Apart from one detail. In the small upstairs window hang thick, red curtains.

The exhaustion that's been weighing me down all morning has vanished, leaving me instead with jittery electricity. The walk back to my house seems to pass in seconds, and before I know it, I am lying flat on my back on the kitchen floor, taking slow deep breaths. Shirley Bassey is sitting on the chaise longue staring at me like I've gone insane, and maybe I have. Because I've found him, I've really found the man who took Katie from me.

Even though I *did* suspect David Cartwright, part of me never truly believed I'd find my man. But the large, bald-headed, tattooed man who works at the club Katie was at, lives right in the location she remembers being in, has the same curtains hanging in his window? All of the pieces are falling, *have fallen*, into place.

Kelly's spiky, mascara-coated false eyelashes hiding her hazel eyes which, if left alone, would have been Bambi-like and charming, flash before me. I wonder how she'll take the news when her boyfriend is found dead. She'll play the grieving partner well, but will there be a part of her that is relieved? The nights spent waiting for him to call while he drinks and cheats, picking up vulnerable girls and ruining their lives? I wonder just how many girls like Katie have had their souls crushed by this man.

No more.

I'm unsure how long I've been lying here, but the hardness of the wood starts to register on my skin, and the chill sends me shivering.

I creakily sit up, startling Shirley Bassey, who seems to have assumed me to be dead, and doesn't appear overly bothered by it. It's past lunchtime and Nina will have been calling me, not to mention that intriguing text from James asking to meet and discuss the case.

In the shower, I turn the dial up to scalding and stand in the burning mist, skin becoming patchy and numb, old scars flashing an angry scarlet. David Cartwright is a big man, and a dangerous one. I need a real plan before I act, I can't risk just bursting in there waving a knife around like Crocodile Dundee. It will be helpful to speak to James and find out what he knows, or suspects he knows, so I can make sure I'm not repeating anything that will raise flags.

Once again, I run through what I know about David Cartwright to make sure I'm not getting carried away. It's not certain, but would it ever be without DNA evidence? I remember the flicker of a tattoo crawling out from his shirt collar. His job on the Pom Pom's door, his lack of hair, his address, his age, his curtains. David Cartwright ticks every box, and I'm going in.

Clean and moisturised, I'm feeling a bit more human as I pull a brush through my hair, the wig having been pushed to the back of my sock drawer. It feels good to be back to my strawberry blond. My cheeks are glowing, and my natural colour makes my features pop. In the mirror, I poke at my hawk-like nose, as if it can be smoothed out with a finger and therefore transform me into someone else.

Today I need to be me though, to be with Nina, and get her money back to her somehow. She is my number one priority along with Katie.

Then I will have to think, research, and plan. I've already decided that this needs to be the last one. James has guessed that the deaths are connected somehow, and even the rest of the idiots down at the police station will cotton on at some point if I keep knocking off every man I dislike. This is the important one though, the one that started it all. The man who ruined my sister's life. And he needs to pay.

David Cartwright's days are numbered.

CHAPTER TWENTY

As opposed to now, when my life is so very uneventful (unless you count all the murders), my childhood was difficult. My mum has always been the same faded human being, and the less said about my dad, the better. One of the only positive adult presences in my life was Dad's brother, Uncle Dale. He would occasionally come to stay when Dad went off the deep end and disappeared for days at a time. Once he took us all the way to Newcastle to watch his favourite team play football. Dale was a good man, even if he was annoyingly obsessed with that football team and motorbikes. I rarely see him now. He still visits Mum semi-regularly, but as I only pop in and out to see Katie, our visits don't often coincide. He has my dad's eyes.

Katie though, she was different. Where my mum was a sallow beige and I was a deep, dark swirling scarlet, Katie was a ray of blinding sunlight in that drab, sad house. I was ten when she was born, and the age difference meant that, although we were sisters and friends, there was a protectiveness I felt for her that has never vanished. I'd sell my soul to keep Katie alive – or take any number of other people's.

This is all to say, that when I met Nina Lee, my life – lonely, quiet, and sad – changed. We were seventeen and my dad had just died. Our house was reeling, in a state of shock that no one knew how to handle. My mother stayed in bed for two weeks, and then I came home from school one day to find the place scrubbed clean and a tin of that sickly lemon-yellow paint open in the hallway. To this day, the smell of paint makes me nauseous.

The silence in my house before my father died was oppressive and tense, and afterwards it resembled the stale quiet of a hospital corridor. But Nina, Nina was never quiet. No one wants to move school at seventeen, and it struck me as a rather cruel thing for her parents to put their daughter through. Until I met them, and realised that they could never be cruel. Like Nina, Mr and Mrs Lee were sunny, practical people who forgave all and got on with life, whatever was thrown at them.

When we met, I'd never truly had a real friend. At seven years old, Katie was a blessing but not exactly the ideal companion for a teenager itching to try out what the world has to offer. And although the quietness and the slightly manic mood swings of my mother felt to me – at that stage – almost calm in comparison to life before, Nina's rainbow joy burst open my world in a wholly unexpected and extremely welcome way.

Nina joined St Anne's secondary school at seventeen and got better grades than anyone else in my class. I was horrified when our teacher designated me as her 'buddy' on her first day, but was quickly overwhelmed by her warmth and we became firm friends. I even tentatively accepted Angela and Izzy when she decided they were fun. She laughed so much, and talked so much. She taught me to experiment with clothing choices that I flinch when I look back on, a confused mixture of embarrassment and warm, pleasant nostalgia. We put on cakey cheap makeup in Nina's parents' bathroom, purchased from the Collection 2000 range in Boots, or furtively pushed into our pockets when the security guards weren't looking. After school, her mother would cook heaped plates of noodles and steaming broths which had flavours I'd never tasted, and I would sit at their table, silently taking in their bizarre, beautiful family dynamic.

There were no flavours in my house.

We're in her childhood bedroom now, largely unchanged since I first saw it at the age of seventeen, the only light coming from the moon through the windowpane and the sliver under the door from the hallway light. Her mum is downstairs making an early dinner, and the smells take me right back to the heady days of making my first friend. Nina is dressed in rainbow pyjamas and is in bed, only her blotchy, miserable face visible above the covers. She moans like a creature from the deep, and I lie down next to her to give her a hug.

'I can't believe he had a girlfriend, Mills. I mean, I also can't believe he is dead. I know that's the worst bit. But sometimes I'm actually *not* sure it's the worst bit, you know? And I feel like, like the *worst person in the world*. So, I remind myself he is dead, and that *that* is a tragedy. And I think of his grandma, who he loved. Then I realise

I'm *making* myself sad to stop thinking about *myself*, and I circle back to how I literally *am* the worst person.'

'You are not the worst person in the world.'

'And then I also think I'm the *stupidest* person in the world. Because what type of *idiot* doesn't realise that their *boyfriend* is already in a relationship! And what type of *idiot* gives their new boyfriend *ten thousand pounds in cash* just because they *ask for it*? And then I realise that I'm also the most *pathetic* person in the world, because I'm so, so *desperate* that I will believe anything just so I can have a boyfriend who loves me.'

'You are neither the stupidest, nor the most pathetic person in the world.' I mumble the words into her hair as I hold her, but I doubt she hears them. Her words are angry and sad and coming through streaming tears and a choked throat. She has been melodramatic since the day I met her, and I expected Hugh's death to hit her hard, despite him being a clear waste of the earth's precious resources. Still, I'm sure it's nothing a night out won't fix.

These walls have posters on them that I haven't seen for many years. Billie Joel Armstrong leers down at us, standing with his Green Day bandmates, wearing a red-and-black tie and too much eyeliner. It's disorientating, I feel like we've whipped back in time. Would I want that, given the chance? When I first came round to Nina's house her room had shocked me. Other than a few times at Uncle Dale's, it had been the first time I'd been in anyone else's house other than my own.

Before the tin of yellow paint, my house was all beige. It was quiet and sad, as if, if it stayed quiet and beige *enough* then no one would notice it was there and, eventually, it would cease to exist. But Nina's was different.

Whereas the walls in my bedroom had been bare, every inch of hers was covered in posters and photos and general bits of rubbish that, at the time, we thought to be quirky. There was so much of her, and my whole being had smouldered with envy in the shadow cast by her bright, burning flame.

Today, I'm just happy to be part of it, in a small and separate way. Her parents smile and nod at me with more warmth than every parental interaction I've had in my own home combined. While Nina suffers this loss, they gather around her like birds, feeding her, petting her, helping her. It's good to feel part of this flock, even though it's circling around a tragedy that is partly of my creation.

Yes, *partly*. Nina did bring the bastard into our lives in the first place, and Hugh was a sleazy, stealing scumbucket who got exactly what he deserved. So don't look at me like that. People make their own beds in which to lie, and I won't be judged for tucking them in at night.

A drunk, a mother, and a serial killer walk into a bar, and the barman says, 'What can I get you, ladies?' And they all sit down to discuss the fourth member of the group, the grieving lawyer. It's Thursday, and I'm sitting in a bar with Izzy and Angela, waiting for Nina to arrive. She is uncharacteristically late.

The week has been ticking by at a painfully slow pace. Nina has taken the news about Hugh even harder than expected, and I've sat with her for days trying to cheer her up. To make up for being distracted all weekend, I've also worked the Message M phone line every single night again. On Monday I saved a woman from an ex-boyfriend. On Tuesday there was a date that was going wrong and turning nasty. On Wednesday an eighteen-year-old had been drugged in a bar, and I helped her and her friend home to safety.

That's not to say I haven't made time for my other mission: I have made daily trips to Dave Cartwright's house to gather intelligence. I've lingered in my car, hood up, and watched him leave for work at the same time each day. There is a large bush in his back garden which I've shoved myself into each night after the Message M phone line quieted. Though desperately inelegant and uncomfortable, this has afforded me a decent view of his routine.

So far, I've learnt that his neighbour has a yappy dog, which is unfortunate but not unsurpassable, and that Dave and Killjoy Kelly are speaking again, though it still sounds fraught. Every night, he calls her on speaker phone while he takes his post-work bath, and I can hear the tinny arguments from the open window. Then he will listen to old pop music for another twenty minutes before turning in. He keeps this ritual religiously, despite often not getting home until 1am on weeknights. I'm not sure exactly what he gets up to in the days – I do have a life – but I've gathered that he leaves for work at six-thirty in the evening. This information is barely worth the cold I've caught from hours spent in a bush.

All in all, I am utterly exhausted. I finally saw Katie yesterday, who I'd been avoiding since my deranged demand for information. I ate spring rolls while she pretended to sip at the spicy pho I'd brought her, and we reminisced about television shows from the noughties. She looked tiny, but she told me how much it cheers her up when I visit, and I've vowed to make more time.

Izzy sighs dramatically. 'Poor woman. Poor Hugh, come to think of it,' she says, shaking her head as if she's in a Spanish telenovela while Angela staggers up to the bar. She must have had a few before we got here because I swear, she is already slurring.

'Why poor *Hugh*? He was a cheat,' I say with a shrug. I really don't understand the pity being thrown around for that guy.

'That's kind of cold, Millie. He wasn't perfect, but the man is *dead*.'

'Doesn't make him not a bastard. Just a dead bastard. Which makes that one less bastard in the world. Things have been sadder.'

Izzy frowns and then looks down into her drink as if she's uncomfortable. Maybe I've gone too far. Don't want to end up like one of those pathetic (almost exclusively male) killers who get away with it all but give themselves away by bragging about it in the pub.

'Sorry, I didn't mean that.' Obviously, I did, I'm the bastard exterminator. 'It's just such a confusing set of emotions, right? Feeling furious at someone for leading on your friend, but then, sorry for them as well? Of course I'm shocked, *horrified* even, by his death.' That should do it.

Izzy smiles and her shoulders relax. 'Of course, babe, of course. It's so weird.'

Izzy chose our meeting place, so instead of The Guinea, we're in an expensive cocktail bar – wood-panelled with red bulbs pulsing under chintzy lampshades, taxidermy birds trapped for eternity under glass domes. Sad little stag horns are mounted on the wall as if killing something so small and runty with a huge gun is an achievement to boast of. The barman, who is trying to force Angela back to her seat so he can earn his tip with table service, is smiley and soft with proud, thick glasses and a small dark moustache. I wonder if he is the kind of man whose personality starts and ends with that moustache, but decide I'm being unkind.

My cocktail, a 'Red Flash', is in a tiny bowl atop a long, thin stem that looks as if it could snap in a strong breeze and is frosted with condensation. It's strong and cold, and in its long spindly glass, I suppose a little like me.

Angela finally returns with a bottle of white wine in a silver ice bucket – clearly the delicate little cocktails weren't doing it for her. I don't think Izzy is even drinking alcohol tonight by the look of it, so I guess I'll have to drink for her. Angela glugs it out into three glasses anyway and gulps at hers. I wonder if someone should be worried about Angela? There isn't enough room in my mind to clear a corner for her right now. But I'm not completely devoid of human emotion and part of me hopes that Izzy volunteers herself for the challenge of being her carer.

As Angela begins a speech on what I think is supposed to be the complexity of grief, I let my mind wander back to those red curtains. Though I've spent days pondering ways and means to take the life of Dave Cartwright, a decision as to the best way to remove him from this earth has yet to be reached. The problem is, there are endless ways to kill a man.

Stab him, shoot him, push him, drug him, burn him, smother him, strangle him, squash him, hit him with a car, a bat, a hammer, a brick, shove him down the stairs, off bridges, over bannisters, under trains. The possibilities are endless. The real issue is that I want the man who hurt my sister to suffer a long and painful death, and I want him to know exactly why he is dying. However, the killing really does have to end after this, and I do not want to get caught by doing a James Bond-esque standoff where I linger for the explanation and dramatics.

'What do you think? Millie?'

'Huh?'

'Nina? Should I call her?' Izzy has clearly grown bored of listening to Angela's monologues.

'Oh, yeah. Go on.'

While Izzy calls Nina to see if she is still coming, I get my own phone out and google 'Slow and painful ways to die'. Before the results, a message pops up saying 'Help is available' in big, bold letters, with a phone number and direction to 'speak to someone today'. I did *not* ask to be judged by a bloody search engine.

Too late, I remember the care I took after killing Karl – not even daring to google the crime. I'm going to have to make sure to clear my browser history. Scrolling down, I find a list titled 'The Most Painful Ways to Die, According to Science' – perfect! Izzy is on the phone now 'hmm'ing and 'yeah'ing sympathetically, so I try to tune her out while I skim-read. Number one is crucifixion, which would be stunning, but I really think it's too much of a risk. Showing off is a clear path to being caught, not to mention the practicalities of my weedy little arms getting Big Dave up onto a cross while he is still alive and kicking. Similar things could be said of 'Being skinned alive' and some of the more medieval methods out there.

'She's not coming, girls!' Izzy announces, throwing her hands up into the air. 'Said that she looks like hell and can't bring herself to leave the bed.' Izzy shakes her head again. I wonder if she is doing it to show off her expensive new highlights.

'Ahh no! Nina! Let's go and get her!' Angela insists, and Izzy gives her a withering look.

'No babe. Let her be. Anyway, ah, I actually have some news that I would like to share. Kind of weird talking about happy things after, well, after what is going on with Nina. So maybe it's best to do it when she's not around anyway. But . . . Josh and I are trying for another baby!'

We 'coo' and 'aww' and I leap to my feet with a huge smile on my face. Honestly, I'm not bothered by the news of another baby in the world, but my happiness isn't fake as I whoop and cheers with Izzy. Because before her announcement pulled me away from my phone screen, I saw something that set my whole body tingling.

I've found the perfect way to kill Big Dave Cartwright.

CHAPTER TWENTY-ONE

Although I'm getting closer to knowing how to dispose of the substandard human who hurt my sister and reduced her to a bedbound hermit, I'm not quite ready to take the plunge. I have one chance, and although I'm keen to get this over and done with, a few days here and there to perfect my idea will be worth it in the grand scheme of things.

The more I think about my plan, the more roadblocks seem to spring up. Everything would be easier if I decided to repeat a previous method, perhaps what I did with Steven, but that offends my artistic nature. I know I swore not to get untangled by dramatics, but Dave needs a special exit.

The weekend sees Dave's schedule slide all over the place, so I let Friday and Saturday pass in a blur of googling and note-taking, plotting out plans that won't ever work, and ones that certainly *would* work but would also result in immediate arrest. In the evenings, I watch my Message

M phone obsessively, leaving it on later and later into the night. I rotate my wigs and change my makeup, lingering outside bars in my car. What started as a project to channel my anger towards men after Katie's attack is becoming more of an obsession the closer I come to taking out the actual man who did it. Each morning I wake late with bags under my eyes and gravel in my throat.

The little money I have in my savings account is dwindling, with no payday in sight. Luckily, my house was paid for by my father's life insurance money, so I won't be homeless, but buying food and paying bills still requires an income. This all needs to end soon – for Katie and for me.

At least Nina is perking up though, as I knew she would, and she is back in her own flat. It's almost time for me to stumble upon the shoebox of cash at the back of her wardrobe, along with the printed note from Hugh that he can't be trusted with it yet and he is leaving it here for safekeeping until he's ready to launch the business. It was the best I could think of in a bit of a pinch, but I think it will work.

Though I've been pretty busy with comforting Nina, visiting Katie, Message M, stalking Dave, and planning, I decide to see James for a Sunday-afternoon walk. I tell myself it's purely to find out more about the murders – Chris has only been mentioned once more in the local paper – but I'd be lying if I said I wasn't looking forward to it. James has been texting me since our last date, and when I'm not thinking of revenge, I'm thinking of his infectious smile, elegant hands, and strong arms. He makes me laugh, and feel relaxed in a way that I have so rarely felt in anyone's company.

I'm early, waiting at the park gate, my hands wrapped around a coffee cup to keep warm. October is in full swing, and the world wants to leave us in no doubt that summer is over. I'm wearing a dress which is split to my thigh and low cut, but with a chunky orange scarf around my neck – a rare splash of colour for me – a thick black coat and warm, knee-high boots. With most of me now covered, it's almost like there was absolutely no point in wearing the tiny dress at all.

'Millie!'

I spin in the direction of the voice, but it's not James. It's *Gina*.

'Hey!' I say in genuine surprise. 'On your way in to Picture This?'

'Oh in a bit, just been shopping.' She holds up a bag from a local tech store – not exactly where I picture her shopping. I assumed she was more of a silk scarf and essential oils kind of woman. 'Working on a little *project*.'

Something is off about Gina. She grins at me manically and sniggers like a malevolent magician.

'Um, okay. Well . . . have fun then.' I do not want her here when James arrives – the smug glee will be too much to handle.

'Daniel Craig is going to get what is *coming to him*, Millie. You *mark my words*.'

'Good . . .'

She walks on, turning halfway up the path to shout back at me, 'Don't let men get away with their . . . their *shit*, Millie!'

'Never in a million years, Gina!'

Who would have thought, I'm starting to like her.

When James arrives, I feel my face split into a smile at

the sight of him. What has got into me? I'm getting like Nina, all romantic and optimistic. He greets me with a hug and his hard, warm body makes my skin feel extra sensitive.

'Hi there, Ms Masters. Looking gorgeous, as always.'

I spent an hour trying to make my face look less tired and drawn, so I appreciate the compliment.

'Flattery will get you everywhere, James.'

'Oh really? Everywhere?'

'Watch it, mate.'

We laugh and begin to walk, finding it even easier to flirt and joke side by side rather than across a pub table. I'm beginning to think that this man might be worth putting real time and effort into when all of this is over, and we have less . . . conflicting interests.

It's a classic autumn day, straight out of a romantic comedy. The sky is blue, and the grass is carpeted with orange leaves. When I shiver, he puts his arm around me and I feel the most content I've been in a very long time.

'How's the job hunt going? Or the investigation into finding what you want to do?'

'Oh slowly. I've always cared about literature. But that's hardly a job, is it? I thought about being a copywriter, or working in a bookshop? How do people know exactly what they want to do?'

He shrugs, and I feel his body move against mine with it. 'God knows. I always wanted to be a detective. Probably from the TV. But also because I wanted to help, you know? I like . . . justice.'

I shiver as he says this and he hugs me tighter, but it's not from the cold. Maybe we are more similar than I realised. Justice. It's what has been driving me for weeks.

'So,' he continues, 'it's not necessarily what you liked

at school. It's maybe what you care about? Like, whether that's beauty, or money, or helping others. Maybe think of it like that?' He laughs and gives his embarrassed shrug. 'Not that I'm a trained careers advisor or anything.'

'No, you're right. I hadn't thought of it like that.'

My hands are turning numb in the icy air, and so we traipse towards a pub at the corner of the park. When we're inside the dark, wood-panelled affair with a roaring fire and a decent wine list, I steer the conversation to murder. Business needs to come first after all.

James tells me about his workload, and about how wound up he is getting with no one taking his ideas seriously at the station. Some bloke reported seeing Chris running toward the bridge alongside a woman with short black hair, but that's about all he managed to gather. I'm not thrilled about the sighting, but the news that it's not being looked into is very welcome. James looks fervent when he speaks of his barely-there theories, and I worry he is becoming obsessed. He should really find a healthier outlet for his emotions. It's reassuring to hear that there has been such little progress though.

'I was told to forget about it,' he says, filling our glasses from the bottle of Malbec. 'Told I'm making mountains out of molehills and seeing links that aren't there. My boss even said that I have an "unhealthy obsession" with these deaths being linked.'

I tut sadly to imply how wronged he is being, and I'm not even faking it.

'What about my friend's boyfriend, Hugh? Do you think that might have something to do with it too?'

'Nah, in the end it didn't look like it.' He looks disappointed in this. All police officers, deep down, are desperate to catch a serial killer. It's what they dream of when they are children, not hours of tedious paperwork and chiding students for stealing traffic cones. Though he comes off as a chilled kind of man, James has a yearning for drama that becomes more obvious each time I meet him.

'It was an anaphylactic shock, which you obviously know. The guy had these little cake things in the kitchen and there's a bakery nearby that sells them two-for-one on Fridays. He probably just saw them on his way home and decided to give them a try. But turns out they are made with some sort of nut flour?'

'Almond flour.'

'Yeah! Yes, almond flour! Anyway, I guess that's quite rare in cakes? I have no idea. He's an idiot for not checking though. People with that serious an allergy usually get used to checking absolutely everything. But from what you said, he wasn't the brightest person.'

'Total moron.'

'Well there you go. The girlfriend, um, the *other* girlfriend, is convinced he would have checked. But there is no evidence to say otherwise.'

'Didn't he have an EpiPen?' Of course I know this case in quite a bit more detail than James, but it's delightful to have someone explain your achievements to you. This must be what it feels like to win an Emmy.

'Well yes, the girlfriend went on about that too. We found it down the back of the sofa. Stupid guy. If you aren't going to watch what you eat, at least keep your life-saving medication in a sensible place. She thought he had two, but the other one didn't turn up. Probably left it somewhere.'

Or it's in my bedroom, tucked into my pen pot.

'My boss was thrilled when he found a stack of cash in the bedside cabinet, thought there might be a gang connection. But the girlfriend – Charlotte, this is – said she'd given it to him to start his business. Sounds like a right waster to me.' He gives his little shrug, then adds quickly, 'Not that I don't care about his death. I shouldn't really insult victims.'

'Your secret is safe with me.' I give James a dazzling smile and clink my glass with his. The cash in the bedside table given to Hugh by Charlotte shouldn't really surprise me, though it does. It's good to hear that the (literal) crumbs of clues I left have been lapped up by the police. The shop selling macarons is a favourite of mine, and is always hugely busy on their two-for-one Fridays. They won't be traced back to me.

'Anyway,' he says with a sigh. 'Less of this. Let's talk about something else. Like . . . I don't know. Halloween? Feeling spooky?'

The conversation flows naturally, and we compete to make each other laugh. When we drain the bottle of wine, we look at each other in hesitation.

'You know, I have wine at mine?' he says with his trademark shrug, and ruffles his dark, floppy hair to distract from the moment. 'If you . . . fancy coming over?'

His eyes are gorgeous, and he is even sexier when he is unsure of himself like this. I'd planned on jumping back on the Message M phone line after this – though my options of help would be limited now that I've drunk too much to drive. But James doesn't know that I've been to his house before.

'Don't you live with your brother? I don't know if I'm up for socialising.'

215

'He's away. On a mini-break with his girlfriend.'

The idea of being back on that street, in that house, is making my head spin. Of stumbling loudly up the stairs I previously stalked up. The house next door, where I left Karl lying all of those weeks ago, now quiet and dark. The other housemates didn't want to live there anymore and the landlord was having to redecorate, according to James. So many things changed that night, in some ways it was the start. But James rests one long finger on the back of my hand, and even this slight touch sends a thrill across my skin.

Standing up, I down the rest of my wine, put down my glass, and hold my hand out to James.

'Let's go.'

The sex is pleasant and intense, if a little sloppy after another bottle of wine in his living room first. Being back on this street means that while James is on top of me, I keep thinking of myself as Rose. When he grabs my hair, I think of hers, and when he collapses back onto the bed next to me, I picture Karl tumbling down those stairs. It's a strange experience. Afterwards, we drowsily talk in bed, me lying across his chest and him stroking my hair.

When silence falls, my phone buzzes – I'd texted Nina his address as we always do when going back home with a man. Despite her belief in true love, she also has a firm belief in safety. I suppose you see bad things working in law. She even carries a can of pepper spray she confiscated off a client in her handbag. You just never know who might be a killer these days.

I fire off a quick response saying all is well and promise to update her in the morning, and then the holes in my plan start to swarm in my mind again. I know I need to get into Dave's house while he is at work next week, possibly tomorrow. So far, I've only watched and listened from outside, but he's a big man who could easily overpower me, so plotting everything out while inside is only sensible. A soft snore escapes James and I smile. It's not long before I fall asleep too, feeling warm and content, thoughts of love and murder swimming in my mind.

CHAPTER TWENTY-TWO

Days pass before I'm finally ready. With the obvious exception of Chris, which I'll admit was a bit of a blunder, I'm becoming better at what I do each time. Every kill has been better researched than the last, and the planning process is becoming almost as thrilling as the act. It's titillating, like foreplay, building up to that glorious crescendo moment when the light fades from their eyes.

Dave goes out to work every evening, and so over the next few days I break into his house twice to scope it out. It's spotlessly clean, which I find surprising for a man I consider loathsome. The house is cheaply decorated with flimsy kitchen units and furnishings that weren't bought any time in the last decade, but the worktops are wiped clean of crumbs, the carpets hoovered, and the bathroom gleaming. In my mind, I'd painted him as little more than one of Gulliver's Yahoos. One doesn't expect a man such as that to have a spotless toilet bowl. But even the worst of people can surprise you.

Thursday is the day I choose to act. It has been almost two weeks since I saw those red curtains, the confirmation I'd been seeking regarding the identity of the attacker. Each day I've been riddled with anxiety, anticipation, and fury, like my blood has turned to bees. As I stare at the little red dot on my wall calendar, I can't quite believe that the moment of retribution is finally here.

There isn't much equipment needed for this murder and Dave doesn't leave his house until 6:30pm, so I have plenty of time to arrange everything. Since Chris went over the bridge, I've been jogging less, but I pull on some running clothes and run eight kilometres at a fast pace to try and settle my nerves. Steering clear of the path up to the suspension bridge, I pace down to the waterfront and along the harbour, dodging couples wrapped up in coats walking fluffy pom poms pretending to be dogs.

At 4:30pm, I arrange everything I need in a small black backpack while Shirley Bassey meows at me in disapproval. Chris's penknife, which I've taken to carrying everywhere, my dark brown wig, some thick-framed glasses, black leather gloves, an iPhone charger, a small torch, and a few other bits and pieces. Leaving a bowl of food out for Shirley, I walk about ten minutes away from my house, put on my wig and glasses, and order an Uber to an address four streets away from Dave's address.

'Had a good day, miss? Just finished work, yeah?' The driver is desperate to talk. I am not.

'Yes, and yes.'

'Nice. Alright for some, yeah! I'm driving until at least 2am.'

'Oh no.' *Maybe you shouldn't have chosen to be a taxi driver if that's an issue.*

'Gotta pay those bills! Gotta keep the missus in new shoes, haven't I? Ha!' I start to fantasise about locking him in his own car boot when we arrive.

'Yeah, she wants some new Skechers. You know those? Have you seen the price of them? Anyway, she is going to go get some new Skechers this weekend, she says. And nothing I'm going to say will stop 'er! You like shoes? Or do you have a different poison?'

'Mostly it's just killing.'

'What was that?'

'Cleaning. Obsessed with cleaning.'

'Well, I wouldn't mind the missus havin' that one!'

Mercifully, we are arriving at our destination, or I don't think I could have kept a lid on it any longer. I back out of the taxi while he is still trying to tell me about his homelife despite me clearly caring less than Vladimir Putin cares about his reputation as a nice guy.

At 5:45pm I arrive on David Cartwright's road. My body feels eerily calm now, stealthy and relaxed. The bees seem to have fallen asleep. I want to see him leave so I can be sure the house is empty. It would be disastrous if I burst in there only to find that he's taken the day off sick and he's sitting in his pants playing *Call of Duty*.

But no, at 6:30pm on the dot, just as every other day, the front door opens and Dave steps out, dressed all in black and ready for his shift playing God to tipsy teenagers wanting to enter the horrifying nightclub he guards like a sphinx. Watching him for these past weeks, I've gotten to know him. He is incredibly punctual, and always looks neat.

I wait twenty minutes longer, just in case today is the day that he has left something behind and hurries back to grab his phone/headphones/Rohypnol. But all seems well.

After countless trial runs, I'm plenty practised at getting into Dave's back garden. The house is an end terrace with a small lane running down the side and a wall, about six foot high, between that and his garden. The wall is old and rough, easily scaled in seconds by anyone fairly fit and able, and you can slide down gracefully behind a bush. Okay, it wasn't so graceful the first few times, but now I feel almost like water.

Entering Dave's house is also easy, because Dave is stupid and unimaginative, something I had my fingers crossed for the first time I moved the flowerpot by the back door. A house key left right by the door – it's basically natural selection.

Within five minutes, I'm in. And now, well, I suppose I wait. Dave won't be back until around 1am, so I've got six and a half hours to kill with little else to do but play on my phone. I have a quick poke around to check nothing is out of the ordinary and then lie down on his bed to reply to James, my hood up so I don't leave hair on the pillow. We've been texting constantly all week, when I wasn't stalking Dave or helping strangers into bed that is. We haven't seen each other again – I haven't had the time – but when this is wrapped up, I'm going to cook him dinner.

Since Sunday, I've continued obsessively working on Message M. Like running, it helps clear my mind and channel my frustrations. Like last week, when I wasn't watching Dave, I was working. Even on Mondays, there is always some cry for help. Always a teenager being followed, a woman being watched, a date turning bad. Every week, there is usually a particular case that sticks with me. This week, it was a seventeen-year-old on a date with a man who had told her he was nineteen but who was at least thirty. He got her drunk then started getting handsy. She panicked, and texted me from the toilets. She looked a lot like my sister. Even more so when she was crying. It's been weeks since I've had a real night's sleep, more than a few broken hours. But the end is in sight. Six hours to go, and this will be over.

It takes a moment to realise where I am and how significantly I have fucked up. The slam of a door has brought me to, blinking the pitch-dark room into focus. I'm lying on David Cartwright's bed, in his home, where I have come to kill him. This was not the plan.

A groan of exhaustion comes from downstairs, followed by the slow thud of feet. With few other options, I drop from the bed and roll under it, reaching back to grab my bag and pull it out of sight just as the door swings open and the light flicks on.

Dave's heavy black boots, perfect for kicking unruly clubbers down the street with, stomp into view. He stops in front of the bed and I remember the neat, army-like precision of the duvet when I arrived, cringing at the thought of the crinkled mess it must be now. I'm not very far under the bed, which is mercifully empty of the usual clutter shoved in this hide-all spot, and I can't risk moving now. I'll just have to hold my breath and pray. I smooth my thumb over the penknife in my pocket – a cornered lion's retracted claws.

A moment of stillness passes, and I hear a slight exhale of air and an almost inaudible mutter, then the rustle of bedsheets as Dave pulls them tight. This guy really is anal. His feet turn as if to leave the room, but then he stops and flops backwards onto the bed.

Dave Cartwright must weigh around eighteen stone, and although the triumphant bed bravely holds his weight, it bulges down into me, squashing my nose into my face. If this guy makes my nose any more bent than it already is, I swear, I'll kill him. Again.

A longer exhale of air tells me that Dave has had a hard night. It would be just my luck if this is the night that his shift was so exhausting he breaks routine and just climbs straight into bed. What would I do? Stay here until 6pm tomorrow? Creep out once I hear him snore and hope he's not a light sleeper?

But luckily, after five minutes of me silently panicking, he heaves himself back up to a sitting position, almost breaking my nose in the process. Pulling off his boots and socks with a grunt, he wriggles his newly free toes on the clean, cream carpet, sinking them into the pile. After another minute, he stands and shuffles out of the room, but it's not until I hear the turn of the tap and the splash of running water that I let myself release a long, careful breath.

Things are not going to plan, but I'm only a quitter when it comes to work, hobbies, relationships, diets, and most friendships. Not murder. So we will roll with what we have. Dave's gone back downstairs while his bath runs, so I allow myself a bit of movement with less fear of being heard. I slip off my own shoes and open my backpack. The painfully slow inching of the zip is the longest, loudest moment of my life. Once it's open, I pull out what I need, and squeeze the knife in my pocket to check it's still there. As I hear the thud of feet on the stairs again, I inch further under the bed.

In the middle of the room, Dave's jacket and t-shirt hit

the floor. His trousers fall around his ankles, followed by his boxer shorts. In a heart-stopping moment, he stoops to pick them all up. Of course make-the-bed Dave wouldn't leave dirty clothes on the floor even for a minute. I hear a rustle of them going into the laundry basket and, when his feet move towards the door, I hear what must be his coat being hung up. Finally, he leaves and the sound of running water stops.

I hear a loud splash and a groan as he lowers his huge body into the water, followed by a satisfied sigh. Beyoncé's 'If I Were a Boy' clicks on.

Show time.

After a few minutes, I edge out from under the bed. Masked by Beyoncé's wailing, I unplug the lamp on Dave's bedside table and plug in the extension cord I've brought with me. Into that, I slot in the charger, at the end of which hangs an iPhone I bought from one of those dodgy stolen phone shops, and a small radio, which I switch on with the volume down to zero. I know that the extension cable is long enough because I tested it while Dave was out. The only thing that could go wrong now is being heard before the time is right, but I'm moving as slickly as a shadow.

Holding the iPhone in my hand, I edge towards the bedroom door. I'm nervous, I'll admit it. My heart is pounding, and it strikes me that I'm taking a ludicrous risk. With Karl, I was saving someone. It was *noble*. Chris was basically stalking me. With Steven and Hugh, I was at least invited into their homes. But this is different. I'm hiding in a man's bedroom, in the middle of the night, intent on killing him. A man three times my size who I know to be dangerous. I could easily be overpowered and arrested, or worse, he could hurt me. Like he hurt Katie. It's almost enough to make me turn back and rethink. Almost.

Turning to look at the window, I focus on the red curtains hanging there. I think of Katie at home in bed, skin and bone, that sad smile she forces to her face when she is trying to please me. This man attacked my sister, and it's time to take him out. Stepping into the corridor, I wince as the floor creaks. But all I can hear from the bathroom is the tinny music of a phone speaker and the occasional splash of water. Reaching my hand towards the doorknob, I pause and take a deep breath. Then the music shuts off.

I freeze. Possibilities whirr through my mind. I've somehow turned it off myself, or he's heard my footsteps and is rushing towards me right this second. I should flee, hide, attack. But then, the whiney voice of *Kelly* echoes around the tiled room and drifts under the door. I almost laugh in relief. The unexpected nap and sudden arrival of Dave has thrown me off; I forgot the crucial nightly phone call.

'Home then, are ya?'

'Ah Jesus, Kelly. I can't be dealing with this right now. It's two in the morning, like.'

'You always call at half one. What have you been doing Dave? *Who is she?*'

Feeling foolish, I pull back my hand and slowly plant a foot on the floor. That could have been a disaster. I hope to God I don't have to listen to this sparring for long. I've had enough of their relationship to last me a lifetime. While their voices rise, I distract myself by looking at the photos framed along the hallway. Dave and Kelly, arms around each other on a beach. Dave with some old people who I take to be his parents. They'll be sad, but they should have raised a better man.

'Listen, Kelly, I'm going, alright? It's been a long night. I'll call you tomorrow. We'll talk. But it's late, and I'm going.'

Beyoncé's voice floods the bathroom again, and as if to demonstrate the fuck you to Kelly, it transitions to 'All the Single Ladies'. Whether I'd come here tonight or not, I'm pretty sure the days until Kelly joins the ranks of them are numbered.

Steeling myself, I step forward and open the bathroom door.

CHAPTER TWENTY-THREE

A huge man in a bubble bath is a surreal sight. His shiny bald head and dumbfounded expression pokes up above the heaps of white foam, and there is a minute when everything, apart from Beyoncé, seems to stop. His baldness and nakedness make him look like a giant baby, and for a wild moment, I want to laugh and call it a day.

Dave's bathroom is white, spotlessly white. The only colour in the room comes from his big head, and the pink sponge that hangs from the tap. The air smells strange, and it takes a beat for me to realise it's the smell of lavender. I've always hated the synthetic smells of bath products.

There is certainly something appealing about making a speech worthy of Liam Neeson in *Taken* before you kill someone, but it isn't always practical. This isn't like killing Hugh, whose strength was sapped from him as I stayed at a safe distance. And although I'm not arrogant, I like to credit myself with enough intelligence that I don't put dramatics *too* far above my own safety. So I've planned what I'll say down to a tee. But I never expected to freeze in the doorway, like a lingering waitress who doesn't know whether to go or stay. As we lock eyes in horror, an outsider watching the scene might not have been able to tell intruder from victim.

But then he begins to move. The spell breaks and I come crashing back into my body, back in the driving seat.

'What the fuck?'

'My name is Millie. I'm here because you raped my sister. You held her down, you raped her, and you sent her on her way. You ruined that girl. You killed something in her. So now, you die.'

Dave opens his mouth to respond to my practised speech, pushing himself upwards as he does so. But I bring both hands from around my back and launch my missiles. A yellow iPhone 5c and a radio.

Have you ever seen a man fry to death? I won't linger on it too much, it wasn't pleasant. Even when it is a man whose death you've pictured, longed for, planned, there are nicer ways to spend an evening.

Wet skin has one hundred times less resistance to electricity than dry skin. That's why you can get a nasty shock from a car battery and still go for a cocktail afterwards, but if someone throws multiple electrical appliances into your bathtub, you can't.

I did my research on what would happen, but I'll admit that it's more, oh okay I'll say it, *shocking* than I imagined. An academic article just can't quite get across the sound of the electric crack, the convulsing body and smell of burning skin, the thrashing water spilling onto the floor.

Dave doesn't make a sound while it happens, and I can

barely move. In the doorway, my body is rigid as he spasms in the water, his face frozen in a grimace of pain. It seems to take an age, but throughout it all, I can't make myself move. Until everything cuts off with a *crack*. The power has gone. I exhale slowly.

Pulling out my torch, I flick it on and pass the light over Dave's body. Water is still sloshing back and forth around him, slowly returning to placidity. His head lolls to the side in the bubbles, eyes wide open but rolled back into his head so that only the whites stare back at me in the torch beam. He looks obscene in the tub, like a Halloween decoration. Never has one of my victims looked so dead, and simultaneously so much like they might spring up and grab me. I shudder, and after I am sure he isn't breathing, I step out into the hallway.

That was a lot. It wasn't the quick jolt of death that I graced Karl, Chris, or Steven with, nor the slow, wander into the underworld that I guided Hugh on. This was both long and violent. Visceral and filmic. The rancid smell of charred meat is slowly filling the hallway, so I pull the bathroom door to. I know I should be moving quickly, but sometimes it pays to take your time. If I rush before I've calmed down, I might make stupid mistakes.

Part of me can't quite believe it's done. I've found the man who hurt my sister, and I've hurt him back. More than that, I've killed him, and in a horrific, painful, degrading way. Naked as a baby, pathetic, wet, defenceless. Closing my eyes, I remember the weeks and months that Katie has hidden away from the world. Her unfinished degree and lank hair, mousy since the highlights grew out. I've fucking done it. Taking a deep breath in, I allow myself a smile.

I'm not quite sure how I'll tell Katie what I've done. She is a pure person and I doubt she'd understand my motivations; she'll feel guilty for her part in all of this. When it hits the newspaper, I'll show her. I'll think of a way to let her know, while keeping my role in it a secret.

I find myself staring at the picture of Dave with his parents. They look nice; the woman in particular has a friendly face. She looks happy to be with her husband and son, her arm around the gigantic Dave who towers over her. The house feels so silent now. Everything outside of my torch beam is pitch black, and the only sound is my ragged breath and the steady drip of water in the bathroom.

For ten months now, my life has been focused on what happened to Katie. In recent weeks it's been all-consuming. Part of me wonders what I'll do with my life now that I've completed my mission, but I suppose that other people manage to fill their time without impassioned vengeance plots, don't they? I should probably get another job, and there is always Message M. There are countless women who need saving from countless men. I allow myself to feel a warm thrill of elation. I've done it. He is actually dead.

I flick the beam to the next frame on the wall, Kelly and Dave on a beach. This one seems recent, though I doubt Kelly's appearance has changed much over time. Once people start getting that much silicone injected into their faces, they start to look agelessly ancient. The next picture is with Dave and a group of men around his age. They are holding their glasses in the air, wrapped up in coats and scarves, mouths open in a frozen roar of jubilation. Flicking the torch around the photo, I look for clues as to the celebration. Behind them, fireworks illuminate the sky, and my eyes catch sight of a New York building, the name of which escapes me. Then I spot something else.

One of the men is wearing a huge pair of novelty glasses, the ones which are made up of the numerals of the year and come out in force on New Years' celebrations. The ones that worked in the early 2000's but became a bit desperate past 2009 where there was a one over your right eye rather than a zero. But these glasses tell me that they are from the year just passed. This picture was taken ten months ago. In New York.

Desperately I push my face up to the photo. The glasses could have been picked up anytime in the past ten months. It doesn't necessarily mean the picture was taken on New Year's Eve; it could be an early January lads' trip. But the men are in a crowd of people, a big one, and the more I look, the more I see. Balloons, more glasses, someone is wearing a glittery top hat. It's New Year's Eve. In New York. The same night my sister was attacked. In Bristol.

The crashing realisation is met with another one, as I whip the torch to my right, back to the picture of Dave and Kelly on holiday. How could I be so fucking stupid? Kelly's in a bikini, and Dave in shorts. A vine tattoo creeps from his shoulder up his neck, but his chest and arms remain entirely bare. How old is this picture? Did I see a magpie on him in the bath?

All is silent from the bathroom, and part of me thinks that, if I open that door, I'll see Dave, relaxing in a bubble bath, eyes closed in slumber. It's such a nice image that I let myself live in it for a moment or two, rather than the present where I've just brutally murdered an innocent man.

Standing in the hallway forever isn't an option. Time is ticking, and I need to clean up and get out of here before the sun rises and early morning commuters climb into their cars. Time to face up to what I've done.

When I open the bathroom door, the smell is what hits me. The scent of lavender is now thick with charred flesh and human shit. Flicking my torch around the room, I survey the damage. Despite my daydream, Dave is unequivocally, utterly, entirely, deceased. The bubbles have started to clear from the water, and his unblemished white chest glows at me in the torchlight. How did I not notice? The floor is soaked, and the iPhone and radio rest on his bulky body under the water. It's so still and quiet and eery, it's unmistakably a room where something very bad has happened.

Standing back in the doorway, I feel once again like I'm in that driving seat, though the car is threatening to spin wildly out of control. Maybe it already has. But I need to snap out of it and sort this out. In the corridor, I leave the phone charger but unplug the now useless radio from the extension cable. I threw both in the water just in case the iPhone wasn't strong enough to do the job alone – I read about cases where a plugged-in phone falling in the bath is enough to kill, but it isn't always. The radio isn't part of the tableau I'm arranging though.

In the bathroom, I try to avoid looking at David's body as I quickly move around the room. I collect his own phone, which had fallen to the floor, and slide it into my pocket, leaving the identical one I brought with me submerged with him. Luckily, I remembered its lurid colour from seeing him use it in Fork It Up. It will be fried and useless, so no one will know the difference. By the cable, I slowly pull the radio from the tub.

The bedroom looks undisturbed, so I quickly check under the bed in case I've dropped anything, pull on my shoes and leave out the back door into the garden.

It's 3:45am and I have a long walk home in a scratchy wig and damp clothes, with a head full of hysterical thoughts.

God, I'm an idiot. An impatient, foolish, trigger-happy idiot. Some of the boxes were ticked, sure, but not *all* of them. The tattoo, the most specific piece of evidence, wasn't verified, and I never even thought to try and check if he was around on New Year's Eve. I just . . . assumed I'd got it right. Assumed he was working that night. That the evidence I gathered was enough. And now I've electrocuted a man in his own bathtub who was guilty only for being bald and working at a shit club.

The smiling face of the woman I assume to be David's mother flashes into my head and I groan audibly. I wonder if she'll have to identify the body, or if that's not necessary when you're found in your own home. I think of Kelly, waiting for his call tomorrow. She's tacky and whiney and has bad extensions, but she doesn't deserve this. David didn't deserve this.

It's gone half past four by the time I'm sitting in my bed with a cup of tea, going over what has happened. Preoccupied by my thoughts, I didn't realise how cold it was on the walk home, and now I'm frozen to the bone. I can't stop thinking about the smell of his body, the noise of the thrashing water, the smiling faces in the pictures.

Now all is said and done, I regret the way I went about the murder, too. Even if it had been the right fucking victim, the dramatics of it were foolish. I'd promised myself not to get caught up in being showy, and what did

I do? Stage a complicated violent death complete with prewritten speech. For the hundredth time, I catalogue the scene, making sure I didn't miss anything. A man in his bathtub. His phone, stupidly plugged into an extension cord running into the hall, is in the water with him. The phone is completely fried, but his girlfriend can confirm that he spoke to her from the bath moments before the recorded time of death. The house shows no sign of forced entry. Surely there is no answer other than an accidental death. Cut and dry. This was supposed to be the last one, but I suppose I'll have to gloss over this little mishap and start again. When I close my eyes, I feel like I'm in the out-of-control car and hear rushing in my ears. But then Shirley Bassey leaps onto the end of my bed and curls as close to my body as she can, her whole form rattling with purrs, and it doesn't take me long to settle in myself.

We all make mistakes.

CHAPTER TWENTY-FOUR

As a child, I never had a sick day. Home was the last place I ever wanted to be, no matter how much I was vomiting my guts up. It was cold – both literally and figuratively. After I met Nina, I would go to her house and tuck myself into her bed while she went to school, sleeping like the dead in a safe, silent tomb. Her parents never seemed to mind. Looking back, I realise they must have seen the bruises.

As an adult, I relish the quiet sanctity of my own home. If I am sick, or sad, tired, or just feeling anti-social, I can push myself under the covers and breathe in the space and silence and *mine*ness of it all. I did this for days after the disastrous death of Big Dave on Thursday. I knew that I needed to get out there and start again on tracking down the man who hurt my sister, and Message M was being neglected, but part of me wanted a rest from it all. I turned off my phone and retreated from the world.

I stayed in touch with Nina though, because she needed

me, and I couldn't pretend I didn't know about Hugh's funeral coming up on Sunday. I was curious anyway. I don't know if you've ever been to the funeral of a man you've murdered, but if not, I suggest giving it a try. It's an interesting experience.

Because of the drama of Nina being Hugh's secondary girlfriend it all felt messy, so we planned to dip in and out, then retreat to the pub.

Nina is holding up remarkably well, and despite her first plunge into madness and sorrow, I can sense her coming back to life. Of her two warring sides, Lawyer Nina is starting to triumph over Incurable Romantic Nina. The funeral will hopefully be the end of this particular saga.

After sleeping for two days straight, I am feeling back to full health and high spirits. Who cares, really, if the wrong man met his untimely end? It's not like random women aren't flicked off the face of the earth day after day after day by their boyfriends and ex-boyfriends and wannabe boyfriends. What is one less man really going to do to the planet?

I meet Nina at a coffee shop near the cemetery. I'm wearing a black dress that feels stylish yet sombre and isn't too low-cut. Nina doesn't own black clothing, so I can tell the dress she's wearing is new, and that she feels uncomfortable in it. We hug and she slides a black Americano across the table at me.

'Thanks for coming. This whole thing, fuck me, it's weird, isn't it?'

'Weird it is, pal.'

'I still can't really believe he had another girlfriend

either.' Nina sighs, gulping down half of her latte in one as though it is a shot of tequila. 'You know, part of me sometimes thinks that someone did it.'

I sip at my own coffee to stall and process what she's said.

'Why do you say that?'

'Because . . . because he was a *bastard*.' She whispers it like it's a sin and God might be listening. 'Wasn't he? Really? The more I've found out about him since, since it happened, the more I . . . He screwed women over. Regularly. What if one of them . . . struck back?'

'Was it you?' I ask with raised eyebrows.

'Ha! Sometimes I wish it was.' She laughs, and then looks at me almost fearfully. 'Shit, that's horrible. I don't mean that. It's his funeral and all.'

'You can be angry, Nina. You can feel whatever you like.'

Silence falls for a few minutes while we both get lost in our thoughts. I'm wondering if Nina would understand if I told her the truth. Maybe she is picturing what it would be like to kill a man like Hugh.

The thing with Nina is that nothing bad has ever really happened to her. Now, I'm not saying that in a resentful way. I certainly do not wish anything bad to happen to her. But in my not-so-humble opinion, trauma is impossible to understand unless you've lived it. Nina has always woken up in a safe bed, knowing she is loved. Her life has been lived wholly within her own control.

Maybe it's part of the reason I love her so much. There are plenty of people like Nina walking around who have never really suffered in their easy, blessed lives, and I despise the vast majority of them. But somehow, even though Nina can never truly understand, she has managed to avoid the naivety that often goes with that state. She knows trauma exists, just not how it works or what it does to you. And I enjoy Nina's normalness, her simple joy in things, her lack of nightmares; I feed off it. For a startling second, I fear that Nina may be broken by this, and it will somehow be my fault.

The moment is broken with the buzz of my phone on the table.

Though I've been avoiding my mobile as much as possible lately, choosing instead to stare at the blank screen of David's that is currently lying under my pillow, James and I have communicated a little over the previous days. His name flashes up on the screen and Nina raises her own eyebrows this time.

'James again, huh?' I had to give her the details of our rendezvous last week. There was no getting out of it after I'd texted when I went back to his. It was fun telling her everything though, especially since I've been keeping so much to myself recently. It also had the added benefit of distracting her from everything with Hugh, and as expected, she quickly became obsessed with my love life instead of her own. 'Answer it!'

I sigh, tap the green icon, and press the phone to my ear, slightly turning away like that might mask the sound of our conversation.

'Hey! Look I can't really talk now, call you back later?'

'Developments, Millie!' he yells. 'There has been another one!'

'What do you mean?' I turn cold and try and keep my face steady. Since sleeping together, James seems to have given up all pretence of discretion when it comes to his

238

work. But I could have done without hearing this news in public.

'Death. Another death. Accident, suicide, murder. Whatever. It's connected, I know it. Can I see you? Today?' James's voice is thick with an excitement which even *I* think is a little morbid, like he's choking on it. *People have died, James, have some compassion.*

'I've got Hugh's funeral today, and Nina needs me. We're going to the pub after the ceremony and—'

'Bring him!' Nina shouts loud enough that James can hear down the phone. 'Come on, James, I need a distraction, and it would be good to meet you!'

'I'd love to!' he shouts back, even though it just deafens me rather than carrying to her. 'I'm at the hospital right now anyway,' he carries on at a thankfully normal volume. 'Idiot brother of mine came back from skiing with a broken leg. He's alright, just getting it checked in a place everyone speaks English. I'll come find you at the pub?'

'Okay, okay. I'll text you the plan, yeah? We'll probably be there in a few hours. Hope your brother is alright.'

I hang up, and before Nina can say anything I finish my coffee and get to my feet. I see she is not too broken to meddle in my affairs, so maybe I shouldn't worry so much about her.

'Let's get going. We can hang around near the crematorium and sneak in the back.

'Okay, okay.' Nina appraises her unusually gloomy outfit in a Lavazza-branded mirror on the wall. 'God, I look depressing. Black makes me so washed out. I wish I didn't have to face them all while I'm looking like shit. All because of *him*.'

'Come here.' I rummage in my bag until I find a lipstick

– Mac's 'Ruby Woo' – and lean over to swipe it across Nina's lips. 'Let's show them who's boss.'

The funeral was unremarkable in all conceivable ways. Hugh's family were as uninspiring as himself, and the cemetery chapel was an ironically soulless room – blank and beige as granola. A bright spark in the proceedings was when the other girlfriend began to sob performatively to the degree that Hugh's aunty had to stop reading about the Valley of Death. I was proud of my friend's stoic face and striking red lips held in a firm line. We lurked at the back of the chapel, uninvited and unnoticed, and slipped out before anyone else.

When I'd been getting ready that morning, I'd wondered if I would feel guilty in the face of one of my victims' family and friends. But even when Hugh's mother made a tearful speech full of clichés about her son being the 'life and soul of the party', a 'good man' who would 'never hurt a fly', and someone who was 'taken too soon', my cold dead heart didn't feel a thing. Well, what do ya know? Maybe I *am* cut out for this.

We've just settled in at our table in The Guinea, choosing to go back to our usual haunt rather than anywhere near the funeral just in case an off-shoot of the wake party came in, when James arrives.

He and Nina hug and smile as if they're old friends, bonded already in Nina's mind by an affection for me. James, ever the gent, buys a round, which gives Nina time to frantically whisper in my ear (at a volume that still carries) about how polite and nice and handsome and kind he seems.

'I bet he doesn't have even *one* secret girlfriend!'

Nina is so robust that having her boyfriend die a gruesome death and then finding out he was a lying, cheating bastard has barely even dented her belief in true love. I knew she could handle it.

James is clearly almost wetting himself with desperation to tell me about the new body, and to be quite honest I am eager to hear, too. However, there is an unspoken agreement in the air that it might be insensitive to talk about brutal murders, seeing as we've just come from a funeral, and we struggle to land on another topic of conversation. Luckily, like the angel from heaven she is, Nina breaks the silence.

'So you're a detective, right? Any interesting cases right now? I'm a lawyer, but mostly family stuff. Bitter men and angry wives fighting over the television, that sort of thing. I've done some criminal law pro bono though. Fancy moving into it one day.'

The irony of me, who you might *technically* describe as a serial killer, drinking with these two pillars of the law is not lost on me.

'Well . . .' James glances at me as if for permission. 'We did actually find a body yesterday.'

'Fuck me! That's much more interesting than arguing over Easter holiday allocation. Tell us everything.'

Like a pipe suddenly bursting, James unloads all that has happened so far, professional discretion be damned. It's surreal, listening to your crimes being reeled off like that. It's how I imagine watching a documentary about yourself must feel. Every time James makes a mistake in the story I flinch. Luckily, they are both so engrossed that they don't seem to notice.

It starts with Karl. James admits that he got a little

fixated on it partly because he was his neighbour, but also insists that, as the rookie, he's less jaded than the rest of his team – cue a dull tangent about how shit his boss is. The fact that James is more *intelligent* than the rest of them isn't explicitly stated, but implied. Arrogance isn't a trait that I particularly mind when I feel it's got cause, and seeing as he is the only member of this braindead police force who has noticed a serial killer is operating in the city, I'll allow it.

We've had a few drinks by this point, and James is showing his trademark lack of discretion. He tells Nina about Karl's missing camera, which is still bugging him. He tells us about Steve, whose bloodstream was full of Rohypnol, and the general consensus that he tried to take a lot of cocaine alone but picked up the wrong baggy. Nina snorted at this.

'So he just had a date rape drug lying around? Serves him fucking right.'

'Well, I shouldn't really say it, as a detective, but I don't think he was the nicest guy. Let's leave it at that.'

'Sounds like the kind of person you come up against with the phone line, Millie!'

James gives me a quizzical look and Nina rambles on. I knew letting them meet was a bad idea. 'Mills runs this phone line,' she explains. 'Called Message M. She saves men from creeps. She's like, a fucking superhero.' Nina sounds drunk.

'She's exaggerating. Anyway, you were saying. You think that it was murder? I don't really get why?'

'Potentially.' He holds my eyes for longer than I'm comfortable with, but the desire to divulge his insider knowledge to Nina is strong enough to overcome his desire to question me further. I don't want him thinking about the phone line too much.

'I don't know,' he finally carries on. 'It just seemed off. The *set-up* seemed off. This guy must have come in, pretty drunk, alone, lined up multiple lines of the wrong drug and taken them in very, very quick succession. When you take too much of that stuff your breathing can stop. But even if it was cocaine, which we are guessing he thought it was, he was playing with fire.'

'People overdose all the time,' I chip in.

'Yeah, they do. But it's pretty rare for a guy like this.'

'Rich people can be idiots too.'

He gives me a quizzical look. 'How did you know he was rich?'

'When people say, "a guy like this" it usually means something to do with class.'

Phew.

'Was anyone seen around the place that night? You checked CCTV?' Nina breaks in, snapping James's attention back to her. I am grateful for it, and vow to keep my mouth shut for the rest of the conversation.

'The CCTV by the front door wasn't working. To be honest, half the CCTV cameras you see around are duds. You can't trust them. I knocked on some doors, but it's a big building with a lot of people coming and going. No one saw anything. And none of his mates seem to have been with him that night or know where he'd been. My boss is against putting a call out in the press for more information, so I've hit a dead end.'

'Well, that says it all, doesn't it?' I say, immediately breaking my vow of silence. My heart is beating fast at the mention of CCTV, which I didn't even consider on the night. What with the David mix-up and now this, I'm feeling shaken. I'm not being anywhere near as careful as I thought I was. 'None of his friends wanted to go out with him. He was a loser, and probably bored and sad, so sat at home and took loads of drugs to perk up his party for one.'

'Well, yeah. Maybe. Anyway, that's not all. Then there was the runner, you might have seen that in the paper?' Nina nodded. 'Well, that was even more suspicious. Listen . . .'

James updates Nina on Chris's final text to his wife, and how Chris hadn't shown any signs of wanting to take his own life before.

'There's nothing on CCTV, but we did have a few people come forward after it hit the papers. Mostly nutters, as always, but someone said they thought they saw the guy talking to a woman in running gear near where he fell. He was driving though, so couldn't be sure.'

'Doesn't sound like particularly compelling evidence,' I say.

'No. I know that,' he says impatiently. 'But get this, the witness said she had dark hair. And in the valley, they found a woman's wig. A black wig.'

'Riiiight,' I scoff, but my heart is beating so hard I'm surprised they don't see it. 'There's probably loads of crap in there. Do you know how many hen dos come to this city? Half of them wear wigs for one "hilarious" reason or another.'

'I don't know, Mills! It could be something?' Nina looks excited. I do not need her to encourage this.

'Well,' says James, 'my boss agrees with Millie. They won't even get it tested in the lab.'

'On the phone, you said there had been another one?' The relief at the wig being ignored registers, but I *need* to know about David.

'Yeah. We found him yesterday after his girlfriend let herself into the flat. He was . . . in the bath. He'd been electrocuted. It *looks* like he'd been using his phone while it was plugged in, and then it fell in the water.'

'Christ alive,' mutters Nina, and I shake my head in shock along with her. 'That would kill you?'

'Yeah, it's not the first time someone's died that way. So that is the fourth man dead – not including your loss, Nina, which seems quite separate. But this time, it's different,' he says with a smug smile in my direction.

My heart plummets. Just my luck I'd be caught out on David who was *an accident*. Sort of. So unfair. I don't know if they'd take that excuse in court though. *'Sorry, your honour, I actually meant to murder someone else. Can we forget that this one happened?'*

'Why's it different?' I sip at my drink to ease my dry throat, and then lean awkwardly back in my chair because I have seemingly forgotten how to just sit normally, and what people do with their limbs, and where they look when they are having conversations, and how much eye contact is weirdly intense and how much is normal, because all if I can think is *why why why is this time different?*

'This time, they were seen.'

CHAPTER TWENTY-FIVE

During my twenty-nine years of life, I've learnt many things. To cook, to clean, to pay my bills and argue with the DVLA about speeding fines. Also, to lie, to kill, and to completely shut down my emotions and exist on auto pilot until something unpleasant is over. That last one comes in pretty handy. James has just told my best friend and me about the evidence he has compiled so far.

It turns out that he doesn't have much information. The brief account from a tipsy neighbour isn't exactly the smoking gun he thinks it is. A woman was spotted in the alleyway by Dave's house the night before his murder, and the neighbour thinks she might have come from his garden. Apparently, it 'looked like she'd just jumped off the wall' but she isn't certain. Someone else noticed a woman on the night of the murder who fit a similar description, but walking along the road.

The woman was described as 'maybe tall-ish with dark hair'. Good luck, coppers.

The real issue is that I was *sure* I *hadn't* been seen. I guess it was inevitable that someone would glance out of the window one of those times I was there, but the fact that I didn't realise gives me chills. I need to be more careful.

I spend the next few days in my house, talking to the cat and decompressing. There are only three interesting things that happen during this time. First of all, the news reports the death of David Alan Cartwright. The details are sparse, but for the first time in my murdering career, I see the words, 'The police are treating this as suspicious'. They have put a call out for any information on a young woman seen in the area, medium-tall in stature with dark hair and of slim build. The gory mode of death hasn't been mentioned, and so the press attention is lacklustre. Like I said, who cares if the wrong man meets his untimely end? Turns out, without the horrifying details, no one.

The second thing is that I bump into a flustered Sean on Tuesday when we are both putting the bins out. Between David, the funeral, and the fact that I am no closer to identifying my sister's attacker, I'd pretty much forgotten about the phone call I'd overheard a week and a half ago.

He is looking thinner and grey in the face, and he jumps out of his skin when I say hello. Almost as if I'm dangerous. Rather than talking my ear off about his grandchildren, the weather, the state of the traffic, the government, or the 'foreigners coming over on rafts from Albania', he hurriedly dumps the bucket he is carrying into the glass collection box with an almighty clatter, and disappears back inside. Interesting. The box is half full with empty wine bottles. Poor old Sean has been trying to drink his problems away.

The third thing is the call from Nina. It is Wednesday afternoon and I am lying in the bath running through the list of tattoo shops I've yet to visit in lieu of a better plan, when her ringtone sounds from my bedroom – since watching Dave fry, I can't bring myself to take my phone into the bathroom, whether it's plugged in or not. After ringing out, it immediately starts up again, so I begrudgingly pull myself from the warm water, wrap my body in a gorgeous white towel I bought myself as a treat to detract from any bathing trauma I may have picked up, and go to find it.

'You don't work at Picture This anymore? Why the fuck didn't you tell me? What happened?'

'You've had a lot on your mind.'

'So? It's weird you didn't tell me. What happened? Rick wouldn't say?'

'Oh, I just couldn't do it anymore Nina. I need to do something else with my life. And you were always on at me to leave anyway!'

'Yeah, well. I didn't expect you to just quit. But congratulations? It's a good thing?' I hear the crackling inhale of her vape down the line.

'Why were you there anyway?'

'I wanted to take you out to lunch. I have a theory.' She takes a deep breath on the other end of the phone. 'It's a woman. All of them. It's a woman, and she is punishing these men.'

'Right. What are you talking about, Nina?'

'Listen, it's not that wild. It's kind of obvious, when you think about it. Think of what James told us – the first one, Karl, had pervy pictures on his computer. Number two, Mr Rohypnol, well that speaks for itself. The third one, the runner, I forget his name . . .'

'Chris.'

'Yes, Chris! I've been looking online, and apparently his wife found out that he'd been texting other women. So, he was a cheat. And the one in the bathtub, well I'm not sure what he did. Yet. But a *woman* was seen leaving the scene!'

I've always said Nina was smart.

'Okay. But think about it. These are just, well, normal men. How many married men are texting other women? How many have pictures they wouldn't want their mothers to see stored on their computers? And yeah, hopefully the Rohypnol is *less* common but—'

'And Hugh, Millie. I know James didn't mention him as part of the pattern. But that's another man dead in a short space of time. Another man who has *just dropped dead*. And who was a cheat. Don't you think that means something?' She inhales loudly on her vape again, smoking fast in her excitement.

'But Nina,' I say with slow patience, like I am talking to a child. 'By that logic, then the killer should be, well, *you*. Are *you* a serial killer, pal? Is that what you're telling me?'

'Sarcasm is the lowest form of wit, Millie.'

'It's the highest, and you know it.'

We bicker back and forth, and I manage to convince her that the police will be thoroughly looking into this. Not her game, not her ball. She finally agrees, but I know Nina, and I know expecting her to actually drop it would be far lower than sarcasm on the wit scale. I had been planning to 'help' her 'find' the money from Hugh this week, but on second thoughts, I think it may be best to leave that until everything has calmed down.

Another few days pass before anything else happens of note. By Saturday morning, all I've achieved is a few more tattoo parlours ticked off the list, and lots of social media stalking of David Cartwright's friends and family. At least I have been back on Message M, or my life would be feeling like a total waste. I am just coming to the conclusion that I have very little chance of getting any further in my mission without more information from Katie, when my phone rings. It's my mother.

My mother does not ring me. We do not talk, unless something about Katie must be communicated that is too big to be confined to a text message. So I am already on edge when I answer the call. She tries to small talk me, because she is a coward, but I push past the 'how are you doing sweetie' and the 'how is work' and the 'have you been doing anything nice' and get right to the point.

'What is it, Mum?'

'It's, well, it's Katie, love.'

'Yes.' I grit my teeth in frustration. This woman. I cannot believe we share genes.

'I'm afraid she took a bit of a turn. She, um, she's in the hospital.'

I'm grabbing my coat and shoes before she's finished her sentence.

'What happened? Explain. Now.'

'Well, I think it was the fireworks last night that did it. We were just having a nice tea with your uncle Dale at home. She'd come downstairs for it and everything, but then these fireworks started and, well, I think it upset her.'

'New Year's Eve,' I muttered, pulling on my boots.

'What was that, love? I think they were left over from Bonfire Night.'

'Nothing. What happened?'

'She went upstairs and didn't come down again, you see. And when I checked on her this morning, she didn't want any breakfast. But then I thought I'd check again a bit later and, well. Oh Millie.'

'What. *Happened*.'

My mother's voice is a whisper, a barely audible crack through the phone. But each word is clear to me, because I already know what they will be.

'She cut herself, love,' she says in a mouse's voice. 'She cut her wrists. There . . . There was a lot of blood.'

'Is she okay? Will she be okay?'

'We . . . We don't know.'

Mental health became a buzzword for millennials, and Gen Z grasped at it with gleeful hands and looks like they are going to refuse to let go anytime soon. I'm not saying it's a bad thing. It's good to take care of yourself and each other, good to understand when you need help or a break. Like me when I accidentally electrocuted the wrong person, I knew I needed to take some time out.

But what really grinds my gears is the hypocrisy. Because although we open our arms wide for any privileged white girl having a bad day, people still turn away in horror at mental illness that is less . . . palatable. I'm not against *anyone* getting help, but when mental illness becomes ugly, or confusing, or inconvenient, most still shuffle off in embarrassment. Where is the offer of a home-working contract for a woman with red raw hands from an hour scrubbing them? Or an embrace for a man tormented by horrible memories that aren't real? Or understanding for my little sister, Katie, lying pale in bed with arms heavily bandaged from wrist to elbow?

As soon as Katie started to unravel, people wanted to look away. Her friends posted on social media about being there for each other, but when she didn't immediately spring back to her carefree university self, their visits turned from encouraging, to awkward, to annoyed, and eventually to non-existent. In my angrier days, I wanted to add them to a hit list. To pick off one by one the people who turned away in embarrassment or disgust when they saw Katie's emotional scars were too deep to paper over with a brave smile.

I'm at the hospital now, sitting by her bed. She is asleep, and she looks so, so small, like a bird who has flown the nest too soon. She is shockingly pale. I suppose because she rarely leaves her room or eats these days, but also because of the blood she lost when she cut her wrists. I'm very aware that it's only by chance that my mother found her in time. If I was a better person, I would live there with her to watch over her all the time. But I can't go back to stay in that house, not even for Katie. The memories are too painful. And she won't leave it.

Her mousy hair is spread out around her face on the pillow, and it conjures an image of Rose. I wonder what she is doing now. Maybe she is a student, and went happily back to her studies. Maybe she only has hazy memories of what happened at all that night. I hope that is the case, and she isn't somewhere else in this building, trying to escape her own mind.

My mother is hovering around, but we haven't really

spoken. I'm so mad, not at her necessarily, but at myself and, mostly, at the man whose name I still don't know, that I can't speak. The doctors come by to tell me that my sister will be okay, and I can hardly contain my relief. But she's lost a lot of blood and will have permanent scarring. The psychologist will be by later and she'll be kept in for the time being. They say that there is nothing I can do.

But I know that's not true.

CHAPTER TWENTY-SIX

After leaving Katie in the hospital, I go for a fifteen-kilometre run. Thank God no one tries to speak to me or they would have gone straight off the bridge or under a car and I don't think I'd have had the head space to stop and look around first. Everything is sliding a tiny bit out of my control. Katie is in hospital, I've murdered the wrong man (not to mention the others, even though they very much deserved it), my best friend seems to be rapidly catching on to what is happening, and the man I'm dating who also happens to be a detective isn't *too* far behind her. No matter how sweet James is, I don't think he'd turn the other cheek when it comes to mass homicide.

But I can still pull this back. Things often go wrong before they go right, or at least that is the case in movies. Then again, Jack sank to the bottom of the ocean and never did get to marry Rose.

I need to find the man who started this so I can end it. James has no evidence of any wrongdoing, not really.

After the killings stop, he'll move on to something else. Another woman or two or three will be beaten to death and it will take up all his time until the motley crew of men found dead this autumn become a distant memory, something to occasionally wonder about during retirement.

Nina is in a weird place right now and she has a habit of becoming fixated on something random when she wants to avoid thinking of something painful. But she'll become busy at work, she'll go on a date with someone who will sweep her off her feet, and she'll move on. We'll all move on. And when Katie hears that the man who did this to her is dead and buried, *she'll* begin to move on too. I know it.

My run calms me. Whereas before I felt like a coil of wire, I now feel as cold and hard and focused as a bullet. The rage is still there though.

Sitting in my house for the evening isn't an option, but I clearly can't socialise with others when I'm feeling like this. So I turn on my Message M phone, drive into town and park in a side alley to wait for a call.

Saturday night is always busy, and I missed last week after the shock of The David Mistake. When I think of the women and girls who might have needed me, I feel a cold stab of guilt. I try to soothe myself with the knowledge that over these past few weeks I've permanently taken out some people who would have caused a lot of harm over their lifetimes, but this is less compelling since my David blunder.

It usually kicks off early, and on a good night, or a bad one, depending on how you look at it, I can end up helping five or six women in one way or another. Around nine o'clock, the texts start pinging in, and I can tell that it's going to be a big one.

There's a woman on a date in a fancy wine bar. She thought he was suave, but he tried to take her back to his after two drinks and started getting aggressive when she said no. After that, I got two underage girls out of a bar where they were being harassed by a group of lads who 'didn't mean no harm, you fuckin' killjoy!' I sent the girls home in a taxi and told them to wait until they were eighteen until they went out drinking again. I found a young woman hiding in a club bathroom because she was sure someone was following her.

It's a lot, this job. Even after just a few days' break, I find myself surprised by the rush of escape, the effect that the girls' relief and their thanks have on me. But also, I recognise there is a deep-seated anxiety and sadness that I can feel in my lungs, that and the bubbling swell of rage. I'm wearing a wig – shoulder length and chestnut – with a hat and too much makeup. I've always tried to keep myself unrecognisable, but ever since Karl, I've tried harder.

I can feel myself buzzing tonight, those bees back in the blood. I'm handling every case with quick efficiency, but with a blunt harshness that isn't usually my style. Every woman I save has Katie's face.

I'm having a word with a barman about keeping a better eye out for his patrons when I feel the phone vibrate in my pocket. I lean forward and tell him in a low and threatening voice that he is a bigoted prick, then head back to the car while opening my messages.

Mostly, jobs are easy and pretty safe, but then you get ones like Rose, where you can see the brink of real, tangible danger. I watch a flurry of texts flow in, it's from a girl who is hurriedly telling her story, followed by a frenzied whisper of a voice note which gives more detail. No misunderstandings here, no lads 'just having a laugh'.

It is garbled and confusing, but from what I understand, there is a guy on her brother's football team that she's met once or twice – twenty-one to her fifteen years. She's flirted with him in the past. She's letting me know this to caveat exactly how much of this is her fault, as if I should be given the opportunity to turn her plea for help down. The guy in question texted her earlier in the evening, telling her that he was having a party and it would be 'cool if she came.'

Her parents were out, and though she'd been told not to leave the house, she jumped at the chance. But when she arrived, she found it wasn't exactly a party. It was him and two of his friends, hanging out in his bedroom. They gave her a cocktail of spirits, that she drank because she didn't want them to think she was uncool, or worse, too young. They *know* she's too young, that's the whole fucking point. It wasn't long before she realised that the other two were leaving, that it was just him, and he was kissing her. She got scared and confused, and when he went to the kitchen to get more drinks, she started texting me.

The last message she sends contains the address, and when I register that it is at least twenty minutes away from where I am, I clutch at handfuls of my fake hair in distress. Running to my car, I shout at Siri to input the address into Google Maps, and I drive.

The speed limit around here is thirty miles per hour, and I'm going over fifty. This child is in trouble and a speeding ticket or two means nothing to me right now. But when I nearly skid wildly out of control taking a corner at full speed I try to slow down; if I crash, I won't be able to do any good at all. Still, as I fly through the night on deserted roads lined with staggering drunks, I pray I'll be quick enough to stop anything more happening, and I vaguely register that in my mind this girl has Katie's face and Rose's soft pink hair.

Finding the address in under fifteen minutes, I slam on the brakes and leave my car parked at a reckless angle. The rage that has been brewing since I saw my sister in hospital has reached a boiling point, bursting out of my every pore. When I catch my reflection in a car window, I'm almost surprised to see that there isn't steam coming out of my ears.

Number 29 Roland Road. I can see a light in the upstairs window. There should be a moment here where I stop and take stock, formulate a plan, but I'm past that. It reminds me unavoidably of the night I barged into Karl's basement, but I don't pause long enough to take a lesson from this. Part of me has been longing to let go completely and give into my rage since the moment that I saw Katie in the hospital. Since even earlier, probably. Since the day she was attacked. Even since I was a child.

Marching up the garden path, I stop at the front door, nothing but darkness coming through the glass. Locked. Of course, it's locked. People don't leave their front doors open. Especially when they have plans with impressionable, drunk young girls. Without thinking, I bend and grab a rock from the side of the garden path. It's heavy and rough.

Hoisting it upwards, I bring the rock down hard against the glass with a resounding *crack*. I hit it again, *crack*, and on the third try, it shatters into the hallway. Pushing my hand through, I turn the handle and the door flies open. I hear a 'What the fuck?' from somewhere, but my legs are moving faster than their brain is, and I'm halfway up the stairs by the time the bedroom door flies open.

A man is standing there, jeans unbuttoned, hair dishevelled. Even in the face of a furious woman storming towards him, he has an aura of arrogance. A regular Romeo. He is undeniably handsome, with the kind of scruffy, floppy hair you see on teen pop stars, and he isn't scared. Men like this aren't scared of women. But they should be.

I say all of this in retrospect. When I play back what happened, my mind slows down enough to give me this image: him, standing in his doorway, framed by the light of his bedroom behind him. Dark brown hair framing his young, chiselled face, a grey t-shirt with the beginning of sweat patches under the arms. The furrowed brow of confusion, the 'who the fuck are you?', the squeak of relief from inside the room. And the *crack* of the rock coming down onto his skull. Over, and over again.

I come to after what feels like a brief holiday from myself. A body is lying at my feet, the artfully dishevelled hair now matted with blood and bits of bone, an arm bent underneath him at an odd, uncomfortable-looking angle – though comfort means nothing here, as there is no chance this man is still alive. I can see one open eye, staring blankly, as blood drips down over the forehead and off the brow onto the carpet.

Looking down at myself, I realise that I'm still holding the rock, which has become as heavy as a sack of lead. I drop it and it rolls backwards, thumping down the stairs with a heavy *thud, thud, thud* on each step. It must have only been seconds that I blacked out, but a whole life can change that time. Or in this case, be snuffed out.

Drawing in a long breath, I try to calm myself. This is not how I am supposed to act, this is madness. This unbridled, unplanned violence has left so much to clear up if I don't want to spend the rest of my life behind bars.

Another noise drifts into my opening consciousness – a low muttered swearing. Looking up, another door off the hallway has opened without me realising. In the doorway stands a man, ashen-faced and stupid. The fug of marijuana is coming from his open door, and he is staring at the body of his friend in gormless confusion.

His slow, heavy eyes finally flick from the bloodied mess on the floor to me, and we stare at each other for a beat. There isn't much time to think of what to do next, there is only one answer really. Stepping over Romeo's body, I reach into my pocket and pull out Chris's knife, flicking out the largest blade.

The mystery housemate backs away, but it's over in seconds. I stab him in the throat as he grabs my arms weakly, pushing me away as I pull out the blade and slam it back into his neck three times. He thuds to the floor and I blink blood out of my eyes, telling myself I had no choice. That he probably deserved it too. He allowed this to happen in a house he was in. He let his friend take advantage of people, while he just sat in his room blunting his brain with weed and closing his eyes to what was going on.

There is that saying that people like to throw around a lot, you know the one, 'The only thing necessary for the triumph of evil is for good men to do nothing'. Well, he did nothing. I didn't.

But mostly, he saw me. He saw my face, saw me covered in blood and standing over the body of his friend. There wasn't anything else that I could do about it. It was him, or me. Murder, or prison. Ironic really, that I had to murder a man to stay *out* of jail.

Leaning against the wall in the hallway, I survey the scene and catch my breath. The blood from both men is like nothing I've seen before. It is soaking into the grey carpet, staining the hallway red from either end as the pools spread and converge. My arms are heavy and aching, Chris's knife still clutched in my fist, and my chest is tight like I've run a marathon. I crouch down, pushing the back of my hand against my mouth to stifle whatever noise is trying to escape. Something wet hits my knuckles, and I realise I'm crying. What have I done?

I've killed a man in blind range. I wasn't even defending myself. I've made no attempt to make this look like a suicide or accident. And then I've killed his friend, someone who didn't even appear to be doing anything wrong. But I couldn't leave a witness. I just couldn't.

I need to get out of here.

But then I hear it, and I realise that for a moment I forgot why I was here at all. From Romeo's room comes a whimper. The stoner wasn't the only witness. How could I forget about little Juliet?

CHAPTER TWENTY-SEVEN

The water is red. I'm lying in a bath of water stained with the mixed blood of two men, with just a drop of my own from where I've clawed at my skin. What I'm doing feels witch-like, but I'm not sure what this spell would achieve. Immortality, hopefully. Along with the rock I'd taken from the scene, my clothes – which are heavy with blood – sit in a pile in the corner of the room and I'm watching Shirley Bassey sniff at them with interest. She pokes out a little pink tongue to lick at my trousers and my stomach lurches.

I rub my hands together to try and remove the last traces of blood on my skin, but I know it's in my hair as well. Reaching across to the various bottles of products, I lie in the hot, red cauldron and scrub at my skin and scalp until I feel raw and new. I drain the bath and start at the beginning.

The car is speeding out of control again, flying through barriers and skidding towards cliffs. This is different to what happened with David Cartwright. That was an

262

honest mistake. Whereas this, even if I was being very generous, I don't think I could brush this off as an accident.

Beating a man to death with a rock, then stabbing someone I presume to be his housemate in the throat is way past mistake territory. Despite it being spontaneous, when I killed Karl, I wiped down every surface and left a scene which could easily have been an accident. David's murder was carefully planned, even if the subject of it was badly chosen. But this . . .

Washing my hair for the third time, I cringe as I think of any DNA or fingerprints I may have left behind. I'm pretty sure that I avoided stepping in the blood on the carpet, so hopefully footprints won't be an issue, but this scene could hardly be painted as an accident or suicide. This was an incredibly clear, incredibly bloody, incredibly incredible double homicide and there is a very good chance I'm totally fucked.

And that's before we even get to little Juliet.

There was a moment, just a fraction of one, where I considered killing her too. But I wouldn't ever do that. Enough innocent women die untimely, violent deaths. None of this was her fault, I was only there to protect her, and if she'd suffered by my hands then there was no way I could have lived with myself. So I told her to stay in the room for a moment while I figured out a plan. Then I found Romeo's phone and deleted their text exchange, and told her to tie something around her eyes before I entered the bedroom so that she couldn't see my face. I collected her, leading her around the bodies to the front door. Before we left the house, I told her that the men had attacked me, and I'd hurt them to save myself, and to save her. She nodded her understanding, shivering and swaying on the spot with a sparkly scarf tied absurdly around her eyes.

I warned her never to mention to a soul that she had been in that house, and that she was to forget about everything that had happened that night.

I admit I also threatened Juliet a little. Just a *little*. She needed to know what was at stake.

'If you tell anyone, *anyone at all*, you were here, then you will be blamed for this,' I said, hating myself more with every word.

'Yes.' The voice was tiny and hushed, as if it was coming from a mouse. I flinched at my words. They're words I've heard before.

'Your DNA will be up there. Do you understand? If I find out you have mentioned it to anyone, you will be in trouble. With the police, and with me.'

'Okay.'

'Delete any messages you've sent this evening. Understand?'

'Yes.'

I drove her most of the way home, dropping her off a few streets away and telling her to wait ten minutes before removing the scarf. She agreed, and I believed her. The girl was in shock, though I'm pleased she didn't see the bodies. In the morning, she'll have to pretend that absolutely nothing of note has occurred. There is a good chance she'll break her word one day, and if that happens, I'll get what's coming to me. Though she doesn't know my name or what I look like, so maybe not.

In trying to save her from trauma, I've given her a whole load of unexpected shit to need therapy about, only she'll have to work through this entirely alone. I push my head under the bath water and stay there as long as I can stand it. Poor girl.

On my way home, I stopped by a public bin where I disposed of the SIM card in my Message M phone. It wouldn't be safe to use that again. I need to distance myself from that number as much as I can, and I'm clearly not in the right headspace for safe vigilantism. Even if this occurrence isn't my undoing, it's only a matter of time before I get caught if I keep acting like I did tonight.

Message M is done.

Light is coming through the bathroom window, dawn is on its way. My skin is raw and wrinkled, and the water is completely clear.

It's midday when I get into my car to go to visit Katie at the hospital. The clothes I wore last night have been put through an intensive washing cycle multiple times and then put into the back of my closet, and I'm feeling better about my prospects. Did you know that only 5.8 per cent of crimes are solved in the UK? A lot of those will be kicking over a bin or some other petty misdeed that the police won't bother investigating, but even when it comes to murder, a *third* of them still go unsolved. And that's with most of them being obvious – the abusive husband found holding the knife, a drunken street brawl outside of a pub full of witnesses.

By my reckoning, unless Juliet blabs and the police can track Message M, it is unlikely I'm going to get done for this. No one suspects a woman of this sort of thing, with good reason really; female killers are rare. There are thousands of avenues down which police will look before landing on a totally unconnected young woman with pathetic, skinny arms – drugs, break-in gone wrong, gang connections. My DNA isn't on the police database as I've never done anything wrong. Okay, fine, I've never been *caught* doing anything wrong. So how would they connect this to me? And even if they eventually do, how long would that take?

I have time. Not unlimited time, but enough to find and dispatch Katie's attacker before focusing on building a new life for us both. Maybe I'll convince Nina to move with us to a different city and start again. But there can't be any more mistakes.

It starts to rain as I hit the ring road, heavy droplets hammering against my windscreen making it difficult to see. I imagine the same rain hitting the door of the house on Roland Road with its broken glass, washing anyway any tiny traces of me.

Hospitals are grim places. We all know the smell of them – the mix of old people, bleach, urine, and boiled cauliflower from the 1980s. How has that not been rectified yet? Surely, with all of the room odourisers, incense sticks, candles, and perfumes in the world, they could fix this small thing that brings misery to one and all? If all spas and 'wellness centres' can smell of a heady mixture of rosemary and eucalyptus, surely they could just try and make this place smell less like death. Stick a load of car fresheners around the place for all I care.

The smell is not the worst thing though. It's the loneliness. All of these people, at their lowest ebb, lying in depressing beds in a depressing ward surrounded by depressing people. If someone does have a visitor, it's usually an adult making a duty visit to their ageing mother, having dragged along their three small children who do not want to be there. They breathe a sigh of relief when they leave Granny there to slowly waste away alone, and escape back to their own lives, full of colour. Loneliness can't be warded off with a candle.

Katie looks embarrassed when I arrive at her bedside, but she's awake. She closes her book without even folding down the page to mark her place and scoots up in bed, fixing an apologetic smile onto her face, like someone who's had too much to drink the night before and is readying themselves to say sorry to their friends for being annoying.

'Mills! You didn't need to come in. I'm fine, really, it's all an overreaction.'

'How are you doing, sis?'

'Oh fine. Fine! Honestly.' She smiles at me again to show just how fine she is, then adds in an undertone, 'Though the people in here are driving me *mad*.'

'Who in particular?'

'Well *she*' – she nods subtly towards a bed opposite and to her right – 'will not stop complaining about the temperature, like it's a bloody hotel. And the one down *there* had a massive group of visitors, including *four* small children. And when they were told to leave, they started having a go at the nurses.'

I raise my eyebrows in mock horror. 'If you could send one of them into the sun, who would it be?'

'*Bed number six*,' she stage-whispers. 'Oh. My. God. She watches *Love Island* on her laptop without headphones and gasps and laughs out loud the whole way through. Reactions like an extra on daytime television.'

I surprise myself by laughing out loud. Despite Katie

lying in hospital, pale and bandaged, it feels incredible to laugh with my sister. She has always been funny. Though I know she is trying to distract me from talking about anything serious, I still haven't seen her this alive in quite a while. Maybe that was the bathtub spell – I transferred the life of those men to my sister. If so, I'd happily kill a hundred times. I don't want to interrogate her too much anyway, and so we happily slag off the ward residents in whispers for the best part of forty minutes until I am told that it is time to leave.

'So, what's happening next, then?' I ask, gathering my things at the slowest speed possible before it becomes obnoxious.

'Maybe *Love Island* will be back on soon? Not much happens here, to be honest, Mills.'

'No, I mean, after *this*,' I say, gesturing to our surroundings. 'Are you coming home soon?'

She flushes, having been lulled into a false sense of security by my lack of questions. I feel guilty, but I can't leave without knowing.

'Um, I'm not sure. They want to keep me here for now, and I might, go . . . somewhere else. After.'

'Oh. Okay.' Questions bubble up in my throat, but I quash them down. *A psychiatric ward? Are you being sectioned? How long for? Can they make you better?* But she's told me enough for now, and I want to leave things on a good note. 'Well, that sounds great. And you look great. I'll come back tomorrow, yeah? Love you.'

I hug her fragile little body and make to leave, but she pulls me back, not letting go of the hug.

'Everything okay?' I whisper. She releases me.

'Yeah, yeah it is. It's . . . No, I'll see you soon.'

I look at her expectantly. A nurse is bustling down the ward, ushering the last visitors on their way. 'Katie, what is it?'

'Nothing, honestly.' But I see her eyes dart to the drawer next to her bedside, so I lean over to open it. There is an envelope inside, my name on the front in her writing.

'Oh, um, yeah,' Katie mutters, her skin flushing. 'I wrote you something, but you don't need to read it. It's just rubbish. I regret writing it.' Her arm moves, but it's injured and slow, and I've already stood up with the letter in my hand. 'Well . . . do *not* read it here then. Wait until you are home. Promise?'

'I promise.'

I push it into my pocket, hug her again, then leave, stopping by the nurses to say thank you. The letter has made me sad, and angry. Katie has apologised to me countless times, which is what this letter will be. Sorry for being so *dull*, sorry for being so *tired*, so *embarrassing*, so *stupid*. Sorry for not eating enough, sorry for getting so thin, sorry for hurting herself, sorry for causing a nuisance. But she doesn't need to be apologetic. *He* needs to be apologetic. She needs to be *angry*.

Despite how I feel, I vow to read it later with a glass of wine.

The rain has cooled to a drizzle, and I'm barely aware of it as I step out of the automatic doors into the fresh air, a blessing after the stuffy stench of hospital sadness. Weaving towards my faded red Micra in the far corner, I'm thinking over Katie's options. Images of outdated lunatic asylums with women chained to beds are battling with those of a country mansion complete with rolling green lawns and lots of yoga.

I'm so caught up in my thoughts that I don't hear my name being called until it's coming from two metres away, and I spin around. My blood freezes, I swear I can feel my heart harden to solid ice in my chest.

'You didn't hear me? How you doing?' James is grinning at me, water droplets shining on his hair, and next to him, stands someone I've met only once.

'This is my brother. Imran.' He gestures at the man next to him wobbling on crutches. I start rummaging in my bag for my keys. 'I told you he got in an accident, right? Idiot. Had to come back to change the plaster over.' He turns to his brother. 'This is the girl I was telling you about.' I can sense James grinning at me, but I let my hair fall in front of my face. *Where* are my keys?

'Nice to meet you,' says Imran, and I mumble something back without looking up. 'I swear I recognise you!' he continues. 'You aren't an accountant, are you? Maybe it's from a conference?'

'Nope. No, no, not an accountant.' I laugh in an unnatural booming way. 'Never could add up. *Totally* crap at maths. I've got one of those faces though, apparently.' I wave my hand over my face, as if the man didn't know what a face was and needed it pointed out. 'Everyone thinks they know me.' My fingers brush metal at the bottom of my bag. 'Ah ha! Sorry, just, um, couldn't find the keys. Now I have them. Anyway, nice to meet you Imran! Hope your leg makes a speedy recovery. See you, James!' I force the key in the lock and pull open the door.

'Oh, okay. See you soon, yeah? I've got some theories to run by you! Maybe tomorrow night?'

James is still speaking through the crack in the door. There is a minuscule spot of blood on the window which

270

I've only just noticed. Fuck, I must get this thing valeted. Murderer 101. I need to get out of here – that's a thought I'm having too much recently.

'Yes! Tomorrow. Let's do that, sure.'

I slam the door the rest of the inch shut and start up the engine. As I pull out of the car park, I can see the men standing in the same place next to my empty spot, talking. Glancing in the mirror one last time before I leave, I see them both turn to watch me go.

CHAPTER TWENTY-EIGHT

I credit myself with an above-average intelligence. I don't hold with all of this false modesty. Women are not expected to brag; we are expected to be humble. If someone tells you that you look nice, you let them know you strongly disagree. If you know you have aced an exam, you must still bemoan how poorly you probably did, and when the results come back, you must look confused and say, 'Well, I wasn't expecting that!'

These are the rules. I understand them, and for the most part, I play by them. Much like the rules of not killing people. I don't boast about that either, it's against the guidelines.

But privately, between you and me, I'm clever. I've always been clever. And all things considered, I've sorted out my own shit. This hasn't resulted in a high-flying job, but that wasn't in the plan. Nina's always said I should try copywriting, and perhaps I will. I just need to get through this first. I need to cover my tracks after the

Romeo killings, find and dispose of Katie's attacker, and make sure James doesn't twig. Then I can move on with my life. Simple.

Pouring out another glass of wine, I exhale deeply to try and calm my nerves. The Golden Guinea is still quiet – it's Sunday afternoon and they don't serve food here. The British desperation for a weekly plate of meat and gravy means that the masses have avoided this place in favour of whatever chain brewery makes the cheapest beef and most plentiful potatoes.

Despite this, my usual table is taken by a smarmy couple, and so I'm ensconced in a leather armchair by the fire, my long legs folded underneath me like a deckchair, my large glass of red hugged to my chest. An old man in the chair opposite has a Highland terrier at his feet, a broadsheet unfolded on his lap. Every time he turns the page the paper crinkles so loudly that the dog wearily raises his head from the floor as if to ask, '*What the fuck is it now?*'

Drinking alone in the day is something I try to avoid. It doesn't scream 'well-adjusted woman who is totally fine'. But I'm panicking. Just a bit. Logically, I know it doesn't pay to panic. It achieves nothing. Panicking, much like sadness, is pure self-indulgence. However, I'm allowing myself this particular self-indulgence for this afternoon.

The old man folds his paper in a cacophony of rustling that makes me jump, splashing wine onto my hand. The deep red against my skin reminds me of the previous night and sends a chill across my body. Rather than further alarm I feel a deep, bone-aching tiredness as I remember that I still need to clean the blood from my car. The old man squeezes past me to the bar and orders a pint of bitter and a glass of water.

'And none of that fancy stuff with the water, if you don't mind.'

'Ah we only do the fanciest stuff around here, Terry,' laughs the barman, as he runs a pint glass under the tap, slopping water everywhere when he plonks it down next to the ale pumps.

'Don't look too fancy to me.'

'We only use Perrier in here. But we pop all the bubbles the night before, see. Was up 'til 2am with a toothpick to get you that glass.'

They laugh and continue bantering back and forth as money changes hands, and soon the ancient bitter-drinker is creaking and crackling back down into his chair. What an easy life this man has. Reading the paper with his dog, drinking his pints, laughing with barmen. I cannot be sure, but I'm willing to bet he wasn't up until the early hours after committing unplanned double homicide, and that he isn't puzzling what to do about a detective who's getting dangerously close to the truth. I wonder if he is a good man, and the thought surprises me. Am I going soft?

My father was a drinker. I can't quite imagine him engaging in friendly over-the-bar chit-chat, but maybe he did. Maybe he used all of his good temper up at the pub, and all that was left rattling around in his body when he came home was rage and bitterness and cruelty. But somehow, I don't believe it. I think that was all he had to give.

If you sit in enough pubs, you'll notice the men like my father. They sit alone, scowling into their glasses, or sometimes partner up with another red-faced man to discuss immigration and gay people.

It's ironic, even funny, perhaps even *hilarious*, that my father thought immigrants or LGBT people were a threat to our country. Not in any particular way you understand, just a 'general threat'. The fact that he was a grade-A bastard who hurt everyone around him, that the biggest threat to the success and happiness of our society is men like him, never seemed to cross his mind.

When I was fifteen, I followed him to the pub. He didn't see me skulking behind him because his mind was laser-focused on where he was going. The place my dad frequented wasn't like this place: no roaring fires, cute dogs or wine lists. His local, The Tap and Barrel, did two-pound pints, free cheese sandwiches on a Friday, and their four walls contained as much pent-up aggression as you could shake a stick at. That evening, I pushed myself into a booth in the corner with a Diet Coke and settled in to watch him.

He had friends, my dad. Even real bastards have friends, because there are so *many* real bastards out there you can always find a tribe of them. Watching him, I saw him laugh, which was something I never heard at home, but he also shouted and ranted, loudly slurping at his lager. At one point in the evening, a woman with short, badly dyed hair and a cast on her leg draped herself around his shoulders. She was sniffing extravagantly in a way that told me she had already taken a few lines of cocaine despite it being eight o'clock on a Wednesday. My father slapped her on the arse and she started shouting things about foreigners, like he'd pressed a button. The whole thing was a real education, and I was just about feeling like I could leave with a greater understanding of who the man who haunted us was, when he spotted me.

Have you felt fear like that? The fear of a familiar, aggressive man fixating on you. Maybe you have, if you're a woman. No one has ever made me cower the way that man did. Memory is a funny thing, and there is a large chance that mine has distorted what happened. Because in my mind, his rage was cartoon-like. His eyes hardened and narrowed to dagger tips, and I remember suddenly feeling the solidness of the chair I was sitting on, the sticky table against the skin of my arms. My whole body was so present.

Nothing happened though, not there. He went to the bathroom, and I ran home. I was punished later when he took a cigarette to my skin – the memory still makes the angry red marks on my leg that I hate so much burn again. I cried while my mum loudly cleaned the kitchen, despite it being 11pm. I remember the sound of the rushing water from the taps.

'How's that air fryer going, Terry? Your wife got you one for your birthday, didn't she?' The barman's voice drifts over my thoughts. He is leaning on the end of the bar, speaking over me to the man and his dog. 'They're the way forward, I've heard.'

'Ah you're right. They are. I did a nice naan bread in there the other day.'

'You didn't!'

'Oh, I did. Anything, you can cook in one o' those. Not sure about the coffee machine the wife got a while back though. A lot of hassle that is. What's wrong with instant?'

'You just wanna make your coffee, don't ya? Don't wanna faff around.'

'It's a lot of nonsense. I've not got the years left in me for grinding beans.'

I lose myself in their inane chatter, like calming waves of water. I fold my legs in to my body and wonder if I'd ever have a life with someone who bought expensive kitchen equipment and made naan bread from scratch.

After my father died, I didn't think about him for years. That probably sounds like a lie, but it isn't. The human brain is a pretty magical thing; you can choose to shut down thoughts you don't want to have and hide them under rocks. Up until that point, most of my waking moments had been consumed by my father. So, I decided no more of my head space would be given to him. Nina, who never knew the whole truth but got the general gist, suggested this wasn't the healthiest attitude, but even best friends need to disagree on some points.

But since Katie was attacked, and especially since Karl died, it's been getting harder to keep those thoughts back. It's all bleeding together in a big mess, and as much as I try to push it all down, it keeps bubbling to the surface. My mother and I haven't spoken about him since he died, and I don't know if she thinks about him. I'm not sure that she has the self-discipline to control her thoughts enough to lock him out. That's on her though, I don't have it in me to help everyone. Especially those who have never helped me.

Sometimes I wonder what has made me the way I am. A cynic, a vigilante, a killer. But I don't have to wonder for long. They made me this way. My father, yes, but my mother is to blame too, for looking the other way. That wouldn't matter in the dock though, would it? *Please, your honour, my mother screwed me up, can she do five of my fifteen years?*

That's not the way it works. You're on your own as soon as you're born, your problems and actions are yours alone. That's why I have no guilt about my victims. Maybe Hugh grew up in a way that makes his deception and greed understandable. Perhaps Karl was abused as a child. Perhaps Steven was desperately depressed. Give a shit? None of those are excuses for their despicable behaviour, and they were judged on their actions, just as I will be. Or would be, if I intended on ever getting caught.

Glancing up at the bar, I see that the barman has gone back to pulling pints for a new group of customers, and old Terry has returned to his paper. Staring at him, his ancient dog nuzzling the hand that hangs from the arm of the chair, I experience a stab of angry envy at his easy contentment. I could have been Terry, or Terry's kitchen-equipment-obsessed wife, or Terry's probably incredibly happy daughter, or even Terry's faithful little dog. But I'm not.

Terry is probably an idiot though.

Katie's letter is in my pocket, and I'm going to read it here, with the insulation of a cosy pub around me. But first, I'll drink, to dull my senses.

There is a buzzing in my pocket and I respond by pouring myself another glass of wine from the bottle I'm two-thirds of the way through. The bees are back in my blood, but they aren't buzzing with rage this time, they are flitting around in constant anxious motion, in a way that makes me feel sick. I don't want to think about my phone, especially about a potential message from James saying that his brother remembers where he had seen me before – skulking around outside on the night that Karl was murdered.

But it won't stop, and the dog is staring at me now, his ears pricked and head cocked. So I down my full glass of Merlot and slide it out of my pocket, just in time to see the call end. It was Nina. I have six missed calls from her, and one message from James that I can read from my lock screen:

Funny bumping into you earlier! Was everything alright? You seemed kind of off?

Maybe I don't have to worry about him as much as I thought. But why the constant phone calls from Nina? Unless I've accidentally stood her up, she is usually a one attempt and then a text message kind of person. As I'm staring at the screen trying to puzzle it out, I get my answer.

A WhatsApp message from Nina comes through, the green notification blooming into view on the screen.

Millie, we need to talk. I know.

CHAPTER TWENTY-NINE

People underestimate women. Not just men, but other women as well. What better example is there than this – I was so concerned about the bumbling detective with the nice smile, I barely gave a thought to the bigger possibility. That Nina, who possesses a large proportion of the facts and is whip-smart, would get there first.

Sure. I knew she was interested in the murders, but as the possibility of Nina finding out what I had been doing had never *seriously* occurred to me, I have no plan for it. Her message said very little, and so I'm not sure what exactly she does know. That I killed Hugh? That I have killed a multitude of people over the course of the last month? That I am tracking down my sister's attacker? That I hid ten thousand pounds in her apartment? It could be any or all of the above. To credit Nina's intelligence, I should assume it is all.

Mine and Nina's friendship is strong. But does that extend to a situation like this? Covering up that your friend is a serial killer? She is a lawyer, after all. She has devoted her life to legal justice.

At home, I get back into the bath, Shirley Bassey watching me from the bathmat, tail waving gently in the air. As an act of machoism, I haven't turned off my phone. I leave it on the tiled floor and mentally register every time it rings, echoing around the room. Nina calls eight more times. When the calls stop, I wait in the water, on tenterhooks to see what exactly will happen next.

The banging on the door makes me jump so much that water slops over the edge of the bath and across the tiles, sending Shirley dashing for safety. The letterbox clangs as it's pushed open, and I hear Nina's familiar voice, raspy from those cigarette-fuelled teenage years.

'Millie? We need to talk. Are you there?'

I've frozen in the water, barely breathing.

'Well, if you are, open the door, or call me, okay? We . . . We need to talk about this.'

The letter box clanks shut, and I breathe out. She was alone. She didn't arrive with a team of police officers armed with battering rams, handcuffs, and tear gas. But I shouldn't kid myself that will last forever. The clank of the letterbox sounds again, followed by a soft thud of something landing on the mat.

Karl, Steven, Chris, Hugh, David, Romeo, and the Stoner. It's been a busy period. Most of them deserved it, perhaps all of them. The stab of guilt when I think about David Cartwright is easily pushed under one of those rocks in my mind. There are always eggs broken when making an omelette. Sucks to be an egg.

My mind is spinning, and I'm well aware that I'm on

the verge of this car finally crashing into a ditch, and being surrounded by wailing sirens and cold metal cuffs.

Hauling my body, which feels like an ancient sack of rattling bones, out of the tepid water, I dry off, and dress in an outfit that makes me feel powerful – high-waisted cigarette trousers, with a sheer black shirt. I put on a full face of makeup, because I can't decide my future when I look like shit, and take a seat in the kitchen, notebook open in front of me.

The clanging sound of something being dropped echoes through the walls from next door and for a bizarre moment I picture Sean and I in the same position. Sitting in our kitchens, trying to figure out the way out of the messes we've created. For a wild second, I wonder if we can be of help to one another, before I remember the way he says 'methinks'.

The noise reminds me of the sound of Nina pushing something through the letterbox, and I pad into the hall to see a folded piece of paper on the doormat. Bringing it into the kitchen, I take my time in opening it, knowing that what is on this scrap of paper could decide my fate.

When I do open it, I'm not ready for the words on the paper. It's an old receipt from Sainsbury's for champagne, tomatoes, and watermelon vaping liquid, and in the middle sits a message in blue ink. It is etched in Nina's rounded handwriting, the type I couldn't imagine on a legal document, and which always felt like a hug. Now though, it feels like so much more than that. It feels like a lifeline. Like oxygen.

I've got you. N x

The police aren't on their way. But I owe Nina an explanation, and I still have James to contend with. This note is more than I could hope for, but it's certainly not a free pass to continue on without another thought. I'd be foolish not to realise that I'm on a precipice, and it won't take much to push me over the cliff. Cold feet from little Juliet, a crisis of conscience from Nina, a moment of brilliance from James. It's time to look at my options.

I can either die, get locked up, or see this all through. Seeing it through would mean successfully completing the plan, persuading Nina never to tell a soul, and probably moving away to start anew. That is, for rather obvious reasons, my preference. However, I'm worrying that it is fast becoming the least likely.

Turning myself in is the coward's way out, and I won't sensibly consider it. What would be the point in all that? Taking my own life at this point also seems counter-productive. I've come through a lot in my time, why would I bow out now? Especially when there is still a slim chance of my preferred outcome actually happening.

No. When you look at the options, it turns out that the way forward is obvious. There may become a time when seeing it through and living a happy life of freedom becomes an impossibility – that is when I can weigh up the pros and cons of the other two options. It may be that I'll have to make that choice quickly, without any buffer period for getting my affairs in order. So, while I'll forge on with my plans, and do so as quickly as possible, I should consider what will be left behind if the worst happens.

Some people are owed an explanation. If I don't make it through this, Katie and Nina will be left hurting and confused. So before I take another step, I should explain everything to them. Slamming my notebook shut, I go upstairs to rifle through my desk, coming up with an old Dictaphone I used during a short stint as a PA (before I was fired for 'attitude' when I refused to lie to my boss's wife about his whereabouts, as if that was in the job description).

Back in the kitchen, I find a bottle of expensive wine, a gift from Nina on my birthday that I've been saving, and pour a large glass. No point keeping the good stuff back if you are planning for your death or incarceration.

I take a deep breath and press record.

'The first man I ever killed was my father.'

When I was five, I saw my father push my mother against the wall so hard that a picture fell and the glass smashed. When I was six, I saw him hit her, and when I was seven, I connected that in my mind with the many cuts and bruises that had patterned her skin as far back as I could remember. When I was eight, he came home drunk and suddenly seemed to notice me, grabbing me so hard it hurt. When I was nine, he raped me for the first time. When I was ten, my little sister was born into my world of pain and fear and fury.

My home wasn't a happy one, but no one apart from my mother – not Nina, not Uncle Dale, not even really Katie – ever understood *quite* how unhappy it was. My mother was a victim, just as I was. She lived in fear of my father's red-hot temper and all-consuming thirst for alcohol that increased year on year. But as an adult, my mother had agency and power that I didn't have at eight years old. She could have packed a bag for both of us and gotten us the hell out of there. She could have reported him to the police. But she didn't. Instead, she cleaned.

I'll never forgive my mother for turning a blind eye to everything that happened in that house. Things weren't easy for her, and perhaps you think I'm cruel for judging her. But you are judged on your actions, just like I will be – not on the extenuating circumstances. In my book, she doesn't get a pass for being scared. If you have a child, you should protect them. That is that.

After Katie was born, the abuse continued for years. Katie was a baby and below my father's notice, just as I had been for the first years of my life. Meanwhile, I'd morphed into a forty-year-old in a child's body, all innocence obliterated. My father grew steadily worse as the years went on, and the house grew steadily cleaner.

Things changed when I was sixteen and Katie was six. Dad came home from the pub around midnight. I could tell from the sound of the door that he was absolutely steaming. You learn things like that in a home like mine – what the sound of the door means.

This particular sound – the drawn-out scuffle of the key not quite finding the lock, the burst open and slam shut – was bad news. I shrank down into my bed, pulling my duvet up to my cheekbones, and began to disassociate. At sixteen, you might ask why I didn't do something about my situation, but it's hard to explain why that didn't seem like a possibility. Where could I go – live on the streets? And it didn't cross my mind to tell anyone. After all, my own mother knew, and didn't do anything to stop it. I didn't know what happened in other people's homes, maybe my situation was common. Deep down I knew it wasn't, but you tell yourself things to get through.

That night I started to drift out of my body as I registered the crashing around in the kitchen, followed by the slow, heavy steps on the stairs. But then something different happened. The footsteps stopped on the upstairs landing. I sat up, confused. Then I heard a new sound. It was the opening of my sister's door, the squeaking of the hinge as it was slowly pushed.

I was out of my bed and in that hallway faster that you can say 'oh shit!' It's another picture branded on me – him standing in Katie's doorway, staring at me like he had been caught in the act. His eyes, for a fraction of a second, widened in surprise. Then it morphed into blankness – just a man checking on his sleeping daughter.

'Sleep tight,' he growled, giving me a wink like we were a team with a secret to keep. He stumbled to his own room, and I tiptoed into Katie's, cuddling up next to her in the bed. I didn't get a moment's sleep that night and feigned sickness to get out of school in the morning.

But it wasn't because I was exhausted that I needed the day at home. It was because I had work to do. The night he opened my sister's door, was the night I knew he had to die.

CHAPTER THIRTY

So you see, I'm good at this killing thing because I've been in training for it for a rather long time. But Dad's death *was* kind of an accident, so I cannot take full credit. I had zero experience in extermination. He was twice my size, three times my weight, and embodied everything that scared me.

Days passed after the incident at Katie's door. Every night I stayed awake until I was sure my father was asleep, often then creeping into Katie's room myself to sleep curled up around her. She was so small and perfect, my little sister. Growing up in that atmosphere wasn't pleasant for anyone, but my mother and I, without speaking about it, tried to shield her from the worst. It was the one thing my mother did right, focusing on Katie. We both knew I was ruined.

The days turned to weeks, and every plan I came up with felt more absurd than the last. How could I, a teenager who had achieved nothing and was loved by no one, possibly defeat *him*? There was a part of me that didn't really believe it could be done. But something had changed in me, nonetheless. My fierce protectiveness over Katie was squashing my own fear. So in lieu of a real plan to kill the bastard, I decided to fuck with him.

I moved his shoes. I hid his car keys. I turned the dial back on his clock, making him twenty minutes late for work three days in a row before he noticed. I suffered because of it. It's not that he knew it was me, but it made him angry, and his anger had a habit of finding me and my mother. But it was worth it, because when his shoes weren't where they should be for the fifth time in a two-week period, I saw something in his eyes I hadn't noticed before – fear. Somehow, the fear I'd lost had transferred to him. He was afraid of himself, afraid he was losing his marbles.

I got bolder. I moved the seat, steering wheel, and mirrors in his car almost daily. I switched his work shoes with trainers. I put cereal in the wrong box. It was small fry. Nothing like watching a man die of anaphylactic shock for screwing over your friend. But it was my first taste of revenge, and it was so, so sweet.

Inspiration came from films, books, and watching his daily routine. I did everything in my power to add a moment of annoyance each day, a little fuck-you from me to him. Reading has always been a pleasure of mine. When you grow up poor and friendless, books are the only non-depressing part of life, and that's because it's about someone else's. At school, lunchtime often found me hiding from other people in the library.

Did you know that there are seventy-four on-stage deaths in Shakespeare's plays? He was a gory guy. They are a real mix of beheadings, snake bites, stabbings, drownings, and more. Full of good ideas, Shakespeare. My favourite play of his wasn't one of the popular ones. *Romeo and Juliet* is foolish – who runs away from fortune and then takes their own life over a man? *Macbeth* has its charms, and *Hamlet*'s general insane demeanour and murderous attitude is always a pleasure. But *Titus Andronicus* was my favourite as a teenager, and will always hold a special place in my heart.

Considered Shakespeare's most violent play, and one of his least respected, there are fourteen deaths over the course of its two-hour-forty-five-minute run time. It includes mutilation, gang rape, human sacrifice, and, crucially, cannibalism in the form of a beautifully baked pie.

So one day, I was hiding in the library, reading this play for the first time. As well as having no friends to hang out with, I was also keeping my head down because I had a black eye. My father had flown into a drunken rage over his car's flat tyre earlier that week. It was actually my fault, to be fair to him, but the response was over the top given that he didn't know that. A punch to the face broke my nose, which never really healed.

Reading this play was eye-opening. The blood thrilled me, the cruelty, the unfairness, the spite. And reading about how two young men are killed, *baked into a pie* and served to their own *mother* was the most horrible, brilliant thing my sixteen-year-old self had ever heard. It gave me a brainwave, and a plan formulated over the afternoon lessons.

When my father went out at night, it was my mother's job to make sure he had a hot meal waiting for him on his return, but recently, as I'd turned sixteen, he'd told me to step up and earn my keep. Half of the week, cooking fell to me. And I knew what I'd be making.

You are rolling your eyes here, aren't you? Well calm down. I didn't bake my dad in a pie. It wasn't even my intention to kill him. Well it was, but eventually, not on *this* occasion.

The following evening, my dad came home from work, changed his clothes, and stalked out the door for The Tap and Barrel with barely a word for his wife or daughters. I made a pie of beef mince, onions, and carrots for us women, and we ate around the table in the pokey kitchen, the cheap plastic tablecloth sticking to our forearms. My sister chattered on about school and Mum and I listened, chiefly communicating through Katie even then. When I'd brought out the pie, my mum looked alarmed at the size.

'I've made him a separate one.'

'That's nice darling.' She'd said it casually, but I could see the anxiety leak out of her like an inflatable ball when it's time to leave the beach. Pump up with fear, deflate with relief. It's an exhausting way to live.

In the oven sat my father's dinner. A beautifully baked pie, almost cartoon-like. Beef mince, carrot, onions, and a healthy dose of rat poison, which I'd found in a box in the shed. I pictured him vomiting, perhaps inducing a bout of humiliating diarrhoea in an inappropriate location. But I didn't know how much to put in – he was much bigger than a rat after all – so I just poured in the lot and hoped he'd be too drunk to notice any taste it may have had, and that the gravy would disguise the colour.

He came home gone midnight steaming drunk, kicking open the front door with a thump that was loud enough to wake the whole house. On that particular evening, I was grinning in the dark, imagining him reading the Post-it note about his food, picturing him staggering to the oven and pulling it out. There was a spike of fear that he would skip dinner or drop it, and the plan would be ruined, but that didn't happen.

An hour or so later, I heard his feet on the stairs. In my excitement, I'd almost forgotten what sometimes happened on nights like this, but the familiar thudding noise brought me back to my senses. The floorboard creaked as he stopped on the landing and my stomach immediately felt full of rocks. Forcing myself to picture the pie helped though. As I'd been doing over the previous month, remembering my revenge made me strong. Even when the door handle turned, I focused my mind on that beautiful, poisonous pie.

Turns out, it was a great night. My father was already feeling ill when he staggered in, so he forced his way into my bed and fell asleep almost at once. After an hour or so of barely moving, I edged out from under his arm, allowing myself a small exhale of relief. Sliding out of the bottom of the bed in silence, I tiptoed to the door to join my sister in her room, when a noise made me freeze. It was a groan.

Spinning around, I confirmed that it was coming from him. He was a big man, and he looked ridiculous in my single bed with the childish pink covers we didn't have the money to replace. His beastly head lay heavily against the sickly pink pillow, his thinning hair sticking to his face with the sweat that was beading on his brow. His dry, thin lips were parted slightly, and once again a groan escaped them.

He better not shit in my bed, I thought.

He did make a mess, but it turns out I didn't mind one bit. I stood by the door, watching him for five minutes or so, when his body violently convulsed and made me jump in fright. It happened again, and he groaned louder, his eyes still shut. I couldn't tell if he was awake at this point or still unconscious, but something certainly seemed to be happening. The third time his body jerked, a fountain of brown sludge burst from his lips, making me jump again and let out a yelp of surprise. The vomit dripped from his open lips onto the sheets, and dribbled down onto the floor. I could see chunks of pie floating in it.

The room stank of beef and beer, it was almost enough to make me sick too. He burped out another gush of beef-flavoured lager. His huge body rolled slightly so he faced the ceiling and he groaned louder, rocking side to side, now shining with sweat that reflected the half-moon shining through the window.

I pressed my back against the door and slid down into a sitting position, fascinated. I'd done this, I'd reduced him to this pathetic beast, a disgusting thing covered in his own vomit. I wasn't sure how long this would last, but I wanted to watch – I'd sneak out before he was sentient.

But that never happened, because the next time the brown sludge burst out of his lips, it bubbled like a volcano in his open mouth, sliding down the side of his face and into his hair.

And then he began to choke.

If you vomit when you are black-out drunk and lying on your back, you will probably be fine. Hopefully you'll have a friend or partner with you – lucky them! – who can roll you over, clean you up, give you a glass of water and argue with you in the morning about it. But *he* had *me*.

Humans have a small cover over the larynx that stops food and drink from being inhaled into their lungs rather than their stomach. When you drink like he did however, the muscles that control the complex junction between windpipe and oesophagus become lazy, or even completely paralysed. Which means all of that beef beer my rat poison was sending flooding out of his stomach was pouring straight back down into his lungs. And he was too plastered to even sit up and cough.

I watched from my position on the floor, knees pulled to my mouth, as he rocked and shook. It was like his life force seemed to cry out in protest as his stupid, fat, useless body inhaled its own sickly vomit. His convulsions grew in intensity, so much so that one of the bed slats snapped with a resounding *crack*, causing a fresh spatter of liquid around the room, a chunk of carrot landing on my pyjama trouser leg. But the bubbling volcano still sat there in his throat, short rasping, rattling breaths ever more audible.

I don't know how long it took. They say time flies when you're having fun, but when you're having *revenge*, I've found it can slow to a delicious crawl. I savoured every second of his death. Even the smell, the filthy mess spreading around him, the nauseating noises of bubbling, hacking, grunts and groans. It all expressed his degradation and powerlessness.

And then an eventual stillness took over him.

I sat there long after that came. That moment when I realised what I'd really achieved was my turning point. I suppose you could say it was my origin story, if you were being trite.

And the best thing was? I had been instrumental in this, sure. But aspiration, choking on your vomit, is a common cause of death for drunks. To this day, I cannot take full credit for his death. He did it to himself, really.

The light was changing by the time I left the room, creeping into my sister's bed and closing my eyes, replaying the scene over and over again, mentally practising what I'd say when I 'discovered him' in the morning.

But it turns out I didn't have to say much at all. Two weeks later, he was buried, the house was yellow, and no one ever mentioned my father again.

CHAPTER THIRTY-ONE

Birds are singing by the time I finish taping my confession. I don't hold back. It started as a way to tell Nina and Katie the truth, but I lost sight of that the more I spoke and it becomes more of a confession for myself, I suppose. Nina always did say I should get therapy.

After explaining about the death of my father, I speak about how I redecorated my room to have bright white walls, with deep red curtains and bedspread – a new space for new memories. It never worked though, and I got out of there as soon as my father's life insurance cleared and I turned eighteen. I speak about meeting Nina while I was still living at home, how she changed my life and gave me hope that I could be normal. I speak about Message M and how that started after Katie's attack.

No one helped me as a kid. Not teachers who must have noticed the bruises, not neighbours who heard the shouting. Certainly not my mother, who knew everything that happened in that house. But I was going to help all the women I possibly could.

I speak directly to Katie. I tell her how she has always been my focus, and how my job in life is to protect her. I apologise for failing in that. How after what happened to her, the anger that has been there all my life came bubbling to the surface. The bees in my blood.

I explain about Karl. And Steven, and Chris, and Hugh, and David, and Romeo, and the Stoner. I hope Nina understands about Hugh; I'm sure she will. Just like how my mother understood why I helped end my father. Though we've never discussed my role in it, I'm sure she knows. I end with a verbal will, making it clear that Katie should inherit my house, and Nina should take anything she wants.

The tiny tape pops out of the Dictaphone when I press eject, and I put it in a manilla envelope with *NINA* scrawled on it. She's a capable woman and I'm pretty sure she'll know what's best to do with it if anything were to happen to me. By the time I crawl into bed, I feel lighter, empty but relieved. As if by saying all of this out loud I've lessened my load. At one point, I even thought I was going to cry. But that is one self-indulgence that there is really no time for.

No point crying over spilt blood.

I'm exhausted and a little drunk, so when I see that my phone has sixty-four notifications, I throw it into the corner of my bedroom, close my eyes, and fall asleep.

Usually, I'm a light sleeper. I suppose so many years of waiting for the bang of the door and the creaking of the floorboards honed my senses to always be alert. But when I wake up today, I know that I've had the deepest sleep I've had for a very long time. The room is glaringly bright, and I can see that it's a rare sunny, November day – the kind where the sky is bright blue and cloudless, but the air has a pleasingly icy bite.

For while, I lie still and try to get a bearing on my feelings. The tape. It's still down in the kitchen, next to an empty bottle of wine. Its existence makes me feel bare and vulnerable, as if I've taken off my armour in the middle of battle. It also makes me feel electrified. Exhilarated. I remember Nina pounding on the door, her note on the mat. *'I've got you. N X'*.

Eventually, my bladder forces me out of bed and to the bathroom, and on the way back I collect my phone from the corner of the room. It's on two per cent battery, which is usually a cause for alarm. But today, what is slightly more alarming is the fact that there are seventy-fucking-eight notifications on the screen: a mixture of missed calls, WhatsApp messages and voicemails. I'm going to need coffee for this.

First, I send a WhatsApp to Nina, who has threatened to break down my door at midday – a time that is fast approaching – to check if I'm okay unless I respond. Ignoring pretty much everything else she's written, I let her know I've been sleeping, to not come round, and that she'll hear more from me soon.

More worryingly are the communications from James. A myriad of missed calls, voicemails, voice notes, texts and WhatsApps. I start easy – WhatsApp.

Hey, can we talk?
Millie?
So, my brother figured out where he recognised you from and I really need to talk to you
Maybe he is wrong, but . . .yeah. Can you call me?

297

Millie?
Hello?
Millie I'm kind of freaking out. Can
you answer your phone?
Christ woman, answer the phone
MILLIE

God people are boring. I lazily scroll down through the increasingly demanding messages. This is bad, though it was expected. But he doesn't out and out accuse me of anything, and the police aren't at my door. So things could be worse.

Shirley Bassey is meowing for food, so I fill up her bowl while I consider the options before me. It appears that James has not informed the police of any suspicions that he may have, and I'll bet he hasn't told a friend either. You can't go around telling people that you suspect the girl you're seeing of being a serial killer. They'd think you insane. He's waiting to hear my side of the story, desperately hoping for an innocent explanation to my being connected to multiple murder scenes.

But Nina's note has given me hope that the truth won't necessarily turn him off me. I remember the excitement in James's eyes when he updated me on the murders, and the way he looked at me when I was at the bar. He's fallen for me, I know it. We have something, and maybe we are more alike than we first appear. He has chosen a job that seeks justice, after all. Which is basically what I'm doing, just with more success. James might understand.

Eventually, I delete all of the voicemails and texts James has sent – life is too short for going through those – and instead, I leave him a short and sweet message apologising for the radio silence and asking him to meet me that evening.

298

Two blue ticks appear, showing it's been read straight away. Has he really been staring at his phone this entire time? Three dots appear to show he is typing. Then vanish. Then appear again, then vanish. Finally, he appears to make up his damn mind and a message appears:

Hey! Good to hear from you. I was getting worried. Yeah tonight works. I'll pick you up at 8? Let me know an address.

Making another coffee, I open the bi-folding doors to my small concrete garden and breathe in the icy air, feeling the sun on my skin. The small red grapes on the vine are growing plump, and if I look at them, I can almost pretend I'm in the south of France. I've never been to France. Furthest I've been is Newcastle to watch the football with Uncle Dale. Would I ever go abroad now? For a moment, I allow the fresh air and thoughts of foreign countries to give me a sense of freedom, even though underneath that I'm hyper-aware of nets closing in around me. The important thing is to avenge my sister before that net pulls shut.

My phone buzzes again. Assuming it is Nina or James again, I pull it out of my pocket ready to cancel the call. But to my surprise, I see it's a landline number that I don't have saved. Unwilling to be tricked into speaking to James, I let it ring out, and see a number one pop up on my voicemail.

'Hi babe, it's Molly right? It's V here from Tattoo Time?' The voice is both upbeat but drawling, as if the owner can't help being a positive person but is aware it doesn't suit the image of goth girl. 'You came in a week or so back? Was just going through some old pictures and found another Magpie we did aaaaages ago, so thought I'd send it to you in case it was up your street. It's probably not the sort of thing you want, 'cause it's part of a sports team logo. But you might like the graphic style? Anyway, give me a call back when you can!'

Interesting. I slide my phone back into my pocket and lie down on the garden sofa with my coffee, staring at the green leaves of the mile-a-minute weaving in and out of the trellis. A team logo. The magpie representing something – a team, a company, even a band hadn't crossed my mind before. As I'm puzzling this over, the very bird lands on the top of the trellis.

I've always liked magpies. They have a slick colour scheme, and the way their black feathers turn petrol green in the right light is so much more beautiful than a gaudy parrot. They take what they want when they want it and are symbolic in a way that appeals to me. One for sorrow.

The sound of Sean's back door sliding open sends my new friend fluttering up into the air. *Fair enough, mate, go while you can. He'll start complaining about foreign birds taking your worms and before you know it, you'll be wanting to leap in front of a passing truck.*

Remaining frozen on the sofa, I try to breathe extra quietly to avoid detection. I wonder how often I have lain here, fearful of him talking to me? How much of my life have I spent *not breathing* just to avoid my neighbour? Once this mess is over, I'm going to move to the countryside and speak to no one but Nina, Katie, and Shirley Bassey for the rest of my existence. Will James be joining me? Not worth thinking about for the time being.

Sean is pacing his own tiny square of a garden, muttering under his breath.

Suddenly, he stops and shouts, 'Fuck!' It makes me jump, but I can't help but agree. Luckily, my movements haven't given me away, presumably because he is rather caught up in his own issues.

'Fuck! Bugger! God. Damn. *It*.' Sean is kicking at what sounds like a tree stump with each word. Christ, he doesn't sound well at all. *Come on, Sean, it's not like you've just been discovered as playing the leading part in multiple murders!* Though that's just an assumption of course. I don't know what he gets up to in his free time.

A loud 'flumpt' sound indicates that his large, gnomish body has flopped down onto a chair. Silence settles between us for a few moments before I hear . . . Is that . . .? Is he *crying* again?

I listen to him sob for at least ten minutes before he pulls himself together and goes back inside, pulling his door to. The sound leaves no real impression on me; there has been enough high emotion around me recently that a few tears barely register. Still, it's intriguing and I wonder if I'll still be around to find out what this was all about.

At seven-thirty, I head out to meet James. I've taken my time getting ready, making sure I look utterly dazzling. If there is ever a time to need to seduce a man, surely this is it. Darkness has fallen and he's going to pick me up on a road nearby – no sense giving him my actual address. This gives me hope, because only a real idiot would agree to get into the car at night with someone they suspect is on a man-murdering spree.

James pulls up in his battered old Mercedes bang on time. He looks nervous but leans over to kiss me hello as I get into the car, before pulling back out into the road. He looks sexy, there are no two ways about it. A black t-shirt and jeans really is an unbeatable look for a man. No need for thinking about it more than that. His biceps are solid and pressing against the t-shirt, his hair is charmingly floppy, thick and glossy. I want to run my hands through it.

A wild part of me sees a future where this will work. Where James and Nina will accept who I am and what I've done. Growing up like I did means that happiness has never been something I assumed I would achieve. Survival, non-misery, and a sense of control are all I've ever aimed for. But as I watch James's long fingers wrap around the gearstick and push into fourth, his other hand gripping the steering wheel tightly, as I see his face turn to me with a quick, warm smile, I allow a different vision to briefly flood the senses.

Lost in these fairy tales, I realise that I have no idea where we're going. Neither of us have spoken much since I got in the car, but we've headed out of town. Suddenly, the car swings to the right down a lane shrouded by trees.

'So, where are we headed? I thought maybe we were going to yours?'

'I need to talk to you. Somewhere private.'

His eyes flick up to the mirror to check the empty road behind him.

'James? Hey, where are we going?'

My annoyance turns to an icy sliver of fear as the future I imagined dissolves. What the fuck is happening?

'JAMES?'

The car swings again, wildly this time, into a clearing off the lane. It jerks to a stop that slams my head forward and back against the headrest. I glare over at him in time to see his index finger pressing a button to the right of the steering wheel, and I hear the *clunk* sound of the doors locking.

CHAPTER THIRTY-TWO

The ticking of the engine cooling fills the void between us. Neither of us move. My brain is quickly recalibrating as I stare at the darkness in front of me. How could I ever have believed I would have my happy ever after with him? That I even deserved it?

Eventually, I turn to look at the man beside me, only to flinch. His large dark eyes are boring into me, his mouth set. He looks good, so it's a shame this is probably the last evening we'll spend together. It's already clear that one of us isn't making it out of here alive.

I'm not speaking first. He brought me here. *If you have something to say, James, go on then. Do your best.*

'It was you.'

'What was?'

'Oh, come on, Millie. I'm not an idiot.'

Debatable. It's taken him rather a long time to figure this out. But I'm not offering up a confession on a plate.

'I don't know what you mean. And frankly, you are

scaring me. You really think it's okay to drive a girl into the middle of the woods and lock the doors?'

'Don't give me the whole damsel in distress thing. It doesn't suit you.'

We sit in silence. He turns away, blowing a strand of hair out of his face with an exasperated puff of breath. He can't bring himself to put the words out there. They seem foolish, even now.

'Look. I know you were there the night my neighbour died. Sorry, was murdered. My brother saw you. You knocked on the door.'

'What are you—'

'And I know you hated your friend's boyfriend, Hugh Chapman.'

'So? He was a prick, I'm sure a lot of people hated him.'

'You run a phone line, helping women? Right? The guy who died in his flat, Steven Baker. He had Rohypnol in there, he wasn't a good guy. He's the kind of guy you . . . protect against. Right?' I open my mouth to speak again but he shuts me down with a glare and holds his hand up between us, like he needs to get everything out in a rush. 'There are others, too. There was the runner, on the bridge? You run, right?'

'Lots of people fucking *run*, James. What the hell are you trying to say here?'

'There was a wig. They found a wig by his body. My boss dismissed it as unimportant, but I think that a woman pushed him off that bridge, and that he grabbed a wig from their head as he went down.'

'A, you sound insane. And B, even if that's true, you seem to be implying that was me because, what, I *run*?'

'I'm not implying. I'm telling you. It was you. There was a doorbell camera on David Cartwright's street.'

Fuck.

'A woman walks past the night he died. Tall, brunette. That wasn't seen as that important either, partly because his death was dismissed as an accident, and partly because it's just a figure walking past. Could have been anyone, for any reason. But I watched it again. You can't see the face, but I recognised the walk. It was you.'

It's hardly a smoking gun, but I figure it's best to stay silent. James rests his head on the steering wheel and exhales deeply, then whips it back around to face me.

'When Imran remembered where he'd seen you before, it all just started slotting into place. What kind of person has a sort of . . . a . . . a fucking *vigilante phone line*? Karl, my neighbour, had these images on his computer. It looked like he'd been assaulting girls. Drugging them and photographing them. Unless they were all models, which I fucking doubt.'

He hits the wheel in anger, and it occurs to me that the anger is directed at Karl, not me.

'Creep.' I say it quietly, reaching out my feelers. No cars have passed us in the time we've sat here, and even if they did, they wouldn't see us unless they were looking. Our lights are off and we're covered by bushes.

'Then the two men the other night. Fuck, that was a fucking mental crime scene. One of them has his head bashed in. He was on the database already. John Towles. He'd been accused of rape twice in the past, but nothing stuck. It's a difficult thing to get a conviction for.'

'Hmm.'

'David Cartwright . . . that one I don't get.' It's as if

James has forgotten I'm here, his eyes are darting around, latching onto unseen things out of the windscreen. 'He seemed like a good guy. I looked into him. No record, not even an accusation. A steady girlfriend who had nothing bad to say about him. Nothing to suggest he was anything other than a stand-up guy, but then he's found dead in his own home. I could almost believe that was unconnected. If it wasn't for that camera footage.'

Silence falls again. Sweat is beading on my palms. James's biceps look less appealing now. They are tense in his frustration, reminding me of my chances in this confined space if he wants to restrain me. Do detectives carry handcuffs when off duty? Do they carry guns? He turns to me again, fully twisting in his seat this time.

'Millie. I know you killed those men. For the most part, I even understand why you did it. I think.'

Here it is. The moment of truth. Is James with me? Or against me?

'Fucking *say something!*'

I sigh, and he looks taken aback. The adrenaline ekes out of me and I'm left feeling so very tired again. It was only last night that I bared my soul on that recording. I don't know if I have it in me for another confessional.

'I need some air.'

'What?'

'I need some air. Open the doors. And we'll talk.'

He considers me, and then obliges. I gratefully inhale the chilly autumn night, while he pulls on a jacket. I perch on the hood of his car, and tentatively he sits next to me. We both stare into the darkness of the trees. I get the sense that, despite the circumstances, James is the kind of person who has always wanted to perch on the hood of a car in the dark with a pretty girl.

'Doesn't it bother you, James? That you know these men are out there, and it's your job to stop them, but you do such a spectacularly shit job at it?'

I pause for a response, but he has nothing to say to this. Maybe he's run out of words.

'You said it yourself. That guy had raped two women, that we know of, but "it's a difficult thing to get a conviction for".'

'*Accused* of raping.'

'Oh come *on*.'

The leaves of the bushes rustle in the breeze and I pull my coat close around me, pushing the collar up to cover my neck.

'They do whatever they want, James. These men. And don't "not all men" me, I know it's not *all* men.'

'I wasn't going to say that.'

'Good. It's *some* men. Enough men. And they need to be stopped. The police don't do that. They apparently can't.' I weigh up my next words, wondering how much to tell him. 'My sister. Katie. She's who I was visiting in hospital the other day. She cut her wrists so badly that she almost bled out and died. She was raped on New Year's Eve, last year. Dropped out of uni after that. Stopped eating. Has barely left her bedroom since.'

'Shit.'

'Yeah. Shit.' I chance a look at him, and he meets my eyes. In the darkness, it's difficult to tell his expression. 'Don't you get tired of that, James? Of doing nothing? Of helping no one? You chose your job for a reason, right? To help people? To get justice for people who need it? That's what I'm doing. What I've done. It's nearly over now anyway.'

'Nearly over?'

'I . . . I didn't exactly mean to do all of this. I just wanted justice for my sister. I need to find the person who hurt her. Then I'm done. I'll move. Start my life again. Do something good.'

'Oh, Millie.' He shakes his head in the moonlight. He looks desperately sad. 'You can't think I can let you get away with this.'

No.

'I'm a homicide detective. You . . . you've killed *seven people*. That I *know* of. And I get it, I get what you're saying. I'm not exactly sad these guys aren't with us anymore. I understand. The system sucks. They deserved punishment. But that's not your job, and they didn't deserve what you gave them. And I can't just pretend I don't know this.'

No. This cannot be happening.

'I care about you. A lot. Which is why I'm not arresting you. I'm letting you turn yourself in. Tonight.'

The manilla enveloped labelled *NINA* flashes across my mind, the preparations I made just in case. But even if I was going to end up dead or in jail eventually, this is too soon. I haven't achieved my goal. I haven't avenged Katie.

'So you're saying you agree with what I've done. But you want me to go to jail anyway? You're saying that the man who ruined Katie's life gets to walk free, but I'm locked up until I'm dead?'

'It's the way the law works, Millie! It's not always perfect, but I've got to believe in it.'

'Not *always* perfect. Right. James, come *on*.' I spin so I'm in front of him and push myself between his legs, grasping his wide, strong shoulders with my hands. I make him look straight at me. 'Those men were *dirt*. *Less* than dirt. They hurt people, hurt women who couldn't defend themselves. And you know yourself that there was nothing the police could do about it, or why would that guy who got his head bashed in – John, was it? – have already done it multiple times? And Karl? The law is not just "not perfect". It's totally *fucked*. It does not work. It does not protect the people who need protecting. Can't you see that I had to do something?'

I shake him, begging him to find sense, but his face is blank.

'Listen to me. Steven, he was preparing to drug me, and we both know it wouldn't have been his first rodeo. Karl? I was called there by a girl who I found unconscious with him taking photographs of her. Chris? He harassed me, frequently. Stalked me.'

'What about David Cartwright?'

'He . . . That's a long story. The point is that sometimes you need to do things differently. Sometimes you need to *act*.'

We stare at each other for a long time, the future hanging in the balance. And then he shakes his head.

'I'm sorry. It's time to go.'

People should listen more. Did he really think I'd come quietly? I'd *just* told him. Sometimes, you need to act.

CHAPTER THIRTY-THREE

The problem with James is that he is too nice. Nina could be mistaken as having this flaw, but once you get past the rainbows and smiles and true love fascination to see the gritty lawyer underneath, you see she isn't. Me? Well, I don't think anyone has ever thought I am 'too nice'. People rarely even think I'm 'nice'.

But James? Despite seeing awful things due to his job, he is bizarrely trusting. What sort of person brings a serial killer to a forest to tell them they know everything and expects it to turn out well?

It takes mere seconds for me to slip back into the car, slam the door, and lock it. He left the keys in the well by the gearstick.

James is pounding on the window, looking at me with a whole mixture of emotions – fury, fear, understanding, all trying to win out on his lovely face. I'm breathing heavily, having not thought past this moment in time. *Shit*. What now? I frantically look for some sort of weapon to protect myself, chiding myself for leaving Chris's knife at home. I find James's handcuffs in the glove compartment – he should have at least put these on me.

James knows everything. He not only guessed it, but I corroborated the story, and it sounds as if he has some evidence. I wish he would stop making so much noise so that I could think.

The risk of being taken into the station is far too great – even if I deny everything, they'll take my fingerprints and DNA, and they are bound to turn up *somewhere*. The stupid man. We could have been happy together. Deep down, he wanted to let me free. Or even go with me. But it's too late now.

Pressing down on the clutch, I stab the keys into the ignition, turn, and the car roars to life. A little more power than the old Micra, bless it. I'm vaguely aware of James switching his tactic from anger to conciliatory.

'Calm down, Millie,' he's yelling through the glass. 'Turn off the car. Let's figure this out. There are options.'

Slipping into reverse gear, I back out of the clearing, through the bushes onto the dark, deserted road. James is following the car, waving his hands manically, as if gestures ever stopped a missile. I reverse quickly once I hit the tarmac, and he stands there in the road with his hands out, like I can't possibly leave if he is in my way.

Options. Like fuck there are, James. There *were* options, and you chose wrong. Fury is building in me. It's been a long time since I was in a relationship, and there had been a chance with James for us to make a rather formidable, fun pair. But he had to screw it up. I wasn't enough for him. Not enough to get in the way of his twisted sense of 'justice'.

Listen, I really don't want to do this. It really isn't my fault.

Taking my foot off the accelerator, I stamp down on the clutch and flick the gearstick into Drive. Then I hit the pedal.

People say that the human brain is quick. I've read that the brain can process certain types of images within thirteen milliseconds. But clearly, the brain is not as quick as a speeding Mercedes.

James hits the hood with an ungodly smack. The force shudders through the car and thin lines appear on the windscreen, radiating out from the point of impact. His body flies onto the roof of the car as I keep driving, thudding loudly to the tarmac behind me. Slamming on the brake, I watch him in the wing mirror. He is lying perfectly still, limbs twisted at odd angles. Not being a complete psychopath, I feel really fucking sad. James didn't deserve to die. But he made some poor choices, leaving me with only one.

When I am certain that there will be no more movement, I pull my hood up around my face and drive on, planning to abandon the car halfway home and walk the rest of the way.

I really didn't think I'd be back here again so soon. I'm lying in the bath, warming my chilled bones after the long walk home. I'm swigging from an old bottle of whisky to heat my blood. Staring up at the ceiling, I inhale to calm myself, but it's no good.

This is it. The end. What the hell was I thinking?

The net has tightened, the bees have stung. Nina knows everything and I have no idea what she is planning to do about it. Who knows what notes James had compiled on the cases? The thought of my name scribbled in a notebook alongside bullet points of his findings didn't cross my mind in that clearing.

Sure, there hadn't been many options, but really, I shouldn't have gone with him in the first place. Why did I get into that car knowing full well what could happen?

Even if James hasn't written down my name, I've killed a detective. The force might be lax at tracking down an elusive killer of some random lout, but they aren't likely to be so cavalier about a hit-and-run of one of their own. In his *own car* no less. Did he tell his brother he was meeting me? If so, I'm well and truly fucked.

On top of that, this death is hitting me differently. James wasn't some guy who preyed on drunk women. He was . . . kind. He was funny. I'd seen a future with him. Sure, we hadn't dated for long, but I'd felt a spark with him that I'd never felt before and I didn't know I could feel. From the possibility of living happily ever after, free and with him at my side, to the certainty of a life of lonely incarceration is like falling off a very high cliff. And I haven't even hit the ground yet.

I am useless. My one point of existence has always been to protect my sister. But I failed, and I have failed at avenging her too. I am no closer to finding out the identity of her attacker. No closer to shutting him down and giving her back a small parcel of her freedom. And now, I am out of time. The police will be here before morning.

So, it's time to make my next choice. I've always chosen to fight, but why? What's the point? I'm a failure. Perhaps I should have let my father kill me all of those years ago – it would have happened eventually, I'm sure. Would

Katie have had a better life? Would Nina have had more fun?

Nina never knew the nasty details, but she has always wanted me to let go of the past. Like that's as easy as moving on from a television series with a disappointing ending, or a jumper that's shrunk in the wash. Your past is you. I am my father's daughter. There is no moving on from that. Anger is what I'm made of. And sadness. And guilt.

Who even knows if the scanty list of information I have in my notebook is correct? Katie was traumatised, she may have misremembered. Maybe she lied to get me off her case. With sick dread, I remember that time we spoke about it, back in January. How in the morning I tried to get more details from her, shouting at her to tell me something, *anything* about the attacker.

'Bald! And . . . tall!' Katie stuttered, fear in her eyes as if I was him and she was back there. 'I've already told you!"

'That's not enough Katie! Did you hear his name? He took you to his house, yes? With the red curtains? But where did you meet him? Tell me that and I'll stop.' She screwed her eyes up tight, shaking.

'His . . . his house. Yes. I met him . . . at the club. Pom Pom's.'

'A name? Any distinguishing features?'

'Just the magpie,' she whispered. 'I've told you. A tattoo of a magpie. Please, please stop. Please stop.'

And I stopped. I was so angry at this man and so desperate for information that I forced it out of her. But I realise now, far too late, that she would have said anything to make me stop asking questions. My fury has sustained me since then, but who have I been thinking of all this time? Is it really her? Or is it me? Is it my own vengeance I've been seeking? After all, can I even say I murdered my father? Or did I merely watch him die?

Pushing myself under the water, I stay there. Is it possible to drown yourself in a bath? Can you override your body's instinctive survival, stop it bursting up for air? I try, and fail. Try again, fail again. A constant loop of failure. I can't even die.

Under the water for the fifth time, I see again James hit the windscreen, see the hairline cracks spiderweb out in the glass. His body lying there in the road. I see David Cartwright in that bath, just like I am now, frying in electric water. I see a flashing montage of Karl's blood, Rose's fanned-out hair, Steven's ratty football scarf, Romeo – or John as he is apparently called – lying with his head caved in. I see his hapless flatmate – wrong time wrong place. Hugh gasping for help, Chris flailing his arms wildly before he falls. And my father in the stillness of the reeking room, a place of so much terror.

Black spots appear across the pictures in my mind and before I can help it, I'm above the water, gasping painfully for air.

In the kitchen, I sit on the chaise longue and stare out into the black of the garden. I realise I'm drunk, and wonder if that is wise, before deciding I don't care. Drunk or sober, I don't think it matters anymore. In one hand, I have my glass of whisky. In the other, I have Chris's knife. It's ready, though I'm unsure who for.

I really *didn't* mean to kill James. I wonder if he has been found yet? It's not the sort of road that gets much traffic on a Monday evening. I imagine pinprick headlights winding down the road. Will the next car see his body, or drive right over him with a thump? Perhaps they've been drinking and they will drive on in horror, thinking it's *them* who's killed him.

Time to face the facts. It's wait to get arrested, or end it now. Do I really want to live out the rest of my days in prison? Wearing some degrading grey jumpsuit and having to speak to idiots? Being flatmates with paedophiles and thieves, greedy money launders and pathetic drug mules? I don't think I can bear that vision of my future. My mind flashes back to the single bed of my childhood bedroom, the door clicking shut after he'd enter.

No, I can't do that.

For someone who has facilitated rather a lot of death, I'm unimaginatively stuck as to how to bring about my own. But after assessing the available options, I decide that hanging might be the best bet. Quick, foolproof – if you read up on knots, which I'm perfectly capable of doing. I can send a text just before I do it and not risk anyone arriving 'just in time'. I think through the process with coldness, my body and mind numb. I feel that old talent of disassociation return.

Making sure the manilla envelope has pride of place in the kitchen, I begin to gather supplies. While looking for a suitable rope, I remember Steven's scarf tucked away in my bedroom. Maybe using that is symbolic of . . . something. Who knows. So I find it, and find the most appropriate ceiling fitting – the bedroom lights which were securely screwed into the joist by a handyman.

As I take a last look around my house, I remember that call from the tattoo lady, V. *It's part of a sporting logo*, that's what she said. I'd meant to look that up, research what else a magpie could represent, but I forgot. Failure.

Grabbing my notebook, I write it down on the list with a question mark, just in case someone finds these scant bullet points in any way useful. And then I turn to write a quick note to Nina, and then to Katie. Most of what I want to say is already on the tape.

But the note to my sister reminds me of something. She wrote me a letter in hospital – I shoved it in my pocket then completely forgot about it. Nina's text in the pub and everything that followed had pushed it out of my mind. My clothes are piled in the corner of the room, never to be washed now. Hunting through them, I locate the black tasselled jeans I wore yesterday and hear a crunch that tells me the envelope is still there.

Sitting down on the bed, I open the envelope and slide out the letter.

CHAPTER THIRTY-FOUR

There's nothing like finding out something that turns your whole world upside down to sober you up.

What the fuck was I thinking? Ending my life? Self-indulgent drivel. There is work to do, and now I know what that work really is.

Katie has written me many notes over the years. She was always a note writer, even when everything was going well. Funny ones about cute dogs she'd seen on the way home from school, complete with biro rendition of said creature. Annoying ones as a teenager left in my bag to tell me she'd borrowed the jacket I'd left there on my last visit, then lost it, accompanied by a smiley face and a plea for forgiveness (always granted). Sweet ones when she could sense I'd retreated into my memories and sadness and anger.

Over the past year, she's left me other notes when I visited. Back to asking for forgiveness, but not for borrowed clothing or broken makeup. Sorry for her sadness, sorry for her inability to fix herself, for how she hadn't eaten or had cut her arm. Always with a promise to do better.

I hated these notes. But the notes came, none the less.

This note though, this note is different. It still said sorry, almost on every line. But it is an apology for something new. Lying.

Sitting on my bed, the whisky tumbler at my feet, I reread the letter. Her writing is wobbly, and I picture her weak, bandaged arm struggling to support her hand as she was scratching this out in her hospital bed.

Dear Mills,

I want to say I'm sorry. I know you hate it when I say sorry, but I have to say it. I know I worry you so much, and I try so hard not to.

But I also want to say sorry for lying. I know you think that I don't notice things, but I do. Recently, you seem different. You asked me questions again, about the night I was attacked, and I worry that you are going mad with it. It's made me feel even more guilty than I do already.

I lied to you about that night. Or some of it anyway. Some of it was true, because it's hard to lie on the spot, isn't it? But I didn't want to give too much away because I didn't want you to know what really happened. I'm sorry.

Truth is, Millie, I know who attacked me. But I worried if I told you, then you would do something you'd regret. Or something I'd regret you doing. We've never talked about Dad, have we?

So I lied. About part of it. Because I can't lose you.

319

And it was too late to go to the police, who would do nothing anyway. But I am sorry.

I need you to move on though, okay? I need you to forget this now? Because that's what I'm going to do. We need to both bury the past, Millie. It's part of us, but it's not all of us. You are brave and clever and funny and kind. I'm in awe of your wit and fierceness and the way you walk through the world without caring what others think. Let's focus on those good parts of us and work with the bad.

I'm sorry, sister. I love you.

Katie

Xxx

There is so much in this short note that I'm floored. Literally, I find, as I notice I'm now sitting cross-legged on the carpet, though I don't remember getting here. So much to unpick. Unfolding my legs, I go downstairs to pour the whisky away, make a coffee, and read it again.

We've never talked about Dad, have we? She knew. About everything, by the sounds of it. Who he was, what I did. How long ago did she realise? All the times I've performed silly dances or made herbal tea for my little sister, and she's known exactly who I am. Seen right through me.

I worried if I told you, then you would do something you'd regret. She knows I'd kill this man if I found out his identity. All the time I've been trying to protect my sister, she's been trying to protect me too. In an instant, I remember her tiny arms around me when we were children, when we'd curl up like quotation marks in her single bed. Occasionally I'd cry, and she'd hug me tighter. I'd forgotten that.

Truth is, Millie, I know who attacked me. The most important line of all. She knows. And the way this letter is written makes me think that if I heard his name, I'd know him too. With a creeping realisation, I realise I do. I won't say that part of me always knew. It didn't, or he would have been dead months ago. But I will say that the knowledge doesn't jar. It makes sense. It fits. Like a corner puzzle piece I've been trying to force into the middle of the sky, the picture is now so obvious.

It's part of a sporting logo, that lady said on the phone. And it's now bright in my mind in stark black and white. The Newcastle United shirt my uncle Dale would wear sometimes when he'd visit. My father's brother, who was there while we grew up. The good man in stark relief to my father. The one who stood by my mother after his death and helped her when she had no one else around her.

Like a lightning storm, memories I'd pushed under the rocks start to force their way through. Lingering eyes and crass comments, which seemed like nothing when I was so focused on my father. After I turned eighteen and left home, I only saw him rarely. But had he *really* never known what my dad was like? Wasn't there a time when he came to stay that I remember him opening the door to the living room and then quickly backing out when he saw me on my knees? What type of man doesn't do anything in a situation like that?

One who doesn't think it's that bad. One who wants the same.

I never knew my grandfather – Dad refused to discuss him, and once my mother told me in hushed tones that 'he wasn't a good man'. Perhaps my father and his brother were abused themselves. It happens. They call it 'the cycle of abuse'. Apparently one in eight boys who are sexually abused go on to become sex offenders themselves. I wonder how someone armed with all the facts would describe me – grown up amid violence, continuing on a path of aggression, just perpetuating the cycle. Keep that circle rolling.

But I'm different to my father and uncle. Because they preyed on the weak and I tackled the strong.

Flicking open my laptop, I google 'Newcastle United magpie' and scroll through hundreds of illustrations of a black and white bird in a top hat, or standing in front of the club name, or clutching a football in its talons. Uncle Dale loves this team, he spoke about them constantly when I was a kid. Is it really so hard to imagine a tattoo of their mascot on his body?

I lied to you about that night. Or some of it anyway. The bald head and the tattoo must have been true. Thinking back, these were the first bits of information she gave me, along with the red curtains. She was supposed to be out with her friends that night, but they were always falling out with each other – she must have decided to stay in while Mum hung out with Uncle Dale. With a start, I think of the red curtains in my old bedroom, the ones I chose after my dad died. A cursed space.

It was only when I pressed Katie harder that she started to talk about the club they'd been in. And what about that restaurant she mentioned that led to the death of David Cartwright? Was it just something she'd plucked out of thin air? A generic Italian restaurant name to shut me up? I've been such an incredible fool.

I open the photo storage app on my phone and spin back through the years. The later ones are full of pictures of Shirley Bassey, or selfies of Nina and me. Occasionally Angela and Izzy crop up. A year before, Katie reappears, smiling, posing, pulling faces. Back further and further until . . . there. A summer's day four years ago. I'd gone to visit Katie and found my uncle Dale at the house with my mother. It had been hot, and he was grilling sausages on the barbeque. It had been so hot in fact, that he'd pulled off his shirt. In the picture, I can only glimpse it. But it's definitely there. The tip of a black and white wing across his chest.

We need to both bury the past, Millie. And we will.

Sleeping isn't easy, but I manage a few hours. Though I was desperate to run straight to Uncle Dale's house last night, it was late and I was exhausted and drunk. I knew that getting some rest would help me think straight – I don't have time to mess up. Before I climbed under the sheets though, I added a hasty addendum to Nina's tape. If something happens to me, I want the truth in the right hands.

Today is the day I'm going to kill my uncle Dale. What happens after that? I have no idea. Maybe I'll escape, maybe I'll be arrested, or maybe I'll go out in a blaze of glory. I honestly don't care anymore. After all of this investigating and plotting and scheming, the answer has been right here all along. I know his address; I even know where there is a spare key to his front door – hanging in my mother's spotless kitchen.

Eating a bowl of cornflakes – one needs fuel for a big day – I flick open the BBC News app on my phone out of habit.

Well, that was unexpected.

323

MAN BADLY INJURED IN HIT-AND-RUN

I'm sorry, *injured*? I'm pretty sure you mean dead. Very dead. I click on the article, again seeing James hit the bonnet, hearing his head crack against the windscreen. *Surely* he isn't still alive? A jolt of joy battles with fear in my body.

Avon and Somerset Police are searching for information pertaining to a hit-and-run that happened last night.

The incident is suspected to have taken place between 9pm and 10pm on Farleigh Lane in South Bristol. A man, 36, who is yet to be identified, remains in hospital. It's unclear what he was doing in the area and no witnesses have yet come forward.

Officers were called to the scene when the man was discovered by a passing car at around 11:30pm.

Paramedics took the victim to the Bristol Royal Infirmary for immediate treatment. The driver fled the scene.

Police are appealing to anyone who may have seen anything suspicious in the area.

James is still alive. Granted, his chances don't sound great. What does 'remains in hospital' really mean? Is he still unconscious? I suppose so, or I'm pretty sure I wouldn't be eating cornflakes in my kitchen. He's not likely to forgive me in a hurry. *As yet unidentified* – yes, his wallet was in the car, which I ditched down a side road a few miles away. So they've not found that yet. At least that will slow them down.

This changes nothing, other than possibly diminishing the time I have left.

I need to kill Dale, and I need to do it fast.

Part of me is relieved that James is alive. He deserves to live. He'll go on to be happy, to meet some other woman. I just need to kill Dale before he wakes up.

My mind roaring, I grab a backpack and start to fill it with things – Chris's knife, the handcuffs I swiped from James's car, duct tape, a dark wig, my leather gloves. The good thing about killing Dale is that it'll be comparatively easy. He knows me. I'll knock on the door, and he'll let me in – or else I'll let myself in with Mum's spare key.

How it goes from there I don't yet know. But I've faced worse foes, and I don't have the time to sit around sketching out intricate plans like electrocution in bathtubs. James could wake up any minute and send the entire police force my way.

Pulling on trainers and a plain black coat that won't grab any attention, I hook the keys to my beloved Micra from the fruit bowl and head to the front door. With a sense of purpose, I pull it open with force and nearly walk right into a waiting fist.

Standing on my doorstep, hand raised in preparation to knock, is Nina.

CHAPTER THIRTY-FIVE

'Sit down. Explain.'

I dare you, even the toughest among you, to defy Nina when she really fucking means business. I stare at her, mouth open for a second before she physically manhandles me back into my hallway and shuts the door behind us.

'I can't,' I sputter pathetically. 'I need to go.'

'Now. Sit.'

She pushes me into a kitchen chair and puts the kettle on, pulling mugs and teabags out of the cupboards with the ease of someone who has been in this house a thousand times before. Meekly as a lamb, I wait where I've been put, watching her stride around my kitchen. Her confidence in the room, the familiarity of her, makes me feel warm, and as she slides a steaming mug across the table along with a plate of biscuits, I realise how long it's been since anyone took care of me.

'So.' She raises both her eyebrows and her mug in invitation.

'Why aren't you at work?' I mumble, and she responds by slamming the cup back down and spilling boiling liquid on the wood.

'*Why aren't I at work?* You really think that's the most important question here?'

I notice that she isn't wearing one of her colourful power suits, but is instead in a bright red jumper and pea green trousers – she must have taken the day off. Nina sighs and pulls out a vape, but after one puff, slams it down next to the mug and retrieves a lighter and a pack of Marlboro Reds from her handbag.

Inhaling deeply, we both wait until a layer of white smoke floats above us.

'Now. Why aren't I at work? Well, let's see. Why do you think I'm not at work, Millie?' I stare at her blankly. No one would have a chance against this woman in court. 'Nothing? Okay. How about your links to multiple murders across the city during the past couple of months or so?'

I swallow and stare at the table, a chastised child who's been caught stealing chocolate bars. Nina takes a few more drags of her cigarette in silence, before continuing.

'You killed Hugh.' It's a statement, not a question. 'I found that money. Thanks for that. A nice surprise. I was only looking for my winter boots with the fur inside. You know the ones?'

I nod.

'Why else aren't I at work? Well, it's not just *my* boyfriend who's attracted trouble, is it? But imagine my surprise when I see in the morning news that *your* new boyfriend has been almost killed in a hit-and-run! What luck we are having!'

'His name was in the news?'

'Not at first. They identified him and added it to the story about twenty minutes ago. You are going to start talking. And you are not going to stop until I know everything. Understand?'

The exhaustion of the past few days, of the multiple confessions, of the disappointment of James turning on me and the guilt of running him down all seems to hit me at once. It must show on my face because Nina, ever the empathist, softens her eyes.

'Millie, understand this: I am your friend. More than that. I am your sister. But please, you need to explain. And you need to get me a fucking ashtray.'

Gratitude floods through me – like the first time Nina took me back to her parents' house, the first time she said, 'Of course we're friends?', the first time she held back my hair when I was sick on a night out, the time she railed against the guy who stood me up, and all the other moments when this wonderful person has been by my side. Relief washes over me. I am not alone.

In the back of a kitchen cabinet, I find the ashtray I used to keep out for Nina before she switched to vaping. At the table, she groans with pleasure while exhaling towards the ceiling.

'God, this is good. Proper tar and smoke, none of that pink watermelon shit.'

'I hear it's just as bad for you anyway. Can give you something called popcorn lung.'

'We all die eventually. Speaking of which?'

'I recorded it for you. On a tape.'

'A tape? How long is this tape?'

'About an hour and a half.'

'For fuck's sake, Millie, summarise.'

'My father abused me as a child. For years. Verbally, physically. Sexually. When he started to notice Katie, I killed him. Well, not on purpose, but kind of on purpose. When Katie was attacked, I promised myself I would kill the person who hurt her. But I guess I got . . . distracted. I was so angry. I *am* so angry. And these men . . . They all got in the way. And they deserved it. Well, most of them did.'

Her face, practised by years of court, is unmoving, but I see her eyes moisten and her throat move as she swallows.

'Succinct.'

'James worked it out. And he wanted me to turn myself in, but I couldn't because I haven't found Katie's attacker yet. Well, I hadn't, I actually *have* now. I ran James over. It was me or him.'

'Fair enough.'

'And . . . and Hugh?' I shoot her a worried look – I did murder her boyfriend after all. 'He was a bastard, pal. But you wouldn't have seen it. You wouldn't have left him. He would have milked you for all you are worth and you do not deserve that. I couldn't have him do that to you and get away with it.'

Nina's face is rigid, I can tell that she is still not over what Hugh did to her and she is consciously steeling herself against the pain of it.

'I understand.' Ever the stoic.

She smokes, and I nibble on the Hobnobs she's put in front of us. We used to do this multiple days a week, and if I try, I can sort of push everything else under a rock and pretend we're back there. Before Katie's attack, before I got behind the wheel of an increasingly erratic and dangerous car going wildly out of control towards my inevitable demise.

'And what have you discovered? About Katie's attacker?'

I tell her about Dale. Nina and I have never spoken about what my dad did to me, but she clearly guessed something along the lines of the truth a long time ago. She takes everything on the chin and has barely flinched during the entire conversation.

'And what is the plan?'

'To go to his house. And kill him, I suppose.'

'You *suppose*? For God's sake, Millie, that's all you've got? Kill him, you *suppose*? What sort of master plan is that? What happens after that?' Her voice has become even raspier with the Marlboro Reds and it comes out as a bark.

'Well, I'll probably go to jail?'

'Not a chance. And for fuck's sake, burn that confession tape. Who do you think you are, Dr fucking Evil?'

I'm behind the wheel of the Micra, this time with Nina, who walked over to mine, in the passenger seat. If the police start looking for me, it's better to not be sitting in the open like a patsy, so we are on the way to her house. On the way, Nina fires questions at me about the crime scenes. Did I wear gloves? Was I ever seen? To the best of my knowledge, did I ever drop anything?

She seems satisfied with my answers. She doesn't once suggest that I abort my plan to kill Uncle Dale. When she asks about anything taken from the scenes, I hesitate, but immediately crumble under her glare. She demands to know where each item is and starts muttering about megalomaniacs and watching too much television under her breath.

'Once this is done, Millie, once Dale is dealt with, this stops. Yes? No revenge plots, no phone lines, no protecting the weak of the world. Got it? You want to help, you do something fucking normal. Work in a women's shelter, join the Samaritans. You don't bash heads in with rocks.'

'Got it.'

'You do as your sister says. As I've always said. You deal with the past, and you learn to move on.'

It feels delightful for someone to be taking charge. For my entire life, it's been me in the driving seat. This must be what having a parent feels like. At hers, over more tea, we discuss the plan. Nina is willing to be by my side until the end, but I point-blank refuse. She is compromised enough already; I'm not sending her into the lion's den.

Instead, we agree that she'll be on call, waiting to step in if anything goes wrong and I need help. No use pointing out that I would never ask her to enter a murder scene in a million years, so I just nod enthusiastically and promise I'll call if I need her.

We decide to wait until nightfall, and spend the rest of the day plotting what will happen inside Dale's house, what the plan is if things go wrong, gathering the supplies we need, and continually refreshing BBC News to see if there is any update on James. But there's nothing. His story has disappeared.

The gas leak is Nina's suggestion. We almost come to blows about the fact that I won't get a final word, but manage to come to a compromise that we are both sort of happy with in the end.

At eight o'clock, darkness has completely fallen. Everything is packed into my backpack, and Nina is looking at me with concern, her calm façade beginning to crack.

'I'm going to be right here, next to my phone, thinking of everything we need to cover to get you out of this mess, okay, pal? You just get in, do what you have to do, and get out.' She inhales, and then suddenly shouts like an army general. 'And no pissing around! No monologues! No explaining why you are doing what you're doing! He'll know.'

'Okay.'

As I climb into my car and wave at my friend, standing in the doorway with a face full of concern and – is that pride? – I can't help but wonder at how my fortunes have changed. Last night, I was completely alone, convinced I was on the brink of capture, with no clue about the identity of the man at the centre of it all. Less than twenty-four hours later, I have the fiercest, most brilliant person by my side, and am heading to the correct address with a solid plan.

Having Nina behind me has made me more determined to come out the other side of this. I want to believe her assertion that she will not let me step foot in jail. If anyone can manage that, she can.

But first, it's time to face Dale. And end this once and for all.

CHAPTER THIRTY-SIX

Uncle Dale lives on the outskirts of the city, which is particularly handy when it comes to CCTV. Nina and I plotted a route that avoids cameras altogether, and I park up in a street nearby feeling like things are, so far, going well. I'm wearing my scratchy brown wig, and black clothes that are easy to move in.

After debating the pros and cons, we decided against collecting the spare key from my mother's. Arriving there might invite unwanted questions, and letting myself in might even startle Dale into calling the police. Besides, what's wrong with his niece knocking on the door to say hello and show off her new hair colour?

Uncle Dale lives in an unattractive, detached house with no discernible personality or charm, the kind with cheap red brick, small, square windows, a grey garage door, and an entirely concrete front 'garden'. As far as I know, he has never been married or had a partner live with him, and in light of everything I now know, this makes him more suspicious. Don't get me wrong, I'm a loner myself. Nothing wrong with the single life. But as I also know, it allows you greater privacy to pursue hobbies others may not approve of.

As I approach the house, I see his favourite motorbike sitting proudly in the drive, telling me he is probably home – which is lucky, because I realise that there is no real plan for Dale not being in, and I don't have the gift of time to wait around. I've seen Dale at my mother's house now and again, but it's been a few years since I have been here. Steeling myself, I walk up to the front door and ring the bell.

I shift from foot to foot on the doorstep, shooting quick glances around me. The neighbouring houses might not be attached, but they are near enough to see me standing at the door if they glance out of the window. I check that my hood covers most of my face and widen my stance to disguise my gender the best I can.

Eventually, I hear movement coming from the other side of the door and prepare a large smile on my face, hitching my backpack further up on my shoulder in preparation. It creaks open and the bloated face of Uncle Dale appears around the door.

Dale has my father's eyes, though I always thought they were far kinder. I realise now that my mind concluded this based on circumstances rather than visual inspection. They are deep set into a ruddy face, sagging with age and mistreatment. His head is smooth and bald, and you can see the folds of skin on the back of his neck when he turns around.

A moment of confused silence beats between us before I remember my lines and pull down my hood.

'Uncle Dale! It's me, Millie. Can I come in?'

He peers at me closely before his face cracks into a grin. His smile was always a key difference between him and my dad. It made him seem like the jolly alternative, the safe one. There were many days as a child when I wished my mother had married this brother instead.

'Millie? Well! I haven't seen you in a while! New hair colour, I see? Come on in, love! Is everything okay?'

Stepping over the barrier, I exhale in relief; step one has gone to plan.

'Yeah, everything's fine, I just wanted to pop by.'

'Now, you want a cup of tea? Or a beer? Let me get you a beer.'

'That would be great, thanks.'

I follow him into the kitchen while he witters on, seemingly genuinely pleased to see me. He probably doesn't get many visitors. Dale's bald head and fat neck perches above the old Newcastle FC football shirt he's wearing, and I cringe at how stupid I've been, how much time has been wasted. How didn't I see it sooner?

'You're sure something's not wrong, is it, love? Didn't expect you to just turn up! Your mum's alright, isn't she? I was round there the other night for dinner. Watched the fireworks one of the neighbours was setting off. Shame you weren't in.' He passes me a bottle of Peroni.

'Oh yeah, Mum's good,' I say, taking a seat at the kitchen table and unzipping my backpack. With a feeling of revulsion, I realise that his presence, perhaps with the bangs of fireworks reminding her of New Year's Eve, must have been what prompted Katie's self-harm that night. 'I just wanted to talk to you about something. It's a little serious, I'm afraid.' He looks alarmed, his eyebrows rising into the large, hairless expanse of his forehead and bottom lip jutting out in concern. 'Would you mind sitting? It's kind of a long story.'

I smile at him gently. Nothing is more disarming than a sad woman.

Dale sits on a high stool at the kitchen island, the same look of concern on his face. He sips at his own beer, pulls out a box of matches and goes to light a cigarette. That's when I lean over and pepper spray him in the eyes.

Nina wasn't fully on board with this plan, I'll say that now. It's not exactly the simplest method of killing, which is what she requested. She wanted a gas leak while he was asleep – get me in and out without being seen. But where is the satisfaction in that? Dale wouldn't even know his time was up. We compromised on me having an exceedingly quick heart-to-heart, explaining to him just what was going to happen, and *then* causing a devastating gas leak.

It's what family is about: compromise.

Dale is screaming and clutching at his face, blinded and in agony. What a wonderful substance this is, I can see why Nina carries it around with her. Working with efficient speed, I slip James's handcuffs onto one of Dale's wrists, pull it through the bar of the kitchen island, and clip on the other.

Nina and I spent about an hour practising efficient handcuffing this afternoon, and I'm proud to now count super-quick restraint as one of my many talents. I will have to pop back over in the morning and remove the cuffs, when he should hopefully look like he has just passed out from the gas leak while having a beer. Pulling out my scissors and duct tape while he rages and sobs, I secure both ankles to the posts of his stool with duct tape, finishing off with a strip across his mouth which has the benefit of shutting him up.

Glancing at my watch, I see that it has only been five minutes and Dale is incapacitated *and* in pain. It's going well.

The muffled weeping from Dale is quietening, and I don't have all day, so I pour a glass of water from the sink, dampen a tea towel and wipe his eyes. They are swollen and red, giving the overall impression that he may be about to explode. They are fixed on me with what I assume is fear, though it's difficult to determine someone's expression when they have been pepper-sprayed and have duct tape across their mouth.

'Hi, Uncle Dale.' I give a cheery little wave.

Now the pain is subsiding I see his brain come back to life, ticking through what on earth is happening to him on this Tuesday evening which seemed to start out exceedingly normal. The moment when he sees the handcuffs is thrilling, and he starts to rock in his stool.

'You will just hurt yourself if you fall. So I'd suggest stopping that.' He stops. It's wonderful to have this much power. Have you tried it? I would suggest finding a way. Now the moment is here, when the man who caused so much pain and suffering is completely under my control, I feel overwhelmed. Excitement is spreading through me, but Nina's voice in my head tells me not to get carried away. No pissing around.

'I don't have all night, Dale, so I'll be quick. You can simply nod or shake your head. Do you understand what I'm doing to you?'

He shakes his head and I roll my eyes. I've no patience for dealing with idiots.

'Obviously I'm here to kill you, Dale. Do you understand that?'

A short pause and a tiny nod. My phone buzzes in my pocket – probably Nina telling me to hurry up.

'Good. We are getting somewhere. And do you understand *why* I'm here to do that? No? Are you sure?'

His eyes are darting around the room, looking for help or a way out. After letting him indulge for a few seconds, I slide the pepper spray further forward on the island and the sound drags his eyes to it like a magnet. He frantically shakes his head.

'You don't? Well, I suppose there are a few reasons. But mainly, I'd like to draw your memory back a short way. To the New Year's Eve just gone?'

His body, which has been in constant motion, suddenly stills as if he's finally met Medusa's eye.

'Ahh there we go. You may remember now? You went to my mother's house, did you not? To share a few drinks with her? Reminisce about the old times? And Katie was there too, right? I don't know why. She was supposed to go out with friends, but maybe she felt ill, or they fell out, or she was just tired. Maybe she came home early. I don't know. That's not important. But she was there.'

We stare at each other for a moment, until I feel my phone buzz again.

'Sorry, Dale, I should check this isn't important. You just continue having a think why you're here.'

Nina, three minutes earlier, sent via Telegram so it can't be traced at a later date:

You should be out by now.

And something else, that makes absolutely no sense.

A voice note. From James.

Staring at the notification for what seems like hours but is probably ten seconds, I square my shoulders and press play. His silky voice fills the echoey kitchen. It sounds rougher than usual, but a lot better than a dead man usually sounds.

'Hello Mille. It's James here. You probably weren't expecting to hear from me. You banged me up pretty successfully last night, but somehow you didn't cause lasting damage and I checked myself out of hospital earlier today. Concussion and a broken arm. They wanted to keep me in, but I insisted on leaving. Because I think it is important that we talk.'

He chuckles. *Chuckles?*

'I paid a visit to your house. Nice cat. The thing about being a police officer is that it's pretty easy to get someone's address. So, I thought I would come and say hello. Maybe I'm a glutton for punishment! Ha!'

It must be concussion. There is no other reason he would be finding all of this so delightful.

'Well, you weren't there. Obviously, you know you weren't there. But I did find an interesting tape lying on the kitchen counter.'

Oh shit. I didn't burn the tape. Nina is going to be so mad. In my defence, there's been a lot going on.

'Thought I'd take it back to mine and have a listen, and, can I just say, *wow*. You killed your dad with a *pie*? That's epic.'

Definitely concussed. Dale's red eyes bulge out at James's words and he rocks in his chair again. I give him a stern glare and he stills.

'I could take this right to the station. I *should* take this to the station. You tried to *kill* me, Millie. I was falling for you and you tried to *kill me?*'

The crackle of recording silence sits with us in the moment, Dale and I both staring at the phone, waiting. Eventually, I hear James sigh.

'But that tape also . . . well, it sort of broke my heart. What your dad did. The things you said on there. And last night. Because I understand, I *do understand*. But I can't let you do this, Millie. I know where you are. You are probably on your way to your uncle's house right now. Am I right? I'm pleased you added that to the tape. I'm a homicide detective. I can't just sit back and let you kill a man, no matter how fucking evil he is. You know that. I don't really know why I'm telling you this. Warning you. I guess because I like you. Or because I've hit my head rather badly. Maybe it's to give you a sporting chance.

'I'll see you soon, Millie. But this time, I won't have my guard down.'

The message ends. I continue staring at the screen. How long will it take for him to find Dale's address? When he says he is coming here, does he mean alone? Or is he sending the full might of the law? How long does it take to mobilise the police in real life, rather than in an ITV drama?

One thing is certain, I don't have time to sit around and write a thesis on the subject. I send Nina a quick Telegram message updating her on what has happened, bracing myself for her disapproval regarding the tape. She immediately sends back a string of exclamation marks.

For a moment I almost forget that Dale is in front of me and he seems to be under the impression that if he stays quiet, I'll forget why I'm here and wander off to find something else to do.

'Look, Dale, I meant to stay longer, I did. I know I don't visit much, so it's a shame that we haven't spent as much time together as I'd planned.' As I speak, I pull up James's contact on my phone and press Call. One last shot. He picks up on the first ring.

'Hello Millie.'

'James . . . I'm sorry. About last night.' He stays silent, so I continue. 'I was terrified. You can understand that, right? But I'm sorry, it's been . . . awful.' I surprise myself by feeling a genuine lump in my throat. Hearing his voice felt warm and comforting. I can almost feel his arm around me, as if we were still walking around that park.

Dale is watching me, and I can only hear James's breathing down the phone. I slide off the stool and start to pace.

'We do need to talk,' I say into the phone. 'I'm in an Airbnb in the countryside. I was scared, and I needed to get away. If I give you the address, will you come?'

It's a desperate attempt to send him in the wrong direction, but it's all I can come up with at short notice. Dale makes a noise behind the tape so I hold the pepper spray can directly in front of his eyes and he falls silent. Finally, James speaks.

'I'm not an idiot, Millie. You are at 38 Middleton Road. Your uncle's house. I'm on my way. Do not move.' Fuck.

'Wait! James! You cannot do this. We had something? Didn't we? We *have* something. I . . . I love you. Please. I love you.'

He is silent again.

'Fuck you, Millie.'

My heart is sinking, his breathing still echoing down the line.

'I wanted to reason with you,' he says in a low voice. 'But . . . saying you fucking love me? You will stoop to anything. You are trying to play me.'

'No, it's tru—'

'Shut up!' He sounds deranged. 'I'm on my way. Do not do anything rash. This is over *now*.'

The line goes dead.

How dare he think I'd do anything rash.

CHAPTER THIRTY-SEVEN

Leaving my uncle firmly handcuffed to the kitchen island, I pace the circumference of the room twice. Deciding that it's always good to keep comrades in the loop, I send Nina an outline of the new plan before opening the door that leads internally from the kitchen to the garage.

Dale is trying to shout for help into his duct tape. I wish he wouldn't because I find it pathetic and I'm getting strong second-hand embarrassment. *We are all stressed here, Dale, we are just not all whining about it.*

Flicking the switch floods the room with an unattractively bright light and I see a concrete floor stained with oil. Three motorbikes take up one half of the garage, and the other half is crowded with a lawn mower, barbeque, tools, and general rubbish. Pushing aside a rake and shovel, I start hunting through, but I can't find what I need. I can still hear Dale's muffled screaming and rocking – he's going to do himself some damage if he's not careful. But a new sound pierces my brain. The distant wailing of a siren.

Here they come.

Frantically now, I dart to the other side of the garage, toppling an expensive bike and pushing aside a helmet and pairs of padded trousers. Then I see them. Three petrol canisters, standing neatly side by side.

They are all full, and I drag them one by one into the kitchen. Dale is craning his head to see what I am doing, but it's probably best I don't stress him out further. He's restrained, but I'll be upset if he manages to somehow topple off his chair and is unconscious for the end of the party.

Once I've dragged the third canister into the house, I slam the garage door. My arms are aching from the strain, but I start to heave them closer to my uncle. When he sees them, his muffled screams resume. The siren is definitely louder now, confirming it was not a figment of my imagination. Unscrewing the lid, I tip the first petrol canister so that a third of it slops onto the floor. When I can lift it, I pour the rest over my uncle's head.

The second canister, I start to splash around the room, making sure to douse the soft furnishings and wood that will catch. Dale is sobbing now, and the siren is growing even louder. I picture that scene in *Thelma and Louise* when they realise they have run out of rope. Part of me wishes Nina was here, holding my hand in the air. Though of course, I don't really. She needs to live.

The last canister, I splash onto myself. I drizzle some onto my head, splash my jacket and trousers. I throw the final drop at Dale. We stare at each other, dripping wet, the acrid smell stinging at my eyes. The smell of petrol has always been something I've found pleasant, but I didn't ever suspect I would die this way.

Never expected my blaze of glory to be so literal.

But the police are on their way, and James has enough evidence to send me away for the rest of my life. I can't face that. I spent sixteen years of my life afraid. And then almost as many years free. I had friends, I ran almost every day and felt the fresh wind on my face. I made myself a home, cared for my cat, built a life driven by *me*. I cannot exchange that for a life behind bars filled with tinned chilli con carne and powdered milk, enforced craft workshops and toothbrush shivs, locked doors and fear.

We've run out of time. James has a tape of my confession. Objects belonging to the victims litter my flat. There are no more minutes, no more choices.

I turn back to Dale.

'You raped my sister. You knew about my dad. You two are the same, and you deserve to burn in hell. Goodbye, Dale.'

He is shaking his head, sobbing, shouting against the duct tape.

'You do not deserve to live. And really, I probably don't either.' I laugh, but I'm crying too. Katie will blame herself, but Nina will take care of her. 'Circle of violence, hey? Raised by violence, live by violence. Maybe it's a good thing it ends with me.'

Pulling out my phone, I tap out a Telegram message to Nina saying I'm sorry, thank you, and that I love her. She deserves a goodbye, and to know this is over so she can untangle any threads that could be traced back to her. I ask her to make sure Katie is okay, and tell her to stay away from men like Hugh. Then I delete the app so that if my phone is found, she won't be implicated. Next, I text Katie a simple message:

I love you. I'm sorry.

Dale's matches are on the kitchen island.

'Any last words?'

He shouts against the duct tape, rocking, his swollen, red eyes streaming with tears.

'Lovely.'

I pull out a match and hold it against the rough edge of the box, ready to end both of our worlds. To end the suffering we cause.

My phone buzzes with an incoming call. It interrupts my dramatic moment, and I roll my eyes. Never a moment's bloody peace. The siren sounds so close now and I know we don't have long. The worst-case scenario would be to be saved, just in time, and be locked up for life while also having my features melted to nothing. But though I try to ignore it, I can't, so I pull it out of my soaking pocket with annoyance. It's Nina.

Without really thinking about it, I answer.

'I've sorted it. Get out. Now.' She clicks off.

I stare at Dale. He stares at me. The sirens are filling my ears. The match is in my hand.

CHAPTER THIRTY-EIGHT

Shit. Shit. Shit.

Peeling off my jacket, I throw it in a puddle of petrol at Dale's feet. Making sure not to stand in the pooling liquid, I kick off my shoes and socks, then slip out of my trousers. Lastly, I chuck my wig after my clothes, thankful that the cheap synthetic fibres have protected my actual hair hiding underneath. At the kitchen sink, I hurriedly rinse my hands and arms the best I can, splashing water down my body.

I tiptoe my way towards where I've left the matches on the island and then to the door, which isn't easy because I've done a damn good job of soaking this place in flammable liquid as thoroughly as if I'm making a Christmas cake.

Standing absurdly in the midst of the petrol-soaked house in my bra, pants and backpack, I open the front door. Finally, I pull the match head along the box and a flame springs to life. Staring at my uncle, handcuffed to his gaudy kitchen island, I shout my final goodbye to the man who ruined my sister's happiness, the brother of the man who ruined mine. In this light, with his face swollen red and tear stained, he looks exactly like his brother. I drop the match.

Heat is instant. Especially when you're basically naked.

The contrast with the cold air is dramatic, and the glass of the windows shatters with an ear-splitting *crack*.

Flames burst into the outside world. Straddling Dale's Triumph motorcycle that sits in the driveway, I insert the key I nabbed from the hook by the door and kick it to life, tearing the skin from the top of my foot against the pedal. The roar takes me by surprise. The air is already full of smoke, a siren wail, the crackling of rising flames from inside, and now the growl of my engine. I can still hear the muffled shouts of my gagged uncle above it all, but deep down I know that must be in my imagination.

I'd love to say I speed off with the grace and pizazz of Angelina Jolie in *Tomb Raider*, but I've never driven this thing before and it takes a second to understand the controls. As I ease into first gear, I'm flooded with blue light and deafened by the wail of a siren and screech of tyres. A single car slams to a stop in the road, driver's door flying open.

James.

He is lit up in a mixture of neon blue and flickering orange, making his dark eyes recess into his face and throwing his sharp cheekbones into relief. I think of the man who came into Picture This, the casual flirting across the counter, the elegant fingers wrapped around the pen. Who would have thought this is where we'd end up?

I can hear more sirens in the vicinity, so he's clearly

called for backup en route, as he threatened. He looks at me, sitting half-naked on this motorbike, and then at the house, where flames flicker at the window.

He makes a choice, the only one a good man could make. He runs into the house, and I twist the accelerator, thrust forward at a speed that nearly snaps my neck, and fly from the scene.

Bristol has been my hometown for my entire life. Other people left, went to university in Edinburgh, or Leeds, or London, coming back for holidays or the occasional long weekend. Some travelled around Asia on gap years with huge backpacks and inflated egos. But I've barely left the city's limits.

Though this may mean my bank of (acceptable) stories to tell at parties is rather slim, it does have the added benefit of me knowing this place like the back of my hand. Staying away from the main roads, I zigzag through the darkness and pray to God no one is staring out of their window tonight.

At one point I slam to a halt at a junction, and I see the depressed face of a teenage boy behind the glass, looking down at me open-mouthed. I wink and rev the engine; no one will believe him anyway.

About half an hour of weaving around town later, I drive straight into a small park by Nina's house and kill the engine. Pushing the bike and myself into a bush and out of sight, I finally breathe.

Nina had shoved me into the bathroom as soon as I walked through the door, telling me I stank of fumes. The police would come here eventually, but not straight away.

James only knows Nina's first name. It would take time to figure out where to go after checking my house.

The shower was steaming hot and smelled incongruously of eucalyptus. The adrenaline stopped me from noticing how cold I was after spending so long outside in my underwear on a November night. With the hot water hitting my skin, pins and needles began to attack my whole body as my blood screamed. Soaping myself all over with Nina's fancy products, I even took the time to wash my hair, breathing in the expensive Aesop scent.

Downstairs, Nina was waiting for me with her head in her hands on the sofa. This concerned me, because she isn't easily rattled, but when she looked up, she smiled.

'Sit, explain.'

So, showered and dressed in a pair of Nina's multicoloured pyjamas, we are now sitting in her living room, staring at each other with wild eyes.

'It was . . . a bit of a shitshow,' I begin.

'You're here, aren't you?'

'Yeah, but I'm not sure for how long. They must be at my house right this second. At some point, they will find your address.' I've gone through the possible ways this could go; there aren't many, and they aren't good. Nina is a great lawyer, but she can't get me out of this. Panicking, my eyes start darting around the room as if I might find an answer there, or an escape route.

'Millie. Trust me. Calm down. Tell me what happened.'

Nina pulls out a cigarette and I flinch at the click of the lighter. As the tip burns red, I imagine the crackle of my own skin in the flames. Would that have been better than what's to come now? It's a toss-up.

Lying my head back against the sofa cushion, I close my eyes and breathe deeply. The smell of this place – the unusual mixture of expensive candles and classic Chinese cooking – calms my mind. I fold my legs, which feel too long and thin, ungainly and transparent, like those of a cellar spider. My arms are empty of blood or muscle.

'James woke up.'

She remains silent and I sigh deeply, exhaling every ounce of air in my lungs, and everything I've been holding on to. I'd given her some information over Telegram earlier, but only the basics. So I take the time to explain properly – about the message from James and having to abandon the slow gas leak plan. About deciding to burn the place down and take me with it.

'Why did you think that would be a good idea?'

She speaks with a soft rasp, as if I'm showing her an ugly jumper I'd ordered online.

'He was on his way. There was too much evidence against me, going down with it all seemed like the best option at the time.'

'I wasn't expecting you to end up naked in a bush with a pretty cool motorbike.'

'No. That was another deviation from the plan.' I left the motorbike in the park, but she'd collected me with a coat to hide my lack of clothing and avoid notice. I pull my arms around my body in a hug. 'He looked . . . so much like my dad.'

'Why did you never tell me about him? I mean, I *guessed* something like this had happened to you. You never mention him, and I've seen the marks on your leg that look like cigarette burns. Always thought you should get some therapy to help you deal with the past in a . . .

different way. But you could have told me. You could have spoken to me.'

'I know. Maybe I should have. It's just not the way I cope with things. I bury them. I've never really believed in all this whining about your problems, though maybe I should have given it a go in retrospect. Instead, I've tried to help other people.'

'Sorry to sound like a fucking motivational poster, but sometimes you have to help yourself first.'

'That is the way it appears to be.'

We sit in silence as I catalogue the ways in which I'm lucky. Few people will ever have a friend like Nina. Sometimes, I believe that the love people receive is evenly distributed, and because I received none from my parents, it was all heaped onto Nina and Katie to give to me. Then I tell myself to grow the fuck up and stop being so crystal-healing about the whole thing.

'Would you like to hear what I've been up to?'

I'm jolted out of my reverie and snap open my eyes. Was I drifting off then? Though I look like I've had the sort of relaxing night in that self-care influencers insist everyone must do on the regular, Nina looks ever the switched-on lawyer. She is used to working late and maintaining focus, and she appears to have approached this as she would any other case. But, you know, on the side of the murderer. Somehow, her red lipstick is still perfect, and I find myself wondering if she reapplied it while I was burning down Dale's house.

'I would, yes,' I say softly, my voice almost as raspy as hers. I suppose I've inhaled a lot of smoke too this evening.

Nina smiles, her apple cheeks and dimples turning her from fierce lawyer to cute child. She pushes her thick glasses up on the bridge of her nose, then pulls the elastic from her hair, which falls in a black sheet around her shoulders. The ripple of shine in the blackness reminds me of the sheen of petrol spreading on the kitchen floor. I shudder again.

'Well after you'd gone, I drove to yours in the Micra and collected up those fucking . . . trophies, or whatever they were.' I flinch. They weren't meant to be trophies, per se. 'The camera, scarf, the knife, the EpiPen, the rock. Nothing from David's house, correct?'

'Nothing.' I didn't want to keep that kill with me.

'Yes, so I shoved those startling pieces of evidence into a bin bag and got them out of the house. Can't *believe* you kept them.' She glares at me while stubbing out her cigarette in an overflowing ashtray.

'You appear to be back to smoking.'

'Shut up.' She points at me with a fresh one. 'This is your fault. Anyway, I'd just arrived home and was settling in to cook some dinner, maybe apply a face mask – while keeping an eye on my phone, of course – when I got your message. James was back up and running, causing a kink in our dastardly plan.'

It almost seems like Nina is enjoying herself, drawing out the tale like a bedtime story. Though surely that cannot be the case because her best friend is about to go to jail.

'My options were limited. As were yours. A plan was just coming together when you sent that text.' She raises an eyebrow, as if my final goodbye was a silly ploy. 'Honestly, Millie. I told you I'd be here to help. You have no faith. By the sounds of it you were about to blow yourself sky high alongside that creep.

'Back into your Micra – no facemask for me! And round I went to James's house.'

'Wait, what?' I sit up ramrod straight now, legs still crossed like I'm meditating. The need for sleep has vanished. 'How did you even know where he lived? Why were you—'

'Will you let me tell it! You gave me his address when you shagged him. It's only a few streets away. So, there I was, speeding round to James's house in your little car, while *he* speeds towards your uncle's. In I went – key under the flowerpot, highly unoriginal – with the little bag of evidence over my shoulder like an evil Santa Claus.'

'No you didn—'

'—and shoved it right under his bed. Then I made an anonymous phone call to 999.'

'Oh my God—'

She put on a high, breathy voice. 'Police, please! You need to get round to 38 Middleton Road quickly. Someone called James Khan is responsible for the deaths of numerous local men, and he is about to attack another. He is a police officer, so I've been scared to come forward, but I can't keep quiet anymore. I won't call again.'

She smiles at me shyly, suddenly modest of her talents of deception. 'I knew you'd be out of there by the time they arrived. Or at least, you'd still have more chance if they'd been tipped off that *he* was the murderer, not you, than if he brought you into the station in handcuffs.'

'And the tape?' I ask, frantic now. 'He took the tape.'

'And he must have been as dumb as you,' she says with a wink. 'He also left it right out on his kitchen table. Maybe you would have made a good pair, in other circumstances.'

Silence falls again while I wrap my head around everything she's just told me. This can't possibly work. Can it? James lives next door to the first victim, and was home when he was killed, alone at the time of the murder when Imran went to the shop. Does he have alibis for the others? He's been at each crime scene, and could have easily tampered with evidence.

Something he said in the pub comes back to me. '*My boss even said that I have an "unhealthy obsession" with these not being accidents.*' They'll believe it. And if not? Well, what is there to tie these cases to me other than his word and a snapshot from a hazy doorbell camera that could be anyone?

'You've *framed James*?'

For the first time, a flash of guilt crosses her face. 'It was him or you, pal. There wasn't a choice. I know you liked him but—'

'Nina. Stop it. You are . . . incredible.'

She beams.

CHAPTER THIRTY-NINE

The police will need to speak to me. Of course they will.

By the end of that fateful evening, we'd concocted an iron-clad cover story and practised it over and over, Nina occasionally shouting at me for repeating lines on retellings.

'No! This cannot sound rehearsed! Every time I ask you a question, you need to answer it differently. Off the cuff. This needs to become real life, not a story. Understand?'

Turns out, Nina is potentially as crazy as I am. Eventually, she let me sleep, but only when it became clear that I could barely remember my own name.

Nina made some calls, and by the next morning, Dale's bike had disappeared from the park. I suppose in her profession you don't just make friends in *high* places. It's morning now, and we are prepared, ready and waiting.

Nina is ready to cry on command – still grieving her recently deceased boyfriend, she has needed her best friend by her side a lot lately, frequently staying over in the spare room. Conveniently, on all of the murder dates. On the other hand, I have practised the shock and confusion of being told not only that my beloved uncle died in a house fire, but that it may also have been caused by the man I've been dating.

But no one comes.

We get our first update along with everyone else – on the local morning news. Having not actually seen the moment Dale left for hell, my chief concern was that he somehow got out of this alive. But the news confirms that a housefire the night before claimed one victim, and that a police officer was taken to hospital. I breathe a sigh of relief.

There is no other update on James's health, but he must be in a bad way. If he could speak, the police would have been knocking on the door already – he knows Nina's best friend and it wouldn't take too long to track down Nina the family lawyer. It is possible for Nina to use some police contacts to find out more, but she doesn't want to risk showing any undue interest.

Coffee is mainlined, thick, dark liquid drizzling out of the Nespresso machine, pink disposable pods thrown one by one into the recycling. After downing another espresso, Nina heads into work, having got over her 'twenty-four-hour sickness bug' and not needing to draw any extra attention to herself, and I go back home.

It feels strange being back here, alone, when I know people have been in here since I left. I don't mind that Nina has gone through my things to collect evidence, of course. But the thought of James sitting in my kitchen, woozy from the head wound and hell-bent on stopping me, sends a chill down my spine. Sitting at the kitchen island, I can picture it like a film. Him coming in, stroking my cat, poking around. Then spying the enticing envelope, Nina's name on it in sharpie pen.

I picture him lying on the chaise longue for over an hour, listening to my exhausted, drunk voice spilling my deepest confessions, though I remember that he'd actually taken it to his own home. I would have sounded vulnerable, and a spike of fury surges in my blood. But it seems that I no longer have the energy to be truly angry. Not like before.

The next update is from my mother. The news of Dale's violent passing has reached her, and she nervously imparts the information over the phone. It didn't occur to me until she rang, that she must have been in the house the night Kate was attacked. Does she know? Would she have done anything to stop it? I very much doubt it.

The conversation is short, and not particularly sweet. Acting takes energy, and that's not something I really want to use up on my mother. What's the point? She's hardly going to shop me in if she suspects anything. Time and again she has proven herself to be someone who looks the other way, no matter what the crime. So rather than feigning shock or asking questions about my uncle's death, I ask how Katie took the news, and there is an awkward pause on the line that tells me that, even if she doesn't know for certain that Dale was the man who hurt Katie, then she's at least guessed.

'Katie doesn't know yet, love. She's still in hospital, and I don't want to worry her too much. She is doing well though, the doctor said.'

'I'll tell her.'

'You're sure?' Her voice is wobbling, from relief or fear or upset, I can't be sure. I never did know this woman very well.

I try to sleep more, and I do drop off at one point. But

the smell of petrol in my nose wakes me with a start, and I wonder if I'll smell this for the rest of my life. When I close my eyes I see the flicker of flames, and picture the crackle of skin. The face morphs between Dale's and my father's. Feelings are always something I've believed to be pretty clear-cut. Anger, sadness, joy, boredom. But I'm feeling something different today that I can't understand, and that makes me uneasy. Perhaps it's a type of closure? Certainly, it isn't guilt.

When I wake again, it's because I've heard a knock at the door. It's what I've been waiting for, though later than expected. Throwing on jeans and a t-shirt, I glance in the mirror to check the makeup is still disguising my lack of sleep and jog downstairs, bullet-pointing my story on my fingers.

But when I throw open the door with a smile, there is no one there. When I was young, kids used to play Knock Out Ginger, deriving uncapped joy from knocking on doors and legging it to slightly disrupt someone's afternoon. But that was before the invention of iPhones. Surely they have better things to do these days?

As I close the door with a creeping sense of dread running down my spine, an envelope on the mat catches my eye. It wasn't there before. A large part of me wants to ignore it and climb back into bed, to destroy it in the food processor or a fire. It's not the white rectangle of a bill or the jolly attention-grabbing colour of junk mail. And the postman comes early, 8am at the latest. This has been hand delivered.

Many words can be used to describe me – psychotic, brave, smart, cruel, lazy, cold, serious, fun, dull. They'd all be true, I suppose. But I don't believe anyone would use the word coward. So I pick it up. The envelope is unmarked, so I sit down in the kitchen and slide it open.

Dear Neighbour of Sean,

Hello there. I would like you to know that the man on your street – Sean Cannon – is a homewrecker who has been sleeping with my husband. If you have one of your own, make sure this man stays far away from them. Do not think I let my husband off without blame; as well as leaving him, I will be informing the neighbours, friends, colleagues, and families of both men.

I have attached photo evidence.

G.

Below the handwritten note, which I can only imagine has been delivered in a similar way to other people on the street, is a printed photograph. Sitting down with shock, I peer at the grainy image of gnome-faced Sean standing in a bedroom stark naked. On the bed in front of him, staring up in delight, is a man that looks like – is it? Could? It? Be? Yes. Daniel Craig.

Not *that* Daniel Craig, obviously. But Gina's cheating husband Daniel Craig. Who has apparently been sleeping with Sean.

Well at least I know what's been keeping him pacing up and down the garden.

Lying back on the chaise longue with the paper clutched to my chest, I imagine Gina on the other end of that phone line, taunting him with the camera footage. Making demands that she must have known he couldn't meet.

Finally extracting her delicious revenge on both the man who broke her heart and his new lover. Well, well, well, maybe Gina isn't that bad after all.

Before I know it, I'm laughing. A slow chuckle turns into hysteria. There are tears running down my face, and I slap my knee as if I'm an animated character displaying full mirth mode. I laugh for a long time, and afterwards, my muscles ache, and my mind feels clear. My cat looks scared.

Four days pass before I hear from the police, who knock on the door on Monday morning. Two officers, a man and a woman, accept a cup of tea and take a seat at the kitchen table. I head them off by saying I'm already aware of my uncle's passing, and the awful circumstances.

'To die in a fire like that,' I say in a horrified whisper. 'Can you *imagine*? Does anyone deserve to die that way?'

'We're glad that you are already aware of this, Miss Masters, and we're sorry for your loss. However, we, er, also have a few other details to run by you?'

The female officer, Officer Shah I think she said she's called, is clearly the junior of the pair, and she says statements as questions, rising up at the end of each sentence. She studiously avoids meeting my eye, even when speaking, and sips at her tea to give herself something to do. Although I can be impatient with timid people, there is something in her demeanour that warms me to her. Her shoulders naturally curl up so she takes up less room, but I can tell she has an internal voice reminding her to take up space, and so she periodically straightens herself. Being a woman, and a woman of colour, in the police force must be tough, and she needs to practise strengthening that backbone.

Her partner, Officer Bauer, is less likeable. He is tall, pale and narrow-shouldered, with long limbs that remind me of that childhood spectre, The Slender Man. When he isn't giving a practised look of false sympathy, his face falls naturally into what can only be called a jeer. When he leans forward, I worry that the sharpness of his pointy elbows might dent my table.

'We need to know where you were on the night of the fire, Miss Masters.' He spreads his fingers on the table as he speaks, and Officer Shah quietly clears her throat.

'Oh, okay. I . . . I guess that you need to ask everyone? Though I wasn't aware it was being seen as anything other than an accident. Oh my God, you aren't saying that this was *deliberate*?'

'Um, well—' Shah begins.

'We aren't saying anything of the sort, Miss Masters. We just need to know everyone's whereabouts while we conduct our enquiry.'

The way he keeps saying my name is irritating. He's clearly learnt it on some sort of course; How To Keep the Public Calm While You Accuse Them Of Murder.

'Well luckily, I know exactly where I was, because I remember my mother calling with the news just after I got home the next day. I was at my friend Nina's house. She's been having a hard time recently, so I've been spending a lot of time at hers.'

'And she would be able to confirm that?'

'Of course.'

'What did you do that evening?'

'We watched a Bond film on Amazon Prime. One of the latest ones. She made pasta.' We'd agreed on this, and it turned out that Nina had even rented the film and let it play while I'd been at Dale's that night, just in case someone was to check. Officer Shah gives an almost imperceptible nod, clearly relieved that I have an alibi. Officer Bauer sighs. It occurs to me that he may know James.

'We need to tell you something else about that night, Miss Masters,' he says delicately. 'Do you know a James Khan?'

'Yes?'

Between them, they explain that James was pulled from the burning building that night, and only woke up in hospital last night. Covering my hand with my mouth, I shake my head gently in the way I've practised in the mirror multiple times a day. Nina already heard he was alive and under police guard in hospital on the legal grapevine, but I'm thankful that James is now finally awake enough to talk. My eyes dampen with tears of relief. He really didn't deserve to die.

Nor does he deserve to go down for crimes he didn't commit.

I also heard from Nina that while he was unconscious, police searched his flat, discovering multiple pieces of evidence that connected him to the murders of Karl Tarneburg, Steven Baker, Chris Drake, Hugh Chapman, John Towles (AKA Romeo) and Paul Marques (AKA the Stoner). But we aren't there yet.

'James Khan has made some claims about *your* involvement Miss Masters, in both this and various other crimes.'

'He – what? Sorry, I need a moment. This is a lot to take in.'

'Of course,' says Officer Shah, uncurling herself and

furrowing her eyebrows in concern. She's on my side. Good to know.

'Mr Khan has told the police that you caused the fire at your uncle's house, and that he arrived too late to stop you. Do you have any idea why he would say such a thing?'

I raise my eyes from my cold cup of tea and look at them, before burying it in my hands and starting to cry.

'Oh God. Oh wow. I just can't believe this,' I mutter through my sobs and into my hands. 'It's a long story, I suppose. There are things I need to tell you. But I – I suppose I should call my lawyer.'

At the station, I sit alone in an interview room until the door swings open, revealing Nina in all her glory. Clad in a lime-green suit with gold buttons and shoulder pads, she lights up the drab room. It occurs to me that, in my usual black garb, I almost belong here among the greys and beiges and browns. Maybe I'll let her convince me to try on a red top or something, when this is all over.

After updating Nina on the conversation so far, we generally chat about what is to come, though we've already discussed everything days earlier – she never believes that these 'private meetings' at the station are actually private. We decided that there was only one option left open to us if James woke up and could speak. Dale is finally out of the picture – I achieved my goal after all.

When the police enter the room, I started to feel the bees in my blood buzz with fear, but Nina raps her nails on the table and I calm. We have got this.

It is time for my confession.

CHAPTER FORTY

Three hours later, we are sitting in The Guinea drinking gin and tonics. I'm feeling shell-shocked, but Nina is taking it in her stride. The barman, the same man from when I was last here less than a week ago, is reading the *Guardian* and the pub is filling with evening punters. The world feels bizarrely normal. I've gulped at my first drink too quickly, and as I down my second one I feel my head start to spin.

There is no evidence to link me to the fire at Dale's, and I have a solid alibi. Even Nina's neighbour, who saw Nina and me enter the house together that day, is prepared to say so. On the other hand, James, about whom the police had had an anonymous tip-off, was found at the scene, his own handcuffs securing the victim.

After answering a few preliminary questions that made me feel as though I was on *Line of Duty*, I tearfully told my story. How I'd met James in my old job at Picture This – they were welcome to ask my old colleague Gina.

How we'd gone on a few dates – why not ask the barmaid of The Portcullis pub where we'd got too drunk? How he'd started to act a little . . . odd. Intense.

James might not really deserve to go down for crimes he didn't commit. But he is prepared to send *me* away, and I've heard that there is only one thing with which to fight fire.

'Intense, how?'

'Oh, just . . . strange? I didn't know him well, but he seemed obsessed with his work. Specifically, these deaths that were happening? They all sounded like accidents, but he would not stop talking about them. It started to freak me out.'

The detectives exchanged a quick glance.

'I'm not a violent person. Talking about death and murder . . . It's not my idea of entertainment. So, I started to pull away from him. And he . . . didn't take it well.' I shot Officer Shah a 'you know how it is' kind of look, and she rewarded me with a smile. 'It also felt kind of unprofessional as well. Like, I didn't know if detectives are supposed to talk about murder scenes they had just been to and stuff?'

Bauer frowned down at his notepad.

'At your house, you mentioned needing to tell us something,' Shah ventured. 'Could you elaborate on that, please? What was on your mind?'

I glanced at Nina, the tearful, scared woman seeking reassurance.

'Go on,' she whispered with encouragement.

'Well, it all reached a head last week. Monday night. He *insisted* that we speak, in person. He sent me like thirty texts in a row. So, he came to pick me up. I was feeling . . . uneasy about him by this point, so I didn't even give him my address. He picked me up a few streets away. I thought we were going to go for a drink but . . .'

Choked up, I buried my face in my hands and inhaled deeply as if trying to regain composure.

'But he had other things in mind. He drove really fast, and wouldn't tell me where we were going. He pulled over into this clearing off a dark road. By this point, I was scared. He started demanding to know why I was avoiding him, and I told him the truth – that I didn't think it was working out?'

Shah's eyes were wide and full of sympathy. She isn't cut out for this job. Bauer's face was of a practised blankness, his skeletal appearance and void expression making him seem like an empty vessel or alien lifeform.

'He got mad. Really mad. We got out of the car, and he was shouting at me. Calling me all sorts of names? Threatening my family members. Oh! And then he must have killed Uncle Dale! It's my fault!' I buried my face in my hands again and everyone let me sit there until I felt ready to continue.

'I . . . I thought he might actually hurt me, so I got back in the car and locked the doors. That just made it worse though. He was banging on the windows, screaming things. I thought he would smash them in. The keys were in there, so I just . . . well I tried to drive away.' I looked apologetic, as if leaving a violent man with a long walk was the worst thing I'd ever done.

'I was going to call him a cab or something. Honest! But in the moment, I didn't know what else to do. Anyway, I tried to drive away, but it was chaotic and dark, and he ran into the road and . . . and . . .'

'What happened next, Millie?'

It made me bristle, hearing Bauer use my first name. This was clearly the second step in that course; When They Start to Open Up, Pretend You Are Their Friend.

'He *ran into the road*! In front of me! I didn't think I hit him hard, and I was terrified. Even more so then. So I kept going. I thought he was fine. Then the next day, he left me this kind of unhinged voice note, and I called him back, but he wasn't making sense. But he did say he was fine and not in hospital or anything. So I figured it was okay.'

There was silence in the room until Nina spoke up.

'My client has told you everything there is to say for now.'

After that, it all wrapped up pretty quickly. They are charging me with reckless driving, but as I was acting out of self-defence, Nina is quite sure that will all soon disappear. Everything went exactly to plan.

As for James, I'm not too sure what will happen. If he has decent alibis, he might get away with being dismissed as a crackpot detective who gets obsessed with crime scenes and steals mementos from the victims, the murders relegated to suicides and accidents aside from the ones in Romeo's flat.

There seems little chance he will escape blame for Dale's murder though. Found at the crime scene, his handcuffs on the victim, my report of threatening my family members, a search for Dale's address on his work account. Why hadn't he called police for backup if he really suspected a murder was about to take place? And what reason would *I* possibly have to set fire to my uncle's home?

'Pal?' says Nina quietly, bringing me back to the here and now of the pub. 'You know you can't run your phone line anymore, don't you?'

'I do. It's over. Message M is closed for business.'

'You helped a lot of people though.'

'Yeah. I know.'

We sip our drinks quietly. I think of those girls in the back of my car, the glitter eyeshadow and the too-short skirts. But I can't be there for everyone. These past few weeks, I've missed so many nights on Message M, and the world has kept turning. It has probably stopped for some people, but I can't be responsible for them all anymore.

'Pal?' she says again. 'Once we've got rid of this charge. What then?'

'I don't know,' I say simply. Because I don't. I have no job, no Message M, no boyfriend. I live in a house paid for by the brothers grim – Dale helped me buy it with Dad's life insurance money, which my mum offered to me out of unspoken guilt and potentially gratitude. The future is a blank.

'Katie is staying in an institution for a bit, did I tell you? I spoke to her on the weekend. She seemed . . . so much better, Nina? Like she is healing.'

'She needed proper help. She has it now. She'll be okay.'

'She will.'

'And you?' she asks.

'Maybe it's time I got out of this city. All the happy memories.'

'Yeah, I've fancied a change for a while.'

It takes a moment before I realise what she is suggesting and notice that she is smiling, but avoiding my eye.

'My company is opening a new office, in Edinburgh. They are looking for people to work there. They've offered me more money. And I'm starting to worry I've completed Bristol Tinder.'

'Apparently it's cold up there.'

'Well, we can always light a fire.'

ACKNOWLEDGEMENTS

I'd like to thank a whole raft of people for making this experience both possible and fun. First of all, a big round of applause for Molly Walker-Sharp, to whom I owe a large part of this creative process, and who also has really nice hair. Which is important in an editor. You should always choose an editor by their hair. Thank you, Molly, for taking a chance on me for this, and for guiding me with wisdom, wit and enthusiasm. I'm still mad at you for leaving, but it did mean I got to put loads of the swearing back in.

And at least you left me with the brilliant Elisha Lundin – so thanks to you too Elisha. It's not always easy taking over a project halfway through, but your incisive notes and excellent direction were invaluable. Millie is a slightly less horrible character thanks to you, and I hope readers appreciate that. You also have nice hair, so it was an easy editorial transition.

And of course, Raphaella Demetris. Rella, you've seen this through from the beginning, and your comments on the story were so helpful. I know just how hard Editorial Assistants and Assistant Editors work, because I used to have that job, and I'm aware you are doing thousands of tasks behind the scenes that absolutely make the success of a book. So thank you, too. I can tell by your hair you'll be extremely senior one day.

That's the editors out of the way. Got to stroke the editors' egos first because they are generally a sensitive type. But there are hundreds of other just as brilliant people in the Avon team that I'd like to acknowledge as part of this and thank for their hard work, even if I haven't met all of them face-to-face at the time of my writing this.

So, thank you to Samantha Luton in sales, Maddie Dunne-Kirby in marketing, Becky Hunter in publicity, Molly Robinson in audio, Emily Chan in production, Vasiliki Machaira, Peter Borcsok, Emily Gerbner and Amanda Percival in the international and rights teams, and of course Sarah Foster who has designed such an incredible jacket. Honestly Sarah, I love this cover. It's going in a frame.

Finally from Avon, I'd like to give a special shout-out to Thorne Ryan, even though she is no longer there. Thanks for hooking me up Thorne, I owe you at least thirty drinks. When I met Thorne she was an assistant, and now she is the boss. She deserves every bit of her shining success.

Outside of HarperCollins Towers, thank you to my parents, who are luckily nothing like Millie's.

They are eternally supportive, encouraging, and loving, and I could never possibly thank them enough. Sorry about all the swearing Mum.

Thanks to my boyfriend Rob, who I am yet to hit with a car. He's one of the fabled Good Guys, and so deserves to live.

To my three brothers, my two sisters-in-law, and their children – I'm stuck with you so it's a good job I like and respect you all. Having a proper family, and a great one, makes me feel very lucky.

To my friends, who make life bright and are a collection of the funniest, smartest people I have managed to discover over the past thirty-odd years.

To my agent, Hannah Todd, who I met after this book deal but who will hopefully be with me for the rest of my career, as she is spectacular, (also great hair!).

And to my dogs, of course, for being my biggest, curliest fans.